**Praise for #1 *New York Times*
bestselling author Linda Lael Miller**

"Miller tugs at the heartstrings as few authors can."
—*Publishers Weekly*

"Miller's astute attention to detail and vivid prose
bring the characters to life with her trademark wit,
warmth and charm."
—*RT Book Reviews* on *The Bridegroom*

"Miller's down-home, easy-to-read style keeps the plot
moving, and she includes...likable characters,
picturesque descriptions and some very sweet pets."
—*Publishers Weekly* on *Big Sky Country*

**Praise for *USA TODAY* bestselling author
Janice Maynard**

"Maynard's deft touch unravels family secrets in
this seething and tempestuous story."
—*RT Book Reviews* on *The Secret Child & The Cowboy CEO*

"For those fans who love a decisive (and Stetson-wearing)
hero who knows what he wants and goes after it,
this one is for you. Here, Maynard proves that
she is at the top of her game."
—*RT Book Reviews* on *Beneath the Stetson*

LINDA LAEL MILLER

The daughter of a town marshal, Linda Lael Miller is a *New York Times* bestselling author of more than one hundred historical and contemporary novels. Linda's books have hit #1 on the *New York Times* bestseller list seven times. Raised in Northport, Washington, she now lives in Spokane, Washington.

JANICE MAYNARD

is a *USA TODAY* bestselling author who lives in beautiful east Tennessee with her husband. She holds a B.A. from Emory and Henry College and an M.A. from East Tennessee State University. In 2002, Janice left a fifteen-year career as an elementary school teacher to pursue writing full-time. Now her first love is creating sexy, character-driven, contemporary romance stories.

Janice loves to travel and enjoys using those experiences as settings for books. Hearing from readers is one of the best perks of the job! Visit her website, www.janicemaynard.com, and follow her on Facebook and Twitter.

#1 *New York Times* Bestselling Author

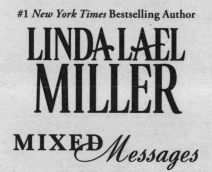

LINDA LAEL MILLER

MIXED *Messages*

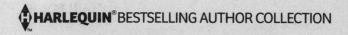

HARLEQUIN® BESTSELLING AUTHOR COLLECTION

Recycling programs for this product may not exist in your area.

ISBN-13: 978-0-373-18090-5

Mixed Messages
Copyright © 2014 by Harlequin Books S.A.

The publisher acknowledges the copyright holders of the individual works as follows:

Mixed Messages
Copyright © 1990 by Linda Lael Miller

The Secret Child & The Cowboy CEO
Copyright © 2010 by Janice Maynard

This edition published by arrangement with Harlequin Books S.A.

For questions and comments about the quality of this book, please contact us at CustomerService@Harlequin.com.

www.Harlequin.com

Printed in U.S.A.

CONTENTS

Dear Reader,

I am, once again, honored to be included in the Harlequin Bestselling Author Collection! And I'm delighted to share this volume with a talented writer like Janice Maynard.

Mixed Messages is an older romance of mine, first published in 1990. Taking another look at it today, I feel it's still quite relevant in this age of celebrity obsession—maybe even more so—although it first appeared pre-internet and pre–social media. The story features a renowned journalist (male), who's interviewed royalty, presidents and movie stars, and an advice columnist with higher aspirations (female). Mark, who'd looked on Carly's little advice column with scorn, soon learns that there's more to her—and more to her writing—than he'd assumed. He also discovers that love is the great leveler…

I hope you'll enjoy this return to what is now a distinctly earlier era. But remember, romance is forever!

Please feel free to visit my website, www.lindalaelmiller.com and check out my contests, my blog and information about upcoming titles.

With love,

MIXED MESSAGES

Linda Lael Miller

For our Wild Irish Rose,
with love

Chapter 1

He was a legend, and he was sitting right across the aisle from Carly Barnett. She wondered if she should speak to him, and immediately began rehearsing possible scenarios in her mind.

First, she'd sort of bend toward him, then she'd lightly touch his arm. *Excuse me,* she would say, *but I've been following your career since high school and I just wanted to tell you how much I've enjoyed your work. It's partly because of you that I decided to become a journalist.*

Too sappy, she concluded.

She could always look with dismay at the dinner on her fold-down tray and utter, *I beg your pardon, but would you happen to have any Grey Poupon?*

That idea wasn't exactly spectacular, either. Carly

hoped she'd be more imaginative once she was work-ing at her new job with Portland's *Oregonian Times*.

Covertly she studied Mark Holbrook as he wrote fu-riously on a yellow legal pad with his left hand, while ignoring the food the flight attendant had served ear-lier. He was tall, and younger than Carly would have expected, considering all his accomplishments—he was probably around thirty-two or thirty-three. He had nice brown hair and could have used a shave. Once he glanced at her, revealing expressive brown eyes, but he didn't seem to see Carly at all. He was thinking.

Carly was deflated. After all, she'd been in the lime-light herself, though in a very different way from Mr. Holbrook, and men usually noticed her.

She cleared her throat, and instantly his choirboy eyes focused on her.

"Hello," he said with a megawatt smile that made the pit of Carly's stomach jiggle.

She, who was used to being asked things like what she would do if she could run the world for a day, came up with nothing more impressive than, "Hi. Don't you like the food?"

His eyes danced as he lifted the hard roll from his tray and took a deliberate bite.

Carly blushed slightly and thought to herself, *Why didn't I just lean across the aisle and cut his meat for him?*

He had the temerity to laugh at her expression, and that brought the focus of her blue-green eyes back to his face. He was extending his hand. "Mark Holbrook," he said cordially.

Carly had been schooled in deportment all her life, and she couldn't overlook an offered hand. She shook it politely, a little stiffly, and said, "Carly Barnett."

He was squinting at her. "You look sort of familiar. Are you an actress or something?"

Carly relaxed a bit. If she was going to recoil every time someone did something outrageous, she wouldn't last long in the newspaper business. She gave him the smile that had stood her in such good stead during the pageant and afterward. "I was Miss United States four years ago."

"That isn't it," Holbrook replied, dismissing the achievement so briskly that Carly was a little injured. "Have you been in a shaving-cream commercial or something?"

"I don't shave, as a general rule," Carly replied sweetly.

Holbrook chuckled, and it was a nice sound, masculine and easy. "So," he said, "you're a beauty queen."

Carly's smile faded, and she tossed her head in annoyance, making her chin-length blond curls bounce. "I'm a reporter," she corrected him coolly. "Or at least I will be, as of Monday morning."

He nodded. "On TV, of course."

Carly heartily resented the inference that any job she might land would have to hinge on her looks. After all, she'd graduated from college with honors back in Kansas, and she'd even written a weekly column for her hometown newspaper. It wasn't as though she didn't have qualifications. "No," she answered. "I've been hired by the *Oregonian Times*."

Mr. Holbrook's eyes were still dancing, even though his mouth had settled into a circumspect line. "I see. Well, that's one of the best newspapers on the West Coast."

"I know," Carly informed him. "I understand it's a rival to your paper." The instant the words were out of her mouth, she regretted letting on that she knew who he was, but it was too late, so she just sat there, trying to look remote.

Holbrook's grin flashed again. "You're behind on your homework, Ms. Barnett," he informed her. "I went to work for the *Times* two years ago."

They'd be working together, if only for the same paper. While Carly was absorbing that discovery, the flight attendant came and collected their trays, and then they were separated by the beverage cart. When it rolled on by, Carly saw that Mr. Holbrook had an amber-colored drink in one hand.

She felt slightly superior with her tomato juice, but the sensation lasted only until she remembered that Holbrook had a Pulitzer to his credit, that he'd interviewed presidents and kings and some of the greatest movie stars who'd ever graced the silver screen. Because she held him in such high esteem, she was willing to allow for his arrogance.

He'd forgotten all about her, anyway. Now that his dinner tray was out of the way, he was writing on the yellow legal pad in earnest.

The plane began its descent into Portland soon after, and Carly obediently put her tray into the upright position and fastened her seat belt. She was nervous about flying in general and taking off and landing in particular, and she gripped the armrests so tightly that her knuckles ached. Even though she'd flown a lot, Carly had never gotten used to it, and she doubted that she ever would

When the plane touched down and then bumped and jostled along the runway, moving at a furious pace, Carly closed her eyes tightly and awaited death.

"It's going to be okay," she heard a voice say, and she was startled into opening her eyes again.

Mark Holbrook was watching her with gentle amusement, and he reached across the aisle to grip her hand.

Carly felt foolish, and she forced a shaky smile. But she had to grimace when the engines of the big plane were thrust into Reverse and the sound of air rushing past the wings filled the cabin.

"Ladies and gentlemen," a staticky voice said over the sound system, "we'd like to welcome you to Portland, Oregon. There's a light spring rain falling today, and the temperature is in the mid-forties. Thank you for choosing our airline, and we hope you'll fly with us again soon. Please remain in your seats until we've come to a complete stop at the gate..."

Mark was obviously one of those people who never listened to such requests. He released Carly's hand after giving it a squeeze, and stood to rummage through the overhead compartment for his carry-on luggage.

"Need a lift somewhere?" he asked, smiling down at Carly.

For a moment she almost regretted that her friend Janet would be waiting for her inside the terminal. She shook her head. "Thanks, but someone will be picking me up."

He produced a business card from the pocket of his rumpled tweed coat and extended it. "Here," he said with mischief in his eyes. "If you need any help learning the ropes, just call my extension."

She beamed at him and replied in the same teasing tone of voice, "I think I'll be able to master my job on my own, Mr. Holbrook."

He chuckled and moved out of the plane with the rest of the mob, glancing back at Carly once to give her a brazen wink and another knee-dissolving grin.

Ten minutes later, when the crowd had thinned, Carly walked off the plane carrying her beauty case and purse. Her best friend from college, Janet McClain, was waiting eagerly at the gate, as promised.

"I thought you'd missed your flight," Janet fussed as she and Carly hugged. Janet was an attractive brunette with dark eyes, and she'd been working in Portland as a buyer for a major department store ever since graduating from college. She'd been the one to suggest that Carly leave home once and for all and make a life for herself on the coast.

"I didn't want to be in the crush," Carly answered. "Is my apartment ready?"

Janet shook her head. "The paint's still wet, but don't worry about it. You can spend a few days at my place—you need to wait for your furniture to arrive anyway."

Carly nodded. In the distance she caught a glimpse of the back of Mark Holbrook's head. She wished she could see if he was walking with anyone, but even at her height of five feet seven inches the effort was fruitless.

"Who are you staring at?" Janet demanded, sensing drama. "Did you meet somebody on the plane?"

"Sort of," Carly admitted. "I was sitting across the aisle from Mark Holbrook."

Janet looked suitably impressed. "The journalist? What was he doing in coach?"

Carly laughed. "Slumming, I guess."

Janet's cheeks turned pink. "I didn't mean it like that," she said, shoving her hands into the pockets of her raincoat. "Did you actually talk to him?"

"Oh, yes," Carly answered. "He condescended to say a few words."

"Did he ask you out?"

Carly sighed. She wished he had and, at the same time, was glad he hadn't. But she wasn't prepared to admit to such confusion—reporters were supposed to be decisive, with clear-cut opinions on everything. "He gave me his card."

After that, Janet let the subject drop even though, these days, judging by her emails and phone calls, she was fixated on the man-woman relationship. She'd developed a penchant to get married and have a child.

They picked up Carly's luggage and had a porter carry it to Janet's car, which was in a far corner of the parking lot. The May sky glowered overhead.

"Well, Monday's the big day," Janet remarked when they had put Carly's bags in the trunk and Janet's stylish car was jetting sleekly into heavy afternoon traffic. "Are you excited?"

Carly nodded, but she couldn't help thinking of home. It was later there; her dad would be leaving his filling station for the day and going home. Since his daughter wasn't there to look after him, he'd probably buy fast food for supper and drive his cholesterol count sky high.

"You're pretty quiet," Janet observed. "Having second thoughts?"

Carly shook her head resolutely. She'd dreamed of working on a big-city newspaper all her life, and she had no real regrets. "I was just thinking of my dad. With me gone, there's nobody there to take care of him."

"Good grief, Carly," Janet immediately retorted, "you make him sound ancient. How old is he—forty-five?"

Carly sighed. "Fifty. And he doesn't eat right."

Janet tossed her an impish grin. "With his old-maid daughter out of the way, your dad will probably fall madly in love with some sexy widow or divorcée and have a wild affair. Or maybe he'll get married again and father a passel of kids."

Carly grinned and shook her head, but as she looked out at the rain-misted Oregon terrain, her expression turned wistful. Here was her chance to live out her dreams and really be somebody besides a beauty queen.

She hoped she had what it took to succeed in the real world.

Carly's new apartment was in Janet's building, and it was a simple one-bedroom unit painted white throughout. Since the walls were still wet, it smelled of chemical fumes.

The carpets, freshly cleaned, were a toasty beige color, and there was a fireplace, fronted with fake white marble, in the living room. Carly looked forward to reading beside a flickering fire in her favorite chenille bathrobe.

"What do you think?" Janet asked, spreading her arms as though she'd conjured the whole place, like a modern-day Merlin.

Carly smiled, wishing the paint were dry and her furniture had arrived. It would have been nice to settle in and start getting used to her new home. "It's great. Thanks for taking the time to find it for me, Janet."

"It wasn't any big deal, considering that I live in this building. Come on, we'll change our clothes, get some supper out and take in a movie."

"You're sure you don't have a date?" Carly asked, following her friend out of the apartment. They had already taken the suitcases to Janet's place.

"He'll keep," Janet answered with a mysterious smile.

Carly thought of Reggie, her erstwhile fiancé, and wondered what he was doing at that very moment. Making rounds at the hospital, probably. Or swimming at the country club. She seriously doubted that he missed her; his career was the real priority in his life. "Are you in love?"

They were all the way to Janet's door before she answered. "I don't really know. Tom is good-looking and nice, and he has a good job. Maybe those things are enough—maybe love is just a figment of some poet's imagination."

Carly shook her head as she followed her friend into an apartment that was virtually a duplicate of the one they'd just left, except for the carpet. Here, it was forest green. "I wouldn't do anything rash if I were you," she warned. "There might just be something to this love business."

"Yeah," Janet agreed, tossing her purse onto the sofa and shrugging out of her raincoat. "Bruised hearts and insomnia."

After that, Carly stopped trying to win her friend over to her point of view. She didn't know the first thing about love herself, except that she'd never been in it, not even with Reggie.

"An advice column?" Carly's voice echoed in her cramped corner office the following Monday morning. "But I thought I was going to be a reporter...."

Carly's new boss, Allison Courtney, stood tall and tweedy in the doorway. She was a no-nonsense type, with alert gray eyes, sleek blond hair pulled tightly into a bun and impeccable makeup. "When we hired you, Carly, we thought you were a team player," she scolded cordially.

"Of course I am, but—"

"A lot of people would kill for a job like this, you know. I mean, think of it. You're getting paid to *tell other people what to do,* for heaven's sake!"

Carly had pictured herself interviewing senators and homeless people, covering trials and stand-offs between the police and the underworld. She knew the advice column was a plum, but it had never occurred to her that she'd be asked to serve in that capacity, and she was frankly disappointed. Calling upon years of training, she assumed a cheerful expression. "Where do I start?"

Allison returned Carly's smile, pleased. "Someone will bring you this week's batch of mail. You'll find all the experts you need listed in your contacts. Oh, and between letters you might help out with clerical work and such. Welcome aboard." With that, she stepped out, closing the office door behind her.

Carly set the box down on her desk with a *clunk* and sank into her chair. "Clerical work?" she echoed, tossing a glance at the computer system perched at her elbow. "Good grief. Did I come all the way to Oregon just to be a glorified secretary?"

As if in answer, the telephone on her desk buzzed.

"Carly Barnett," she said into the receiver, after pushing four different buttons in order to get the right line.

"Just seeing if it works," replied a bright female voice. "I'm Emmeline Rogers, and I'm sort of your secretary."

Carly felt a little better, until she remembered that she was probably going to spend as much time doing office work as writing. Maybe more. "Hi," she said shyly.

"Want some coffee or something?"

Carly definitely felt better. "Thanks. That would be great."

Moments later, Emmeline appeared with coffee. She was small, with plain brown hair, green eyes and a ready smile. "I brought pink sugar, in case you wanted it."

Carly thanked the woman again and stirred half a packet of sweetener into the hot, strong coffee. "There are supposed to be some letters floating around here somewhere. Do you know where they are?"

Emmeline nodded and then glanced at her watch. Maybe she was one of those people who took an early lunch, Carly thought. "I'll bring them in."

"Great," Carly answered. "Thanks."

Emmeline slipped out and returned five minutes later with a mailbag the size of Santa's sack. In fact, Carly was reminded of the courtroom scene in *Miracle On 34th Street* when the secretary spilled letters all over her desk.

By the time Emmeline had emptied the bag, Carly couldn't even see over the pile. She would have to unearth her computer and telephone before she could start working.

"I couldn't think of a way to break it to you gently," Emmeline said.

Carly took a steadying sip of her coffee and muttered, "Allison said I'd be helping out with clerical work during slack times."

Emmeline smiled. "Allison thinks she has a sense of humor. The rest of us know better."

Carly chuckled and shoved the fingers of her left hand through her hair. Until two weeks ago, when she'd made the final decision to break off with Reggie and come to Oregon, she'd worn it long. The new cut, reaching just a couple of inches below her earlobes, had been a statement of sorts; she was starting over fresh.

Emmeline left her with a little shrug and a sympathetic smile. "Buzz me if you need anything."

Carly was beginning to sort the letters into stacks. "If there's another avalanche," she responded, "send in a search party."

Her telephone and computer had both reappeared by the time a brisk knock sounded at her office door. Mark poked his head around it before she had time to call out a "Come in" or even wonder why Emmeline hadn't buzzed to announce a visitor.

"Hi," he said, assessing the mountain of letters with barely concealed amusement. He was probably off to interview the governor or some astronaut.

Carly gave him a dour look. "Hi," she responded.

He stepped into the tiny office and closed the door. "Your secretary's on a break," he said. He was wearing jeans, a plaid flannel shirt and a tan corduroy jacket.

"What I need is a moat stocked with crocodiles," Carly retorted with a saucy smile. She wasn't sure how she felt about this man—he produced an odd tangle of reactions that weren't easy to unravel and define. The impact of his presence was almost overwhelming—he seemed to fill the room, leaving no space for her—and Carly was both intrigued and frightened.

She was at once attracted to him, and defensive about her lack of experience as a journalist.

Mark drew up the only extra chair, turned it around backward and sat astraddle of it, resting his arms across the back. "What are they going to call this column now? 'Dear Miss Congeniality'?"

"I wasn't Miss Congeniality," Carly pointed out,

arching her eyebrows and deliberately widening her eyes.

"Little wonder," he replied philosophically.

Carly leaned forward in her chair and did her best to glower. "Was there something you wanted?"

"Yes. I'd like you to go to dinner with me tonight."

Carly was putting rubber bands around batches of letters and stacking them on her credenza. A little thrill pirouetted up her spine and then did a triple flip to the pit of her stomach. Even though every instinct she possessed demanded that she refuse, she found herself nodding. "I'd enjoy that."

"We could take in a movie afterward, if you want."

Carly looked at the abundance of letters awaiting her attention. "That would be stretching it. Maybe some other time."

Idly Mark picked up one of the letters and opened it. His handsome brow furrowed as he read. "This one's from a teenage girl," he said, extending the missive to Carly. "What are you going to tell her?"

Carly took the page of lined notebook paper and scanned it. The young lady who'd written it was still in high school, and she was being pressured by the boy she dated to "go all the way." She wanted to know how she could refuse without losing her boyfriend.

"I think she should stand her ground," Carly said. "If the boy really cares about her, he'll understand why she wants to wait."

Mark nodded thoughtfully. "Of course, nobody expects you to reply to every letter," he mused.

Carly sensed disapproval in his tone, though it was

well masked. "What's wrong with my answer?" she demanded.

"It's a little simplistic, that's all." His guileless brown eyes revealed no recriminations.

Without understanding why, Carly was on the defensive. "I suppose you could come up with something better?"

He sighed. "No, just more extensive. I would tell her to talk to a counselor at school, or a clergyman, or maybe a doctor. Things are complex as hell out there, Carly. Kids have a lot more to worry about than making cheerleader or getting on the football team."

Carly sat back in her hair and folded her arms. "Could it be, Mr. Holbrook," she began evenly, "that you think I'm shallow just because I was Miss United States?"

He grinned. "Would I have asked you out to dinner if I thought you were shallow?"

"Probably."

Mark shrugged and spread his hands. "I'm sure you mean well," he conceded generously. "You're just inexperienced, that's all."

She took up a packet of envelopes and switched on her computer. The printer beside it hummed efficiently at the flip of another switch. "I won't ever have any experience," she responded, "if you hang around my office for the rest of your life, picking my qualifications apart."

He stood up. "I assume you have a degree in psychology?"

"You know better."

Mark was at the door now, his hand on the knob. "True. I looked you up. You majored in—"

"Journalism," Carly interrupted.

Although his expression was chagrined, his eyes twinkled as he offered her a quick salute. "See you at dinner," he said, and then he was gone.

Thoroughly unsettled, Carly turned her attention back to the letters she was expected to deal with.

Resolutely she opened an envelope, took out the folded page and began to read.

By lunchtime, Carly's head was spinning. She was certainly no Pollyanna, but she'd never dreamed there were so many people out there leading lives of quiet desperation.

Slipping on her raincoat and reaching for her purse and umbrella, she left the *Times* offices and made her way to a cozy little delicatessen on the corner. She ordered chicken salad and a diet cola, then sat down at one of the round metal tables and stared out at the people hurrying past the rain-beaded window.

After a morning spent reading about other people's problems, she was completely depressed. This was a state of mind that just naturally conjured up thoughts of Reggie.

Carly lifted her soft drink and took a sip. Maybe she'd done the wrong thing, breaking her engagement and leaving Kansas to start a whole new life. After all, Reggie was an honest-to-God doctor. He was already making over six figures a year, and he owned his sprawling brick house outright.

Glumly Carly picked up her plastic fork and took a

bite of her salad. Perhaps Janet was right, and love *was* about bruised hearts and insomnia. Maybe it was some kind of neurotic compulsion.

Hell, maybe it didn't exist at all.

At the end of her lunch hour, Carly returned to her office to find a note propped against her computer screen. It was written on the back of one of the envelopes, in firm black letters that slanted slightly to the right. *This guy needs professional help. Re: dinner— meet me downstairs in the lobby at seven. Mark.*

Carly shook her head and smiled as she took the letter out of the envelope. Her teeth sank into her lower lip as she read about the plight of a man who was in love with his aunt Gertrude. Nothing in journalism school, or in a year's reign as Miss United States, had prepared her for dealing with things like this.

She set the letter aside and opened another one.

Allison popped in at five minutes before five. "Hello," she chimed. "How are things going?"

Carly worked up a smile. "Until today," she replied, "I had real hope for humanity."

Allison gestured toward the computer. "I trust you're making good use of Madeline's contacts. She made some excellent ones in the professional community while she was here."

Madeline, of course, was Carly's predecessor, who had left her job to join her professor husband on a sabbatical overseas. "I haven't gotten that far," Carly responded. "I'm still in the sorting process."

Allison shook a finger at Carly, assuming a stance and manner that made her resemble an elementary school librarian. "Now remember, you have deadlines, just like everyone else at this paper."

Carly nodded. She was well aware that she was expected to turn in a column before quitting time on Wednesday. "I'll be ready," she said, and she was relieved when Allison left it at that and disappeared again.

She was stuffing packets of letters into her briefcase when Janet arrived to collect her.

"So how was it?" Janet asked, pushing a button on the elevator panel. The doors whisked shut.

"Grueling," Carly answered, patting her briefcase with the palm of one hand. "Talk about experience. I'm expected to deal with everything from the heartbreak of psoriasis to nuclear war."

Janet smiled. "You'll get the hang of it," she teased. "God did."

Carly rolled her eyes and chuckled. "I think he divided the overflow between Dear Abby, Ann Landers and me."

In the lobby the doors swished open, and Carly found herself face-to-face with Mark Holbrook. Perhaps because she was unprepared for the encounter, she felt as though the floor had just dissolved beneath her feet.

Janet nudged her hard in the ribs.

"M-Mark, this is Janet McClain," Carly stammered with all the social grace of a nervous ninth grader. "We went to high school and college together."

Carly begrudged the grin Mark tossed in Janet's direction. "Hello," he said suavely, and Carly thought, just fleetingly, of Cary Grant.

Mark's warm brown eyes moved to Carly. "Remember—we're supposed to meet at seven for dinner."

Carly was still oddly starstruck, and she managed nothing more than a nod in response.

"I take back every jaded remark I've ever made about love," Janet whispered as she and Carly walked away. "I've just become a believer."

Carly was shaken, but for some reason she needed to put on a front. "Take it from me, Janet," she said cynically, "Mark Holbrook may look like a prize, but he's too arrogant to make a good husband."

"Umm," said Janet.

"I mean, it's not like every dinner date has to be marriage material—"

"Of course not," Janet readily agreed.

A brisk and misty wind met them as they stepped out onto the sidewalk in front of the *Times* building, and Carly's cheeks colored in a blush. She averted her eyes. "I know he's the wrong kind of man for me—with all he's accomplished, he must be driven, like Reggie, but—"

"But?" Janet prompted.

"When he asked me out for dinner, I meant to say no," Carly confessed, "but somehow it came out yes."

Chapter 2

Carly arrived at the *Times* offices at five minutes to seven, wearing an attractive blue dress she'd borrowed from Janet and feeling guilty about all the unread letters awaiting her at home.

She stepped into the large lobby and looked around. She shouldn't even be there, she thought to herself. When she'd left home, she'd had a plan for her life, and Mark Holbrook, attractive as he might be, wasn't part of it.

An elevator bell chimed, doors swished open, and Mark appeared, as if conjured by her thoughts. He carried a briefcase in one hand and wore the same clothes he'd had on earlier: jeans, a flannel shirt and a corduroy jacket.

"This almost makes me wish I'd worn a tie," he said,

his warm brown eyes sweeping over her with admiration. Another of his lightning-charged grins flashed. "Then again, I'm glad I didn't. You look wonderful, Ms. Congeniality."

Carly let the beauty-pageant vernacular slide by. Although she'd had a lot of experience talking to people, she felt strangely shy around Mark. "Thanks," she said.

They walked three blocks to Jake's, an elegantly rustic restaurant-tavern that had been in business since 1892. When they walked in, the bartender called out a good-natured greeting to Mark, who answered with a thumbs-up sign, then proceeded to the reservations desk.

Soon Mark and Carly were seated in a booth on wooden benches, the backs towering over their heads. A waiter promptly brought them menus and greeted Mark by name.

Carly figured he probably brought a variety of women to the restaurant, and was inexplicably annoyed by the thought. She chose a Cajun plate, while Mark ordered a steak.

"Making any progress with the letters?" he asked when they were alone again.

Carly sighed. She'd probably be up until two or three in the morning, wading through them. "Let's put it this way," she answered, "I should be home working."

The wine arrived and Mark tasted the sample the steward poured, then nodded. The claret was poured and the steward walked away, leaving the bottle behind.

Mark lifted his glass and touched it against Carly's. "To workaholics everywhere," he said.

Carly took a sip of her wine and set the glass aside. The word "workaholic" had brought Reggie to mind, and she felt as though he were sitting at the table with them, an unwelcome third. "What's the most important thing in your life?" she asked to distract herself.

The waiter left their salads, then turned and walked away.

"Things don't mean much to me," Mark responded, lifting his fork. "It's people who matter. And the most important person in my life is my son, Nathan."

Even though she certainly wasn't expecting anything to develop between herself and Mark, Carly was jarred by the mention of a child. "You're not married, I hope," she said, practically holding her breath.

"No, I'm divorced, and Nathan lives in California, with his mother," he said. There was, for just an instant, a look of pain in his eyes. This was quickly displaced by a mischievous sparkle. "Would it matter to you—if I were married, I mean?"

Carly speared a cherry tomato somewhat vengefully. "Would it *matter?* Of course it would."

"A lot of women don't care."

"I'm not a lot of women," Carly responded, her tone resolute.

He shrugged one shoulder. "There's a shortage of marriageable men out there, I'm told. Aren't you worried that your biological clock is ticking, and all that?"

"Maybe in ten years I'll be worried. Right now I'm interested in making some kind of life for myself."

"Which you couldn't do in the Midwest?"

"I wanted to do it here," she said.

Mark smiled. "Exactly what kind of life are you picturing?"

Carly was beginning to feel as though she was being interviewed, but she didn't mind. She understood how a reporter's mind worked. "Mainly I want to write for a newspaper—not advice, but articles, like you do. And maybe I'll buy myself a little house and a dog."

"Sounds fulfilling," Mark replied.

There was so little conviction in his voice that Carly peered across the table at him and demanded, "Just what did you mean by that?"

He widened those guileless choirboy eyes of his and sat back on the bench as though he expected the salt shaker to detonate. "I was just thinking—well, it's a shame that so few women want to have babies anymore."

"I didn't say I didn't want to have babies," Carly pointed out. Her voice had risen, and she blushed to see that the people at the nearest table were looking at her. "I *love* babies," she clarified in an angry whisper. "I plan to breast-feed and everything!"

The waiter startled Carly by suddenly appearing at her elbow to deliver dinner, and Mark grinned at her reaction.

She spoke in a peevish hiss. "Let's just get off this topic of conversation, all right?"

"All right," Mark agreed. "Tell me, what made you start entering beauty pageants?"

It wasn't the subject Carly would have chosen, but she could live with it. "Not 'what,'" she replied. "'Who.' It was my mother. She started entering me in contests when I was four and, except for a few years when I was in an awkward stage, she kept it up until I was old enough to go to college."

"And then you won the Miss United States title?"

Carly nodded, smiling slightly as she recalled those exciting days. "You'd have thought Mom was the winner, she was so pleased. She called everybody we knew."

Mark was cutting his steak. "She must miss you a lot."

Carly bent her head, smoothing the napkin in her lap. "She died of cancer a couple of weeks after the pageant."

When Carly lifted a hand back to the table, Mark's was waiting to enfold it. "I'm sorry," he said quietly.

His sympathy brought quick, stinging tears to her eyes. "It could have been worse," Carly managed to say. "Everything happened almost instantaneously. She didn't suffer much."

Mark only nodded, his eyes caressing Carly in a way that eased the pain of remembering.

"How old is Nathan?" she asked, and the words came out a little awkwardly.

Mark's voice was hoarse when he answered. "He's ten," he replied, opening his wallet and taking out a photo.

Nathan Holbrook was handsome, like his father, with brown hair and eyes, and he was dressed in a baseball uniform and was holding a bat, ready to swing.

Carly smiled and handed the picture back. "It must be difficult living so far away from him," she commented.

Mark nodded, and Carly noticed that he averted his eyes for a moment.

"Is something wrong?" she asked softly.

"Nothing I want to trouble you with," Mark responded, putting away his wallet. "Sure you don't want to go take in a movie?"

Carly thought of the pile of letters she had yet to read. She gave her head a regretful shake. "Maybe some other time. Right now I'm under a lot of pressure to show Allison and the powers-that-be that I can handle this job."

They finished their meal, then Mark settled the bill with a credit card. He held her hand as they walked to his car, which was parked in a private lot beneath the newspaper building.

Barely fifteen minutes later, they were in front of Janet's door. Mark bent his head and gave Carly a kiss that, for all its innocuousness, made her nerve endings vibrate.

"Good night," he murmured, while Carly was still trying to get her bearings. A moment after that, he disappeared into the elevator.

"Well?" Janet demanded the second Carly let herself into the apartment.

Carly smiled and shook her head. "It was love at first sight," she responded sweetly. "We're getting married tonight, flying to Rio tomorrow and starting our family the day after."

Janet bounded off the couch and followed Carly as she went through the bedroom and stood outside the bathroom door while she exchanged the dress for an oversize T-shirt. "Details!" she cried. "Give me details!"

Carly came out of the bathroom, carrying the dress, and hung it back in the closet. "Mark and I are all wrong for each other," she said.

"How do you figure that?"

Turning away from the closet, Carly shrugged. "The guy sends out mixed messages. He's very attractive, but he's bristly, too. And he's got some very old-fashioned ideas about women."

Janet looked disappointed for a moment, then brightened. "If you're not going to see Mark anymore, how about fixing me up with him?"

Carly was surprised at the strong reaction the suggestion produced in her. She marched across Janet's living room, took her briefcase from the breakfast bar and set it down on the Formica-topped table with a thump. "I didn't say I wasn't going to see him again," she said, snapping the catches and pulling out a stack of letters.

After tossing her friend a smug little smile, Janet said good-night and went off to bed. Carly looked with longing at the fold-out sofa, then made herself a cup of tea and set to work.

Although there was no sign of Emmeline when Carly arrived at work the next morning, suppressing almost continuous yawns and hoping the dark circles under her eyes weren't too pronounced, a memo had been taped to her computer screen.

Staff meeting, the message read. *Nine-thirty, conference room.*

Carly glanced at her watch, sat down at her desk and began reading letters again. It was almost a relief when the time came to leave her small office for the meeting.

The long conference room table was encircled by people, and they all seemed to be talking at the same time. An enormous pot of coffee chortled on a table in the corner. Carly poured herself a cup of coffee and sat down in the only empty chair in the room, shaking her head when a secretary came by with a box full of assorted pastries.

She saw that Mark was sitting directly across from her. He grinned and tilted his head slightly to one side in a way that was vaguely indulgent.

Mixed messages again, Carly thought, responding with a tight little smile.

The managing editor, a slender, white-haired man with the sleeves of his shirt rolled back to his elbows and suspenders holding up his pants, called the meeting to order.

Carly listened intently as he went over the objectives of the newspaper and gave out assignments.

The best one, a piece on crack houses for the Sunday edition, went to Mark, and Carly felt a sting of envy. While he was out in the field, grappling with real life, she would be tucked away in her tiny office, reading letters from the forlorn.

Mark sat back in his chair, not drinking coffee or eating doughnuts like the others, his eyes fixed on Carly. She was relieved when the meeting finally ended.

"So," boomed Mr. Clark, the managing editor, just as Carly was pushing back her chair to leave, "how do you like writing the advice column?"

Carly glanced uncomfortably at Mark, who had lingered to open a nearby window. *Now's a nice time to think of that,* she reflected to herself, and Mark looked back at her as though she'd spoken aloud.

She remembered Mr. Clark and his affable question. "I haven't actually written anything yet," she answered diplomatically. "I'm still wading through the letters."

Mark was standing beside the table again, his hands resting on the back of a chair. "You're aware, of course," he put in, "that Ms. Barnett doesn't have any real qualifications for that job?"

Carly looked at him in stunned disbelief, and he favored her with a placid grin.

Mr. Clark was watching Carly, but he spoke as though she wasn't there. "Allison seems to think Ms. Barnett can handle the work," he said thoughtfully, and there was just enough uncertainty in his voice to worry the newest member of his staff.

Carly ignored Mark completely. "You won't be sorry for giving me a chance, Mr. Clark," she said.

The older man nodded distractedly and left the conference room. Carly was right behind him, but a sudden grip on her upper arm stopped her.

"Give me a chance to explain," Mark said in a low voice.

The man had done his best to get her fired, and after she'd uprooted herself and spent most of her life savings to move to Oregon, too.

"There's no need for explanations," she told him, wrenching her arm free of his hand. "You've made your opinion of my abilities perfectly clear."

He started to say something in response, then

stopped himself and, with an exasperated look on his face, stepped past Carly and disappeared into his office.

She went back to her office and continued working. By noon she'd read all the letters and selected three to answer in her column. The problems were clear-cut, in Carly's opinion, and there was no need to contact any of Madeline's experts. All a person needed, she thought to herself, was a little common sense.

She was just finishing the initial draft of her first column when there was a light rap at the door and Allison stepped in. She hadn't been at the staff meeting, and she looked harried.

"Is the column done by any chance?" she asked anxiously. "We could really use some help over in Food and Fashion."

Carly pushed the print button on the keyboard and within seconds handed Allison the hard copy of her column.

Allison scanned it, making *hmm* sounds that told Carly exactly nothing, then nodded. "This will do, I guess. I'll take you to F&F and you can help Anthony for the rest of the day. He's at his wit's end."

Carly was excited. She wouldn't be accompanying the police on a crack-house raid like Mark, but she might at least get to cover a fashion show or a bake-off. Either one would get her out of the building.

Anthony Cornelius turned out to be a slim, good-looking young man with blond hair and blue eyes. Allison introduced Carly, then disappeared.

"I've been perishing to meet you," Anthony said with a straight face. "I would have said hello at the staff meeting, but it got a bit stuffy and I couldn't *wait* to get out of there."

Carly smiled. "I know what you mean," she said as Anthony gestured toward a chair facing his immaculate desk.

"I saw the video of your pageant, you know. You were splendid."

"Thank you," Carly demurred. She was getting a little embarrassed at the reminders of past glories.

Anthony gave a showy sigh. "Well, enough chitchat. I'm just *buried* in work, and I'm desperate for your help. There's a cooking contest at the St. Regis Hotel today, while the mall is putting on the biggest fashion show *ever*. Needless to say, I can't be in two places at once."

Carly hid her delight by crossing her legs and smoothing her light woolen skirt. "What would you like me to do?"

"You may have your choice," Anthony answered, frowning as he flipped through a notebook on his desk. "Fashion or food."

Carly had already thought the choice through. "I'll take the cooking contest," she said.

"Fabulous," Anthony responded without looking up from his notes. "St. Regis Hotel, two-fifteen. I've already sent a photographer over. I'll see you back here afterward."

Eagerly Carly rose from her chair and headed for the door. "Anthony?"

He raised his eyes inquiringly.

"Thanks," Carly said, and then she hurried out.

After collecting her purse, notebook and coat, Carly

set off for the St. Regis Hotel, which turned out to be within walking distance of the newspaper office. She spent several happy hours interviewing amateur chefs and tasting their special dishes, and she even managed to get them to divulge a few secret recipes.

Returning to her office late that afternoon, having forgotten lunch entirely, Carly absorbed the fact that a new batch of letters had been delivered and sat down at her computer to write up the piece on the cooking contest.

Anthony turned out to be a taskmaster, despite his gentle ways, and Carly willingly did three rewrites before he was satisfied. She was about to switch off her computer and go home for the day, taking a briefcase full of letters with her, when a message appeared unbidden on the screen.

"Hello, Carly," it read.

Frowning, Carly pushed her big reading glasses up the bridge of her nose and typed the response without thinking. "Hello."

"How about having dinner with me again tonight? I'll cook."

It was Mark.

"No, thanks," she typed resolutely. "I never dine with traitors."

"I'll explain if you'll just give me the chance."

"No."

"Will begging help?"

Carly shut off her computer, filled her briefcase with letters and left the office. She walked to the department store where Janet was employed and found that her friend was still working.

After consulting a schedule, Carly caught a bus back to the apartment building and was overjoyed when the manager, Mrs. Pickering, greeted her with the news that her car and furniture had been delivered.

"I made sure they set up the bed for you," the plump, middle-aged woman said as Carly turned the key in the lock.

The living room was filled with boxes, but the familiar couch and chair were there, as was the small television set. The dining table was in its place next to the kitchenette.

Carly set her briefcase and purse down on the small desk in the living room, then lifted the receiver on her telephone. She heard a dial tone and smiled. Her service was connected.

Feeling unaccountably domestic, Carly thanked Mrs. Pickering for her trouble and set out immediately for the parking lot. Her blue Mustang, one of the prizes she'd won as Miss United States, was in its proper slot.

Taking the keys from her purse, Carly unlocked the car, got behind the wheel and started the engine. She drove to the nearest all-night supermarket and bought a cartful of food and cleaning supplies, then came home and made herself a light supper of soup and salad in her own kitchen.

She dialed Janet's number and left a message, then called her father, knowing he'd be up watching the news.

Don Barnett picked up the telephone on the second ring and gave his customary gruff hello.

"Hi, Dad. It's Carly."

She heard pleasure in his voice. "Hello, beautiful," he said. "All settled in?"

Carly sat down in her desk chair and told her father all about her apartment and her new job.

He listened with genuine interest, and then announced that Reggie was engaged to a nurse from Topeka.

"It didn't take him long, did it?" Carly asked. She wasn't sure what she'd expected—maybe that Reggie would at least have the decency to pine for a month or two.

Her father chuckled. "Having a few second thoughts, are you?"

"No," Carly said honestly. "I just didn't think I was quite so forgettable, that's all." They talked a little longer, then ended the call with promises to stay in touch.

Carly was feeling homesick when a knock sounded at her door. She had never been very close to her mother, despite the inordinate amount of time they'd spent together, but her dad was a kindred spirit.

She put one eye to the peephole and sighed when she saw Mark standing in the hallway.

She opened the door to the length of the chain and looked out at him uncharitably. "Aren't you supposed to be participating in a crack-house raid or something?"

He flashed one of his lethal grins. "That's tomorrow night. May I come in?"

The living room was still filled with unopened boxes,

and Carly was wearing her pink bathrobe. Her hair was probably a mess, too. And this man had tried to get her fired just that morning.

Despite all these things, Carly unfastened the chain and opened the door.

Mark was wearing jeans and a navy-blue football jersey with the number "39" printed on it in white, and he carried a bouquet of pink daisies.

Carly eyed them with a certain disdain, even though she secretly loved daisies. "If you think a few flowers are going to make up for the way you sandbagged me this morning—"

Mark sighed. "I was trying to get Clark to move you to another assignment."

"I'll be lucky if you didn't get me booted out instead," Carly replied. Grudgingly she took the daisies, carried them to the kitchenette and filled a glass with water.

When she turned around, she collided with Mark, and, for several excruciatingly sweet moments, her body seemed to be fused to his. She was possessed by a frightening and completely unexpected urge to bare herself to him, to feel his flesh against hers.

She shook her head as if to awaken herself from a dream and started to step around him.

He pinned her against the counter, using just his hips, and Carly felt heat rise from her stomach to her face as he took the daisies and set them aside. His voice was a low, rhythmic rumble.

"I'm not through apologizing," he said, and then he

bent his head and touched Carly's lips tentatively with his own.

She gave a little whimper, because she wanted so much to spurn him and could not, and the kiss deepened. He shaped her mouth with his, and explored its depths with his tongue.

Even with Reggie, the man she'd planned to marry, Carly had been able to withstand temptation easily. With Mark, things were startlingly different. He had overridden her resistance, stirring a sudden and brutal need within her with a simple kiss.

Carly found herself melting against her kitchen counter like a candle set close to a fire. She had a dizzy, disoriented feeling, as though she'd just stepped off some wild ride at a carnival.

With a little chuckle, Mark withdrew from her mouth only to nibble lightly at the length of her neck. He cupped her breast with his hand, and beneath the terry cloth her nipple pulsed to attention.

She moaned helplessly, and Mark lifted her onto the counter. Then he uncovered the breast he had aroused and began to suck gently on its peak.

Carly drew in a swift breath. She knew she should push him away, but she couldn't quite bring herself to do that. What he was doing felt entirely too good.

He traced her collarbone with kisses and then bared her other breast and took its pink tip boldly into his mouth.

Carly gave a strangled groan and let her head fall back against the cupboard door. With one of her hands, she clutched Mark's shoulder, and with the other she pressed the back of his head, holding him close to her.

She clasped his waist between her knees, as though to keep from flying away, and when she felt his hand move down over her belly, she could only tremble. When he found her secret, and began to caress it with his fingers, she started and cried out softly.

"Shh," he said against her moist, well-suckled nipple. "It's all right."

Carly, who had never given herself to a man before, sought his lips with her own, desperate for his kiss. He mastered her mouth thoroughly, then went back to her breasts. He continued his gentle plundering, and Carly's heels rose to the counter's edge in a motion of abject surrender.

Mark kissed his way down her belly and wrung a raw gasp from her throat when he took her boldly into his mouth. He gripped Carly's ankles firmly, parting her legs until she was totally vulnerable to him.

A fine sheen of perspiration covered her body as he attended her, and her hair clung, moist, to her forehead and her cheeks. She writhed and twisted, murmuring nonsense words, while Mark drove her toward sweet damnation.

She cried out at the fiery tumult shuddering through her body, surrendered shamelessly to the searing pleasure. And when it was over, tears of confusion and relief trickled down her cheek.

Gently Mark released her ankles so that she could lower her legs. He closed her robe and kissed her damp brow softly.

"Oh, God," Carly whispered, as shame flowed into her, like water rushing into a tide pool.

Mark traced her lips with the tip of one finger, and considered her with kind eyes. "Chemistry," he said, and then, to Carly's utter amazement, he turned away.

She scooted off the counter and stood for several moments, waiting for her knees to stabilize. Mark had already reached the door, and his hand was resting on the knob.

Carly cinched the belt of her bathrobe tightly. She couldn't believe it. This man had aroused her thoroughly, had subjected her to a scorching climax—and now he was *leaving*. "Where are you going?"

The insolent brown eyes caressed her as he opened the door. "Home."

"But..."

There was a touch of sadness to his smile. "Yes," he said, answering her unspoken question, "I want you. But we're going to wait."

Carly was finally able to move. She stumbled a few steps toward him, filled with resentment because he'd made her need him so desperately and then dismissed her. "You would have been the first," she taunted him, her voice barely above a whisper.

His eyes slid over her slender body, which was still quivering with outrage and violent appeasement. "I'll be the first," he assured her, "and the last."

And then he was gone.

Chapter 3

Carly didn't see Mark the next day, but another message appeared on her computer screen late in the afternoon, just as she was getting ready to go home.

"Nice coverage on the food contest," it said, "but telling 'Frazzled in Farleyville' to get a divorce was truly cavalier. Who the hell do you think you are, Dr. Phil?"

Carly sighed. All her life, her view of the world had been pretty clear-cut: this was right, that was wrong; this was good, that was bad. Now she was faced with a man who could melt her bones one moment, and attack her most basic principles the next.

She poised her fingers over the keyboard for a few minutes, sinking her teeth into her lower lip, then typed, "If you don't like my column, Holbrook, do us both a favor and stop reading it."

Mark's response took only seconds to appear. "That's what I like," it jibed. "A rookie who knows how to heed the voice of experience."

"Thank you, Ann Landers," Carly typed succinctly. "Good night, and goodbye." With that, she shut down the system, gathered up her things and left the room.

Somewhat to her disappointment, there were no computer messages from Mark the next day or the one after that, and he didn't appear in any of the staff meetings, either.

Carly told herself she was relieved, but she was also concerned. She worried, at odd moments, about Mark's undercover assignment with the police. A thousand times a day she wondered how soon word would leak out if something went wrong...

A full week had passed when she encountered Mark again, at a media party in the ballroom of a downtown hotel. He was wearing jeans, a lightweight blue sweater and a tweed sports jacket while all the other men sported suits, and he still managed to look quietly terrific.

His eyes flipped over Carly's slinky pink sheath, and instantly her nipples hardened and pressed against the glimmering cloth. "Hi," he said, and the word was somehow intimate, bringing back Technicolor memories of the incident on her kitchen counter.

Carly's cheeks went as pink as her dress, and she folded her arms in self-defense. "Well," she said acidly, "I see you survived the crack raid."

Mark took hold of her elbow and gently but firmly

escorted her through the crush of television, radio and newspaper people toward the lobby. "We need to talk."

Carly glared at him. "I think it would be best if we just communicated through our computers. Better yet," she added, starting to move around him, "let's not communicate at all."

He captured her arm again, pulled her back and pressed her to sit on a bench upholstered in royal-blue velvet. He took a seat beside her and looked into her eyes, frowning. "What did I do now?"

She straightened her spine, drew a deep breath and let it out again. "That has to be the most obtuse question I've ever heard," she said stiffly.

"I doubt it," Mark retorted, before she could go on to say that she didn't appreciate his criticism and his nonchalant efforts to get her fired. "Considering that you've probably been asked things like, 'How do you walk without your tiara falling off?' and 'What contribution do you think tap dancing will make to world peace?'"

Carly leaned close to him and spoke through her teeth. "I'd appreciate it, Mr. Hotshot Pulitzer Prize Winner, if you would stop making comments about my title!"

His wonderful, damnable brown eyes twinkled. "Okay," he conceded, "just answer one question, and I will."

Carly was cautious. "Fair enough," she allowed huffily. "Ask away."

"What was your talent?"

"I beg your pardon?"

"In the pageant. When the other semifinalists sang

and danced and played stirring classical pieces on the piano, what did you do?"

Carly swallowed and averted her eyes.

Mark prompted her with a little nudge.

"I twirled a baton," she blurted out in a furious whisper. "Are you satisfied?"

"No," Mark replied, and even though he wasn't smiling, his amusement showed in every line of his body. "But I'll let the subject drop for the time being."

"Good," Carly growled, and sprang off the bench.

Mark pulled her back down again. "Lighten up, Barnett," he said. "If you can't take a little ribbing, you won't last five minutes in this business."

Carly's face was flushed, and she yearned to get out into the cool, crisp May evening. "So now I'm thin-skinned, as well as incompetent."

He chuckled and shook his head. "I never said you were incompetent, but you're damned cranky. I can't figure out which you need more—a good spanking or a very thorough session on a mattress."

That was it. Carly had reached the limit of her patience. She jumped up off the bench again and stormed back into the party.

She would have preferred to walk out of that hotel, get into her car and drive home. But she knew contacts were vital, and she wanted to meet as many people as she could.

She stayed an hour and a half, avoiding Mark, passing out and collecting business cards. Then she put on her shiny white blazer and headed for the parking lot.

She had unlocked the door and slid behind the wheel

before she realized that Mark was sitting in the passenger seat. Surprise and fury made her gasp. "How did you get in here? This car was locked!"

He grinned at her. "I learned the trick from Iggy De-Fazzio, a kid I interviewed when I was doing a piece on street gangs."

Carly knew it wouldn't do any good to demand that he leave her car, and she wasn't strong enough to throw him out bodily. She started the ignition and glared at him. "Where to, Mr. Holbrook?"

"My place," he said with absolute confidence that he'd get his way.

"Has anybody ever told you that you are totally obnoxious?"

"No, but my teenage niece once said I was totally awesome, and I think she meant it as a compliment."

Carly pulled out into the light evening traffic. "You must have paid her."

Mark spoke pleasantly. "Pull over."

"Why?"

"Because I can't grovel and give directions at the same time," he replied.

Wondering why she was obeying when this man had done nothing but insult her since the moment she'd met him, Carly nonetheless stopped the car and surrendered the wheel to Mark. Soon they were speeding down the freeway.

"So," he began again brightly, "when you were twirling your baton, were the ends on fire?"

Carly reached out and slugged him in the arm, but

a grin tugged at the corners of her mouth. "Is this your idea of groveling?"

He laughed. "Meet anybody interesting at the party?"

"Two or three TV newscasters and a talk-show host," she answered, watching him out of the corner of her eye. "I'm having dinner with Jim Benson from Channel 37 Friday night."

Mark's jaw tightened for just a moment, and he tossed a sidelong glance in her direction. "He's a lech," he said.

"If he gets out of line," she replied immediately, "I'll just hit him with my baton."

Mark cleared his throat and steered the car onto an exit. "Carly—"

"What?"

"We got off on the wrong foot, you and I."

Carly folded her arms. "Whose fault was that?"

He let out a ragged sigh as they came to a stop at a red light. "For purposes of expediency," he muttered, "I'll admit that it was mine. Partly."

"That's generous of you."

The light changed, and they drove up a steep hill. "Damn it," Mark bit out, "will you just let me finish?"

Carly spread her hands in a motion of generosity. "Go ahead."

He turned onto a long, curving driveway, the headlights sweeping over evergreen trees, giant ferns and assorted brush. "I have a lot of respect for you as a person."

"I haven't heard that one since the night of the junior

prom when Johnny Shupe wanted to put his hand down the front of my dress."

The car jerked to a stop beside a compact pickup truck, and Mark shut off the ignition and the headlights. "I get it," he snapped. "You're mad because I only took you part of the way!"

Carly wanted to slap him for bringing up the kitchen-counter incident, even indirectly, but she restrained herself. "Why, you arrogant bastard!" she breathed instead, clenching her fists. "How dare you talk to me like that?"

He got out of the car, slammed the door and came around to her side. Before she thought to push down the lock, he was bending over her, his lips only a whisper away from hers. "This is how," he replied, and then he kissed her.

At first, Carly resisted, stiffening her body and pressing her lips together in a tight line. But soon Mark's persuasive tongue conquered her, and she whimpered with unwilling pleasure, sagging limply against the back of the car seat.

Presently he took her arm and ushered her out of the car and into the house. By the faint glow of the porch light, Carly could see that it was an old-fashioned brick cottage, with wooden shutters on the windows and a fanlight over the door.

In the small entryway he kissed her again, and the sensations the contact stirred in her pushed all thoughts of their differences to the back of her mind.

"It looks like there's one thing we're going to have to get out of our way before we can make sense of what's happening to us, Carly," he said when the kiss was over. He smoothed away her blazer with gentle hands.

Carly, who had been an avowed ice maiden in high school and college, was suddenly as pliant and willing as a sixteenth-century tavern wench. Her body seemed to be waging some kind of heated rebellion against the resolutions of her mind.

She knew she should get into her car and go home, but she couldn't make herself walk away from Mark.

He led her into a pleasantly cluttered living room where lamps were burning and seated her on the couch. Carly watched as he lit a fire on the hearth, then shifted her gaze to a desk facing a bank of windows. A computer screen glowed companionably among stacks of books and papers.

"I do a lot of my work at home," Mark explained, dusting his hands together as he rose from the hearth. "You can't see it now, of course, but there's a great view of the river from those windows."

Carly was still trying to shore up her sagging defenses, but the attempt was largely hopeless. Mark's kisses had left her feeling as though she'd been drugged.

He left the room briefly and returned with a bottle of wine and a couple of glasses. Taking a seat beside Carly on the cushiony sofa, he opened the bottle and poured.

Carly figured her chances of coming out of this with her virginity intact were slim—and getting slimmer. The crazy thing was, she didn't want to leave.

Mark handed her a glass, and she took a cautious sip.

"I'm really very bright, you know," she said, feeling defensive. "I got terrific grades in college."

He smiled, set his goblet on the coffee table and swung her legs up onto his lap. "Umm-hmm," he said, slipping off her high-heeled shoes one by one and tossing them away.

Some last vestige of pride made Carly stiffen. "You don't believe me!"

Mark ran a soothing hand over her right foot and ankle, and against her will she relaxed again. "I'd be a fool if I didn't," he answered quietly. "There were over a hundred applicants for your job at the *Times*, and all of them were qualified."

Carly was pleased. "Really?"

Mark took advantage of the sexy slit on the side of her pink dress to caress the back of her knee. "Really," he said.

She put her glass aside, feeling as though she'd already consumed a reservoir full of alcohol. On the hearth the fire crackled and snapped. "I really should go straight home," she said.

"I know," Mark agreed.

"I mean, it's possible that I don't even *like* you."

"I know that, too," he responded with a grin.

"But we're going to make love, aren't we?"

Mark nodded. "Yes," he said, and then he stood and drew Carly off the couch and into a gentle embrace. He kissed her lightly on the tip of the nose. "If you really want to go home," he said, "it's okay."

Carly let her forehead rest against his chest and slid her arms around his waist. "God help me," she whispered, "I want to stay."

He put a finger under her chin and tilted her head

back so he could look into her eyes. He moved his lips as though he meant to speak, but in the end he kissed her instead.

Again, she had the sensation of being swept into some kind of vortex, where none of the usual rules applied. When Mark lifted her into his arms, she laid her head against his shoulder.

He carried her up a set of stairs, along a hallway and into a room so large that Carly was sure it must run the entire length of the house. She noticed a fireplace, the shadowy shapes of chairs and, finally, the huge bed.

Made of dark wood, it stood on a U-shaped ledge, dominating the room. It was a place where a knight might have deflowered his lady, and Carly was filled with a sense of rightness, as well as desire.

Mark carried her up three steps and set her on her feet. She stood still as he unfastened the back of her dress and then lowered it to her hips.

The moonlight flowing in through the long windows that lined the opposite wall gave Carly's skin the translucent, pearly glow of white opals, and she felt beautiful as Mark stepped back to admire her. His eyes seemed to smolder in the dim light of the room.

After a while, he bent to kiss the pulse point at the base of her throat, and Carly trembled. She felt as though she'd been created for this moment, as though she'd worked toward it through not just one lifetime, but a thousand.

"Mark," she whispered, and that one word held all her confusion, all her wanting.

In slow, methodical motions, he took away her slip

and bra and panty hose and laid her, naked, on his bed. "So beautiful," he said hoarsely, and Carly raised her hands over her head in unconscious surrender as she watched him shed his clothes in the shadows.

"I've never—"

He interrupted her with a soft, reassuring kiss. "I know, sweetheart," he said. "I'll be as gentle as I can." And then he lay on his side on the mattress, caressing her breast with his strong hand, toying with the straining nipple, tracing the lines of her waist and hip.

"Mark," Carly moaned. He had kindled a blaze within her that night in her apartment, and now it burned so hot that it threatened to consume her.

He bent to suckle at her breast, and she whimpered in welcome, entangling her fingers in his rich, glossy hair. He allowed her to fondle him for a time, then caught both her wrists in his hand and lifted them above her head again, making her deliciously vulnerable.

With his other hand he made a light, fiery circle on her belly, sweeping lower with each pass until he found the core of her womanhood.

Carly's flesh pulsed against his palm as he made slow, steady rounds, and she felt herself grow moist in response. She arched her neck, her breath coming in shallow gasps, and instinctively spread her legs.

And still Mark suckled her breasts, first one and then the other. Her nipples were taut and wet from his tongue, and she was sure she would die if he didn't satisfy her.

She began to plead, and he left her breasts to position himself between her thighs. As he had once before, he clasped her ankles and set her feet wide of her body, holding them firmly in place.

By the time he burrowed through to take her into his mouth, the rest of her body was as moist as her hard, jutting nipples. She pressed her heels deep into the mattress and gave a lusty cry as he feasted on her womanhood, and her hips writhed in concert with the teasing parries of his tongue that came later.

She flung her hands wildly, first clawing at the bedspread, then gripping his shoulders, then delving into his hair. The short tendrils around her face were dewy, clinging to her forehead and her cheeks as she strained for the relief only nature could provide.

Passion racked her violently, and her body quivered as she thrust it upward to meet the teasing strokes of Mark's tongue. "Finish me," she pleaded without breath. "Oh—Mark—*finish me!*"

He complied fiercely and wrung a sobbing shout from her, cupping his hands under her bottom, holding her high, supporting her until the storm raging inside her body subsided. When the tempest had ceased, he lowered her gently to the mattress, where she lay trembling and filled with wonder.

"Mark," she wept.

Slowly he kissed her moist forehead, her eyelids, her cheeks. He drank from her breasts again, sleepily at first, and then with growing thirst. When he mounted Carly, parting her legs first with a motion of one knee, she welcomed him, though she knew he was about to change her forever.

She moved her hands up and down his muscle-corded

back while he drew at her nipple and, finally, she could wait no more.

She clasped his buttocks in her hands and pressed him to her, and he submitted with a groan.

His entry was slow and careful, and every inch he gave Carly only made her want more. There was a brief, tearing pain as he passed the barrier that had sealed her depths to all but him, but in some strange way it made the pleasure keener.

Moaning when he was inside her to the hilt of his manhood, Mark dragged the pillows down from the head of the bed and stuffed them under her so that she was raised to him, in perfect alignment for pleasure.

His second thrust was gentle, but when she urged him with soft, fiery words, he delved deeper.

Carly encircled his waist with her legs and clenched as if to crush him, and the coupling became a tender battle. Near the end, when they were both wild with need and trembling with exhaustion, he caught hold of her hands and thrust them high above her head. While she cursed him with words of love, he held himself still inside her for a long moment, then made a final lunge.

Carly flung back her head and gave a low, guttural wail as her body spasmed around him. He answered with a shout of amazed ecstasy and filled her with his warmth.

They lay like stone for a long time, neither able to speak or move, and then Mark got up from the bed and lifted a still-befuddled Carly into his arms. He carried her into the bathroom and set her, dazed, on the edge of a deep marble tub.

His body was lean and agile as he adjusted the spigots and fetched two enormous white towels from a shelf. He set them close at hand, then eased Carly gently into the water. When it reached a certain depth, he flipped a switch, and powerful jets made the warmth swirl and bubble around her.

Mark turned off the faucets, then got into the tub behind Carly, his powerful legs making a boundary for hers, his arms resting lightly around her waist. He bent to kiss her bare shoulder.

She tilted her head back and looked up at him, only then able to speak. "If I'd known it felt that good, I'd have been promiscuous," she said.

Mark laughed and then nibbled at her nape. "Me, too," he said, and that made Carly twist to look up at him, a broad smile on her face.

"Come on," she said. "You're not going to tell me that was your first time. Even I'm not *that* naive."

He shook his head, and his wonderful eyes were sparkling at her naïveté. "No, babe—you were the only virgin in attendance. But I can honestly say I've never felt exactly that way before."

Carly settled deeper into the water, leaning back against his hairy chest. "I bet you say that to everybody."

He chuckled and moved his lips against the back of her head. "Wrong again," he replied, and then he dipped a hand into the swirling, soothing water and bathed Carly's breasts, one by one.

It was another beginning.

Soon he was caressing her, and she was surrendering, wanting to melt into him again.

When she had to confront him with her need or perish from it, she shifted so that she was facing him and kneeling between his legs.

"You like being in charge, don't you?" she crooned, taking a fresh bar of soap from a brass dish, dipping it into the water, turning it between her hands until they were slick with suds.

Mark leaned back, resting his head on the edge of the tub, and grinned insolently. "You didn't seem to mind it a little while ago. In fact, my guess would be that it beat twirling a flaming baton all to hell."

Slowly, sensuously, she began to lather his broad chest, making soapy swirls in the down that covered it, teasing his nipples with a mischievous fingertip. "There must be some symbolism in that," she conceded huskily. "But I don't quite see it."

He tilted his head even farther back and closed his eyes with an animal sigh of contentment, and it struck Carly that even surrender required a kind of confidence.

"Think, Barnett," he teased. "Think."

Carly didn't want to think. She wanted to bathe this man, and then turn him inside out, just as he'd done to her. And because of the things he'd taught her, she had a pretty good idea how to go about it.

She took her time washing him, and he submitted, but then he claimed the soap and everything was turned around. Soon every inch of Carly was scrubbed to a delicate ivory pink, and she was limp as the cloth Mark had used to cleanse her.

He got out of the tub, lifting her after him, and flipped off the jets under the water. Then he pulled the plug and wrapped one of the huge towels around Carly like a sling, using it to draw her close to him.

She felt his staff rising hard and insistent between them.

"Oh, Mark," she whispered sleepily, "I can't—not again."

"That's what you think," he replied, his lips against her forehead. And he took her back to his bed, where he dried her and laid her out on the sheet like a delicacy to be enjoyed at leisure.

He joined her beneath the covers, knelt between her legs so she couldn't close them to him, and slid his hands under her bottom to lift her to his mouth.

"I mean it," she whimpered as he placed her legs over his shoulders. "I can't—"

He disciplined her with a few flicks of his tongue, and she moaned as heat surged through her tired body, giving it new life.

Mark chuckled against her hardening flesh. "That's what I thought," he said, and he held her firmly in place while she rode helplessly on his lips, her head twisting from side to side in delirium.

He was ruthless. Carly was drenched with perspiration within minutes, and she locked her heels behind his head when he brought her to climax.

After that she begged him to take her and then let her sleep, but he wouldn't. He put her in a new position and made her perform again, and he granted her no quarter until the last shuddering tremor had been

Mixed Messages

drawn from her and her cries of pleasure had died away in the darkness.

Finally she gathered the strength to take revenge. She fell to him, like a starving woman would fall to food, and began to consume him.

At last, Carly had found the way to prevail in the age-old war of lovers, and she was no more merciful to Mark than he had been to her. He groaned like a man in fever, and the sound aroused Carly as much as his caresses and kisses had.

When he could bear no more, he lifted her head and held it from him, gasping as he struggled to catch his breath. Then, ever so gently, he pressed Carly back onto the mattress and took her in a long, slow stroke.

Because his pleasure had excited her so much, she immediately began to convulse, the lower part of her body buckling wildly as he made love to her. Through a sleepy haze she heard him rasp her name, and she felt him stiffen upon her in final release. Then they both were still, and the night rolled in like folds of black velvet and claimed them.

In the morning Carly awakened to the sound of a man whistling. Her aquamarine eyes flew open in alarmed chagrin as she remembered where she was and how she'd behaved in Mark Holbrook's arms.

She sank her teeth into her lower lip. It was morning, and she was going to have to go home in her slinky pink evening dress.

Just then Mark came out of the bathroom. He was wearing a towel around his hips and there was a toothbrush jutting out of his mouth. He gave Carly a foamy grin, opened a drawer, took out a striped pajama top and tossed it to her.

She scrambled into it, using the blankets to hide behind, and he laughed and went back into the bathroom.

Carly needed a shower, but she wasn't about to pass Mark to get one. Knowing a house that large must have at least one more bath, she hurried out of the room. She found what she sought at the opposite end of the hall and, after locking the door, stepped hastily under a spray of hot water.

When she was clean, she put on the bra, panty hose and slip she'd worn the night before. She was about to shimmy into the dress when a knock sounded at the door.

"It's early, Carly," Mark said cheerfully, as though this were a perfectly ordinary morning. "I'll go over to your apartment and get your things if you'll give me the key."

She pressed her cheek to the door panel, embarrassed to be sending a man for such personal items as clothes and underwear and makeup, but she named off the things she wanted. When she was sure he was gone, she stepped out into the hallway, only to find Mark leaning against the opposite wall, grinning at her.

He moved his gaze slowly, possessively, over her figure. "Like I said," he told her in a voice that was as effective as a kiss or a caress, "it's early."

Chapter 4

Carly dodged back into the bathroom and slammed the door, and Mark responded with a laugh.

"Regrets?" he asked.

"Yes!" Carly shouted back. She shoved both hands through her hair. "Go away and leave me alone."

"Cranky," he observed in a resigned tone. "Maybe I should have tried the spanking."

Carly turned the lock, then went to the sink and started the water running full blast. She hummed loudly to let Mark know she wasn't paying any attention to anything he was saying—if he was saying anything.

Fifteen minutes had passed before she dared peer into the hallway again.

Mark was gone then—the house seemed to echo with

his absence—and Carly put his pajama top on over her underthings and stepped out of the bathroom.

On her way to the kitchen, where she hoped to find coffee perking, Carly passed through the living room. Once again the computer caught her eye. Since Mark wasn't around to see, she ventured over to the desk, sat down in the chair and squinted at the words on the screen.

Excitement brought her to the edge of the chair as she read backward through what was apparently a stage play. The story centered around the painful demise of a marriage, and it was so gripping that Carly forgot her quest for coffee, rummaged through her purse for her glasses and read on.

She didn't stop until she heard a car door slam in the driveway. The sound brought her back to the present with a jerk, and it suddenly occurred to her that Mark might not want her reading his play. Her heart beating double time, she pressed her finger to the "Page Down" key and held it there until the original material was back on the screen.

She was in the kitchen, pouring coffee into a mug, when Mark came in carrying her garment bag and beauty case. He gave her a curious look, and she had the uncomfortable feeling that he was picking up on her guilt.

It's a good thing you're not a spy, Barnett, she thought, reaching out for the things Mark had brought her. "Thanks."

He gave her a light kiss on the forehead. "You're

welcome," he answered, and the words had a teasing quality to them.

Carly took another sip of her coffee, then set it aside. If she was going to be at work on time, she'd have to get a move on. "How long have you been up?" she asked idly, remembering that Mark's computer had been on when they came in the night before.

He'd poured coffee for himself, and he grinned at her over the rim of the mug. "A couple of hours. I do some of my best writing before the birds get up."

Carly hesitated in the kitchen doorway. She felt strangely at home in Mark's house and his pajama top, and that was disturbing. "Your piece on the crack-house raid was good," she conceded. The article had had top billing in the Sunday edition, and Carly had marveled as she'd read it.

Mark opened the refrigerator and took out eggs, bacon and a carton of orange juice. "Thanks, Barnett," he said briskly. "I'd love to stand here listening to praise all day, but I've got things to do, and so do you."

Carly felt rebuffed. Until he'd spoken, there had been a certain cautious, morning-after closeness between them. Now there was an impassible force field.

Carly turned around and headed back toward the bathroom.

When she came out, ready to leave for the newspaper office, Mark was at his desk. The play was gone from the screen, replaced by some kind of colorful graph, and he was leaning back in his chair, talking on the telephone.

He dismissed Carly with a wave of his hand—

the way he might have done the paperboy or a meter reader—and she was stung. *Apparently,* she thought glumly, *I've served my purpose.*

She gathered up her purse and the clothes she'd worn the night before and went out to get into her car. Her spirits lifted a little when she found a single yellow rosebud lying on the seat.

At the office, another mailbag full of letters awaited her, as well as three frantic messages from Janet.

Sipping the cup of coffee Emmeline had brought to her, Carly dialed her friend's work number. A secretary put her right through.

"You didn't come home last night!" Janet said, dispensing with the usual "hello."

Carly smiled, even though there was a heavy place in her heart because she'd given herself to the wrong man. "Are you moonlighting for the FBI these days, or what?"

Janet let out a sigh. "I was just worried, that's all. I mean, you're new in town, and there are some real creeps out there—"

"I'm fine, Janet," Carly insisted moderately, getting out her glasses with one hand and slipping them onto her face. Judging by the bulges in the mailbag sitting on her desk, it was going to be a long day.

"You were with Mark Holbrook!" Janet cried, obviously excited at having solved the mystery.

Carly was annoyed. "Janet—"

"I don't mind telling you, I'm impressed."

"Good. I'd hate to think I wasn't living up to my image," Carly said a little stiffly.

Janet made Carly promise that they'd go out for pizza and salad that night after work, then rang off.

Carly immediately set herself to the task of reading and sorting her mail, and her brow crumpled into a frown as she scanned letter after letter berating her for telling "Frazzled in Farleyville" to get a divorce. It was beginning to seem that the public heartily agreed with Mark's assessment of her advice.

She was still reading and disconsolately munching on Cheeze Crunchies from the vending machine in the lounge, when Mark popped into her office at one forty-five that afternoon.

By then she was really feeling cranky. She'd been writing her column for less than two weeks, and everybody in Portland hated her. "What do you want?" she snapped.

Mark grinned in a way that reawakened some of the perturbing feelings she'd had the night before, when they'd somehow gotten past their many differences and visited a new part of the universe. "I came to see if you'd like to go out for lunch, then maybe take in a matinee or something."

Carly took a sip of diet cola and set the can down with a solid thump. "Some of us can't come and go as we please," she replied, glaring at him through the big lenses of her reading glasses. "*Or* take off to a movie in the middle of a workday."

He drew up a chair and sat down with a philosophical sigh. "My older sister is like you. When she gets overtired, and doesn't eat right—" he paused and nodded toward the Cheeze Crunchies "—her blood sugar drops and she takes on the personality of a third-world leader. It's not a pretty sight."

Carly took off her glasses, tossed them aside and rubbed her eyes wearily. "Don't you have to work or something?"

"I'm between assignments," he answered.

The intercom on Carly's desk buzzed, and she pushed the button and said, "Yes?"

"There's a lady psychologist on the phone," Emmeline announced, "and she's hopping mad because you told 'Frazzled in Farleyville'—"

"To get a divorce," Carly finished with a sigh. Her head was pounding. "Put her on," she added with resignation, pushing another button so Mark wouldn't be able to overhear the psychologist's side of the conversation.

He leaned forward to help himself to a Cheeze Crunchy. "It's gonna be a bloodbath," he said, and settled back to watch.

Carly narrowed her eyes at him, then spun her chair around so that her back was turned.

The psychologist introduced herself and proceeded to tell Carly off. "In essence, *Miss* Barnett," the woman finished, "you should be demoted to a position where you can't possibly do any more harm!"

Calling on all her poise-under-pressure training, Carly replied that she was sorry if she'd offended anyone and hung up. When she turned her chair around again, Mark was gone, and the discovery gave her an empty feeling.

Half an hour later she was called into the managing editor's office.

Fully expecting to be fired, to have to go home to her dad in utter disgrace, Carly obeyed the summons, never letting any of her insecurities show.

"We've had some complaints about the way you're handling the advice column," Mr. Clark said when Carly was seated in a chair facing his imposing desk. His expression was sober, and she resisted an urge to bite her lower lip.

She waited in dignified silence.

A smile broke across the editor's face. "And that's good," he boomed. "Means they're reading you. You're shaking them up, jolting them out of their complacency. Which is not to say you couldn't be a little more careful."

Carly's relief was overwhelming. "I'll be sure to check with an expert on the trickier questions," she promised.

Mr. Clark was sitting back in his chair now, his fingers steepled under his chin. Carly was clearly not excused from the hot seat. "Liked your work on the cooking contest," he said. "How would you feel about taking on more varied assignments like that one? We're thinking of picking up one of the syndicated advice columns instead of running our own, you see."

Carly could barely keep from leaping over the desk and kissing Mr. Clark. "I would enjoy that," she said moderately.

"Good, good," responded the editor as his phone buzzed. As he reached for the receiver, he mused, more to himself than to Carly, "Maybe we'll put you on the fathers' rights piece with Holbrook. Get a woman's side of it."

Carly nodded. She wasn't sure how she felt about working with Mark—God knew, he was a genius and she'd kill for the opportunity to learn from him, but he was also the man who had taken her to bed the night before and calmly turned her inside out. If she did get to share the assignment, she would just have to make damn sure she kept her mind on business.

Mr. Clark dismissed her with a kindly gesture, and she rushed out of his office, feeling better than she had all day. When she returned to her desk, she found a turkey sandwich from the corner deli waiting for her, along with a note. "Eat this that others might live. Mark."

Carly couldn't help smiling. She sat down at her desk and made short work of the sandwich, then spent the rest of the afternoon conferring with experts over the telephone. She was determined that that week's column wouldn't generate a storm of protest like the first one had.

If Mark was still in the building, he didn't come near Carly again, and she was both relieved and disappointed as she caught the elevator to the parking garage at five-thirty. She scolded herself that she mustn't fall into the age-old female trap of expecting too much just because she and Mark had been to bed together. He had probably put a check by her name in his book of conquests and moved on to the next prospect.

The thought made Carly sad, and she was feeling moody again when she got home. There, she dumped her garment bag, kicked off her shoes and exchanged the clothes she'd worn to the office for a pair of stretchy exercise pants and a T-shirt. What she needed, she decided, was a good workout.

After fetching a clean towel from the linen closet, she went downstairs to the building's small but well-equipped gym and began going through the program she'd outlined for herself. When she was finished, she felt better.

She encountered Janet in the upstairs hallway. "You're the first woman I've ever known who looked good in sweat," her friend commented with a shake of her head.

Carly blushed, thinking of the last time she'd been worked up enough to perspire, and opened the door of her apartment. "Gee, thanks," she said with a grin. "And here I thought I didn't have anything going for me."

Janet laughed and set her briefcase and purse down on Carly's table. "Right. You were Miss United States and now you're dating a famous journalist. You're a pathetic case if I've ever seen one."

Opening her refrigerator door, Carly took out two diet colas and set them on the table. "I'm not 'dating' Mark Holbrook," she said.

Janet's lips twitched a little; she was obviously fighting back a smile. "I can't understand why you're so touchy about this, Carly—most women would shout it from the rooftops. After all, the guy is merely sensational."

Carly filled two glasses with ice and brought them to the table, sitting down with a sigh. She shrugged, averting her eyes. "He has this affectionate contempt for me, Janet—I know he sees me as a brainless little beauty queen in way over her head—"

"But," Janet pointed out moderately, "you spent the night with him."

"I don't know how to explain that," Carly said with a weary sigh.

"You don't have to explain it," Janet reasoned. "You're a grown woman, after all."

Carly bit her lower lip for a moment. Janet was right, of course, but she still felt a need to confide her feelings to someone, and she couldn't think of a better candidate than her best friend. "I never had any trouble turning guys down when they came on to me," she said quietly. "Even with Reggie—well, it was just easy to say no. But all Mark has to do is kiss me and I turn into this— this red-hot mama."

Janet let out a peal of laughter. "*Red-hot mama?* God, I didn't think anybody said that anymore!"

Carly flushed. "Janet, this is serious!" she hissed. "That man can try to get me fired, he can make remarks about my title, he can as much as tell me I'm incompetent. And then he just turns right around and takes me to bed! Doesn't that make me a woman-who-loves-too-much or something?"

Her friend was kindly amused. "Maybe it just makes you a woman-who-loves, period. Give yourself a break, Carly, and stop analyzing everything to death." She paused and glanced at her watch. "Are we still going out for salad and pizza?"

Carly nodded. "It'll have to be an early night, though. I've got a lot of work to do."

With that, Janet went to her own apartment to change clothes and Carly headed for the shower. Twenty minutes later she was dressed in gray cords and a soft matching sweater, and the doorbell rang. Tossing her makeup bag into a drawer, she made her way through the living room and pulled open the door, expecting to see Janet standing in the hall.

Instead she found Mark, and he didn't look well.

"What's the matter?" Carly asked, stepping back to admit him.

He moved his eyes over her with weary admiration. "It's a personal problem—nothing you need to worry about."

Carly closed the door. "Then why are you here?"

He shoved one hand through his rumpled brown hair. "I'm not sure. I guess—after last night—I thought I could talk to you."

She came to stand in front of him and looked up into his eyes. "You were right—you can."

"You're on your way out." There was no note of accusation in his voice, only a quiet statement of fact.

"Janet and I are going to a pizza place, that's all. You're welcome to come along."

He grinned in a way that tugged at her heart. "Thanks, Barnett, but I don't think I'm up to snappy repartee."

She laid her hands on his upper arms. "Talk to me," she said softly.

He sighed again. "My mother called me an hour ago. Jeanine—that's my ex-wife—was in an accident on the freeway. Nathan was with her, and he's in the hospital with a broken arm."

Carly's eyes went wide with sympathy and alarm. "Then you've got to go down there."

"It isn't that simple."

"Why not? Nathan is your son—he's a little boy, and he's hurt—"

"And his mother has a restraining order against me."

Carly was quiet for a long time, absorbing the implications. "You were violent?" she asked in a whisper, and even as she uttered the words, she couldn't imagine Mark doing any of the things that usually prompted ex-wives to take legal measures to protect themselves and their children.

"No, but I was angry—damn angry. And that was all Jeanine needed. She went to a lawyer and told him I was dangerous."

Carly let her forehead rest against Mark's shoulder for a moment, breathing in concert with him, feeling his frustration and pain in a strange, fundamental way. Finally she looked up at him with tears in her eyes. "Do you want me to go with you?"

He smiled, pulled her close and kissed the top of her head. "No," he said. "I just need to know you're thinking about me, and that you'll be here when I get back."

"Mark—"

He tilted her chin up and gave her a soft, hungry kiss, and all the reactions Carly feared so much immediately set in. If he'd wanted her then and there, she would have given herself to him, and the idea frightened her.

"I'll call," he said.

Carly only nodded and followed Mark to the door, watching him as he left. Janet came in almost unobserved, dressed in designer jeans and a sweatshirt.

"Looks serious," she remarked.

"Let's go get some pizza," Carly replied.

Although Carly tried to have fun with her friend, she was essentially preoccupied. She and Janet came home early.

When she arrived at work the next morning, she stopped by Mark's office, being as subtle as possible, and peeked in. The place was spacious and cluttered, and it smelled of Mark's cologne. And it was empty.

She stepped out, closing the door and wondering how this man had made her care so deeply in such a short time. She had too much of herself invested in Mark, and she had no idea how to back away.

There were flowers waiting on her desk—pink daisies exploding from a pretty cut-glass vase. *It's too soon to talk about love,* the card read, *but I think I'm seriously in like. With you, of course. I left the key to my front door with your assistant, just in case you might want to be there when I get home. Soon, Mark.*

A rush of feeling swept over Carly. She put it down to "like" and switched on her computer.

When Emmeline came in with the customary cup of coffee, she brought the key to Mark's house. To her credit, the woman neither asked questions nor made a comment.

Carly spent a busy day reading letters and talking with various authorities, and when her deadline arrived, she had a solid column to turn in.

She went to Mark's that first night, which was silly because she knew he wouldn't be there. She walked through the house, checking to make sure all the doors and windows were locked, then sat down at his desk.

One of the drawers was sticking out, and Carly tried to close it.

It promptly jammed, and she reached inside.

She hadn't actually meant to snoop. Still, when Carly drew her hand out of the drawer, there was a manuscript in it.

Carly realized she'd found a printout of the play he'd been writing, and she couldn't resist flipping to the opening scene. She would just read a line or two, then put it away.

Moments later, however, Carly was in another dimension. She wasn't aware of time passing, or of the dying light at the windows, or the view of the Columbia River. She read, filled with awe and a singular heartbreak, to the very last page.

Tears brimmed in her eyes as she put the play back in its drawer, and just then the phone rang. Feeling like a prowler, but nonetheless a responsible one, Carly groped for the receiver and sniffled, "Hello?"

"Hi." The voice was Mark's.

Carly gave a guilty start and dashed away her tears with the back of one hand, trying to cover her discomfort with a joke. "Your burglar alarm doesn't work," she said.

He chuckled. "I didn't turn it on. I'm glad you're there, Carly—it's almost as good as having you here would be."

"How's Nathan? Did you get to see him?"

"One question at a time, Scoop. Nathan's going to be fine—I think I'm in worse shape than he is."

"And Jeanine?"

Mark hesitated for a long moment. "She's as difficult as ever."

"But she wasn't hurt in the accident?"

"No."

"What about the restraining order? Was there any trouble?"

"I called my parents' attorney when I got here and had it lifted. I'll tell you all about it when I get home tomorrow night."

Carly felt a wifely warmth at the idea. "Maybe I'll stop by after work, then," she said.

Mark's voice was a slow, sensual caress. "Bring your toothbrush."

She squirmed slightly and let the remark pass. "Thanks for the flowers—they're lovely."

They talked for a few minutes longer, then said reluctant good-nights.

During the drive back to her apartment, Carly thought about Mark's play. His talent was truly formidable, and his words had moved her on a very deep level. She should have told him that she'd read his work, she knew, but the truth was she hadn't dared. The play was about a man and a woman and a child, and in it the dissolution of the family had been portrayed with painful clarity.

It didn't take a genius to figure out that Mark had

written about his own divorce, or that he felt a tragic sense of loss where his young son was concerned.

The subject of Mark's previous marriage seemed to be sacred ground; Carly didn't know how to broach it. She felt almost as though she'd read his diary, tapped his phone or opened his mail. And yet there was a certain exaltation in her, too, because the play had such a poignant beauty.

Arriving at her own building, Carly carried in her purse, briefcase and mail. There was a wedding invitation from Reggie and the nurse from Topeka, and she rolled her eyes as she tossed it onto the desk with the other things.

After changing her clothes, Carly again went to the small gym to work out. When she returned, she showered, made herself a light supper and started reading the briefcase full of misery she'd brought home from the office.

Although she tried, Carly was unable to keep her mind on the letters from readers of her column. Her thoughts kept straying to Mark, and his play. She wanted so much to tell him she'd read it, and that it was wonderful.

But she was afraid.

The next day was hectic, as usual, and Carly didn't have time to think about anything but her work. At six-thirty she got into her car, where a small suitcase was waiting, and drove to Mark's place, stopping off at a supermarket on the way.

When she reached his isolated house, there was no

sign of his car, though the compact pickup was parked in its usual place.

She unlocked the door and went inside. "Mark?" she called out in a hopeful tone of voice, but there was no answer.

Carly carried her luggage into Mark's room, changed into jeans and a T-shirt, then went back to the living room. With considerable effort, she managed to start a blaze in the fireplace, and she put some music on— Mozart.

She was in the kitchen, chopping vegetables for a salad, when she saw his car swing into the driveway. Her heart leaped with an excitement it wasn't entitled to, and she hurried out to meet him.

He needed a shave, and he looked haggard, but his grin transformed his face. "Hi, Scoop," he said hoarsely when she slipped her arms around his waist.

Carly reached up to touch his cheek. "Aren't you going to kiss me?"

He laughed and gathered her against him, and when his mouth touched Carly's, it was as though someone had draped a wet towel over an electric fence. The charge was lethal.

She was breathless when he finally released her. "I hope you didn't eat on the plane," she managed to say, "because I want to cook for you tonight."

Mark reached into the car for his suitcase and assumed a look of comical surprise. "You cook, as well as twirl the baton and tell total strangers to get divorced?" he teased. "My God, Barnett—is there no end to your talents?"

She gave him a saucy look over one shoulder as she led the way toward the gaping front door. "I've got talents galore."

He laughed and followed her into the house.

While Carly broiled the steaks she'd bought, and baked the potatoes, Mark showered and changed clothes. When he joined her on the little patio off the kitchen, he was wearing jeans and a football jersey, and his rich brown hair was still damp.

"I could get used to this," he said, standing behind Carly and slipping his arms around her waist. His lips were warm and tantalizing against her neck.

Carly pretended to bristle, though the fact was that she wouldn't have protested if Mark had hauled her off to bed right then. "You're a chauvinist, Mr. Holbrook."

"I know," he said, lifting her hair to kiss her lightly on the nape.

She was trembling when she turned in his arms and gazed into his eyes. She had to tell him she'd read his play now, while things were so good between them. "Mark, I—"

He silenced her by laying an index finger to her lips. "Later," he told her. "Whatever it is, please save it until after the food, and the loving."

During the meal Carly and Mark didn't talk about Nathan, or Mark's trip. Instead they discussed some of the funnier letters Carly had received and the answers she'd been tempted to give.

They laughed, and the sound of it healed injured places deep inside Carly. Once, tears came to her eyes because it felt so good just to be sitting across the pic-

nic table from Mark, watching the changes in his face
as he talked or listened.

He was rinsing their dishes and putting them into the
machine when Carly told him the advice column might
be discontinued. She watched closely for his reaction,
then felt relief when he grinned and said, "They'll probably find a place for you."

Carly drew a deep breath and leaned against the
breakfast bar. "Actually," she said, "they already have,
sort of."

Mark looked at her curiously. "Don't keep me in suspense, Scoop—are they sending you on assignment to
the White House or what?"

She ran the tip of her tongue over her lips. "I'm probably going to be working with you," she answered, "on
a piece about fathers' rights. Mr. Clark wanted a woman's view on the subject."

He sighed, slammed the dishwasher door closed and
shoved one hand through his hair. "Great."

Carly went to him and laid her hand gently on his
arm. "Mark, I'm not Jeanine," she said in a quiet voice.
"I don't have any axes to grind."

He drew her close and buried his face in her hair. "I
missed you so much," he said hoarsely.

Chapter 5

Mark knelt in front of the fireplace, adding wood to the blaze, while Carly sat on the couch, her legs curled beneath her. The white wine in her glass sparkled and winked like a liquid jewel.

"Things are happening pretty fast between us," she said.

He looked back at her over one shoulder. "Is that a problem?"

Carly thought, taking a leisurely sip of her wine. "Yeah, when you consider we don't even know what it is."

Mark joined her on the couch, taking her wineglass from her hand and setting it beside his on the coffee table. "Don't look now, Barnett, but I think it's passion," he said, easing Carly down onto the cushions and then poising himself over her.

He was so incredibly brazen, but Carly couldn't find it in her heart to protest. She wanted to feel his weight pressing down on her, wanted to lose herself in the multicolored light show his lovemaking would set off in her head.

Mark drank the wine from her lips, then shaped her mouth with his and delved into her with his tongue. Carly felt as though he'd already taken her, and an electrical jolt racked her body. With a whimper, she flung her arms around his neck and responded without reservation.

Mark was gasping when he broke the kiss and slid downward over her body. Carly raised her T-shirt and opened her bra of her own accord, and his groan of pleasure at the sight of her naked breasts vibrated under her flesh.

She cried out in acquiescence when he caught one of her nipples in his mouth and grazed it lightly with his teeth, and dug her fingers into his muscular back.

Before, Mark had taken his sweet time loving her, but that night there was a primitive urgency between them that would brook no delays. While he drank from her breast, Mark was unsnapping her jeans and pushing them down.

She kicked off her shoes, and Mark relieved her of the jeans. She lay before him in just her underpants, with her bra unhooked and her T-shirt bunched under her armpits, and for all the indignity of that she felt beautiful because his brown eyes moved over her with reverence.

"Take me," she whispered, letting the backs of her hands rest against the soft material of the couch on either side of her head.

He bent his head and nipped at her lightly through the silky fabric of her panties until she was moaning softly and beginning to writhe.

Then his clothes were gone as quickly as Carly's. He knelt between her legs, hooking his thumbs under the waistband of her panties, drawing them downward.

"Don't think you're going to get off this easy, Scoop," he teased, finding her entrance and placing himself there. His eyes glittered with desire as he gazed down into her face. "I plan to keep you busy for a long time."

Carly groaned as he gave her an inch then she clawed frantically at his bare back. "Please, Mark—don't make me wait—"

His response was a long, fierce stroke that took him to her very depths. He cupped his hands beneath her bottom, lifting her into position for another thrust.

"Faster," Carly fretted.

He chuckled. "Does this mean you missed me?"

"Damn you, Mark Holbrook!"

After that, he loved her in earnest, with fire and fever, and when the hot storm broke within her, she sobbed his name.

He covered her face with light, frantic kisses as he climaxed, his mouth on her eyelids, her cheeks, the underside of her chin. In those treacherous moments, Carly felt cherished as well as thoroughly mastered.

When it was over, he fell to her, taking solace in her softness in the age-old way of men. His breath came hard and his words, spoken against her cheek, were labored. "If this gets…any better…I'm going to need… respiratory therapy."

Carly laughed softly and laid her hands to either side of his face. "Look at me, Mark. I've got to tell you something before I lose my courage."

He raised his head, his brown eyes mischievous. "You used to be a man," he guessed.

Carly's delight erupted in another burst of amusement. "Wrong."

"You have a prison record."

She couldn't let the game go on any longer. "I read your play, Mark," she blurted out. "I found it and I read it."

He studied her somberly for a long time, then thrust himself upward and reached for his clothes.

"Mark?"

"I heard you, Carly."

"I don't blame you for being angry—I shouldn't have snooped. But it was fabulous—really fabulous."

He got back into his jeans and stormed across the room to his desk.

Carly dressed awkwardly while he wrenched open the drawer, found the screenplay and flung it toward her, its fanfold pages spreading out over the floor. "Mark—"

"You like it?" he rasped. "It's yours. Take it. Line bird cages with it!"

"What is the matter with you?" Carly demanded, snapping her jeans. When he didn't answer, but just stood gazing out through the dark windows, she knelt and gently gathered the play up from the floor. She handled it like the broken pieces of something she'd cherished. "Do you know what I'd give to be able to write like this?"

He turned around then, and to Carly's relief he was much calmer. "You'd have had to feel the pain," he said. "Believe me, the price is too high."

She held the manuscript to her breast like a child as she stood. "I *did* feel the pain, Mark—that's what makes it such a wonderful piece of work—"

"Look," Mark interrupted sharply, "I don't give a damn that you read it, all right? But it represents another part of my life and I can't talk about it—I don't want to be reminded."

"I can keep it?" Carly ventured cautiously. "I can take it home?"

"Do whatever you want."

Carly was filled with sadness as she carried the play across the room and tucked it into her briefcase. She should have known Mark would be angry; she'd been trespassing in the deepest reaches of his soul.

"Carly?"

She felt his hands, strong and gentle, on her shoulders. "I'm sorry, Mark," she whispered.

He turned her to face him. "No," he said huskily. "I'm the one who was wrong. I apologize."

She managed a broken smile. "We both knew this wasn't going to work, didn't we?" she asked.

He gave her a slight shake. "Of course it's going to work," he argued. "It has to."

She prayed she wouldn't cry. "Why?"

"Because I need you, and I hope to God you need me, that's why. Because I think maybe I love you."

"You 'think maybe'?" Carly asked, hugging herself. She felt shaky and confused. "What the hell kind of statement is that?"

Mark caught her by the belt loops at the front of her jeans and hauled her toward him. "I'm doing the best I can here, Carly, so how about helping me out a little?" he said, his face very close to hers. "I don't *know* if this feeling is love—I don't even know if there's any such thing as romantic love—but damn it, I feel *something* for the first time in ten years and I don't want it to stop!"

Carly drew a deep, shaky breath. "You're probably just horny," she said in a tone of resignation.

Mark laughed like a comical maniac, hoisted her up over one shoulder and gave her a sound swat on the bottom. "You may be right," he agreed.

"Put me down!" Carly gasped. "I'm about to throw up."

"I love these romantic moments," Mark answered, carrying her toward his bedroom in exactly the same position. "I feel like Errol Flynn."

"You're an idiot!"

He hauled her up the steps to his bed and flung her down on the mattress. "Will you lighten up, Scoop? Something poignant is happening here."

"Like what?"

Mark stretched out beside her. "Damned if I know, but like I said—I sure don't want it to end."

Carly didn't know whether she was happy or sad,

whether she wanted to laugh or cry, but tears filled her eyes and she said, "Hold me."

The next morning, she was careful to go to work in her own car, hoping no one at the newspaper would guess what was going on between her and Mark. But that night she went back to his house, and he cooked spaghetti.

They laughed and talked and made love, but they didn't discuss Mark's play. Or the assignment they might be sharing.

Friday was hectic. The decision to end the advice column had been made, and Carly felt responsible for its demise to some degree. After all, there had been the "Frazzled in Farleyville" incident.

She still had her office, however, and Mr. Clark announced in a special staff meeting that she and Mark would be working together for the time being. Carly could not have been happier, but there was something disturbing about the remote look she saw in Mark's eyes when he looked at her.

"We'll start working on the story tonight," he announced peremptorily, when everyone else had left the conference room.

Carly swallowed. "I can't."

He raised his eyebrows. "You can't?" he echoed, with a maddeningly indulgent note in his voice. "Why not, pray tell?"

Carly dragged in a deep breath and let it out with a whoosh. "I've got a dinner date. Jim Benson, remember? Channel 37?"

Mark walked over to the door and calmly pushed it shut. "Break it," he said.

Hot pink indignation throbbed in Carly's cheeks. "I beg your pardon."

He was glaring at her. "You heard me, Carly."

Carly had no feelings for Jim Benson one way or the other. She just wanted to establish contacts, to "network" the way other people in the media did. She struggled to stay calm. "Look, it's no big deal. Besides, when I made this date, there was nothing going on between you and me."

"And now there is," Mark pointed out evenly.

Carly laid her hand on his arm. "It's only dinner," she said, and then she left the conference room.

Mark didn't follow.

Back at her apartment, as she showered and dressed, Carly decided it would probably be a good thing if she saw other men. After all, whatever it was that had flared up between her and Mark had come on fast, and she'd had little or no chance to distance herself from the situation.

The other side of that coin, of course, was that Mark would have just as much right to date other women. And the prospect didn't appeal to Carly at all.

Jim Benson arrived promptly at seven. He was tall and handsome, with dark hair and streaks of premature gray at his temples, and bright blue eyes. He took in Carly's soft yellow dress with obvious appreciation.

As she and Jim were leaving the apartment, they encountered Janet, who stood there in the hallway, clutching a grocery bag and staring at them with her mouth open.

Carly knew there would be a message on her answering machine when she got home. "My best friend, Janet McClain," she explained as she and Jim descended in the elevator.

Jim laughed. "When people gape like that, I get this overwhelming compulsion to see if my fly's open."

Jim's car, a sleek sports model, was waiting in the parking lot, and he chivalrously opened the door for her. He turned out to be a very nice guy, the kind of man Carly might have gotten serious about if she hadn't met Mark first.

When they'd reached the restaurant and were settled at their table, Jim said very companionably, "You must know Mark Holbrook, if you work at the *Times*."

Carly nodded thoughtfully. "Sometimes I wonder how well," she murmured.

"He and I have been good friends for a long time," Jim went on. "I hope you won't mind that I invited him and his date to join us for drinks later."

Carly had been sipping ice water, and she nearly choked at this announcement. "Tell me the truth," she said when she'd composed herself. "You didn't invite Mark—he invited himself."

Jim grinned. "Well…"

Carly had picked up her table napkin during her choking spell; now she tossed it down angrily. "Why, that sneaky—"

"Am I missing something here?" the newscaster asked politely.

Carly sighed. Jim was too nice; she wasn't going to play games with him. "The truth is, Mark and I have been seeing each other, and something's going on. I don't know whether it's love or not, but it's pretty heavy, and he was upset when I told him I was keeping my date with you."

A grin spread across Jim's face. "So he just wants to unsettle you?"

"I'm afraid so," Carly said with a nod and another sigh. "I'm sorry, Jim."

He shrugged. "No reason we can't be friends." He picked up his menu and opened it. "The shrimp scampi is good here."

Carly had no appetite at all now that she knew Mark was going to show up at any minute, but she ordered the shrimp and did her best to eat.

She and Jim were in the lounge, later, when he said, "Don't look now, but your partner just walked in. Let's dance and give him a thing or two to think about."

The idea sounded good to Carly. She smiled warmly and allowed Jim to lead her onto the small dance floor. Even though it nearly killed her, she didn't look to see who Mark was with.

"Is he watching?" she asked.

Jim chuckled and drew her closer. "Oh, yes. If that expression in his eyes were a laser beam, he'd be doing surgery on me. The kind you don't recover from."

Carly laughed. "And the woman?"

"Weatherperson from Channel 18. Very cute."

Before Carly could maneuver into a position where she could get a look at Mark's date, he walked right onto the dance floor. Carly was pulled from Jim's arms into Mark's long before he took the trouble to grind out, "May I cut in?"

"No," Carly answered, but when she tried to pull away, he restrained her. "This is ridiculous."

He arched one eyebrow. "All right, I admit it—I'm jealous as hell."

Carly smiled acidly, her eyes widening in mock surprise. "No!"

He gave her a surreptitious pinch on the bottom, and she gasped and stiffened in response. "You've made your point, Barnett—I don't have any rights where you're concerned. But you're going to have to give up dating other guys, unless you want me tagging along."

"Why should I?" Carly asked. "Give up dating other guys, I mean."

"Because I l-like you."

"Well, I *l-like* you, too. Maybe I even love you. In spite of the fact that you're acting like a badly trained baboon tonight." The music stopped. "How about introducing me to your date, Mark?"

He cleared his throat, took her hand and started toward the table where Jim and the weatherperson were sitting, already deep in conversation. "I told you he was a lech," Mark whispered.

"And he told me you were his friend," Carly scolded.

"I was, until he made a move on you," Mark responded, still talking under his breath.

Jim stood when he saw Carly, and an unreadable look passed between the two men. Mark pulled out Carly's chair for her and, when she was seated, sat down beside the weatherperson.

"This is Margery Woods," he said. "Margery, Carly Barnett."

The young woman's brown eyes were round with admiration. "Miss United States—"

"Let's not talk about me," Carly broke in.

"But I saw your pageant—I recorded it. I record all the pageants."

Carly looked to both Mark and Jim for rescue, but neither of them offered it. In fact, they both looked amused, as though they'd set up some tacit conspiracy. "That's—that's nice," she said. "Have you been dating Mark long, Margery?"

That question wiped the complacent look from Mark's face.

"On and off for about six months," Margery responded with a philosophical sigh. Then she gave her date an affectionately suspicious glance. "But I've heard rumors that he's running around with some bimbo at the newspaper office."

Carly managed to swallow the sip of white wine she'd taken without choking on it, but just barely. She gave Mark a look that said, *just you wait, fella,* then changed the subject.

By the time Jim drove her home, she was exhausted. "I'm sorry," she said again at her door. "Tonight was probably a real drag for you."

He smiled and kissed her lightly on the forehead. "Actually it was the most fun I've had in weeks. If it helps any, I can tell you that Mark's in love with you."

The words gave Carly a soft, melting feeling inside. "It helps," she said.

"That's what I was afraid of," Jim answered with a grin and a shrug. He kissed Carly again and walked away.

As soon as Carly was inside her apartment with the lights flipped on and the door locked behind her, she saw that she had messages. Kicking off her high-heeled shoes and pushing one hand through her hair, she played the first message.

"Who was that hunk?" Janet's voice demanded without so much as a hello. "I mean, I know who he is because I've seen him on television. What I meant was, what are you doing going out with him when you've got this hot thing going with Mark Holbrook? You'd better call me *tonight,* Carly Barnett, or our friendship is over!"

Carly grinned as she moved on to the next message.

"Carly, honey, this is your dad. I was just calling to see how you're doing. Give me a ring tomorrow sometime, if you have a chance—I'll be at the filling station."

Her throat thick, because she would have liked very much to talk with her father and maybe get some perspective on the situation with Mark, Carly sank into the desk chair to hear any further messages.

"Okay, I acted like a caveman," Mark's voice confessed. "It's pretty strange, Scoop—I'm sorry, and yet I know I'd do the same thing all over again. I'll pick you up in the morning for breakfast and we'll get started on the new project. Bye."

She wondered what her dad would think of Mark

Holbrook and his high-handed but virtually irresistible methods. Her teeth sinking into her lower lip, Carly glanced at the clock on her desk and wished it wasn't so late in Kansas.

The sudden jangling of the telephone startled her so much that she nearly fell off her chair. Knowing the caller was probably either Mark or Janet, she answered with a somewhat snappish "Hello."

"Hi, baby," her father's voice said.

"Dad!" Carly looked at the clock again. "Is everything okay? Are you sick?"

He chuckled. "Do I have to be sick to call my little girl?"

Carly let out a long sigh. "I'm so glad you did," she said. "I really need to talk to you."

"I'm listening."

Carly's eyes stung with tears of love and homesickness. Her dad had always been willing to listen, and she was grateful. "I think I'm falling in love, Dad. His name is Mark Holbrook, and he's utterly obnoxious, but I can't stay away from him."

Her father laughed affectionately. "Did you think it would be bad news to me, your falling in love? I'm happy for you, honey."

"Didn't you hear me, Dad? I said he was obnoxious! And he is. He's got this Pulitzer Prize, and he's always making comments about my title—"

"There are worse problems."

"I think he's going to ask me to move in with him," Carly burst out.

Don Barnett was quiet for several moments. "If he does, what are you going to say?"

Carly swallowed hard. "Yes. I think."

If her father had made any private judgments, he didn't voice them. "You're a big girl now, Carly. You have to make decisions like that for yourself."

Carly sighed. "Maybe I should hold out for white lace and promises," she mused.

Her dad chuckled at that. "Even when you've got those things, there aren't any guarantees. The name of the game is risk."

It seemed like a good time to change the subject. "Speaking of risk, Dad," Carly began with a smile in her voice, "are you still eating your meals over at Mad Bill's Café?"

He laughed. "Bill's going to be real hurt when I tell him you said that."

Five minutes later, an impatient knock at Carly's door terminated the conversation. She said goodbye to her father, went to the peephole and looked out.

Her arms folded, Janet was standing in the hallway, wearing her bathrobe.

Carly opened the door, and her friend swept into the room.

"You didn't call," Janet accused.

"I was talking with my dad," Carly answered, grinning as she went into the kitchen to put on the teakettle. A nice cup of chamomile would help her sleep.

Janet followed her into the kitchenette. "Well? What's going on? Is it over between you and Mark?"

Carly chuckled and shook her head. "No, but it sure

is complicated. Jim is just an acquaintance, Janet—I want to make contacts."

There was a pause while Janet inspected her freshly polished fingernails and Carly got mugs down from the cupboard, along with a box of herbal tea bags. "Maybe you could fix me up with him," she finally said. "Jim, I mean."

Carly smiled. "Sure," she said gently. "I'll see what I can do."

"You're a true friend," Janet beamed. But then she glanced at her watch and frowned. "I'd better not stay for tea—I'm putting in some overtime tomorrow. Let me know when things are set."

"I will," Carly promised, following Janet to the door and closing and locking it behind her.

It was very late and Carly had to be up early the next morning herself, but even after drinking the chamomile tea, she couldn't go to sleep. She got Mark's play out, carried it to bed and began to read.

Again she was awed by the scope of the man's talent—and a little jealous, too. No matter how hard she worked, it would be years before she was even in the same ballpark. In fact, in her heart Carly knew she would never be the caliber of journalist Mark was, and she wondered if she would be able to live with that fact and accept it.

Long after she had set the play aside and turned out the light, Carly lay in the darkness, thinking about it, envisioning it produced on a stage or movie screen. It would be remarkable in either medium.

A wild idea she barely dared to entertain came to

her. The temptation to send the work to an agent was almost overpowering. After all, Mark had said the play was hers, that she could do what she wanted to with it.

Carly sighed. He'd been upset at the time.

Finally, after much tossing and turning, she was able to go to sleep.

It seemed to Carly that no more than five minutes could have passed when her eyes were suddenly flooded with spring sunlight from the window facing her bed. At the same time, Mark—it had to be Mark—was leaning on the doorbell.

Grabbing for her robe, Carly shrugged into it and went grumpily to the door. Sure enough, the peephole revealed Mark standing in the hallway.

Carly let him in, prepared for a lecture.

"You're not ready," he pointed out. "What kind of reporter are you, Barnett? There's a whole world out there living, dying, loving and fighting. And here you are—" his eyes ran mischievously over her pink bathrobe "—standing around looking like a giant piece of cotton candy."

Carly retreated a step and cinched her belt tighter. She knew the perils of standing too close to Mark Holbrook in a bathrobe. "I'll be ready in ten minutes," she said.

"Make it five," Mark retorted, glancing pointedly at his watch. "We have a plane to catch."

Carly stared at him. "A plane?"

Mark nodded, his hands tucked into his hip pockets. "If we're going to write about fathers' rights, Scoop, you're going to have to do a little research on the subject. We'll start by introducing you to Nathan."

"But I can't just leave—"

"Why do you think Clark gave me this story?" Mark interrupted. "He knows I've got my guts invested in it. And you're my assistant. Therefore, where I go, you go. Now hurry up."

Carly hurried into the bathroom, showered, and hastily styled her hair and put on light makeup. After that, she pulled a suitcase out from under the bed.

"How long are we going to be gone?" she called out.

Mark appeared in her doorway. He was sipping a cup of coffee, and he looked impossibly attractive in his jeans and Irish cable-knit sweater. "Long enough for you to see that women aren't the only ones who sometimes have their rights trampled on," he responded.

Carly wasn't about to comment on that one—not before breakfast. She packed as sensibly as she could, tucking the play into her suitcase when Mark wasn't looking, and left a message for Janet saying she'd be away on business for a while. Finally she and Mark set out for the airport in his car.

After they'd bought their tickets and checked in their baggage, they went to a busy restaurant for breakfast. Carly left the table for a few minutes, and when she returned, there was a long velvet box beside her orange juice.

Her hand trembled a little as she reached for it and lifted the lid to find a bracelet of square gold links. She was unable to speak when she lifted her eyes to Mark's face.

He took the bracelet from the box and deftly clasped it around her wrist. "I can't pretend this trip is strictly business, Carly," he said, his eyes warm and serious. "I guess what it all boils down to is, I'm asking you to move in with me."

Chapter 6

"I need some time to think," Carly said softly, gazing down at the bracelet in stricken wonder. The words sounded odd even to her, especially in light of what she'd told her father the night before, about saying yes if Mark asked her to live with him. Being confronted with the reality was something quite different, though, and whatever it was that she and Mark had together was still fragile. She didn't want to ruin it.

She was trying to unfasten the bracelet when Mark's fingers stopped her.

"It's all right, Carly," he said quietly. "No matter what you decide, I want you to keep the bracelet."

They finished their breakfast in a silence that was at once awkward and cordial, then went to board their plane.

Once they were settled in their seats and their air-craft had taken off, Mark was all business. He pulled a notebook and a couple of pens from his briefcase and started outlining his basic ideas about the piece on fa-thers' rights. He listened to Carly's input thoughtfully and even condescended to use some of it.

By the time they landed in San Francisco, they had the basic structure of the article sketched in.

In the cab that brought them into the city, they ar-gued. Mark naturally felt that fathers got a bad deal, as a general rule, when it came to questions like custody and visitation rights. Carly responded that he was preju-diced, that many fathers didn't care enough about their children to pay support, let alone visit or seek custody.

The taxi came to a stop in front of an elegant house overlooking the Bay, and Carly was surprised. She hadn't paid attention when Mark gave directions to the cabdriver.

"We're not staying in a hotel?"

Mark grinned as he held the car door open for her. "My parents would regard it as an insult," he answered.

Soon they were standing on the sidewalk with their luggage, the cab speeding away down the hill. And Carly was nervous.

"This isn't fair, Mark. You didn't warn me that I was going to be meeting your family."

"You didn't ask," he said as a plump woman in a maid's uniform opened the front door and came out onto the porch.

"They're here!" she called back over one shoulder.

Mark was holding Carly's suitcase, but she grabbed

it. "How are you going to present me?" she whispered out of the side of her mouth. "As the woman you want to live with?"

"I detect hostility," Mark whispered back just as a tall, striking lady with white hair came out of the house, beaming with delight.

Carly knew immediately that this was Mark's mother, and she smiled nervously as Mrs. Holbrook kissed her son's cheek. "It's so good to see you again, darling."

"It's only been a few days, Mom," Mark pointed out, but the look in his eyes was affectionate. "This is Carly," he added, slipping his free arm around her waist.

Carly smiled and offered her hand. "Hello."

Mrs. Holbrook's grasp was firm and friendly. "Welcome, Carly. I'm very pleased to meet you." She turned resigned eyes to Mark. "There is a problem, though."

"What?" Mark asked, starting toward the door.

Mrs. Holbrook stopped him with two words. "Jeanine's here."

Carly felt a wild urge to turn and chase the taxi down the street.

Mark paused on the step, frowning down into his mother's concerned face. "What the—"

Before he could finish, a tall beauty with auburn hair and Irish green eyes appeared in the doorway. Her complexion was flawless, and her gaze moved over Mark in a proprietary way, then strayed to Carly.

"So," she said, her voice icy. "This is Mark's beauty queen."

Although the words had not been particularly inflammatory, Carly felt as though she'd been slapped.

She lifted her chin and met Jeanine's gaze straight on, though she didn't speak.

Mrs. Holbrook linked her arm through Carly's and politely propelled her toward the door, forcing Jeanine to shrink back into the entryway. "Don't be rude, dear," she said evenly. "Carly is my guest."

The maid led the way up the stairs, depositing Carly in a lovely room decorated in muted mauve and ivory. There was an inner door that probably led to Mark's quarters.

Sure enough, he came through it five seconds after Carly had popped open her suitcase.

"I should have warned you," he said, giving her a light kiss on the mouth. "Here be dragons, milady."

"Thanks a lot," Carly said furiously. She was still smarting because Jeanine had called her a "beauty queen," and because she had a pretty good idea where the description had come from.

Mark's eyes were dancing as he shrugged and spread his hands. "Don't feel bad, Scoop—I didn't like her, either. That's why we are divorced."

"How did she know we were coming?" Carly demanded in a furious whisper.

Mark sighed and sat down on the edge of Carly's four-poster bed. "Mom probably told her."

"It must be nice to be let in on little things like that!" Carly spat, pacing. She had half a mind to call a cab and head straight for the airport. The trouble was, half a mind wasn't enough for the task.

Mark reached out and pulled her easily onto his lap.

She struggled, he restrained her, and she gave up with an angry huff.

He unbuttoned her blouse far enough to kiss the cleft between her breasts, resting his hand lightly on her thigh.

Carly felt as though someone had doused her in kerosene, then touched a match to her. "Mark, not here. Not now."

"Umm-hmm," he agreed, pushing down her bra on one side and nonchalantly taking her nipple into his mouth.

She stiffened on his lap, unwilling to free herself from his spell even though she knew it was desperately important to do so. "Mark," she moaned in feeble protest.

He raised her linen skirt, and dipped his hand inside her panties. His lips never left her breast. "Umm," he said.

Carly swallowed a strangled cry of delighted protest as he found her secret and began to toy with it. "You—are—an absolute—*bastard,*" she panted.

He chuckled and nuzzled her other breast, nipping at it through the thin, lacy fabric of her bra. "No question about it," he admitted. And he slid his fingers inside Carly and plied her with his thumb.

She clutched his shoulders, and a soft sob of rebellious submission escaped her as he worked his singular magic. She felt a fine mist of perspiration on her upper lip and between her breasts as he made her body respond to him. She let her head fall back in surrender. "So—arrogant—"

He slipped his tongue beneath the top of her bra to find her nipple. "You love it," he said when he paused to bare her for his leisurely enjoyment.

That was the worst part of it, Carly thought, writhing helplessly under Mark's attentions. She *did* love it.

Her climax was a noisy one, despite her efforts to swallow her cries of release, and Mark muffled it by covering her mouth with his own. When she sagged against him in a sated stupor, he withdrew his hand and calmly fastened her bra, buttoned her blouse and straightened her skirt.

When he set her on her feet, she swayed, and he steadied her by grasping her hips in his hands.

He stood, kissed her gently on the mouth, then disappeared into his room.

Mark hadn't been gone five minutes when a light knock sounded at the outer door. Carly had been sitting on the window seat, staring out at the Bay and wondering whether what she felt for Mark was love or obsession, and she was grateful for a distraction.

"Come in," she said quietly.

Mrs. Holbrook stepped into the room. "Lunch is nearly ready," she said with a smile. "I do hope you're hungry, my dear. Eleanor makes a very nice crab salad sandwich."

Carly smiled lamely and hoped her clothes weren't rumpled from those wild minutes on Mark's lap. "That sounds marvelous," she answered. She didn't have the courage to ask if Jeanine was still present and, fortunately, she didn't have to.

"Jeanine is gone, for the time being at least," Mrs.

Holbrook volunteered. "I should have known better than to tell her I was expecting you and Mark."

Carly lowered her eyes for a moment. The phrase "beauty queen" was still lodged in her mind like a nettle, and she wondered why Mark hadn't spoken of her as a journalist, or even an assistant. It hurt to be defined with a long-defunct pageant title when she'd worked so hard to learn to write. "It's all right, Mrs. Holbrook," she said.

"Please," the woman said gently, holding out a hand to Carly. "Call me Helen. And what do you say we give Mark the slip and have our sandwiches in the garden? He's on the telephone with his father."

Carly smiled and nodded, and she and Helen went downstairs together.

The garden turned out to be a terrace lined with budding rosebushes and blooming pink azaleas. There was a glass-topped table with a pink-and-white umbrella and a splendid view of the Golden Gate. A salty breeze blew in from the water, rippling Carly's hair, and she had a strange sensation of returning home after a long, difficult journey.

"Did you know Mark wrote a play about his marriage and divorce?" she asked when the maid had brought their sandwiches, along with a bone-china tea service, and left again.

"I'm not surprised," Helen said, and there was a sad expression on her still-beautiful face. "He deals with most things by writing about them."

Carly had known Helen Holbrook for less than an hour, and yet she felt safe with her. "It's absolutely brilliant," she went on. Just recalling the powerful emotions the play had stirred in her almost brought tears to her eyes. "And he's not going to do anything with it."

Helen sighed. "Sometimes," she reflected, "I delude myself that I understand my son. Mostly, though, I accept the fact that he's a law unto himself."

Carly nodded. "He gave me the play," she said. "He told me I could do anything I wanted to with it—that it was mine."

Helen's gaze met Carly's, and in that instant the two women came to an understanding. "Then I guess you'd be within your rights if you took certain obvious steps," Helen said.

Before Carly could respond, Mark appeared in the gaping French doors that led from an old fashioned, elegantly furnished parlor. He was carrying a sandwich and a tall glass of ice tea. He winked at Carly, in a tacit reminder of the episode upstairs, bringing a blush to her cheeks.

"Jeanine's bringing Nathan over in an hour," he said.

Carly felt like an intruder, but didn't move from her chair. And she knew then that they hadn't flown to San Francisco to work on the article, but to come to terms with Mark's past.

Helen looked extremely uncomfortable. "Jeanine's been drinking more and more lately," she finally confided.

Carly was about to make an excuse and retreat to her room when Mark reached out and closed his hand over hers, indicating that he wanted her to stay. She felt a charge go through her that probably registered on the Richter scale.

"And she was drunk when she had the accident," Mark ventured.

His mother pressed her lips together in a thin line for a long moment, then said, "I think so, but she denies it, of course."

Mark slammed his fist down on the glass tabletop and bounded out of his chair to stand facing the Bay, his hands gripping the stone wall that bordered the garden. "One of these days she's going to kill him."

Carly longed to help, to change things somehow, but of course there was nothing she could do.

Mark finally came back to the table, but he was too restless to sit. He put one hand on Carly's shoulder and squeezed, and she pressed her fingers over his.

Helen's lovely blue eyes moved from Carly's face to her son's. With a perceptive smile, she rose from her chair. "I think I'll make myself scarce for a little while," she announced, and then she vanished.

Carly stood and slipped her arms around Mark's waist. "I like your mother," she said.

He kissed her briefly. "So do I, but I don't think she's the topic you really want to discuss."

Carly shook her head, resting her hands on the lapels of his lightweight tweed jacket. "You're right. I want to know how you met Jeanine, and what made you fall in love with her."

"I didn't 'meet' Jeanine—I've known her all my life," Mark answered, and there was a hoarse note of resignation in his voice. "We were expected to get married, and we didn't want to disappoint anybody, so we did."

"You must have loved her once."

Mark shook his head. "I didn't know what love was," he answered huskily. "Not until Nathan came along. As soon as Jeanine realized how much I cared about our son, she began using him against me."

I know, Carly wanted to say. *I read your play.* But she only stood there, close to Mark, her head on his shoulder, her eyes fixed on the capricious Bay.

"I want him back, Carly," he went on. "Not just for weekends, or holidays or summer vacations. For keeps."

She wasn't surprised. "From what you've said," she answered softly, "the chances of that aren't too good."

"I can fight her. I can sue for custody."

Carly turned so that she could look up into Mark's face. She saw determination there, and fury, and she had a glimmer of what he'd meant when he'd spoken so bitterly of fathers' rights. Her heart went out to him. "You might lose," she said.

"Life is full of risks," he answered.

Carly and Mark were in the parlor when Jeanine returned, bringing Nathan with her.

He was a handsome, serious boy, so like his father that Carly's heart lurched slightly when she saw him. He was wearing jeans and a red-and-blue striped T-shirt, and there was a cast on his left arm, covered with writing.

He beamed, showing a gap where his two front teeth had been. "Hi, Dad," he said a little shyly.

Carly noticed the tears in Jeanine's eyes as she stood

behind her son, and felt a moment's pity for the woman. Perhaps Mark had been telling the truth when he said he'd never loved Jeanine, but Carly knew for certain that Jeanine had once loved him. Maybe she still did.

"Come here," Mark said huskily, and the child rushed into his arms.

"Have him back by nine o'clock," Jeanine said crisply, her chin high. "And don't give him sugar. It makes him hyper."

Mark ruffled his son's rich brown hair and nodded at Jeanine, and that was the extent of his civility. Carly was relieved when the other woman left the room.

"I want you to meet somebody," Mark told the boy, putting an arm around Nathan's shoulder and gently turning him toward Carly. "This is my—friend, Carly Barnett. Carly, this is Nathan."

Carly held out her hand in a businesslike way, and Nathan shook it, looking up at her with solemn, luminous eyes.

"Hello," he said.

Again Carly had that peculiar sensation of déjà vu that she'd had in the garden. She could have sworn she'd met Nathan before. "Hi," she replied, smiling.

He crinkled his nose. "Mom said you were a queen. I thought you'd be wearing a bathing suit and a crown," he informed her.

Carly laughed. "I'm a reporter," she said, spreading her hands. "No queens around here."

Once Mark had hustled them out the door, they drove to Fisherman's Wharf in Helen's sedate Mercedes and watched the street performers. There were mimes and banjo players and even acrobats, all combining to give the place the festive flavor of a medieval fair.

Carly busied herself exploring the little shops for an hour or so, while Mark and Nathan sat quietly on a bench, talking. Occasionally she checked on them, and it twisted her heart that the expressions on their faces were so serious.

Having no real idea what ten-year-old boys liked, Carly selected a deck of trick cards in a magic shop, along with a bottle of disappearing ink. When Mark and Nathan had had an hour to talk, she joined them.

To her relief, they looked delighted to see her.

"I'm hungry," Nathan announced.

Mark glanced at Carly in question, and she shook her head. She was still full from lunch.

He bought hot, spicy sausages for himself and Nathan, and they ate as they explored the waterfront. When the wind off the water became chilly, they went back to the car.

"I bought you something," Carly told Nathan a little shyly, holding the bag from the magic shop out to him.

He reached between the car seats to accept the gift. "Thank you," he said politely. The bag crackled as he opened it. "Wow! *Disappearing ink!*"

Mark was pulling the expensive car into traffic. "Just don't spill it. Your grandmother wouldn't appreciate that."

Nathan gave a peal of delighted laughter. "She'd never know, Dad—it would disappear!"

They went to an adventure movie after that, and then to dinner at a rustic place on the waterfront.

By the time the evening was over, Nathan was asleep in the backseat of Helen's car, the deck of magic cards still clasped in his hand.

Just looking at him made Carly's heart swell inside her until it seemed to fill her whole chest.

Mark brought the car to a stop in front of a town house on a steep, winding street, and Jeanine appeared on the porch as he awakened his son. "Come on, Buddy," he said quietly. "It's time to hit the sack."

Nathan woke up slowly and gave Carly a sleepy grin. "Would you sign my cast? Please?"

Carly swallowed and nodded, rummaging through her purse until she found a pen. She wrote her name beneath Pauly Tosselli's, and drew a heart beside it.

"Thanks," Nathan said. "When you come back, I'll know a whole bunch of card tricks."

"Okay," Carly replied in a small voice.

She waited in the car while Nathan and Mark approached the house. When Mark returned, his expression was strained.

She laid a hand on his arm. "It's progress, Mark. A few weeks ago Jeanine wouldn't even let you see him."

"She smells like she spent the afternoon at the bottom of a bourbon bottle," he answered tightly.

They drove back through darkened, picturesque streets that could only have belonged to one city.

"You neglected to mention," Carly ventured teasingly, her hand caressing the leather-upholstered car seat, "that your parents are rolling in money."

Mark relaxed a little and flashed her a grin. "Darn. I was going to tell you I'd started as a lowly paperboy."

"Is this the old stuff, or are you *nouveau riche?*"

"It's been around a few generations—my great-great-grandfather was a forty-eighter."

"A what?"

"He got here a year before the other guys."

Carly laughed. "And more than a hundred years later you're still carrying on the tradition," she said.

Mark's grin broadened and took on a cocky air. "Yeah."

When they reached the Holbrooks' house, Mark's father was home. He was an imposing man with a full head of snow-white hair, a ready smile and a firm handshake.

"So this is the reporter I've heard so much about," he said, winning Carly's heart with a single sentence. "It's about time my son had a little competition."

The four of them had nightcaps together and talked, and then Carly excused herself, wanting to give Mark and his parents some private time.

She almost jumped out of her skin when she came out of the guest bathroom, freshly showered and dressed in an oversize T-shirt, to find Mark sitting cross-legged in the middle of her bed. He was wearing a pair of black-and-gray striped pajama bottoms and nothing else.

"Eleanor laid them out for me," he said a little defensively when Carly giggled. "The least I could do was wear them."

"Get off my bed, Mr. Holbrook."

He fell back against the pillows, pretending to pull at an arrow lodged in his chest, and when Carly bent over him to repeat her order, he grabbed her and flung her down on the mattress beside him.

Her squirming struggles ended, as usual, when he kissed her. She wrapped her arms around his neck and scooted close to him.

Presently he tore his mouth from hers, his eyes dancing. Rising off the bed, he pulled Carly with him and led her toward the inner door, one finger to his lips.

His room was shadowy, but she could make out pennants on the walls, and framed pictures of athletes. "Do you know how long I've fantasized about this?" he whispered.

"What?"

He set her down on the edge of the bed and bent to subdue her with another kiss. "This," he finally answered long moments later when she was rummy and disoriented. "Sneaking a girl into my room."

Carly giggled. "Come on. You don't expect me to believe you never tried that!"

"I tried, and my mother, Helen the Terrible, always caught me. She'd rap on the door and say, 'This is a raid.' It always threw cold water on the moment, if you know what I mean."

Despite their bantering, Carly was trembling with excitement. She sighed when Mark laid her back on the mattress and began raising the T-shirt. Finally he pulled it off over her head, and she lay before him, naked except for a mantle of shimmering moonlight. Her nipples tightened and flushed dark rose under his perusal.

"You're so beautiful, Carly," he said, his voice low

and husky. His hand came to rest lightly on her belly. "So remarkably beautiful."

She reached up and clasped her hands behind his head. "Come here and kiss me," she said, and drew him down to her mouth.

He moved his hands in ever-broadening circles. With his fingers he explored her satiny thighs, then parted them to venture into the tangle of silk.

Carly tried to wriggle farther onto the mattress, but Mark wouldn't let her. He kissed his way down her body until he was kneeling beside the bed, the undersides of her knees clasped gently in his hands.

"I can't be quiet," she choked out in a panic. "Not if you do that."

"Then don't be quiet," he answered, and Carly pressed the corner of a pillow against her mouth to stifle her involuntary cry when he took her into his mouth.

She tossed her head from side to side as he enjoyed her, and she bit down on her lower lip to keep the noise to a minimum.

Mark was ruthless. He brought Carly to an excruciating release that arched her back like a swan's neck, his hands fondling her breasts as she whimpered, swamped in pleasure, unable to stop the violent spasms of her body.

Finally she collapsed to the mattress, gasping for breath, her skin glistening with perspiration.

Mark wouldn't let her rest. Seated on the floor now, with his back to the bed, he made her stand over him while he teased and tempted her, always stopping just short of appeasing her.

When she pleaded in broken gasps, he laid her down and came into her in a long, gliding thrust. After a few measured strokes, Carly's feeble control snapped. She hurled her body upward to meet his as a resonant string was plucked deep inside her, its single note shuddering throughout her body.

But her greatest satisfaction was in hearing Mark groan as her flesh consumed his, drawing on him with primitive greed. He was made to give everything.

"Are you using anything?" he gasped a full fifteen minutes later when they were both coming out of their dazes.

Carly laughed. "Now's a nice time to think about that, Holbrook. I love it when the man takes responsibility."

He lifted his head from her breast, and the moonlight caught something strange and somber in his eyes.

"It's okay," she said softly, entangling her fingers in his hair. "I bought something while we were out."

"Carly." The name came out as a rasp.

She stroked the sides of his face. Maybe he hadn't made up his mind what he felt, but she knew her side of things. She was desperately in love. "What?"

"If I asked you to, would you give me a baby?"

Carly gazed up at him for a long time before she answered. "That depends on whether you planned to walk off with the little dickens or let me have a hand in raising it."

"We'd raise it together."

She sighed. "How do we know we wouldn't want to break up in six months or six years?"

"How does anybody know that, Carly? If everybody had demanded a guarantee, the human race would have died out before the dinosaurs did."

"I'd need some promises from you, Mark. Some pretty heavy-duty ones."

He lowered his head to her breast and circled the nipple with his tongue, causing it to jut out in renewed response. "How's this one, Scoop? As long as you want me, I'll be around."

Carly's eyes were wet. "This is scary," she said. "A month ago I was minding my own business, getting ready to come out here and start a new job. I'd never met the man who could get past my defenses. Now all of a sudden I'm lying in bed with you and talking babies."

Mark raised himself to look into her face, and kissed away her tears. "I know what you mean," he said, his voice a gentle rasp. "It's kind of like being caught in an avalanche."

Carly's laughter caught on a sob. "Such tender, romantic words."

Just then there was a light knock at the door.

"It's a raid!" Mark whispered, and jerked the covers up over Carly's head.

"Good night, son," his father called from the hallway.

Chapter 7

The Holbrooks held an impromptu brunch the next day, and Carly was surprised at the variety of people who attended on such short notice. Mark introduced her to a bank president, a congressman and a film agent before she'd even finished her orange juice.

When Jeanine arrived, he excused himself and approached his ex-wife. Carly knew he was going to ask for custody of Nathan, and she crossed her fingers for him and stepped out onto the terrace to look at the Bay. The fainter blue of the sky and the deep navy of the water blended into azure at the horizon, and Carly yearned to hide the sight in her heart and carry it away with her.

"Lovely, isn't it?"

Carly turned, a little startled, to see Edina Peters, the film agent. "Yes," she said. "I could look at it forever."

Ms. Peters, a petite, well-dressed woman in her mid-forties, smiled, the spring sun glinting in her bright brown hair. "Who knows? Maybe you lived here in another life and were very happy. That would account—at least in part—for that look of controlled sorrow I see in your face."

Pushing a lock of windblown hair back from her forehead, Carly changed the subject. "Have you known the Holbrooks long?"

"Yes," she answered simply.

Carly was never sure, when she looked back on that moment, what made her say what she did then. "Mark wrote a play, and it's fabulous."

Edina's interest was obviously piqued. "I'm not surprised. After all, he has achieved a certain amount of success. Did he ever tell you that he was writing potboilers for detective and science-fiction magazines before he was even out of high school?"

Carly smiled and shook her head. She could easily picture Mark in that room where he'd made love to her, hurriedly penning stories on a yellow legal pad. "He's remarkable."

"Is he going to show the play to anyone?" Edina asked carefully.

Still leaning against the terrace railing, Carly interlocked her fingers and sighed. "He gave it to me," she said.

"*Gave* it to you?"

Carly shrugged, drinking in the view, taking solace in it. "I wouldn't put my name on it, or anything like that."

"Of course not," agreed Edina, who had no way of knowing what Carly's scruples were.

"I'd like to show it to someone, just to find out whether or not my instincts are right. Would you be willing…?"

Except for a glint in Edina's eyes, there was no outward sign of her eagerness. "I'd be happy to. And, naturally, I wouldn't do anything without talking to you first."

Carly nodded, went upstairs by the back way and took the manuscript from her suitcase. Edina was waiting in the kitchen when she came down, and her slender white hand trembled slightly as she reached for the play.

"Now remember," Carly said firmly, "I'm only looking for your opinion. I don't have the authority to sell Mark's work."

Edina nodded, gave Carly her card and left the party five minutes later.

Carly returned to the brunch to find that Mark had finished his talk with Jeanine. She knew it hadn't gone well by the strained look in his eyes and the muscle that kept bunching along his jawline.

She slipped her arm through his and pulled him into an alcove. "Well?"

"She said no."

Carly reached up to still the angry muscle. "You didn't really expect her to say yes so easily, did you? Good heavens, Mark, Nathan is her *son*."

He let out a ragged sigh. "Jeanine's an alcoholic," he said.

"That doesn't mean she doesn't love her child," Carly reasoned. "What you're asking is the hardest thing in the world for a woman to do." She thought fleetingly of the play, and felt an ache inside—and an urge to run after Edina Peters and ask her to give the manuscript back.

Mark pushed back the sleeve of his forest-green sweater and checked his watch. "We've got to catch a plane in two hours, Scoop," he said in a lighter tone. "Maybe we'd better start inching toward the door."

Carly stood on her toes to kiss his cheek. "It's so nice of you to keep me advised of our schedule," she mocked with a twinkle in her eyes. "First you tell me we're coming down here because of the piece on fathers' rights, without giving me any idea of how long we're staying, then you present me to your family, then you calmly announce that we're leaving in two hours. Is there anything else I should know, Mr. Holbrook?"

He leaned toward her and grinned, lifting his eyebrows a degree. "Yeah. You should know that when we get back to Oregon, I'm going to take you to bed and make love to you until you collapse in exhaustion."

A blush colored Carly's cheeks, and she turned away, infuriated that he could arouse her so thoroughly in a room full of people, then leave her to wait hours for satisfaction.

Forty-five minutes later, after Mark had spent a little more time with Nathan, he and Carly said goodbye to his family, got into a cab and headed for the airport.

The fact that she'd given the play to an agent was preying on Carly's conscience by then, but she didn't have the courage to confide in Mark. She pushed the subject to the back of her mind and the two of them brainstormed the fathers' rights issue during the flight back to Oregon.

"Are you coming home with me?" Mark asked as they landed.

Carly twisted the exquisite gold bracelet on her wrist. "No," she said after nervously running the tip of her tongue over her lips. "I think we need some space."

He didn't comment on that until they were out of the plane and on the way to the baggage-claim area.

"What's going on, Carly?" he demanded as they rode the escalator. "I thought things were pretty good between us."

Carly felt sad. "They are," she answered. "But they're volatile, too. I don't want this relationship to go up like a bomb and crash to the ground in flaming pieces, and it could if we push too hard."

He gave her a weary grin. "I hate to admit it, Scoop, but you may be right. But *damn,* I really wanted to make love to you tonight."

Again Carly blushed. "Well—you could come to my apartment for dinner. It's just that I don't think we should live together. Not yet."

His brown eyes caressed her. "Fair enough, but what about that baby we talked about?"

Carly glanced anxiously around to see if anyone was eavesdropping on their conversation. "I think we should forget that, at least until after this thing about

Nathan's custody is ironed out. Creating a child isn't something you do on impulse, Mark, and besides…" She paused, swallowed and averted her eyes for a few moments before going on. "You can't replace one child with another."

He sighed, slipped an arm around her waist and pulled her close against his side. "All right, Scoop, you win. But we can at least *practice,* so that when we do make a baby, we'll get it right."

Carly laughed, but inside her there was a great sadness. For all her sensible decisions, what she really wanted was to pack up everything she owned, move into Mark's house and start a baby right away.

What she *didn't* want was to end up divorced in a few years because they'd tried to do things too quickly.

After collecting their baggage, Carly and Mark drove to his place. Carly waited in the car while he collected his laptop and a change of clothes. They stopped briefly at a Chinese restaurant, then retreated to Carly's apartment.

The light on her answering machine was flickering, and Carly had already pushed the button and started to play the message before she realized there might be messages she didn't want Mark to hear.

Sure enough, Janet's voice filled the living room. "I'll bet you're off in some romantic hideaway with that fantastic man you're dating, you fink. Call me when you get back."

Mark, who was sitting on the couch, opening the bags from the Chinese place, paused long enough to polish his fingernails against his shirt and toss Carly a cocky grin.

Subtly she went back to the machine and pressed the Off button. Then she kicked off her shoes and curled up beside Mark on the cushions. They watched an old movie on TV while they ate casually from the cartons, occasionally feeding each other, and the progression to the bedroom was a natural one.

Carly went in to change her clothes, and in the ancient way of men, Mark followed her.

"Remember what I told you in San Francisco?" he teased, his voice a low, throaty rumble as he stood behind her, his lips moving against her nape.

In spite of herself, Carly trembled. His words hadn't been far out of her mind since he'd spoken them. "Yes," she managed as he lifted her tank top and closed his hands over the bare, full breasts beneath.

He nipped at her earlobe. "What did I say?"

Carly wondered if there were other women in the world who'd gone from virgin to vamp in one easy lesson. "Y-you said you were going to t-take me to bed and make love to me until I c-collapsed."

Mark turned her in his arms and pulled the tank top off over her head. Her plump breasts bobbed with the motion, and two patches of color throbbed in her cheeks. He lifted her up, and she wrapped her legs around his waist, her arms encircling his neck.

He was kissing her collarbone, the warm, quivering tops of her breasts. He found her nipple and suckled, and she flung back her head in ecstatic surrender, pulling in her breath. His glossy brown hair was like silk between her fingers.

"Tell me what you want, Carly," he paused to mutter.

"You," Carly answered in a helpless whisper. "On top of me, inside me   part of me…"

Mark laid her down on the bed and pulled away the shorts and panties she'd just put on. His eyes glittered with desire as he entered her.

Their time together was everything it had ever been, and more. Carly thought, at times, that she could not endure the pleasure, that she would be unable to survive it. When the tumult had overtaken them, when glory had been reached and shared, they lay quietly for a long time, shadows slipping over them. And Carly wept.

"What?" Mark asked gruffly, brushing away her tears with his thumbs.

"I want this to work," Carly managed to respond, feeling silly and bereft. "I want so much for this to work."

Mark kissed her, not in a demanding way, but in a gentle, reassuring one. Then he got up and held out his hand to her. "That part of it is up to us, Scoop—it's not like we're at the mercy of a whimsical fate or anything."

He led her to the bathroom and they showered together, then Mark dried himself with a towel and began putting his clothes back on. Carly, wearing her pink robe, stood in the doorway, watching him, thinking what a marvel he was. His body was beautifully sculpted, like one of Michelangelo's statues come to life.

"You're leaving?" she asked softly.

He paused in the hunt for his other shoe long enough

to plant a kiss on her forehead. "Yes. You're all done in, babe. You need some rest."

Carly swallowed. "I guess loving you is exhausting work," she said.

Mark stopped and recoiled comically, like a victim in one of the old Frankenstein movies. "Did I actually hear it? The L word?"

Carly nodded. It was so hard, taking the risk, laying all her feelings on the line when he might just walk out and never come back. "I love you, Mark."

He came to her, gripped her shoulders gently in his hands and searched her face. "Carly, I'm going to owe half of next year's income when I say this, because I bet all my friends I'd never let it happen, but I love you, too. And it's not like anything I've ever felt before."

She was too moved to speak, so she just nodded again, and he kissed her lightly and went back to the search for his shoe.

"Get some shut-eye, Scoop," he said. "Tomorrow we start working in earnest." After that, he kissed her once more and left.

Carly locked the apartment door after him and let her forehead rest against the wood.

Presently she turned around and made her way to the desk. She listened to a series of messages while she gathered up the cartons and bags left on the coffee table from their Chinese meal. Abruptly she stiffened when Edina's voice filled the room.

"Carly, you were right—this play is wonderful. I read it at one sitting. We've simply *got* to persuade Mark to let me market it. Call me back at the number I gave you on Monday morning, and we'll formulate a plan."

Carly's knees weakened as she imagined what would have happened if she hadn't stopped the machine after Janet's message played. She dropped the debris from dinner into the trash and made her way somewhat shakily to the telephone.

Janet answered on the third ring.

"It's me," Carly said, and then she began to cry.

Her friend was there in less than a minute. "What's wrong?" she asked, taking in Carly's mussed hair, bathrobe and tear-reddened eyes.

"I'm in love with Mark!" Carly wailed.

Janet smiled gently as she pressed her friend into a chair and then went to the kitchenette, talking loudly to be heard over the sound of water running into the teapot. "Now there's stunning news," she called. "Nobody would have guessed you were crazy about the guy or anything."

Carly got out of the chair and followed her friend's voice, watching as Janet took mugs and tea bags from their respective places. "I've done something sneaky and underhanded," she went on, sniffling. "He's probably never going to forgive me."

Arms folded, Janet leaned against the kitchen counter to wait for the water to boil and sighed. "What could you have done that was so bad?" she asked skeptically.

Carly bit her lower lip for a long moment before answering. "I showed his play to an agent without telling him first."

Janet's pretty eyes went round. "You did what?"

"It seemed like a good idea at the time," Carly reasoned fitfully. "And I told the agent I didn't have the power to sell it. But she called back a little while ago—it was just lucky that Mark didn't hear the message—and I have an awful feeling she's not going to be able to control her enthusiasm."

The teakettle whistled, and Janet poured boiling water into the two mugs and carried them past Carly to the table, where they both sat down.

"You're right," Janet said. "I think you're in very big trouble."

Carly nodded miserably, her fingers curved around the steaming mug. "I thought it would be okay," she said. "I mean, he *said* I could do what I wanted to with it, and his mother and I tacitly agreed that somebody in the business ought to look at it. That might even have been why she invited Edina to the brunch."

Janet didn't pursue the subject of the Holbrooks' brunch. "You've got to tell Mark what you did before he hears it from somebody else," she said. "It's your only chance, Carly. If the agent calls him and starts raving about what a hit the movie's going to be, he'll be furious with you."

Carly's throat ached, and she was on the verge of tears again. "Do you suppose I did this on purpose, Janet? You know, to sabotage myself, to keep things from being too good?"

"You've been watching too much trash TV," Janet said, dismissing the idea with a wave of one hand. "You did it because you love the man, and you want to see him get the recognition he deserves. Thing is, your methods leave something to be desired, kid."

Mark's laptop was still sitting on the coffee table—they'd never gotten around to actually using it—and the sight filled Carly with guilt. With shaking hands, she lifted the mug full of tea to her mouth.

"He'll probably be mad at first," Janet went on when Carly didn't speak. "But he'll see that you meant well when he calms down."

Remembering how Mark had exploded when she'd confessed that she'd *read* the play, Carly had her doubts about what his reactions would be when he learned she'd shown it to someone else. Now, she guessed, she'd see how much—or how little—Mark loved her. She grimaced.

"There's always the sneaky way out," Janet suggested. "You could call the agent, tell her to send back the play and never breathe a word about it to anybody—after which you conveniently forget to mention the blunder to Mark."

Carly dismissed the idea with a shake of her head and, "I'd never have a moment's peace for worrying that he'd find out."

Janet gestured toward the phone. "Call him. I'll be down the hall if you need me." With that she got out of her chair, carried her cup to the sink and then left the apartment.

Carly stared after her, her thumbnail caught between her front teeth, but she didn't make the call. No, she reasoned, she wouldn't do that until after she'd spoken to Edina in the morning and asked her to send the play back.

She made herself another cup of tea, selected a book from the shelves underneath the living room window and went to bed. It seemed lonely without Mark.

Fluffing her pillows behind her, Carly opened the new adventure-espionage novel she'd bought at the grocery store and began to read. By the time she'd gone over the same paragraph for the third time, she gave up.

There were dark circles under her eyes when she got up the next morning, and no matter how skillful she was with her makeup, she couldn't hide them. She had tried Edina's office number twice, without success, when Mark showed up.

The moment he got a look at her face, he frowned and put a hand to her forehead. "You're not looking so good, Scoop. Are you sick?"

Yes, Carly thought miserably. "No," she said out loud.

He didn't look convinced. "I can start the interviews without you," he said. "And I'll bring my notes by later, so we can go over them."

"Mark, I'm new on this job. I don't want to mess up—"

"One day won't make a difference, Carly. And, like I said, I can get the legwork done without you."

Stubbornly Carly shook her head. She grabbed an orange while Mark reached for the laptop, and they set out to begin their day's work. It was ten o'clock before she got a chance to sneak out of Mark's office at the *Times,* where they'd been arranging interviews with divorced fathers, and put a call through to Edina.

"Did you talk to Mark?" the agent asked immediately.

Carly sat on the corner of her desk, the telephone receiver pressed to her ear. "No," she said. "I shouldn't have given you the play without talking to Mark first. I want you to send it back."

There was a short, stunned silence on the other end of the line. "Ms. Barnett, this is a very special property, and I could have half a dozen producers fighting over it by nightfall."

"I just wanted your opinion, remember?" Carly said, pulling her reading glasses off and setting them aside on the desk with a clatter. "Please. Just express it back to me—"

"I can't do that, I'm afraid. I'm going to call Mark myself. We're old friends—maybe he'll listen to reason."

Carly fairly leaped off the desk. "You can't do that," she cried in a frantic whisper. "He'll be furious— "

Edina sighed indulgently. "Mark is quick-tempered, I'll give you that. But once he's had time to think—"

"Send back the manuscript!" Carly broke in.

"If Mark asks me to—personally—I will."

Rage and panic filled Carly as the door of her office opened and Mark peered around it. "Ready to go out and talk to the man in the street?" he asked.

"Goodbye," Carly said into the receiver, and slammed it down.

Mark's eyebrows drew together in a frown. "Who was that?"

Carly tried to smile, and failed. She wanted to tell Mark the truth, but she was afraid.

They went back to work after that, and for the next three days, they were busy. By the time Mark was ready to draft the first version of the article, Carly was sure they'd talked to every divorced father in Portland.

Mark worked on the computer on his desk at home, and the keys clicked rapidly as his fingers raced to keep up with his thoughts. Carly stood behind him, one hand resting on his shoulder, reading the little words as fast as they appeared on the screen.

"Biased," she commented, when he finally reared back in his chair and pushed the Print button. "Some of these guys are card-carrying sewer rats and you know it. I could go to their wives and get an entirely different story!"

Mark turned far enough in his chair to give Carly a challenging look. "So do it," he said.

Carly pulled her notebook from her purse and reached for the phone. "Okay, I will," she replied, already punching out a number. She'd have to do some investigating to reach most of the ex-wives of the men she and Mark had interviewed, but she had information on a few.

When Carly arrived home late the following night, Janet brought her an express package that had been left with her by the building manager. Carly opened it right there in the hallway and found Mark's play inside.

Unconsciously she raised one hand to her heart in a gesture of relief.

Janet looked horrified. "You mean you haven't told him?"

"We've been so busy with the assignment—"

"Thin ice," Janet said as Carly left her to walk down the hallway to her own door. "You're walking on thin ice."

In the privacy of her own apartment, Carly stood holding the manuscript, her lower lip caught between her teeth. Despite everything she'd said about telling Mark, Edina had returned the play. That meant she'd changed her mind—didn't it?

She laid the play down on the table and went to the desk. As usual, she had several messages. Carly played them, steeling herself against an angry call from Mark or some kind of threat from Edina, but all the messages were from women she'd been trying to reach for interviews.

In calling them back and taking notes, Carly was able to forget her outstanding problem for a while. She wrote rapidly, nodding to herself as the divorced mothers told stories about the former husbands she and Mark had interviewed about fathers' rights.

Late that night when she'd roughed in the outline for the first draft of her article, Carly held Mark's play in both hands for a moment, then dropped it into her desk drawer. *Out of sight, out of mind,* she thought with a pang of guilt.

She spent the next day interviewing, and the day after that squirreled away in her office, writing. She had just turned the finished product, an article rebutting Mark's, in to Allison when she was called to Mr. Clark's office.

Filled with nervous excitement, Carly obeyed the summons.

After telling her to sit, Mr. Clark launched right into the assignment. There was a new shelter for battered women opening in the city, and the director had some innovative ideas. He wanted Carly to get an interview.

Carly fairly danced out of his office. Here was her chance to really show what she could do. *Carly Barnett, girl reporter,* she thought with a happy grin. She stopped by Emmeline's desk.

"Is Mark—Mr. Holbrook in yet?"

Emmeline shook her head, seemingly unconcerned. "His hours are flexible," she said. "He pretty much sets them himself."

Carly sighed and nodded, then vanished into her office. She had work to do.

Mark stood gripping the telephone receiver, a glass of orange juice in his free hand, his body rigid with shock.

"So you see," Edina Peters finished up, "I really think it's time you stopped hiding this jewel of a play in your desk drawer and let me sell it. It could be adapted for the screen in five minutes, and we're talking major money here, Mark."

His muscles finally thawed, and he flung the orange juice at the fireplace. Glass shattered against brick. But his voice was deadly calm. "Carly showed you the play," he said like a robot, even though Edina had already told him that. He guessed he was hoping the agent would say no, she'd made a mistake, it had been someone else.

"She meant well," Edina said. "Afterwards she had an attack of conscience and begged me to send it back to her. I did—after making a few copies."

Mark closed his eyes tightly. His stomach twisted inside him, and an ache pounded at his nape. *Carly*, he thought, and the name splintered against his spirit the way the glass had against the fireplace.

"Mark?" Edina prompted.

He felt sick. He forced himself to speak evenly, to relax his grip on the receiver. "I'm here, Edina," he rasped.

"Will you let me sell it?"

My guts are in that play, he thought. *It's an open door to my soul.* "No," he answered.

"But—"

"The discussion is over," he broke in. And then he hung up the telephone with only a moderate amount of force.

He'd planned to work at home that day on a human-interest piece he and Clark had been discussing, but now that he knew what Carly had done, he could only think of one thing—confronting her. Resolute, he strode into the bathroom, stripped off the shorts and T-shirt he'd worn for a late-morning run and showered.

He dressed hastily, and drove away from the house with his tires screeching on the asphalt. He shouldn't have trusted Carly, he thought as he sped down the freeway. He shouldn't have loved her.

He jammed one hand through his hair and cursed

when he heard a siren behind him, then glanced into his rearview mirror. A silver-blue light whirled on top of the squad car—sure enough, he was the man the officer wanted to see.

Filled with quiet rage, Mark pulled over to the side of the road and waited.

Chapter 8

Carly had been down in the morgue in the basement of the newspaper building, reading up on past articles about shelters for battered women, and her heart did a little leap when the doors whisked open in the lobby to reveal Mark.

Her instant smile faded when their eyes linked, however, and she knew in that moment that she'd waited too long to tell him about the play. She wanted to explain, but when she tried to speak, no sound came out of her mouth.

Mark jabbed a button on the panel and the doors closed. The look in his eyes was cold and remote. "I guess I didn't lose those bets with my buddies after all," he said, his voice as rough as gravel in a rusty can. "I wasn't in love—just lust."

Carly sagged against the wall of the elevator, her hands gripping the stainless-steel railing. "That was cruel," she said. "I had a reason for what I did."

He struck another button, and the elevator stopped where it was. His hands came to rest against the wall on either side of Carly's head, and his eyes bored into hers. "Oh?" he rasped.

She swallowed, wanting to duck beneath his arm and start the elevator going again, but unable to move. She was like a sparrow gazing into the eyes of a cobra. "I wanted a professional opinion," she managed to say. "I was h-hoping to persuade you to let *Broken Vows* be produced."

Mark ran the tip of one index finger down the V of her blouse in a impudent caress. "And make lots of money? The joke's on you, baby—I already have a fortune. And until an hour ago I would have given you anything you wanted."

Carly's eyes stung with tears of humiliation and frustration. "Will you stop being a melodramatic bastard and listen to me, please? I don't give a damn about your money—I never did! I wanted to see the play produced because something that good should be—"

"Shared with the world?" he interrupted acidly, arching one eyebrow. "Come on, Carly—that's a cliché."

"I'm not the one who said it," she pointed out, battling for composure. "You did."

He turned away, touched another button and set the elevator moving again. "Goodbye, Carly," he said. His broad shoulders barred her from him like a high, impenetrable wall, and when the doors opened on their floor, he stepped out.

Carly couldn't move, she was so filled with pain. And she let the elevator go all the way back to the lobby before she pressed the proper button. Reaching her floor, she hurried into her office, glancing neither right nor left, and closed the door.

She was sitting behind her desk, still trying to pull herself together, when Emmeline buzzed her and announced, with a question in her voice, that Helen Holbrook was on the line.

"Hello, Helen," Carly greeted Mark's mother sadly, not knowing what to expect. Despite their conversation in the garden that day in San Francisco, the woman was probably furious with her, and Carly steeled herself to be harangued.

"Edina told me about the play," Helen said, her voice calm. "She said Mark wasn't pleased that you'd shown it to her."

Recalling the way he'd looked at her in the elevator, the cold, bitter way he'd spoken, Carly was anguished. "I'd say that was an understatement," she got out. "He doesn't want to have anything to do with me now."

Helen sighed. "Mark can be positively insufferable. He's hardheaded, just like his father."

A despairing smile tugged at the corners of Carly's mouth. "You're being very kind," she said, "but there's something else you're trying to tell me, isn't there?"

"Yes," Helen confessed in a rush. "Carly, something has happened, and I don't want Mark to be told about it over the telephone. I must ask you to talk to him for me."

Images of another automobile accident, with Nathan seriously hurt, filled Carly's mind with garish sounds and colors. "What is it?" she whispered.

"Jeanine has crashed her car again," Helen said sadly. "Nathan wasn't with her, thank God, but naturally he's very upset."

Carly's forehead was resting in her hand. "And Jeanine?"

"She's in a coma, Carly, and not expected to live."

Carly squeezed her eyes closed, remembering the beautiful auburn-haired woman who had once been Mark's wife. "My God."

"Jeanine has her parents, but Nathan needs Mark. Carly, could you please go to him and tell him, as gently as you can, what's happened?"

After swallowing hard, she nodded and said, "Yes." Her heart twisted inside her to think how frightened Nathan must be. "Yes, Helen, I'll tell him."

"Thank you," Helen replied with tears in her voice. Then she added, "I'll try to reason with Mark while he's here. He loves you, and he's an idiot if he throws away what you've got together."

Carly thought of the look she'd seen in Mark's eyes and grieved. She knew that as far as he was concerned, their relationship was over. "Thanks," she said softly. Then the two women said their goodbyes and hung up.

Carly found Mark in his office, standing at the window and glaring out at the city. His name sounded hoarse when she said it.

He turned to glower at her.

"Mark, there's been an accident," she said in measured tones. She saw the fear leap in his eyes and added quickly, "Nathan wasn't hurt—it's Jeanine. She's—she's not expected to live."

The color drained out of Mark's face, and Carly longed to put her arms around him, but she didn't dare. In his mood, he would probably push her away, and she knew she couldn't bear that. "Dear God," he said, and turned around to punch out a number on his telephone.

Carly slipped out of the office and closed the door.

Mark left five minutes later without saying goodbye, and Carly went into the women's restroom and splashed cold water on her face until she was sure she wouldn't cry. Then she went back to work.

When quitting time came, the relief was almost overwhelming. She stuffed her files and notes into her briefcase, snatched up her purse and drove home in a daze. When she pulled into her parking space in the apartment lot, she was ashamed to realize the drive had passed without her noticing.

She went to her apartment without stopping for the mail or a word with Janet, dropped all her things just inside the door and then raced into her room, flung herself down on the bed and sobbed.

After a while, though, she began to think that if Mark was so easily angered, so lacking in understanding or compassion, she didn't want him anyway.

At least, that was what she told herself. Inside, she felt raw and broken, as though a part of her had been torn away. Carly showered, put on shorts and a summer top and went downstairs to exercise.

When she got back to her apartment, the phone was

ringing. Carly made a lunge for it and gasped out an anxious hello, praying the caller was Mark. That he'd come to his senses.

She was both disappointed and relieved to hear her father's voice. "Hello, Carly."

Instantly Carly wanted to start blubbering again, but she held herself in check. Her dad was hundreds of miles away, and there was nothing to be gained by dragging him into her problems. "Hi, Dad. What's up?"

"I just thought I'd tell you that I liked that piece you sent me about the food contest. That was really good reporting."

In spite of everything, Carly had to smile. Don Barnett wasn't interested in soufflés and coffee cakes, she knew that. He called purely because he cared. "Thanks, Dad. I'm expecting a Pulitzer at the very least."

He chuckled. "I never was very good at coming up with excuses. I want to know what's the matter, and don't you dare say 'nothing.'"

Carly let out a ragged sigh. "I finally fell head over heels and it didn't work out."

"What do you mean, it didn't work out?" her dad demanded. "What kind of lamebrain would throw away a chance to make a life with you?"

"One named Mark Holbrook."

"Is there anything I can do?"

"Yeah," Carly answered, making a joke to keep from crying. "You can eat a banana split in my honor. I'd like to drown my sorrows in junk food, but if I do, none of my clothes will fit."

"Maybe you should just get on a plane and come back

here, sweetheart. Ryerton may not be a metropolis, but we do have a newspaper."

Carly was already shaking her head. "No way, Dad— I'm standing my ground. I have as much right to live in Portland and work at the *Times* as Mark does."

"Okay, then I'll come out there. I'll black his eyes for him."

Carly smiled at the images that came to her mind, then remembered that Jeanine was lying in a hospital, near death, and was solemn again. "I'm okay," she insisted. "If you want to come out and visit, terrific. But you're not blacking anybody's eyes."

"Maybe I'll do that. Maybe I'll just get on an airplane and come out there."

"That would be great, Dad," Carly said, knowing her father wouldn't leave Kansas except under the most dire circumstances. He hadn't been on a plane in twenty years.

Five minutes later, when Carly hung up, she dialed the Holbrooks' number in San Francisco, and Mark's father answered.

"Hello," he said when she'd introduced herself, and there was a cool note in his voice.

Carly wondered what Mark had told him about her. "I'm sorry to bother you, but I wanted to know if there was any news about Jeanine."

Mr. Holbrook sighed. "She's taken a turn for the better," he said. "The doctors are pretty sure she'll survive, though how long it will take her to recover completely is anybody's guess." His voice was a degree or two warmer now. "Shall I ask Mark to call you when he comes in, Carly?"

She shook her head, forgetting for a moment that Mr. Holbrook couldn't see her. "No!" she said too quickly. She paused, cleared her throat and tried to speak in a more moderate tone. "Please don't mention me to Mark at all."

"But—"

"Please, Mr. Holbrook. It will only upset him, and he needs to be able to concentrate on helping Nathan right now."

Mark's father didn't agree or disagree; he simply asked Carly to take care of herself and said goodbye.

Jeanine was lying in the intensive care unit, tubes running into her bruised and battered body, her head bandaged. She opened her eyes when Mark took her hand, and her fingers tightened around his.

"Nathan...?" she managed to rasp.

"He's safe, Jeanine."

Tears formed in the corners of her eyes. "Are you— taking him home?"

It wouldn't be a kindness to lie to her, Mark decided. Jeanine needed to know their son would be loved and taken care of. "Yes," he said, still holding her hand. He didn't love her—since his relationship with Carly he'd come to realize that he never had—but it hurt him to see her suffering.

"I was drinking," she said clearly, her eyes pleading with Mark to understand.

He nodded. "You need some help, Jeanine."

She tried to smile. "Maybe it's hopeless."

Mark shook his head. "You'll make it," he said hoarsely, even though he had no idea whether that was true or not. Jeanine was in serious trouble, and they both knew it.

"Take care of Nathan," she finished. And then her eyes drifted closed and she slept.

Mark went out into the hallway to find Jeanine's father and mother waiting. They both had deep shadows under their eyes.

"Was she upset that you're taking Nathan?" his former mother-in-law asked.

Mark shook his head. "She knows I love him," he said, pitying these people, wanting to ease their pain but not knowing how. "I'm sorry you have to go through this."

The Martins nodded in weary unison, and Mark left them to keep their vigil.

When he arrived at his parents' home, his mother was waiting up for him. She served him a cup of de-caffeinated coffee and launched right into her lecture. "You're a fool, Mark Holbrook. An absolute idiot."

He sighed and rubbed his tired, burning eyes with a thumb and forefinger. "Mother, I'm not in the mood for this."

"I don't care what you're in the mood for," Helen retorted. "Carly showed Edina that play because she hoped some professional feedback would convince you to let it be produced, and for no other reason."

Mark had been cherishing secret dreams of leaving the newspaper business to write plays for over a year, but he hadn't meant for *Broken Vows* to be seen by any-one. He'd written it in an attempt to clear his mind of the pain. "When I was married to Jeanine," he said slowly, "I didn't know where she was or what she was up to half the time. As you already know, I had some pretty un-pleasant surprises. I don't want to live like that again."

"Carly is nothing like Jeanine, and in your heart, you know that. Besides, I believe you love her."

Mark sighed. He was tired, and he ached from the core of his spirit out. "Carly is more like Jeanine than you'd like to think, Mother," he said evenly, "and as for loving her—I'll get over it."

"Will you?" Helen challenged. "Don't be so sure of that, my dear. You can't turn love on and shut it off like a faucet, you know."

He thrust himself out of his chair and bent to kiss his mother's forehead. "Give it up," he said with quiet firmness. "It's over between Carly and me."

Upstairs, Mark carefully opened the guest-room door and stepped inside. Nathan lay sprawled on the bed, arms and legs askew, his eyelids flickering as he dreamed.

Gently Mark brushed his son's hair back from his forehead. *I wanted you to come and live with me, buddy,* he told Nathan silently, speaking from his heart, *but I didn't expect it to happen like this. Honest.*

The child stirred, then opened his eyes. "Dad?" he asked on a long yawn.

Mark sat down on the edge of the bed. "Sorry, big guy. I didn't mean to wake you up."

"Is Mom okay?"

"Yeah," Mark answered. "But she has to stay in the hospital for a while."

Nathan accepted that with the sometimes remarkable stoicism of a ten-year-old. "I can visit her, can't I?"

In that moment the decision was made. Mark would return to San Francisco, buy a town house and build a life for himself and his son. Maybe he would even write a play—one that didn't touch every raw nerve in his soul, one he could bear to show to an agent. "Sure you can visit her," he said. "Now get some sleep. You've got school tomorrow."

Nathan screwed up his face. "I have to go to *school?*"

Mark chuckled. "No," he teased. "Of course not. A fifth-grade education will take you a long way in the world." He started to rise off the bed, but Nathan stopped him with one anxious little hand.

"Dad, where's Carly? Is she going to live with us?"

Those two simple questions left Mark feeling as though he'd just stepped into the whirling blades of a giant fan. *Carly,* he thought, and the name was a lonely cry deep in his spirit. "Carly's in Portland, doing her job," he managed to say, after a moment or two of recovery. "And no, it's just going to be the two of us for a while, buddy."

For a moment Nathan looked as though he might cry. Mark could see that the kid had been spinning dreams of a real home and a regular family in his head, and seeing his disappointment was painful. "Mom said Carly probably had a baby growing inside her. Does she, Dad?"

Mark swallowed, and it felt like he'd gulped down a

petrified grapefruit. *God, I hope not,* he thought. "No," he said forcefully, trying to convince himself as well as Nathan. "No, big guy, there isn't any baby."

Emmeline looked concerned as she handed Carly her morning coffee. "I guess you know that Mr. Holbrook is leaving the paper and moving back to San Francisco," she said.

Carly felt as though Emmeline had just flung the scalding contents of the cup all over her. "N-no," she answered, avoiding the secretary's gaze and fumbling in the depths of her purse for her glasses. "No, I hadn't heard about that."

"Oh," said Emmeline, and her voice was small and confused. "I'm sorry if I said anything I shouldn't have."

Carly took her glasses from their case and poked them onto her face. "What Mr. Holbrook does is nothing to me," she lied, flipping on her computer. She'd been living at the battered women's shelter for three days, pretending to be hiding from a violent husband, and she was ready to write about the experiences of the people she'd met there.

Emmeline couldn't seem to let the subject drop. "His ex-wife was hurt in an accident, you know, and he's got custody of his son now. I guess he didn't want to uproot the kid and make it so he couldn't see his mother."

"You're probably right," Carly answered, deliberately sounding distracted and preoccupied.

Finally Emmeline took the hint. She slipped out of Carly's office with a muttered goodbye and closed the door behind her. The moment she was alone, Carly slammed one fist down on the desk and whispered, "Damn you, Holbrook. Damn you to hell."

Fortunately the article absorbed her attention for the rest of the day. As she was leaving that evening, she passed Mark's office and couldn't help noticing that Emmeline and several of the other assistants were inside hanging streamers.

"There'll be a going-away party tomorrow," Emmeline called to her.

Carly nodded and bit her lower lip. She hadn't had to say any goodbyes to Mark; he'd said them for her. She made up her mind to busy herself outside the office the next day.

She spent a miserable night, finally falling asleep in the wee hours of the morning, only to be awakened by a wave of nausea with the rising of the sun. One hand clasped over her mouth, she made a dash for the bathroom.

"Oh, great," she complained, staggering to the kitchen for a cup of chamomile tea, "now I've got the flu."

The tea settled her stomach, though, and after a shower Carly felt better. She also felt guilty about staying away from the office just because of Mark's going-away party.

Resolutely Carly put on one of her best outfits—a pink silk suit from Hong Kong—and took extra care with her hair and makeup. She walked into the newsroom half an hour later, a Miss United States smile on her face, her briefcase swinging jauntily at her side.

When she was sure no one was watching, she fairly

dived into her office and leaned against the door, feeling as though she'd just picked her way through an emotional mine field.

She switched on her computer and opened her briefcase, planning to go over her notes for a proposed article and hide out until Mark had heard a round of for-he's-a-jolly-good-fellow and left. Then Mr. Clark called an unexpected meeting.

Carly felt like a martyr being summoned from the dungeon for execution. She stood, smoothed her skirt and checked her hair and lipstick in a small mirror pulled from her purse. Then she walked bravely down the hall to the conference room.

Thanks to some cruel fate, she was seated directly across from Mark, and he was making no effort at all to ignore her. His solemn brown eyes studied her thoughtfully while he turned an unsharpened pencil end over end on the tabletop.

Carly willed him to look away, and he seemed to sense that, refusing to give in. Finally she dropped her eyes, her cheeks burning, and devoutly wished she'd followed her original instincts and called in sick that day.

Mr. Clark got up and made a speech about what an honor it had been to work with Mark Holbrook and how they were all going to miss him. Everyone tittered when he mentioned Mark's plans to write a play—everyone except Carly, that is. Her eyes shot to his face in angry question.

He responded with an infuriating grin.

After what seemed like a millennium, Mr. Clark finished raving about Mark's accomplishments and suggested that everyone take time for cake and punch. Carly slipped out of the conference room and hurried in the opposite direction.

Even in her office she could hear the laughter and the talk, and it made her heart turn over in her chest. Mark, gone. It was almost impossible to believe that after today she wouldn't so much as catch a glimpse of him or hear his voice in the hallway.

She hadn't had such a hard time holding back tears since the time she'd set the stage curtains on fire with one of her flaming batons during the Miss Feed and Grain pageant. She'd been fourteen then, and she felt younger than that now.

The only thing to do was work. That, her father had always told her, was the salve that healed every wound.

She turned to her computer and sat back in her chair when she saw the message that popped up on her screen.

Goodbye, Scoop. Better luck next time.

That did it. Carly's tears began to flow, and she couldn't stop them. She was standing at the window, gazing out at the city and frantically drying her cheeks with a wad of tissue, when she heard a gentle rap at the door.

She was afraid to turn around—afraid Mark would be standing there, afraid he wouldn't. "Yes?"

"The party's over, Carly," Emmeline's voice said quietly. "I'll cover for you if you want to go home."

Carly was a trouper, and she knew the show had to go on, no matter what kind of show it was. But the front she was hiding behind was teetering dangerously, and she needed to be alone. She nodded without looking at the assistant, grimly amused that she'd thought no one in the office knew about her affair with Mark.

What a naive little idiot you were, she scolded herself, gathering up her purse and turning off the computer. She left her briefcase behind, under no delusion that she would get any worthwhile work done that night.

When she arrived at her apartment, she stayed only long enough to exchange her silk suit for cut-off jeans and a turquoise T-shirt. She went to a matinee at the mall, where she cried silently all through a comedy, then had supper at a fast-food place. When she still couldn't face going home after that, she went to another movie.

She never remembered what that one was about.

In the morning Mr. Clark called her into his office and asked her if she was aware that she was covered by a company health plan. "You don't look well, Ms. Barnett," he finished.

It's only a broken heart, Carly wanted to reply. *In about sixty years it will probably heal.* "I guess I'm just a little tired," she said, hoping he wouldn't decide the job was too much for her. Being demoted or getting fired would be beyond bearing.

"I liked that piece you did on battered women. It was damn good."

Carly was reassured, if only slightly. "Thank you. I've been thinking about a piece on women entrepreneurs—"

Mr. Clark waved her into silence. "No, that's been done too much lately. There's a river rafting expedition leaving on Saturday—one of those things meant to give executives confidence in their inner strength. I'd like you to go along on that. It's going to last about three days."

Carly thought of pitching through rapids and spinning in whirlpools and felt her flu symptoms returning, but she managed a brilliant smile. "That sounds exciting," she said.

"Of course, we'll send a photographer along, too. That way, if one of you drowns, the other one can still bring back the story." Mr. Clark beamed at his joke, and Carly dutifully laughed.

Carly took down the information he gave her and left the office early. She had preparations to make, and she was going to need hiking boots, flannel shirts and a sleeping bag, among other things. She went shopping and bought more things than she could possibly have carried without help from the sales staff.

On the way home her car mysteriously headed toward Mark's house instead of the apartment building. She knew he wasn't there as soon as she reached the end of the driveway, but she didn't leave. She just sat, her eyes brimming with tears, remembering how she and Mark had talked and laughed and made love in that house. She'd given him her virginity there, and no matter how many men she might meet in the future, she would never forget that first night in Mark's arms.

She touched the gold bracelet he'd given her, then fumbled open the catch. Stepping up onto the porch, she dropped the glimmering chain through the mail slot. Then Carly hurried back to her car, started the ignition and left.

That night she slept, but it was only because of nervous exhaustion. And in the morning she was sick again. Evidently, she decided, she'd caught some kind of intermittent flu. She made herself a cup of herbal tea, forced it down and presently felt better.

She spent the day at a local high-school gymnasium, sitting on the bleachers with a lot of other potential adventurers, listening to the head river rafter explain what was involved in the expedition. He said the trip wasn't for weaklings, and anybody who couldn't stand three measly days grappling with the wilderness should just go home and forget the whole thing.

That option sounded good to Carly, but she had her job to think about, so she stayed. Besides, she needed to stay busy in order to keep herself from dwelling on Mark and all the things that could have been.

She drove home that night and found a message from Jim Benson, the anchorman, on her machine. He obviously knew that Mark had left town, and he wanted to know if Carly would have supper with him after the six o'clock newscast.

"What the hell?" Carly said to her empty apartment. Life was like a river, and she had to raft down it. She called Jim back and left a message with his assistant that she'd meet him at the station at seven o'clock.

Chapter 9

Jim's gaze was filled with gentle discernment as he joined Carly in his office after the newscast. "You're as gorgeous as ever," he said, "but you look as though somebody's been batting you around like a croquet ball."

Carly managed a smile. That 'somebody' was Mark Holbrook and they both knew it. "And this is a pity date, is that it?"

Jim chuckled and shook his head. "Nothing so magnanimous," he said. "I'm still nursing a vain hope that when you get over Mark, you'll begin to see that I'm a nice guy with prospects."

She slipped her arm through his. "I already know you're a nice guy. If you weren't, I wouldn't be here."

He escorted her out of the station by a back way,

and opened the door of his fancy sports car for her. "I know of a great seafood place," he said. "Does that sound good?"

Thanks to the strange case of flu that had overtaken her in recent days, Carly didn't have much of an appetite for anything. But she smiled and tried to look enthusiastic as she nodded.

"I've got to ask you a question," she said when they were zipping along the freeway. "How did you know it was over between Mark and me?"

Jim gave her a sidelong look. "He told me. Like I said once, Carly, I've known Mark for a long time."

Carly bit down on her lower lip to keep from asking what Mark had said about her. Probably Jim was one of those buddies he'd talked about, the ones he'd bet that he'd never fall in love.

She didn't care, damn it. She *wouldn't* care.

"If you love Mark," Jim said reluctantly, "don't write him off just yet. Between getting custody of his son and what's happened to Jeanine, I don't guess he's thinking straight. He needs some time to adjust."

"He's planning to 'adjust' in San Francisco—or didn't he tell you that?"

"He told me."

Carly gazed out the window for a long time; there was an emotional storm gathering inside her and she didn't want Jim to see her face. "I love him," she said presently in a small, choked voice, "but it's probably better that we ended it when we did. Mark is temperamental—I would have spent the rest of my life walking on eggshells, worrying that I'd offended him somehow. Who needs it?"

Jim chuckled ruefully. "What am I doing? I should be trying to impress you with what a terrific guy I am." He paused to draw a deep breath, then let it out again. "Carly, Mark isn't a temperamental man—he's practical and pragmatic, like any good journalist. None of this stuff is typical of him."

Carly finally dared to look at Jim again. "What are you saying?"

"That meeting you caused some kind of upheaval in Mark's emotions. If I know him—and believe me, I do—he's still reeling from the shock. Given time and distance, he'll realize he's being a jerk."

Although she had no intention of waiting around for Mark to forgive her, Carly was comforted by Jim's words. They gave her hope that one day the hurting would stop and she could go on with her life without limping inwardly. "I have this friend who wants to go out with you," she said, remembering Janet's request to be "fixed up" with Jim.

He grinned. "The good-looking one with the grocery bag who was standing in the hall the first time we went out?"

Carly nodded, smiling. "That's Janet. She's a wonderful person."

Jim laughed. "We're a pair, you and I. Will somebody tell me why I'm sitting next to one of the most beautiful women in America, extolling the virtues of some other guy?"

"That's easy," Carly answered softly. "It's because

you're a sensational person yourself. Watch out, Jim— I'm starting to get the idea that there might be a few nice men out there after all."

Dinner was enjoyable, though Carly wasn't able to eat much. After Jim brought her home, she took a bubble bath and went to bed with a book. And her thoughts strayed to Mark with every other word.

On Friday afternoon, her extra clothes and sleeping bag stuffed into a canvas backpack, Carly got into her car and drove southeast to the town of Bend, where the river expedition would begin. It was late when she finally found the riverside park where the others had camped, and she noticed first thing that the mosquitoes were out in force.

"Don't be a negative thinker," she muttered to herself, getting out her backpack and making her way toward the camp.

The others were gathered around a huge bonfire, and they all looked at home in their skins, as Carly's grandmother used to say. It was evident that river rafting was nothing new to most of them, but Carly already had motion sickness just thinking about it.

Wearing her trusty smile, along with jeans, hiking boots, a flannel shirt and a lightweight jacket, she joined the gathering.

The house Mark selected was in a good part of San Francisco, just far enough from his parents' place to promote good relations. The windows in his den offered a view of the Bay, and Nathan wouldn't have to change schools in the fall.

To Mark's way of thinking, the place was perfect.

Except, of course, for the fact that Carly wasn't there.

He reached into the pocket of his sports jacket and touched the bracelet she'd dropped through the mail slot at the house in Portland. Sometimes he fancied that he could feel her warmth and incredible energy still vibrating through the metal.

With a sigh, Mark stepped closer to the windows and fixed his gaze on the Bay. The furniture wouldn't arrive for another week, so there was no place to sit.

Life without Carly was like running in a three-legged race, he reflected; what should have given him more mobility and freedom only made it more awkward to move. He thrust his hand through his hair.

"Dad?"

He turned to see Nathan standing uncertainly in the doorway. "Am I allowed in here?" he asked.

Mark frowned. "Why wouldn't you be?"

Nathan lifted one of his small shoulders in a shrug. "Mom didn't like me to go in her living room. She was afraid I'd spill something on the carpet."

With some effort, Mark kept himself from expressing his irritation. Being annoyed with Jeanine wouldn't do anyone any good. "Things are different here, big guy," he said as the boy came to stand beside him. "We're not going to worry much about the carpets."

Nathan looked up at him and flashed the gapped grin that always gave Mark's heart a little twist. "I used to have to go to bed at nine o'clock," he said, obviously hoping Mark would shoot another rule down in flames.

"You still do," Mark replied.

"Darn."

"Hello!" a feminine voice called suddenly in the distance. "Is anybody home?"

"Grandma," Mark and Nathan told each other in chorus, and left the room to go down the stairs and greet Helen.

"I've come bearing gifts," she said, indicating the bucket of take-out chicken she carried in one arm. "Am I invited to stay for dinner?"

Mark smiled at his mother, while Nathan rushed forward to collect the chicken.

"She can stay, can't she?" the boy asked, looking back over his shoulder.

"No," Mark teased. "We're going to hold her up for the chicken and then shove her out through the mail slot."

The three of them ate in the spacious, brightly lit kitchen, at a card table borrowed from the elder Holbrooks. When the meal was over, Mark sent Nathan upstairs to take his bath.

"I still think both of you should be staying at our house," Helen fretted when she and Mark were alone.

Mark grinned and shook his head. "We're having a great time camping out in sleeping bags and living on fast food."

"If you're having such a 'great time,'" Helen ventured shrewdly, "then how do you account for that heartache I see in your eyes?"

Mark's grin faded. "It shows, huh?"

Helen nodded. "Yes. Mark, when are you going to

admit you were wrong, fly up to Portland and ask that lovely young lady to forgive you?"

He sighed, glad his mother couldn't possibly know how many times he'd made plans to do just that, only to stop himself at the last second. Carly was just getting started on her career, and he had to make a solid home for Nathan. He told himself it would be better if they just went their separate ways.

"She's already dating Jim Benson," he said, hoping that would throw Helen off the subject for good. "I was a passing fancy."

"Nonsense. When the two of you were in a room together, the air crackled. I don't care if she's dating a movie star and an underwear model on alternate nights—Carly loves *you*."

Mark was fresh out of patience. "Well, I don't love her—okay?"

"Liar," Helen responded implacably. "Don't you think I can see what's happening to you? You're being eaten alive by the need to see her."

"You've been reading too many romance novels, Mother," Mark replied evenly. What she said was true, he reflected to himself, and he damned her for knowing it.

Helen got out of her chair with a long-suffering sigh and began gathering up the debris from their impromptu dinner, only to have Mark stop her and take over the task himself. He wasn't about to start depending on other people, even for little things.

When she was gone and Nathan was asleep in a down-filled bag on the floor of his bedroom upstairs,

Mark got out his laptop, set it on the card table and switched it on. After a few minutes of thought, he poised his fingers over the keyboard.

"Carly," he typed without consciously planning to.

"Now that's brilliant, Holbrook," he said to himself. "Neil Simon is probably sweating blood."

He sat back in his chair, cupping his hands behind his head, and closed his eyes. In his mind he saw Carly dancing with Jim Benson that night when she'd insisted on keeping her date with the guy. And even though Benson was one of the best friends he'd ever had, his nerve endings jangled just to think of another man holding Carly, kissing her, taking her to bed.

He cursed. Carly wasn't going to go to bed with Jim or anyone else, not for a while, he told himself. She was too sensible for that.

Then he recalled the way she'd responded to him, the soft, greedy sounds she'd made as he pleasured her, the way she'd moved beneath him. His loins tightened painfully, and her name rose to his throat in an aching mass. She was a healthy, passionate woman and, in time, she would want the release a man's body could give her.

In anguish, Mark thrust himself out of his chair and stormed across the room to the telephone. He picked it up from the floor and punched out her number before he could stop himself, not knowing what he would say, needing to hear the sound of her voice.

Her machine picked up, and Mark leaned against the wall in mingled disappointment and relief. "Hi, this is Carly," the recorded announcement ran. "If you're a friend, I'm off braving the wilds of the Deschutes River, and I'll be back on Tuesday morning. If you're a potential burglar, I'm busy bathing my Doberman pinscher, Otto. Either way, leave a message after the beep. Bye."

Mark closed his eyes and swallowed, unable to speak even if he'd had words to say. He hadn't expected hearing her voice to hurt so much, or to flood his mind and spirit with so many memories.

He replaced the receiver gently and went back to his computer, but no words would come to him. Finally he turned the machine off and went upstairs, where he looked in on Nathan.

The boy was sleeping soundly, a stuffed bear he wouldn't have admitted to owning within easy reach. Mark smiled sadly, closed the door and went on to his own room.

It was more of a suite, actually, with its own sizable bathroom and a sitting area that had probably been a nursery at one time. The walls were papered in pink-and-white stripes, the floor was carpeted in pale rose, and the place had an air about it that brought whimsical things to mind—sugar and spice and everything nice.

He allowed himself another bleak smile, imagining a baby girl with Carly's big blue-green eyes and tousled blond hair. The knowledge that such a child might never exist practically tore him apart.

Resolutely Mark stepped out of the sitting room and closed the door behind him. In the morning, he told himself, he'd see about having it redone to suit a confirmed bachelor.

Carly unrolled her sleeping bag and spread it out on the ground near two other women who hadn't bothered to include her in their conversation. The photographer the newspaper had sent along was a man—a very uncommunicative man.

After removing her boots, she crawled into the bag in her jeans and shirt, listening to the hooting of an owl and the quiet, whispering rush of the river.

The sky was bejeweled with stars, and the tops of ponderosa pines swayed in the darkness. It was all poetically beautiful, and there was a rock poking against Carly's left buttock.

She got out of the bag with a sigh and moved it over slightly, but when she lay down again, the ground was still as hard and ungiving as ever. A desolate feeling overcame her; she was surrounded by strangers, and Mark didn't love her anymore.

She began to cry, her body shaking with sobs she silenced by pressing the top of the sleeping bag against her mouth. It wasn't fair. Nothing in the whole damn world was fair.

After a long time Carly fell into a fitful, exhausted sleep, and she awakened with a start, what seemed like only minutes later, to find the gung-ho leader crouching beside her.

He was handsome, if you liked the Rambo type, but Carly wasn't charmed by his indulgent grin or his words. "Wake up, Girl Scout," he said. "Everybody else is practically ready to jump into the rafts."

Horrified, Carly bolted upright, squirmed out of the sleeping bag and was instantly awash in nausea. She ran for the log shower rooms.

When she came out feeling pale and shaky and having done what absolutions she could manage, an attractive dark-haired woman wearing khaki shorts and a plaid cotton blouse was waiting. There was a camera looped around her neck.

"Feeling better?" she asked, offering a smile and a handshake. "My name is Hope McCleary, and I didn't come on this trip willingly."

Carly swallowed, glad to see a friendly face. "Carly Barnett," she answered. "And I was sort of shanghaied myself—I'm doing a piece for a newspaper."

Hope grinned. "With me it's a magazine. I work for a regional publication in California."

Carly felt a little better now that she'd found a buddy.

The two women walked back to the campsite together, and Hope helped Carly roll up her sleeping bag and stow it, with her backpack, in one of the rafts. The stuff was carefully covered with a rubber tarp.

Rambo sauntered over and looked Carly up and down with disapproving eyes. "You missed breakfast," he said.

Carly felt her stomach quiver.

"Maybe she wasn't hungry, all right?" Hope snapped, putting her hands on her hips and glaring at him. "Give her a break!"

Rambo backed off, and Carly looked at Hope with undisguised admiration. "Admit it—you're really an angel sent to convince me that life is worth living after all."

Hope grinned and shook her head. "I'm no angel, honey, but you're right about part of it—life is *definitely* worth living." She paused to pull in a breath. "Like I

said, I'm just a humble magazine editor from San Francisco. Where do you live, Carly, and what newspaper
do you write for?"

A pang went through Carly at the mention of the city
that had charmed her so much. She might have visited it
often if things had worked out between her and Mark.
"I'm from Portland—my managing editor wants the
scoop on adventure among executives. I guess I'm lucky
he didn't want me to run with the bulls in Palermo."

Hope laughed and laid a hand on Carly's shoulder.
"A woman called Intrepid," she said. "But you are a little green around the gills. Are you sure you wouldn't
prefer to stay here and just question everybody when
we get back?"

Carly would have given her rhinestone tiara for a
room at the Best Western down the highway, but she
wasn't about to let the weak side of her nature win out.
"I'm going on this trip," she said firmly.

Soon they were seated in one of the rafts, wearing
damp, musty-smelling orange life preservers and listening to Rambo's final speech of the morning. Everybody, he said, was responsible for doing their share of
paddling. His eyes strayed to Carly when he added that
one slacker could send a raft spinning into the rocks.

She sat determinedly on the wet bench, her jeans
already soaked with river water, staring Rambo in the
eye and silently praying that she wouldn't throw up.

Soon they were off, skimming down the river between mountains fringed with ponderosas and jack
pines. The dirt on the banks had a red cast to it, and
here and there the color had seeped into the trunks of

trees. Carly got over being scared and was soon paddling for all she was worth.

Diamond-clear water sprayed her, and her morning
tea rose to her throat a couple of times, but all in all the
experience was exhilarating.

The convoy of three large rafts traveled until noon,
then Rambo led them ashore for lunch. Shivering with
cold and with the delight of finding a new area where
she was competent, Carly drank tea and cheerfully chatted with the others.

After thirty minutes Rambo herded them all back
into the boats again and they were off.

Several breathless hours later they stopped for the
night, making camp in a glade where a stone circle
marked the site of the last bonfire.

Carly plundered through her backpack for dry
clothes, then went into the woods to change. When she
returned, there was a fire blazing and food was being
brought out of the boats in large, lightweight coolers.

Reminding herself that a Girl Scout always plans
ahead, Carly hung her wet jeans and shirt on a bush,
with the underwear secreted behind them.

She jumped when she turned and came face-to-face
with Rambo. He was grinning down at her as though
she'd just greased herself with chicken fat and entered
a body-building competition.

"What was your name again?" he asked. Apparently,
now that he'd decided Carly had a right to live, he was
going to be chummy.

She barely stopped herself from answering, *Call me*

Intrepid. "It's Carly," she said aloud. "Carly Barnett. And you're…?"

His dark brows drew together in a frown. "Weren't you listening during orientation?" he demanded. "It's John. John Walters. Remember that." Displeased again, he turned and stormed away.

Carly raised one hand to her forehead in a crisp salute.

Hope came to her, laughing. "Come on, Carly—let's go gather some wood before he decides you're plotting a mutiny."

"I just can't seem to please that guy," Carly told her friend, following Hope into the woods.

"Do you want to?" Hope asked over one shoulder.

Carly chuckled. She was feeling stronger by the minute. It was nice to know she was a survivor, that she wasn't going to die just because Mark had left her without so much as a backward look. "No, actually. There's bad karma between Rambo and me."

They found enough dry wood to fill their arms and returned to camp.

"Have you ever thought about writing for a magazine?" Hope asked as they dropped the firewood beside the blaze in the middle of the clearing.

Carly shrugged. "No, but that doesn't mean I wouldn't like to try it. Why?"

"You're obviously a very special lady, Carly, and I'm looking for someone to replace a staff writer at the end of the month. Could you send me some clips as soon as you get back to Portland?"

Carly was intrigued. Mentally she sorted through the

pieces she'd done for the *Times*—the inside view of the shelter for battered women, the rebuttal to Mark's article on fathers' rights, the coverage of the food contest. "I don't have much, I'm afraid," she said finally. "I haven't been working for the paper all that long."

Hope shrugged. "Just send me what you can," she said.

That night was pleasant in a bittersweet sort of way. Everyone sat around the camp fire, full of roasted hot dogs and potato salad, and sang to the accompaniment of John Walters's guitar. The pungent perfume of the pines filled the air, and the river sang a mystical song begun when the Ice Age ended.

And Carly's heart ached fit to break because Mark wasn't there beside her calling her Scoop. She wondered now why she'd been so insulted at his jibes over her title; it seemed clear, in retrospect, that he'd only been teasing.

"Who was he?" Hope asked as they rolled their sleeping bags out, side by side, within six feet of the fire. Some of the other people had small tents, but most were stretching out under the stars.

"Who?" Carly countered, hedging. She didn't know whether talking about Mark would ease her heartache or get her started on another crying jag.

"The guy who left you with that puppy-loose-on-a-freeway look in your eyes, that's who."

Carly sat down and squirmed into her bag. "Just somebody I used to work with," she said. *And sleep with,* added a voice in her mind. *And love.*

Hope was looking up at the splendor of the night

sky, her hands cupped behind her head. Her voice was too low to carry any farther than Carly's ears. "You're going to have his baby, aren't you?"

For a moment the ground seemed to rock beneath Carly's sleeping bag. Her hands moved frantically to her flat abdomen, and her mind raced through the pages of a mental calendar.

"Oh, my God," she whispered, squeezing her eyes shut.

"Sorry," Hope said sincerely. "I thought you'd already figured it out."

Carly sank her teeth into her lower lip. The nausea, the volatile emotions—she should have known.

"What are you going to do?" Hope asked.

"I have no idea," Carly managed to say. But there were things she did know. She was going to have the baby, and she was going to raise it herself. Beyond that, she couldn't think.

"You should tell him, whoever he is," Hope said.

"Yeah," Carly agreed halfheartedly. Mark had a right to know he was going to have another child, but she wasn't sure she had the courage to tell him. He might think she was trying to rope him into a relationship he didn't want, or he could hire lawyers and take the child away from her. After all, he'd planned to sue Jeanine for custody of Nathan.

Hope was quiet after that, and Carly lay huddled in her sleeping bag, imagining the ordeals of labor and birth with no one to lend moral support. After a long time she fell asleep.

She woke with the birds, went off to the woods to be sick and began another day.

That morning her raft overturned, and she and Hope and eight other people were dumped into the icy river. As Carly fought the current, her mouth and nose filled with water, her eyes blinded by the spray, she prayed. *Please, God, don't let anything happen to my baby.*

She made it to shore, half-drowned and gasping for breath, and so did everyone else who'd been spilled out of the raft, but their sleeping bags and backpacks were gone.

A camaraderie had formed between the travelers, though, and the others pooled their extra clothes to help those who'd lost their packs. Rambo had spare blankets in the lead raft.

"This is going to make one hell of a story," Hope said as she stood on the shore beside Carly, soaking wet, snapping pictures as the overturned raft was hauled toward the bank.

Carly could only nod. When she got back to the office, she was going to ask Mr. Clark for a nice, easy assignment—something like skydiving, or jumping over nineteen cars on a motorcycle.

For all of it, she was sorry the next afternoon when the trip ended and pickup trucks hauled the exhausted, exhilarated rafters back to the original camp.

Since Carly had lost everything but the clothes she'd been wearing when the raft tipped over the day before, she was spared the task of packing her gear. She and Hope stood by her car, talking.

"Be sure you send me those clippings, now," Hope said as the two women hugged in farewell.

Carly smiled and nodded. She was never going to forget what a good friend Hope had been to her on this crazy trip. "Take care," she said, slipping behind the wheel of her car.

That day's spate of morning sickness had already passed, and Carly was possessed of a craving for something sweet. She stopped at a doughnut shop and bought two maple bars that were sagging under the weight of their frosting.

"Here's to surviving," she said, taking a bite.

The drive back to Portland was long and uneventful. When Carly arrived, she staggered into the bathroom, without bothering to look through her mail or play her telephone messages, and took a long, steaming-hot shower.

When she'd washed away the lingering chill of the river and the aches and pains inherent in sleeping on the ground, she ate another maple bar, brushed her teeth and collapsed into bed.

Arriving at the paper the next morning, she immediately shut herself up with her computer and started outlining her article. She barely raised her eyes when Mike Fisher, the photographer who'd been sent on the trip with her but kept mostly to himself, brought in the prints.

Carly flipped through them, smiling. Her favorite showed her crawling out of the river with her hair hanging in her face in dripping tendrils and every line in her body straining for breath. *And for her talent, ladies and gentlemen,* she thought whimsically, *Miss United States will nearly drown.*

She made a mental note to ask for a copy of the photograph, then went back to work. Almost as an afterthought, she asked Emmeline to send her clippings to Hope in San Francisco.

A full week went by before Carly allowed herself to dream of moving to California and joining the staff of one of the most successful magazines published on the West Coast. When Hope called and offered her a job at an impressive salary, Carly accepted without hesitation.

Maybe she couldn't have Mark Holbrook, but nobody was going to take San Francisco away from her.

Chapter 10

Janet gave Carly a tearful hug in the parking lot behind their building. "Be happy, okay?" she said.

Carly nodded. Happiness was a knack she hadn't quite mastered yet, but she had the baby to look forward to and the challenge of another new job in another new city. "You, too," she replied. Janet was dating Jim Benson regularly, and things looked promising for them.

The two women parted, and Carly got behind the wheel of her car and began the drive to San Francisco. She would live in a hotel until she found an apartment, and her dad was breaking all precedent to fly out for a short visit.

Carly wanted to tell him about the baby in person.

As she wended her way out of Portland, she considered his possible reactions. After all, in Don Barnett's day women just didn't have babies and raise them alone—they married the father, preferably before but sometimes after conception.

Mentally Carly began to rehearse what she would say. By the time she drove into San Francisco two days later, she had her story down pat.

When Carly checked in at the St. Dominique Hotel, she was told that her father had arrived and wanted her to call his room immediately.

He met her in the hotel lobby, looking like a real-estate agent in his black slacks, white shirt and blue polyester sports jacket. His graying brown hair was still thick, and his skin was tanned. Carly was pleased to realize he'd been spending a reasonable amount of time out of doors, away from the filling station.

She hugged him. "Hi, Dad."

Don kissed her lightly on the forehead. "Hello, doll," he answered, and his voice was gruff with emotion.

Carly was tired from her trip, and she wanted to have something light to eat and lie down for a while, but she knew her dad had been eagerly awaiting her arrival. She couldn't let him down. "How was the flight out?" she asked as she dropped her room key into her purse.

He grinned broadly. "Wasn't bad at all. In fact, there was this cute little stewardess passing out juice—"

Carly laughed. "They call them 'flight attendants' now, Dad. But I can see that you're up-to-date on your flirting."

He smiled at that, but there was a look in his eyes that Carly found disturbing. "For all this success you're having," he said as they gravitated toward one of the hotel's restaurants, "there's something really wrong. What is it, button?"

Tears were never very far from the surface during these hectic days, and Carly had to blink them back. She waited until they'd been seated in a quiet corner of the restaurant before answering. "Dad, I hate to be so blunt, but it wouldn't be fair to beat around the bush. I'm pregnant, and there's no prospect of a wedding."

Don was quiet for a long moment, his expression unreadable. But then he reached out and closed a strong, work-callused hand over Carly's. "That character with the Pulitzer Prize?" he asked. "I knew I should have blacked his eyes."

Carly couldn't help smiling at her dad's phrasing. "That's him," she said. Her eyes filled, and this time there was nothing she could do about it.

"Does he know?"

"Not yet. I'll send him a registered letter after I'm settled."

Her father looked nonplussed. "That's what I like to see—the warm, human touch."

Carly averted her eyes. "It's the best I can do for now. I'm taking things one minute at a time."

"You in love with him?"

Carly sighed. "Yeah," she admitted after a long moment. "But I'll make it through this, Dad." She paused, thinking of that photograph of her crawling out of the Deschutes River. "I'm a survivor."

"There's more to life than just surviving, Carly. You shouldn't be hurting like this—you deserve the best of everything."

"You're prejudiced," Carly informed him as a waiter brought menus and water.

Don studied his choices and chose a clubhouse sandwich while Carly selected a salad. During the meal they discussed the latest gossip in Ryerton and Carly's prospects of finding an apartment at a rent she could afford.

"You need money?" her dad asked when they'd finished eating and were riding up in the elevator.

Carly shook her head. "There's still some from the endorsements I did," she answered.

"But a baby costs a lot," Don argued.

She waggled a finger at him. "I'll handle it, Dad," she said.

At the door of her room, he kissed her forehead. "You go on in and take a nap," he ordered. "As for me, I'm headed over to take the tour at the chocolate factory."

Carly touched his face. "We have a date for dinner, handsome—don't you dare stand me up."

"Wouldn't think of it," he answered. "It isn't every day a fella gets to go out on the town with a former Miss United States on his arm."

With a laugh and a shake of her head, Carly ducked inside her room and closed the door.

There were a dozen yellow rosebuds waiting in a vase on the desk. The card read, *Welcome aboard, Carly. I'm looking forward to working with you. Hope.*

Carly drew in the luscious scent of the roses and made a mental note to call Hope and thank her as soon as she'd had a shower and a brief nap. When she awakened, though, it was late, and she had to rush to dress and get her makeup done.

Wearing a pink-and-white floral skirt and blouse, Carly met her father in the lobby, bringing along one of the rosebuds for his lapel. They had dinner at a place on the Wharf, then took in a new adventure movie.

The next morning Carly called Hope first thing, thanked her for the flowers and made arrangements to meet for lunch. Hope said she'd had her assistant working on finding an apartment for Carly, and there were several good prospects for her to look at.

"You're spoiling me," Carly protested.

"Nothing is too good for you, kid. Besides, I want to hook you before you find out what a slave driver I am."

Carly laughed, and the two women rang off. Three hours later they met at one of the thousand-and-one fish places on the Wharf for lunch.

"I can see where Carly gets her good looks," Hope said to Don when the two had been introduced.

Don blushed with pleasure, and Carly reminded herself that he was still a young man. Half the single women in Ryerton were probably chasing him.

Lunch was pleasant, but it ended quickly, since Hope had a busy schedule back at the magazine's offices. Carly promised to report for duty at nine sharp the following Monday, then accepted the list of apartments Hope's assistant had checked out for her.

She and her father spent the afternoon taxiing from one place to another, and the last address on the list met Carly's requirements. It was a large studio with a partial view of the water, and it cost more to lease for six months than her dad had paid to buy his first house outright.

Carly left a deposit with the resident manager, then she and Don went back to the hotel.

She was exhausted, and after calling the moving company in Portland to give them her new address, she ordered a room-service dinner for herself and Don. They had a good time together seated at the standard round table beside the window, watching a movie on TV while they ate.

"You going to be okay if I go back home tomorrow?" Don asked when the movie was over and room service had collected the debris from their meal. "I hate to leave you way out here all by yourself. It's not like you couldn't find somebody in Ryerton who'd be proud to be your husband—"

Carly laid her index finger to his lips. "Not another word, Gramps. San Francisco is my town—I know it in my bones—and I'm going to stay here and make a life for myself and my baby."

Respect glimmered in her father's ice-blue eyes. "Maybe you could come home for Christmas," he said.

"Maybe," Carly answered, her throat thick.

Her dad left then, and Carly took a brief bath, then crawled into bed and fell asleep. She didn't open her eyes again until the reception desk gave her a wake-up call.

Carly and Don had breakfast together, then he kissed her goodbye and set out for the airport in a cab. Even though he'd obviously been reluctant to leave her, he'd been eager, too. The filling station was the center of his life, and he wanted to get back to it.

At loose ends, Carly went to the offices of *Californian Viewpoint* to tell Hope she'd found an apartment.

Hope was obviously rushed, but she took the time to show Carly the office assigned to her.

"You didn't forget," Carly began worriedly, "that I'm pregnant?"

Hope shook her head, and her expression was kind and watchful. "I didn't forget, Barnett. And your dad told me who the father is—I must say, I'm impressed. With genes like yours and Holbrook's, that kid of yours is going to have it all."

Carly laid her hands to her stomach and swallowed. "I should skin Dad for spilling the beans like that. When, pray tell, did he manage to work *that* little tidbit into the conversation?"

Hope smiled. "When we were having lunch and you went to the restroom. Does Mark know you're here in San Francisco, Carly?"

"No," Carly said quickly. Guiltily. "And he doesn't know I'm pregnant yet, either, so if this is one of those small-world things and he's a friend of yours, kindly don't tell him."

Cocking her head to one side and folding her arms, Hope replied, "It is a small world, Carly. I went to college with Mark."

Carly sighed. "I suppose that means I'm going to be running into him a lot," she said.

Hope was on her way to the door. "Worse," she said, tossing the word back over one shoulder. "I want you to interview him about his new play." With that, Carly's new boss disappeared, giving her employee no chance to protest.

There was no escape, and Carly knew it. She'd signed a lease on an expensive apartment and she needed her job. She was going to have to face Mark Holbrook, in person, and tell him she was carrying his child.

All through the weekend she practiced what she would say and how she'd say it. She'd be cool, dignified, poised. Mark could have visitation rights if he wanted them, she would tell him. If he offered to pay child support, she would thank him politely and accept.

Despite two solid days of rehearsal, though, Carly was not prepared when she rang the doorbell at Mark's town house at ten-thirty Monday morning.

Nathan answered, and his freckled face lit up when he saw who'd come to call. "Carly!" he cried.

She smiled at him, near tears again. "Yeah," she answered. "Learn any good card tricks lately?"

The child nodded importantly and stepped back to admit her. "You're here to see my dad, aren't you?" he asked, his voice and expression hopeful. "He's really going to be surprised—he was expecting a reporter."

He's going to be more surprised than you'd ever guess, Carly thought, but she smiled at Nathan and nodded. "Where is he?"

"I'll get him," Nathan offered eagerly.

Carly shook her head. "I'd rather not be announced, if that's okay with you."

The boy looked puzzled. "All right. Dad's in his office—it's up those stairs."

Carly drew a deep breath, muttered a prayer and marched up the stairway and along the hall.

Mark was sitting at his computer, his back to her, his hands cupped behind his head.

Carly felt a pang that nearly stopped her heartbeat. "Hello, Mark," she said when she could trust herself to talk.

He swiveled in his chair and then launched himself from it, his face a study in surprise.

All weekend Carly had been hoping that when she actually saw Mark, she'd find herself unmoved. The reality was quite the opposite; if anything, she loved him more than she had before.

His expressive brown eyes moved over her, pausing ever so briefly, it seemed to Carly, at her expanding waistline. "What are you doing here?" he asked, his tone lacking both unkindness and warmth.

Carly shrugged. "I'm supposed to interview you for *Californian Viewpoint.*"

"What?"

"I work there," she explained, wondering how she could speak so airily when her knees were about to give out.

"You've living in San Francisco?"

She nodded.

"Oh." Mark looked distracted for a moment, then said abruptly, "Sit down. Please."

Gratefully Carly took a seat in a comfortable leather chair. Her hands trembled as she pulled her notebook out of her oversize handbag, along with a pencil. "Hope tells me you're writing a new play."

Mark looked confused. "Hope?"

"McCleary. Editor of *Californian Viewpoint* and your friend from college."

"Oh, yeah," Mark replied, and his gaze dropped to Carly's stomach again. Was the man psychic?

Carly crossed her legs at the knee and smoothed her soft cotton skirt. "A photographer will be along in a few minutes," she said. "Before we get started, how's Jeanine doing?"

Although Mark still looked a little off balance, he was obviously recovering. The ghost of a grin tugged at one corner of his mouth. "She's out of the hospital and attending regular AA meetings," he answered.

"Obviously Nathan is still with you."

Mark nodded. "He's had a lot of upheaval in his life during the past few years. Jeanine and I agreed not to jerk him back and forth between her place and mine."

In the distance the doorbell chimed, and Mark frowned at the sound.

"My photographer," Carly said brightly, though she begrudged the precious few moments she'd had with Mark and didn't want to share him.

"Great," Mark said, and the word was raspy.

Carly had been introduced to Allen Wright, the photographer, that morning in Hope's office. Besides his talent with a camera, she'd learned, he was a computer whiz.

True to form, Allen barely greeted Carly and Mark before zeroing in on Mark's computer and looking it over. A handsome young man with brown hair and blue eyes, he turned to grin at the master of the house. "Nice piece of equipment," he remarked.

Mark was looking at Carly; she could feel the heat and weight of his eyes. That extraordinary brain of his was probably developing one-second X rays of her uterus. "Yeah," he said pensively. "Great equipment."

Carly urged Allen to take the candidly posed photos needed for the layout and then shuffled him out the door.

When he was gone, she turned to Mark, her eyes feeling big, her teeth sunk into her lower lip. She was going to have to tell him now but, God help her, she couldn't find the words.

He made it all unnecessary. "My baby?" he asked in a husky voice, his gaze dropping again to Carly's stomach.

Her face flushed with color. "Who told you?" she demanded. "My dad? Hope?"

"Nobody had to tell me," Mark said, shoving splayed fingers through his hair.

Carly picked up her notebook again. "Let's just get the interview out of the way, okay? Then we can go our separate ways."

Mark shocked her by wrenching the notebook from her hand and flinging it across the room. "How the hell can you be so calm about this?" he demanded. He was gripping her upper arms now, forcing her to look at him. "Did you think I was just going to say, 'Oh, that's nice,' and read off my entry in *Who's Who* for your damned article?"

Carly pulled free. "I told you about the baby, Mark. That's the end of my obligation."

"The hell it is," he grated.

Carly's old fear that Mark might want to take her child from her when it was born resurfaced in a painful surge. "I'd better send someone else to do the interview," she said stiffly.

With a harsh sigh, he turned away from her. "I'd rather just get it over with, if it's all the same to you."

Legs trembling, Carly made her way back to her chair and sank gratefully into it. Mark picked up her notebook and brought it back to her.

"I want a place in this baby's life, Carly," he said.

She nodded briskly, unable to look at his face, composed herself and asked, "How's the new play going?"

"Well enough," Mark answered, falling into his own chair. "But I think I prefer nonfiction."

It was a relief to have things on a professional level again. "Does that mean you'll be going back into the newspaper business?"

He considered the question for a long moment, then shook his head. "I think I'd like to do books," he responded finally.

"Starting with?"

"One about what's happening in China, I think. I'd like to write about how the cultural and political conflicts interweave."

"Doesn't the prospect of danger bother you?" Carly asked, only marginally aware that *she* was the one troubled by the idea of Mark risking life and limb.

He lifted one shoulder in a shrug. "There are a lot of

hazards in everyday life," he reasoned. "I can't hide in a closet, hoping the sky won't fall on my head."

Carly lowered her eyes for a moment, then shifted the conversation back to the craft of writing plays. "How about your *Broken Vows?*" she asked moderately. "Whatever became of that?"

Mark smiled sadly. "Not a subtle question, Scoop, but I'll answer it anyway. Edina sold it to a movie producer, and it's being filmed in Mendocino even as we speak."

Shock and fury flowed through Carly's veins like venom, and she scooted forward in her chair. "After all you put me through, Mark Holbrook, you went ahead and *sold* that play?"

He nodded. "I read it and decided I'd been a jerk about the whole thing."

Carly recalled Jim Benson saying that Mark would eventually come to exactly that realization. It was too bad, she reflected to herself, that he hadn't felt any compunction to tell *her* about his change of heart.

She supposed there was someone else in his life now, and the thought filled her with pain.

"Well," she said, standing. "I'd better get back to the magazine and start writing." She offered her hand. "Thanks for the interview."

The moment Carly was gone, Mark raced up the stairs, down the hallway and into his bedroom suite. In the nursery a painter's helper was just getting ready to strip the pink-and-white striped paper from the walls.

"Stop!" Mark yelled, making the guy jump in surprise.

He didn't stay to explain, however. He ran back downstairs to his office and flipped through the phone book until he found the number for *Californian Viewpoint*.

When the receptionist answered, he identified himself and asked for Hope.

Carly sat at the computer in her office, her fingers making the keys click with a steady rhythm as she worked on the draft of her article about Mark. A rap at her door interrupted her concentration, and she raised her eyes to see Hope standing in the chasm.

She pulled off her glasses and set them aside on the desk. "I told him," she said.

Hope nodded, her eyes eager. "And what did he say?"

"Not much, actually. He wants to be part of the baby's life."

Hope closed the door. "Didn't he —well—ask you to dinner or anything?"

Carly gave her boss a wry look. "No, Yenta, he didn't," she answered. And then she sighed and sat back in her chair. "This is going to be an odd situation, I can see that right now. It'll be like being divorced from a man I was never married to in the first place."

"There isn't any hope that the two of you might get back together?" The editor looked disappointed, like a kid who'd expected a pony for Christmas and gotten a stick horse instead.

"Even if Mark Holbrook came to me on bended

knee," Carly said with lofty resolution, "I wouldn't take
him back. He was absolutely impossible when I showed
that agent his play—there was no reasoning with him.
If you think I want a whole lifetime of *that,* you're a
candidate for group therapy."

Hope had drawn up a chair, and she leaned forward
in it, looking at Carly in amazement. "You gave someone his play, without even *asking* him about it?"

Carly swallowed. "I know it sounds bad, but you
have to consider my motives—"

"What would *you* do if you'd written a play and
somebody snitched it and passed it on to an agent?"

"I'd have a fit," Carly answered defensively. "But
I'd also forgive that person, especially if I happened
to love him."

Hope let out a sigh that made her dark brown bangs
rise from her forehead. By tacit agreement the two
women dropped the subject of love. "How did the interview go?"

"It was great," Carly answered, her gaze drifting
toward the window. She could see a bright red trolley
car speeding down a hill, looking for all the world as
though it would plunge into the Bay. She swallowed
hard. "After all of it, he's letting them produce the play.
It's being made into a movie in Mendocino."

"So in a way you won," Hope reasoned, spreading
her hands.

"Right," Carly answered forlornly. "I won."

At the end of the day Carly went home to her apartment, where she'd been roughing it, waiting for her fur-

niture to arrive. Her new kitten, Zizi, greeted her at the
door with a mewling squeak.

Whisking the little bundle of white fur to her face,
Carly nuzzled the cat and laughed. There was something about a baby—no matter what species it was—
that always lifted her spirits.

She fed Zizi the nutritious dry food the pet store had
recommended, then changed her cotton skirt and blouse
for cut-off jeans and tank top. She was just opening a
can of diet cola when the telephone rang.

He won't call, Carly lectured herself as she struggled
not to lunge for the phone. *So don't get your hopes up.*

For all her preparations, her voice was eager when
she lifted the receiver and said, "Hello?"

"Hi, Carly," Janet greeted her. "I'm calling with big
news."

Carly closed her eyes for a moment, knowing perfectly well what her friend's announcement would be.
She was happy for Janet, of course, but she felt a little
left out, too.

"Jim and I are getting married!" Janet bubbled.

Carly smiled. "That's great," she said, and she meant
it.

"I want you to be my maid of honor, of course."

Always a bridesmaid, Carly thought. She knew she
was feeling sorry for herself, but she couldn't seem to
help it. She generated enthusiasm befitting the situation. "What colors are you going to use?"

"Pink and burgundy," Janet answered without hesitation.

Carly remembered when she'd first arrived in Portland, and Janet had been talking about getting married. At that time her ideas about the institution had been practical, but hardly romantic. "Have you decided that love isn't a myth after all?" she asked.

Janet laughed. "Have I ever. Jim's my man and I'm nuts about him." She paused. "Speaking of nuts, have you and Mark been able to touch base or anything?"

Carly sighed. "I interviewed him this morning," she said sadly. "And I told him about the baby."

All the humor was gone from Janet's voice. "Don't tell me he didn't ask you to marry him on the spot?"

"Of course he didn't," Carly replied breezily. "It's over between Mark and me—has been for a long time."

"Right," Janet replied, sounding patently unconvinced. "Now that the two of you are in the same city again, the earthquake people had better keep an eye on the Richter scale."

Carly shook her head. "It's really over, Janet," she insisted. Her words had put a definitive damper on the conversation, and it ended about five minutes later.

Zizi came to amble up Carly's bare legs and sit down on her stomach. "Reooow," she said sympathetically.

"Ain't it the truth?" Carly sighed, sweeping the kitten into one hand as she got back to her feet. She cuddled Zizi for a few moments, then put her down again. There was no sense in moping around the apartment, waiting for a call that was never going to come. She'd go down to the market and pick out some fresh vegetables and fish for supper.

After finding her purse, she left the apartment. She

walked to the market, since it was a warm August evening and the sun was still blazing in the sky.

She chose cauliflower, and broccoli and crisp asparagus, then purchased a pound of fresh cod. As she climbed back up the hill to her building, she was filled with a sort of lonely contentment. Maybe her life wasn't perfect—whose was? But she lived in a city she was growing to love, worked at a job that excited her and, come winter, she would be a card-carrying mother.

Those things were enough. They had to be.

Carly didn't know whether to be alarmed or encouraged when she saw Mark's car parked in front of her building. When she went inside, she found him sitting on the bottom step, a big bouquet of pink daisies in his hand.

Her traitorous heart skipped over one beat as he stood, a smile lighting his eyes. He took her grocery bag from her and handed over the flowers.

Carly looked at him with wide, worried eyes. "What do you want?"

"Now there's a cordial greeting," he observed, putting a hand to the small of Carly's back and propelling her gently up the stairs. "I guess I should be grateful you aren't shooting at me from the roof."

"If this is about the baby…" Carly began as she stopped in front of her door and rummaged in her purse for the key.

"It's about you and me," he said in a husky voice. "Carly, I came here to ask you to marry me."

She'd forgotten how old-fashioned Mark could be.

Obviously he meant to do his grim duty, however distasteful he might find it.

She stepped into the apartment, snatched her groceries from Mark's arms and shoved the riotously pink daisies at him. "Don't trouble yourself," she snapped, and slammed the door in his face.

Chapter 11

Carly closed her eyes and leaned against the door, Mark's knock causing the wood to vibrate.

"I'm not leaving until you hear me out, Carly," he called. "And I'm as stubborn as you are—I can keep this up all night, if necessary!"

"Go away!" Carly cried as the kitten, Zizi, brushed her ankles with its fluffy, weightless body.

"I'm not going anywhere," Mark retorted. "Damn it, let me in—I have things to say to you."

Carly shook her head, even though there was no one to see the gesture. "Give me one good reason why I should listen to anything you have to tell me."

He was silent for a moment, and the knocking stopped. "Because inquiring minds want to know," he finally responded.

Carly's lips curved into an involuntary smile. She crossed the room to set her grocery bag and purse on the counter by the stove.

The knocking started again. "Carly!"

She sighed. At this rate the neighbors would be summoning the police any second. "All right, all right," she muttered, returning to the door and sliding the bolt. "Come in!"

Mark stepped inside the spacious studio, looking irritated. He fairly shoved the pink daisies at her. "Here," he snapped.

"Thanks," Carly retorted just as shortly, but there was a softening process going on inside. Mark was getting to her in spite of her efforts to keep him at a distance.

She found a cut-glass vase in one of the cupboards and put the flowers into it with water. Then she set them on the sunny windowsill above the sink.

She stiffened when she felt Mark's hands come to rest, ever so gently, on her shoulders. He said her name hoarsely, and turned her to face him.

"I was wrong."

Carly jutted out her chin. "You can say that again."

The merest hint of a smile flickered in his eyes. "But I won't," he answered. "Carly, I love you. And I need you."

"Why?" she asked in an ironic singsong voice. "You've got everything—a son, money, a career anyone would envy—why do you want me?"

"Why do I want you?" He arched one eyebrow, and his voice was gruff. "Because you gave my life a dimension and a perspective it's never had before or since. With you I was one hundred percent alive, Carly."

She touched her upper lip with the tip of her tongue, watching Mark with wide eyes. "I know what you mean," she admitted softly, reluctantly. "I've got a great job, and I've proven to myself that I can make it on my own. And for all that, something vital is missing."

Mark's dark gaze caressed her. "Please," he said, "give me a chance to prove to you that I'm nothing like that jerk who threw such a fit over a play."

Without moving at all, he had pulled her to him. She came to rest against his strong chest, her body trembling, and he moved his hands over her back, soothing her. She slipped her arms around his waist, telling him physically what she could not say in words.

His lips moved, warm, against her hair. "I know now that I was scared of what I felt for you, Carly—and then there was getting Nathan back and Jeanine's accident. I distanced myself from you, thinking that would keep us both from getting hurt, but it didn't work." He paused to draw in a deep, ragged breath. "I promise I'll never do that again, sweetheart. When we have problems in the future, we'll stand toe-to-toe until they're worked out—agreed?"

Carly lifted her head and nodded. "Agreed."

He curved a finger under her chin. "I love you," he said, and then he lowered his mouth to hers.

Carly gave a little whimper as he kissed her, and her arms went around his neck. The feel of his hard frame against her set her flesh to quivering beneath her clothes.

He rested one of his hands, fingers splayed, against her belly. The muscles there leaped against his palm in response, and Carly smiled as she drew back from the kiss. In a few months he would be able to lay his hand there and feel the movements of their child.

"Marry me," he said, kissing her neck. He unsnapped her jeans and slid his fingers down over the warm flesh of her abdomen to find the swirl of silk.

Carly's head was light, and her eyes weren't focusing properly. She gave a little moan as Mark toyed with her. "Yes," she whispered, "oh, yes..."

He chuckled as he spread his left hand over her bottom, pushing her into the fiery attendance of his right. "It would be convenient if you had a bed, Scoop."

"Oooooh," Carly groaned, closing her eyes and letting her head fall back. During those moments, her every emotion and sense seemed to center on the motion of Mark's fingers.

He left her swaying and dazed in the middle of the room, while he gathered the three large and colorful floor pillows she'd bought in an import shop and arranged them on the floor.

It never occurred to Carly to protest when he came back to her and spread her gently on the pillows, a prize to be examined and savored. He stripped her methodically, kissing her insteps when he'd tossed aside her shoes, nibbling at the undersides of her knees when he'd taken away her cut-off jeans. He removed her T-shirt next, and then, with excruciating slowness, her bra.

Carly cupped her hands beneath her breasts, lifting

them to him, offering them. He shed his jacket and shirt and flung them aside before bending, with a low groan of pleasure, to catch one pink gumdrop of a nipple between his teeth.

Carly writhed on the soft pillows, her heels wedged against the hardwood floor, while Mark suckled her. Then he hooked a thumb under the waistband of her panties, her last remaining garment, and drew them down.

She wriggled out of them, kicked them away, and Mark stayed with her breast, as greedy as a thirsty man just then allowed to drink. Desperate, she found his hand and pressed it to the warm, moist delta between her legs.

He chuckled against her nipple and began moving his palm in a slow, titillating circle. Carly's body followed him obediently, yearning for his attentions.

He left her breast to kiss his way down over her belly, and Carly clutched at the floor in anticipation though, of course, the waxed wood would grant her no purchase.

She felt his lips on her still-flat abdomen. "I'm going to make your mom really happy," he promised the little person inside.

A great shudder shook Carly; she knew what Mark was going to do to her, that he would make her perform a physical and spiritual opera before he let her up off those pillows, and she couldn't wait another moment.

"Oh, God, Mark," she whispered, "now—please, now."

He parted her with his fingers, gave her a single flick with his tongue.

Carly cried out in lusty delight, not caring who heard, and sank her teeth into her lower lip when she felt Mark position himself between her knees. She covered her breasts with her hands, not because she wanted to hide them, but because she could not lie still. Mark made her show herself again.

"I want to see them," he said, his voice low and rumbling. Then he went back to the taut little nubbin of flesh that awaited him so eagerly.

He was greedy, and Carly clamped a hand over her mouth to stifle her cries of pleasure. Immediately, firmly, he removed it, and the gesture told Carly that he would demand an unrestrained response from her. He would hear every sound, see every inch of her flesh.

She gave a series of choked gasps as he took hold of the undersides of her knees, lifting and parting them so she was totally vulnerable to him. And then, having conquered her completely, he was ruthless.

He brought her to a thunderous crescendo that had her writhing beneath his mouth, and the sounds of her triumphant submission echoed off the walls and the ceiling.

She had known he wouldn't permit her to reach only one climax, no matter how soul shattering it might be. His own pleasure was in direct proportion to the heights Carly reached. Still, knowing these things, she pleaded with him.

He only chuckled, nibbling at the inside of her thigh while she came down, trembling and moist with exertion, from the top of a geyser. "We haven't even begun," he said.

Soon she was bobbing on the crest of an invisible spray of energy again, her back arched, her eyes dazed and sightless, her hair clinging to her cheeks and forehead. And Mark was already arousing her anew long before she'd recovered.

The instinct for power gave her the strength to open his jeans and reach inside, pressing her palm against his magnificence, closing her fingers around it.

He groaned, and his wonderful eyes rolled closed. "Oh, Carly..." he grated out. "Carly."

She caressed him until he was muttering in delirium, then maneuvered him so that he was lying sprawled on the pillows, as helpless as Carly had been earlier. She finished stripping him, bold as the queen of some primitive tribe, and bent to touch him lightly with her tongue.

He gave a guttural cry, and Carly felt a sweep of loving triumph. She had Mark where she wanted him, and she wasn't going to let him go until she'd enjoyed him thoroughly, because she had won the battle and he was the spoils.

His submission was glorious, full of honor, and Carly loved him with a sweet and tender violence.

Finally, though, he stopped her, his hands clenched on either side of her head. She watched his powerful chest rise and fall as he struggled for the breath to speak. "Inside you," he managed after a long time. "I want to be inside you."

Carly would not give up her position of dominance— this time it would be Mark who lay beneath the pleasure, drowning in its splendor.

She placed a knee on either side of his hips and

guided him to her portal with one hand, smiling when he buckled beneath her in a desperate search.

Splaying her hands over his heaving chest, feeling his nipples tighten under her palms, she allowed him only a little solace. He tossed his head from side to side, half-blinded with the need of her, and Carly loved him all the more for his ability to surrender so completely.

"More?" she teased.

"More," he pleaded.

She was generous, giving him another inch of sanction. His skin was moist beneath her hands, and she could feel an underlying quiver in his muscles as he struggled for control.

He arched his neck, his eyes closed, and Carly bent forward to kiss and nibble the underside of his chin. Then she felt him clasp her hips, and she knew the game was almost over.

Sure enough, he pressed her down onto him in a strong stroke that immediately set her afire. She groaned as he raised his fingers to her nipples and rolled them into tight little buttons.

He made another pass into her, and the tiny muscles where the magic lay went into wild spasms, making Carly toss back her head and cry out over and over again in satisfaction. When she finally went limp, Mark shifted her so that she lay beneath him, and took her in earnest.

At peace, she watched in love and wonder as pleasure moved in his eyes. She spread one hand over his muscular buttocks as he strained to give himself up to her, while the other traced the outline of his lips.

His teeth clamped lightly on her finger when he stiffened suddenly, emptying himself into her. And this
time the cry that filled the shadowy room was Mark's,
not Carly's.

He fell onto the pillows beside her when it was over,
curving an arm around her waist and holding her close
against his chest. They lay in silence for a long time,
but even then there was some kind of dynamics going
on between them.

It was a mystical mating process, fusing their two
spirits together at an invisible place. Carly's eyes filled
with tears as one indefinable emotion after another
swept over her.

She was Mark's, and he was hers, and not just until
the next time they disagreed over something, either. By
a process she could not begin to understand, an age-old
link between them had been reinforced.

Carly kissed Mark's shoulder and closed her eyes.

Beyond the fenced boundaries of the little church-
yard, Kansas stretched in every direction. Plump ma-
trons in colorful dresses chattered, while men smoked
and talked about their crops and "them politicians back
in Washington," whom they held in a healthy and typi-
cally American contempt. Children zigzagged throughout, filled with exuberance because the ripe summer
was still with them and because there would be cake
and punch aplenty at the reception.

Clad in her mother's gossamer wedding dress, her
arm linked with Mark's, Carly stood a little closer to
her husband. The limo he'd hired to drive them from

the church to the reception at the Grange Hall glistened like a sleek silver ghost at the curb.

Carly smiled at the stir it caused.

"Came all the way from Topeka," she heard some-one say.

Mark broke off the conversation he'd been having with Carly's father and his own, and grinned down at her. Something unspoken passed between them, and then they were getting into the plush car, Carly grap-pling with her rustling voluminous skirts of lace and satin. Her bouquet of pink daisies and white rosebuds lay fragrant in her lap.

She gave a happy sigh.

Mark chuckled and leaned over to kiss her cheek. "I love you, Mrs. Holbrook," he said.

She beamed at him, answering with her eyes.

The driver obligingly turned on the stereo, filling the car with soft, romantic music. It was his way of telling the newlyweds, Carly figured, that he wasn't listening in on their conversation.

They talked with their foreheads touching about their brief upcoming honeymoon in Paris. After that, Carly would be returning to San Francisco and Nathan and the magazine, while Mark jetted to the Far East to gather material for his book on China.

Whether or not he would get into the country re-mained to be seen. Carly suspected he had contacts who would be willing to smuggle him over the border, but she didn't allow herself to think about the possible ramifications of *that*, because she wasn't about to spoil the happiest day of her life.

When the limo pulled up in front of the ramshackle Grange Hall, which had never been painted, there were already a number of wedding guests waiting, and country-and-western music vibrated in the hot August sunshine.

Mark and Carly went inside, and Mark immediately pulled her into his arms for a dance. This delighted the onlookers, who loved a wedding almost as much as a rousing cattle auction.

Playfully Mark touched his lips to hers, and everyone clapped and cheered with delight.

"Show-off," Carly said, one hand resting lightly on his nape.

He laughed. "Me? Tell me, Mrs. Holbrook—was *I* the one who put on a sparkly outfit and twirled flaming batons in front of a whole nation?"

Carly's cheeks warmed. "You're still going to be teasing me about that in fifty years, aren't you?"

Mark pulled her a little closer. "Yup," he said.

After that, Carly danced with her father, then with Mark's father, then with Nathan.

"You look real pretty in that dress," her stepson said.

Carly smiled. "Thanks—you're looking pretty handsome yourself." She wanted to touch his hair, but she held back, unwilling to embarrass him. "You don't mind about my taking your dad away to Paris for a week?" she asked.

Solemnly Nathan shook his head. "And you don't need to worry when he goes to China, either. I'm pretty tough, and I won't let anybody hurt you."

Carly's heart swelled with love. "Okay," she said. "I won't give it a thought."

Toward the end of the song, Mark tapped his son on the shoulder to cut in. "Judging from the look on your face, I've got some pretty strong competition in that kid."

She smiled, glad to be close to her husband again. "He's one terrific guy," she agreed. "He just told me not to be afraid when you go to China, because he's tough and he can take care of me."

Mark searched her face. "*Are* you worried about me going to China, Scoop?"

"Of course I am," Carly answered. "What kind of wife would I be if I didn't consider the dangers? But I'm determined not to stand in your way where your career is concerned, and I expect the same courtesy from you."

It was time for more photographs and for the cutting of the giant cake decorated with white sugar doves and scallops of pink frosting.

They posed and exchanged sticky, crumbling bites of cake, and a collective sigh of approval arose from the guests when Mark took Carly into his arms and gave her a sound kiss.

"For better or for worse, Mrs. Holbrook," he said, his voice a hoarse whisper, "and for always, I love you."

Happy tears sprang into her eyes for the hundredth time that day. "Could I say something to you?"

He smiled. "Anything, as long as you never say goodbye."

"I'm so glad I met you," Carly told him. "And so glad I'm a survivor."

He kissed her. "So am I, Scoop. So am I."

She gazed up at him with loving eyes. "One more dance before we go?"

Mark nodded.

They whirled around the dance floor, unaware now of the guests, and the teetering cake, and the mountains of beautifully wrapped presents. Mr. and Mrs. Mark Holbrook were, for those precious moments, aware only of each other.

San Francisco
One year later...

Carly wore jeans and a blue T-shirt, and the baseball cap Nathan had given her on Mother's Day sat firmly on her head, the brim covering her nape. Riding on her back, papoose style, was Molly, who watched her father approach with solemn aquamarine eyes.

Out on the diamond, Nathan was speeding between third base and home. The ball came in from left field; the pitcher caught it and hurled it to the catcher.

Nathan dived, sliding into home plate on his belly, his hands outstretched.

"Safe!" yelled the umpire, who was, like everybody else on both teams, a kid from the neighborhood.

Reaching the place where his wife and daughter stood, Carly still unaware of his approach, Mark leaned over to give Molly a light kiss on the forehead.

She rewarded him with a gurgling chortle and a, "Da-da!"

Carly spun around at that, her eyes big in her dusty,

gamine's face. Her baseball cap fell off onto the ground when she flung her arms around Mark's neck.

He kissed her soundly, even though he knew he'd hear about it from Nathan. In his son's world, a guy just didn't kiss a woman in front of everybody in the neighborhood like that.

"How was China?" Carly asked. Her voice was throaty and low, and her eyes were filled with a blue-green come-hither look.

"Same as always," Mark answered gruffly. He'd made two trips since he and Carly were married. "Big. Isolated. Awesomely beautiful."

"I think we should go home and discuss this," Carly crooned.

He bent to pick up her fallen baseball cap and put it back on her head. This time the brim stuck out to the side, giving her a jaunty, Our Gang kind of look. "You're absolutely right, Mrs. Holbrook," he responded, his body tightening at the luscious prospect of being alone with her in the shadowy privacy of their bedroom. "But what about the short person here?"

Carly grinned. "Molly's due for a nap," she replied, "and Nathan will be out here playing baseball until you come back and drag him home for supper."

He lifted his brown-haired daughter out of the back sling and kissed her glossy curls. "You do look tired, kid," he told the child, his expression serious.

Molly's lower lip curled outward as though he'd insulted her, then she tossed back her head and wailed.

Twenty minutes later, when her mother had washed

her face and hands and given her a bottle, Molly closed her enormous Carly eyes and went immediately to sleep.

Mark led his wife out of the nursery and into their bedroom, taking off her baseball cap and tossing it aside. "As for you, Mrs. Holbrook," he said, "you're about to spend some quality time with your husband."

He saw the tremor of pleasure go through her, watched as her cheeks turned a delicious apricot pink. And he knew he loved her as desperately as he ever had.

"Mark," she began shyly, "I need a shower...."

He nodded. "So do I," he answered, catching hold of her T-shirt and lifting it off over her head.

Her breasts, full ever since she'd given birth to Molly, seemed to burgeon over the tops of her lace bra, and the sight of them filled Mark with a grinding ache that would take a long time to satisfy. He anticipated the feeling of a nipple tightening in his mouth, the arch of Carly's body against him, the little purring groans that would escape her throat.

He brought down one side of the bra and bent to taste her.

They undressed each other in a slow, romantic dance they'd learned together, and when they were naked, Carly led Mark into the bathroom. He adjusted the spigots in the double-size shower and drew her underneath the spray of the water with him.

Taking up the soap, Carly turned it beneath her hands, making a lather. Then she began to wash her husband, to prepare him for a sweet sacrifice that would be offered on their bed.

His muscles quivered beneath his flesh as she soaped

him all over, gently washing away the loneliness, the grit, the frustration of being parted from her. She was kneeling before him, washing his feet, when she looked up at him through the spray and ran one slippery hand up the inside of his thigh.

He felt his Adam's apple bob in his throat as he swallowed. "Carly," he managed to grind out just as she closed her mouth over him.

He entangled his fingers in her dripping hair and let the crown of his head rest against the shower wall, and he tasted warm water when he opened his mouth to moan in helpless pleasure. She gripped his tensed buttocks then, as though she feared that he would leave her.

His knees weakened as she continued to pleasure him, and he wondered how long he could stand before her. He was on the verge of slipping to the floor of the shower as it was.

"Carly," he choked out, and he tried to lift her head from him, but she would not be deterred.

Only seconds later his raw cry of surrender echoed in the shower stall, stifled by the sound of the water.

They lay naked in the middle of the bed, arms around each other, legs entwined. Carly's head rested on Mark's shoulder.

"That was your last trip to China," she said, hardly able to believe he'd really said he wouldn't be leaving her again for a long time.

With his hand he cupped her breast possessively. "I'll be underfoot from now on," he said. "Even though

I'll be writing a book, your friends will all think I'm a house husband."

Carly laughed, but the sound caught in her throat as Mark's thumb moved back and forth across her nipple. She purred as warm pleasure uncurled within her. "We could use one around here," she said, stretching as Mark continued to stroke her. "You see, the Holbrook family is about to get bigger again."

He reared up on one elbow to search her face with those wonderful, luminous brown eyes of his. "We're having another baby?" he asked hopefully, as though such a thing could happen only once in an aeon.

Carly held up two fingers. "It's a double play, Mr. Holbrook," she answered, her throat thick with emotion, "and our team is about to score."

Mark laughed for joy, and there were tears glistening in his brown eyes, but his body was conducting an independent celebration all its own. He parted Carly's legs and lay between them, letting her feel his heat and his power and his vast love for her.

His face somber again, he slipped his hands under her bottom and lifted, then went into her in one unbroken stroke. And Carly welcomed him with her whole soul.

Mark Holbrook was home to stay.

* * * * *

Dear Reader,

The Grand Teton Mountains in Wyoming, icons of the American West thanks to famed photographer Ansel Adams, offer some of the most beautiful scenery in the world. My husband and I have visited the area several times. On one particular trip, I was lucky enough to run into Harrison Ford and his wife on the street in the small, charming town of Jackson! He was quiet and reserved, but he signed an autograph for me. During the entire encounter, which lasted all of three minutes, my husband stood ten feet away with a video camera and *never* turned it on. Men!

The autograph is displayed in my office with a color movie still from one of the Indiana Jones films where "Harry" is wearing his famous leather hat. Framed in weathered barn wood, the combo is one of my prized possessions.

I've always wanted to set a book in Wyoming because I am fascinated by men like Harrison Ford and my hero, Trent. These are tough, macho guys who are perfectly comfortable doing hard, dirty manual labor on a ranch and yet can move seamlessly into the glittering world of wealth and privilege.

My heroine, Bryn, has suffered a few hard knocks in her short life—who hasn't? But for her young son, she is strong enough and brave enough to face the man who broke her heart. I hope you enjoy their story, and I hope your travels may one day take you to Jackson Hole and the Tetons.

I also invite you to read about the Kavanagh family: seven wealthy, sexy brothers who live in the mountains of North Carolina in the resort town of Silver Glen. Next up is Aidan's story, *Christmas in the Billionaire's Bed*, due out December 2014. Still available: *A Not-So-Innocent Seduction* and *Baby for Keeps*. And don't forget the Men of Wolff Mountain, an exciting series available as ebooks: *Into His Private Domain*, *A Touch of Persuasion*, *Impossible to Resist*, *The Maid's Daughter*, *All Grown Up*, *Taming the Lone Wolff* and *A Wolff at Heart*.

Happy reading,

Janice

THE SECRET CHILD
& THE COWBOY CEO

Janice Maynard

For Caroline and Anna,
who shared with us one wonderful Wyoming summer.
A van, an X-Cargo and the open road…
six weeks of fun…memories to last a lifetime.

Chapter 1

A half-dozen years... One look from those fabulous eyes and she could still make him act like a foolish kid.

Trent felt his heart slug hard in his chest. Oxygen backed up in his lungs. *Dear God, Bryn.*

He dragged the remnants of his self control together and cleared his throat, pretending to ignore the woman standing beside his father's bed.

Her presence in the room made him sweat. The lust, loathing and sharp anger teeming in his gut made it impossible to act naturally, particularly since he wasn't sure if the anger was self-directed or not.

His father, Mac, watched them both with avid curiosity, giving his son a canny, calculating look. "Aren't you going to say something to Bryn?"

Trent tossed aside the damp towel he'd been using to

dry his hair when he walked into the room. He folded his arms across his bare chest, then changed his mind and slid his hands into his back pockets. He turned toward the silent woman with what he hoped like hell was an impassive expression. "Hello, Bryn. Long time no see."

The insolence in his tone caused a visible wince to mark her otherwise serene expression, but she recovered rapidly. Her eyes were as cool as a crisp Wyoming morning. "Trent." She inclined her head stiffly in a semblance of courtesy.

For the first time in weeks, Trent saw anticipation on his father's face. The old man was pale and weak, but his voice was strong. "Bryn's here to keep me company for the next month. Surely she won't aggravate me like all those other cows. I can't stand strangers poking and prodding at me...." His voice trailed off, slurring the last few words.

Trent frowned in concern. "I thought you said you didn't need a nurse anymore. And the doctor agreed."

Mac grunted. "I don't. Can't a man invite an old friend without getting cross-examined? Last time I checked, this was *my* ranch."

Trent smothered a small, reluctant grin. His father was a grouch on his best days, and recently, he'd turned into Attila the Hun. Three nurses had quit, and Mac had fired two more. Physically, the Sinclair patriarch might be on the mend, but he was still mentally fragile.

It was a comfort to Trent that, although exhaustion marked Mac's face, he was as ornery as ever. The heart attack he'd suffered two months ago, when his youngest son was found dead of a heroin overdose, had nearly cost the family *two* lives.

Bryn Matthews spoke up. "I was happy to come when Mac contacted me. I've missed you all."

Trent's spine stiffened. Was that a taunt in her perfectly polite words?

He forced himself to look at her. When she was barely eighteen, her beauty had tugged at him like a raw ache. But he'd been on the fast track already, an ambitious twenty-three-year-old with no time for a young wife.

She had matured into a lovely woman. Her skin was the same sun-kissed ivory. Her delicate features were framed by a thick fall of shiny black hair. And her almost-violet eyes gazed at him warily. She didn't appear unduly surprised to see him, but he was shocked right down to his bare toes. His heart was beating so hard, he was afraid she'd be able to see the evidence with her own eyes.

She was dressed more formally than he had ever seen her, in a dark pantsuit with a prim white blouse beneath. Her waist was narrow, her hips curvy. The nononsense cut of her jacket disguised her breasts, but his imagination filled in the details.

Bitterness choked him. Bryn was here to cause trouble. He knew it. And all he could think about was how badly he wanted her in his bed.

He ground his teeth together and lowered his voice. "Step into the hall with me." He didn't phrase it as a request.

Bryn preceded him from the room and turned to

face him across the narrow space. They were so close he could see a pulse beating in the side of her throat. And he caught a whiff of her familiar, floral-scented perfume. Delicate…like she was. The top of her head barely came up to his chin.

He ignored the arousal jittering through his veins. "What in the hell are you doing here?"

Her eyes flared in shock. "You know why. Your father asked me to come."

Trent growled low in his throat, wanting to pound a hole in the wall. "If he did, it was because you manipulated him into thinking it was his idea. My brother Jesse's not even cold in his grave and yet here you are, ready to see what you can get."

Her eyes flashed, reminding him she had never lacked for gumption. "You're a self-righteous ass," she hissed.

"Never mind." He cut her off, swamped with a wave of self-loathing. She was a liar. And she had tried to blame Jesse for another man's sins. But that didn't stop Trent from wanting her.

He firmed his jaw. "Apparently you couldn't be bothered to make it to the funeral?"

Her lips trembled briefly. "No one let me know that Jesse had died until it was too late."

"Convenient." He sneered. Only by whipping up his anger could he keep his hands off her.

The hurt that flickered in her gaze made him feel as if he was kicking a defenseless puppy. At one time he and Bryn had been good friends. And later—well… there had been a tantalizing hint of something more.

Something that might have developed into a physical relationship, if he hadn't screwed things up.

Bryn had been innocent, not-quite-eighteen, and Trent had freaked out over his reaction to her. He had rejected her clumsily when she asked him to be her date for the senior prom, and she was heartbroken. A few weeks later, she and Jesse started dating.

Had Bryn done it to hurt him?

Trent couldn't blame Jesse. Jesse and Bryn were the same age and had a lot in common.

Bryn's face was pale. Her body language said she wanted to be anywhere other than in this hallway with him.

Well, that was too damn bad.

He leaned forward to tuck a strand of her hair behind her ear, whispering softly, "If you think I'll let you take advantage of a sick old man, you're an idiot." He couldn't stop himself.

Bryn's chin lifted and she stepped sideways. "I don't care what you think about me, Trent. I'm here to help Mac. That's all you need to know. And I'm sure you'll be on your way back to Denver very soon…right?" In another situation the naked hope on her face would have amused him. But at the moment, he couldn't escape the irony.

He cocked his head, wishing he could discern the truth. Why had she really come back to Wyoming?

He shrugged. "Tough luck, Bryn. I'm here for the foreseeable future.… I got tapped to take a turn running the place until the old man is back on his feet. So you're stuck with me, sweetheart."

Her cheeks flushed, and her air of sophistication vanished like mist in the morning sun. For the first time he saw a hint of the girl she had been at eighteen. Her agitation made him want to soothe her when what he should be doing was showing her the door.

But his good sense was at odds with his libido. He wanted to crush her mouth beneath his, strip away the somber-looking jacket and find the curves he would map in detail.

The past beckoned, sharp and sweet.... He remembered one of the last times he and Bryn had been together before everything went so badly wrong. He had flown in for his dad's birthday party. Bryn had run to meet him, talking a mile a minute as soon as he got out of the car. She was all legs and slim energy. And she'd had a crush on him.

She would have been mortified if she'd realized he had known all along. So, on that long-ago day he had treated her with the same easy camaraderie that had always existed between them. And he'd done his best to ignore the tug of attraction he felt.

They were not a match in any way.

At least that's what he'd told himself.

Now, in this quiet hallway, he got lost for a moment, caught between the past and the present. He touched her cheek. It was soft...warm. Her eyes were the color of dried lavender, like the small bouquets his mother used to hang in the closets. "Bryn." He felt the muscles in his throat tighten.

Her gaze was guarded, her thoughts a mystery. No longer did he see naked adoration on her face. He didn't trust her momentary docility. She might be trying to play him for her own advantage. But she'd soon find that she was no match for him. He'd do anything to protect his father. Even if it meant bedding the enemy to learn her secrets.

Without thought or reason, his lips found hers. Their mouths clung, pressed, moved awkwardly. His hands found the ripe curves of her breasts and he caressed her gently. He thought she responded, but he couldn't be sure. He was caught up in some weird time warp. When sharp daggers of arousal made him breathless, he jerked back, drawing great gulps of air into his starving lungs.

He ran his hands through his hair. "No." He couldn't think of a follow-up explanation. Was he talking to her or himself?

Bryn's face was dead-white but for two spots of hectic color on her cheekbones. She wiped a shaky hand across her mouth and backed away from him.

Distress filled her eyes and embarrassment etched her face.

She turned and walked away, her gait jerky.

He watched her go, his gut a knot the size of Texas. If she had come again to try to convince them that Jesse had fathered her child, she would get short shrift. It would be in extremely bad taste to accuse a man who wasn't here to defend himself.

Remembering Jesse at this particular moment was a mistake. It brought back every single moment of torment Trent had experienced when his baby brother started dating the woman Trent wanted. The situation had been intolerable, and only by keeping himself in

Denver, far away from temptation, had Trent been able to deal with it.

But in his heated fantasies, during the dead of night, it was Bryn, always Bryn. He'd told himself he was over her. He'd told himself he hated her.

But it was all a lie....

Bryn didn't have the luxury of locking herself in her room and giving way to the storm of emotions that tightened her throat and knotted the muscles between her shoulder blades. Why couldn't Mac's son Gage have been here...or Sloan? She loved both of them like brothers and would have been happy for a reunion. But Trent... Oh, God, had she given herself away? Did he know now she had never gotten over her fascination with him?

She couldn't allow herself to think about what had just happened...refused to acknowledge how she enjoyed the way his hard, naked chest felt beneath her hands. Had she pushed him away or leaned into him?

Don't be a fool, Bryn. Nothing can come of going down that road but more hurt.

When Bryn was sure Mac was napping, she went out to the car to retrieve her suitcase and carry-on. Trent had disappeared to do chores. Bryn was grateful for the respite from his presence.

She stood, arms upraised, and stretched for a moment, shaking off the stiffness from the long flight and subsequent drive. She had forgotten the clearness of the air, the pure blue of the Wyoming sky. In the distance, the Grand Tetons ripped at the heavens, their jagged peaks still snowcapped, even in mid-May.

Despite her stress and confusion, after six years of exile, the familiar Crooked S brand entwined prominently in the massive wrought-iron gates at the end of the driveway felt like a homecoming. The imposing metalwork arched skyward as if to remind importunate visitors, "You're nobody. Trespass at your own risk."

The four boys used to call it the "Crooked Ass Ranch." Mac hadn't thought the irreverence funny.

Before going back inside, Bryn studied the house with yearning eyes. Little had changed since she had been gone. The sprawling two-story structure of timber and stone had cost millions to build, even in the mid-seventies when Mac had constructed it for his young bride.

The house rested, like a conqueror, on the crest of a low hill. Everything about it reeked of money, from the enormous wraparound porch to the copper guttering that gleamed in the midday sun. The support beams for the porch were thick tree trunks stripped of bark. Flowering shrubs tucked at the base of the house gave a semblance of softness to the curb appeal, but Bryn wasn't fooled.

This was a house of powerful, arrogant men.

Back inside, she picked up her phone and dialed her aunt's number. Even though the Sinclairs' ranch was in the middle of nowhere, Mac had long ago paid for a cell tower to be built near the house. With enough money, anything could be bought, including all the trappings of an electronic society.

When Aunt Beverly answered, Bryn felt immediately soothed by the familiar voice. Six years ago her mother's older sister had taken in a scared, pregnant teenager and had not only helped Bryn enroll in community college and find a part-time job, but when the time came, she had also been a doting grandmother, in every sense of the word, to Allen.

Bryn chatted with a cheer she didn't feel, and then asked to speak to her son. Allen's tolerance for phone conversations was limited, but it comforted Bryn to hear his high-pitched voice. The family next door had two new puppies. Aunt Beverly was taking him to the neighborhood pool tomorrow. His favorite toy fire truck had lost a wheel. "Love you. Bye, Mommy."

And with that, he was gone.

Beverly came back on the line. "Are you sure everything is okay, sweetheart? He can't make you stay."

Bryn squeezed the bridge of her nose and cleared her throat. "I'm fine…honestly. Mac is weaker than I expected, and they're grieving for Jesse."

"What about you?"

Bryn paused, trying to sort through her chaotic feelings. "I'm still coming to terms with it. He didn't break my heart. What we had was more hormones than happily-ever-afters. But he nearly destroyed my world. I never forgave him for that, but I didn't want him dead." Her throat thickened, making it hard to speak.

Beverly's gentle words echoed her strength. "We've gotten by without the money all this time, Bryn. It's not worth losing your pride and your self-respect. If they give you trouble, promise me you'll leave."

Bryn smiled, though her aunt couldn't see her. "Allen deserves a share of the wealth. And I'll put it in a special account for his college education and whatever else he might need down the road. It will give him a secure future, and that's important. I'll be home in four weeks. Don't you worry about me."

They chitchatted a few more minutes, but then Allen demanded Aunt Beverly's attention. Bryn clicked the phone shut and blinked rapidly to stave off a wave of loneliness and heartache. She had never been away from her baby more than a night or two.

Allen would be fine. She knew that. But she felt like she'd been given a life sentence without parole.

She changed into comfortable jeans and a petal-pink sweater. It was time to check on Mac.

She tiptoed as she neared his room. He needed his rest desperately. Fortunately, this entire wing of the house was quiet as a tomb, so maybe he was still sleeping. Everything in his luxurious but masculine suite was designed for comfort, so as long as his medication was relieving any pain, he should be recovering on schedule.

But she knew as well as anyone that grief manifested itself in serious and complex ways.

Her foot was moving forward to enter the room when she realized Trent was sitting on the side of his father's bed. She caught her breath and drew back instinctively.

Trent murmured softly, the conversation one-sided as Mac slept. Bryn couldn't make out the words. Trent stroked his father's forehead, the gesture so gentle a huge lump strangled her throat.

The old man was feeble and frail in the large bed. His

eldest son, in contrast, was virile, strong and healthy. Seeing Trent show such tenderness shocked her. He had always been a reserved man, self-contained and difficult to read. Striking and impressive, but a man of few smiles.

His steel-gray eyes and jet-black hair, dusted with premature silver at the temples, complemented a complexion tanned dark by the sun. Despite the years he'd been gone from Wyoming, he still retained the look of one who spent much of his time outdoors.

She swallowed hard and forced herself to enter the room. "When is his next doctor's appointment?"

Though her words were soft and low, Trent snatched back his hand and rose to his feet, his expression closed and forbidding. "Next Tuesday, I think. It's written on the kitchen calendar."

She nodded, her voice threatening to fail her. "Okay." She tried to step past him, but he put a hand on her arm.

Trent was raw with grief over the loss of his brother. He could barely contemplate the possibility of losing the old man so soon after Jesse's death. How could Bryn still turn him inside out? His grip tightened. Not enough to hurt her, but enough to let her know he wouldn't be a pushover.

He put his face close to hers, perhaps to prove to himself that kissing her was a temptation he could withstand. "Stay out of my way, Bryn Matthews. And we'll get along just fine."

This close he could see the almost imperceptible lines at the corners of her eyes. She was not a child anymore. She was a grown woman. And he saw in one brief instant that she had suffered, too.

But then she blinked and the tense moment was gone. "No problem," she said, her voice quiet so as not to wake her patient. "You won't even know I'm here."

Trent strode outdoors blindly, feeling suffocated and out of control. He needed physical exertion to clear his head. A half hour later, he slung a heavy saddle over the corral rail and wiped sweat from his forehead. Working out at the gym in Denver wasn't quite the same as doing ranch labor. The chores here were hard, hot and strangely cathartic. It had been a decade since Trent had played an active role in running the Crooked S. But the skills, rusty as they might be, were coming back to him.

He had repaired fences, mucked out stalls, hunted down stray calves and helped the vet deliver two new foals. Up until yesterday, his brothers, Gage and Sloan, had done their part, as well. But they were gone now— for at least a month —until one of them returned to relieve Trent.

A month seemed like a lifetime.

Trent's father employed an army of ranch hands, but in his old age, he'd become cantankerous and intolerant of strangers—reluctant to let outsiders know his business. He'd fired his foreman not long before Jesse's death. The tragedy had taken a toll on all of them, but Mac had aged overnight.

Even now, eight weeks after Jesse's death, Trent was blindsided at least once a day by a poignant memory of his youngest brother. The coroner's report still made no sense. Cause of death: heroin overdose. It was ridiculous. Jesse had been an Eagle Scout, for God's sake. Had someone slipped him the drug without his knowledge?

Trent finished rubbing down the stallion and glanced at his watch. He'd fallen into the habit of checking on the old man at least once an hour, and with Bryn around, that routine was more important than ever. He didn't trust her one damn bit. Six years ago she had lied to weasel her way into the family. Now she was back to try again. The next few weeks were going to be hell.

Especially if he couldn't keep his traitorous body under control.

Chapter 2

When Trent stormed out of the room, albeit quietly, Bryn couldn't decide if she was disappointed or relieved. He made her furious, but at the same time, she felt so alive when he was around. Six years had not changed that.

She sat at Mac's bedside for a half hour, just watching the rise and fall of his chest. In some ways, it was as if no time had passed at all. This man had meant the world to her.

When he finally roused from his nap and shifted upright in the bed, she handed him a tumbler of water, which he drained thirstily and placed on the bedside table.

He stared at her, his expression sober. "Do you hate me, girl?"

She shrugged, opting for honesty. "I did for a long time. You broke your promise to me." When her parents, Mac's foreman and cook, died in a car accident years ago, Mac had sat a fourteen-year-old Bryn down in his study and promised her that she would always have a home on the huge Wyoming ranch where she had grown up.

But four years later that promise was worth less than nothing. Jesse, spoiled golden child and chillingly proficient liar, turned them all against her in one insane, surreal instant.

Mac shifted in the bed. "I did what I had to do." His words were sulky…pure, stubborn Mac. But knowing how much he had suffered softened Bryn's heart a little.

In spite of herself, forgiveness tightened her throat and squeezed her chest. Mac had made a mistake…. They all had made mistakes, Bryn included. But Mac had done his best to look out for her after her parents were gone. Until it all went to hell.

Then he'd sent her to Aunt Beverly. Punishment by exile. Bryn had been crushed. But six years was a long time to hold a grudge.

She sighed. "I'm sorry Jesse died, Mac. I know how much you loved him."

"I loved you, too," he said gruffly, not meeting her eyes.

His behavior bore that out. Mac hadn't forgotten her. For six years he'd sent birthday and Christmas presents like clockwork. But Bryn, hugging her injured pride like the baby she was, promptly sent them back every time.

Now shame choked her. Did Mac's one moment of weakness erase all the years he'd been like a grandfather to her?

She took a deep breath. "I came back to Wyoming because you asked me to. But even if you hadn't, I would have been here once I knew Jesse was gone. We have to talk about a lot of things, Mac." Like the fact that she wanted a paternity test to prove that Jesse was Allen's father. And that her son was entitled to his dead father's share of the Sinclair empire.

Mac's lips trembled, and he pulled the blanket to his chest. "There's time. Don't push it, girl." He slid back down in the bed and closed his eyes, effectively ending the conversation.

Bryn stepped into the hall, leaving the bedroom door open so she could hear him call out if he needed her. The study was only steps away. She couldn't help herself...she went in.

The room seemed benign now, not at all the way she remembered it in her nightmares. That dreadful day was etched in her memory by the sharp blades of hurt and disillusionment. She'd considered herself an honorary Sinclair, but they had sided with Jesse.

"What are you doing in here?"

Trent's sharp voice startled her so badly, she spun and almost lost her balance. She placed a steadying hand on the rolltop desk and bit her lip. "You scared me."

His scowl deepened. "I asked you a question, Bryn."

She licked her lips, her legs like jelly. "I wanted to send my son an email."

Trent's face went blank, but she saw him clench his

fists. "Don't mention your son in my presence," he said, his voice soft but deadly. "Not if you know what's good for you."

Bryn could take the knocks life dealt her, but no one was going to speak ill of her baby while there was breath in her body.

She squared her shoulders. "His name is Allen. And he's Jesse's son. I know it, and I think deep in your heart, you and Mac and Gage and Sloan know it, too. Why would I lie, for heaven's sake?"

Trent shrugged, his gaze watchful. "Women lie," he said, his words deliberately cutting, "all the time—to get what they want."

For the first time, she understood something that had never before been clear to her, especially not as an immature teenager. When Mac's flighty young wife abandoned her family years ago, the damage had run deep.

The Matthews family had come along to fill in the gaps. For more than a decade, Bryn and her mother had been the only females in an all-male enclave. And Bryn had assumed that trust was a two-way street. But when Jesse swore that he had never slept with Bryn, Mac and Trent had believed him. It was as simple as that.

Bryn chose her words carefully. "I don't lie. Maybe you've had bad luck with the women in your life, but I can't help that. I told the truth six years ago, and I'm telling the truth now."

He curled his lip. "Easy for you to say. With Jesse not here to defend himself."

She tamped down her anger, desperate to get through to him. "Jesse was a troubled boy who grew into a troubled man. You all spoiled him and babied him, and he used your love as a weapon. I have the scars to prove it. But Jesse's gone, and I'm still here. And so is my son. He deserves to know his birthright—his family."

Trent leaned back against his wall, the hard planes of his face showing no signs of remorse. "How much do you want?" he said bluntly. "How big a check do I have to write to make you leave and never come back?"

The bottom fell out of her stomach, and her jaw actually dropped. "Go to hell," she said, her lips trembling.

He grabbed her wrist as she headed for the door. "Maybe I'll take you with me," he muttered.

This time, there was no pretense of tenderness. He was angry and it showed in his kiss. Their mouths battled, his hands buried in her hair, hers clenched on his shoulders.

At eighteen she'd thought she understood sex and desire. After Jesse's betrayal, she'd understood that his love was an illusion. As was Mac's…and Trent's.

Now, with six years of celibacy to her credit and a heart that was being split wide open with the knowledge that she had never stopped loving Trent Sinclair, she was lost.

The kiss changed in one indefinable instant. She curled a hand behind his neck, stroking the short, soft hair that was never allowed to brush his collar. His skin was warm, so warm.

She went limp in his embrace, too tired to fight anymore. Her breasts were crushed against his hard chest. Her lips no longer struggled with his. She capitulated to the sweetness of being close to him again. A sweetness tainted with the knowledge that he thought she was a liar. That she had tried to manipulate them all.

Gradually, they stepped away from a dangerous point of no return. Trent's expression was closed, his body language defensive.

She nodded jerkily toward the desk. "I'll use the computer later. I'm sure you have work to do."

When he didn't respond at all, she fled.

Trent was not accustomed to second-guessing himself. Confidence and determination had propelled him to success in the cutting-edge, fast-paced world of solar and wind energy. When he'd received the call about his father's heart attack, Trent had been in the midst of an enormous deal that involved buying up a half-dozen smaller companies and incorporating them into the already well-respected business model that was Sinclair Synergies.

Except for some start-up cash that had long since been repaid, he'd never relied on his father's money. Trent was damned good at what he did. So why was the CEO of said company cooling his heels in Wyoming shoveling literal horseshit?

And why in the hell couldn't he read the truth in a woman's eyes? A woman who had stayed in his heart all these years like a bad case of indigestion.

Had Jesse lied? And if so, why? Mac, Sloan, Gage and Trent had doted on the little boy who came along three years after his one-after-the-other siblings. Jesse had suffered from terrible bouts of asthma, and the entire family rallied whenever he was sick. So, yeah—

maybe Bryn was right. Maybe they *had* catered to Jesse's whims, especially when their mother bailed on them. But that didn't mean Jesse was a bad person.

Heroin overdose. Trent shifted uneasily in Mac's office chair. Going through the books was proving to be more difficult than he'd anticipated. Jesse had never been a whiz at math, so God knows why Mac put him in charge of the finances. His youth alone should have been a red flag. And his inexperience.

Already, Trent was uneasy about some ways money had been shifted from one account to another. A heart-to-heart with Mac was in order, but until the old man was a little steadier on his emotional feet, Trent would hold off on the questions.

Which brought him back to Bryn. What was Mac thinking? Why had he brought Bryn back to Wyoming?

Trent shoved back from the desk and stood up to stretch, his eyes going automatically to the magnificent scene outside the window. Wyoming was his birthplace, his home. And he loved it. But it had not been able to hold him…or Gage or Sloan, either, for that matter.

Gage had developed a bad case of wanderlust at an early age…and Sloan—well—Sloan's brilliance was never going to be challenged by ranching. Had Jesse felt the need to be his father's heir apparent? It didn't fit what Trent knew of his baby brother's temperament, but what else could explain Jesse's role in running the ranch?

At one time the Crooked S had been the largest cattle operation in a six-state area…back when Mac was in his forties and had a brand-new twenty-year-old bride at his side. Now it was nothing more than acres of really valuable land.

What would become of the ranch when Mac was gone?

Trent waited until he heard Bryn talking on the phone in her bedroom before he went back in to check on his dad. Mac was sitting up in bed, and already his eyes seemed brighter, his skin a healthier shade. Had something as simple as bringing Bryn home wrought the change?

Trent sat down in a ladderback chair near the foot of the bed and hooked one ankle over the opposite knee. He put his hands behind his head and leaned back. "You're looking better."

Mac grunted. "I'll live." The two of them had never been much for sentimentality.

Trent smothered a smile. "Do you feel like going for a ride? I need to pick up a few things in town. Might do you good to get out for a couple of hours."

His father seemed to wilt suddenly, as though his burst of energy had come and gone in an instant. "Don't think I ought to try it yet. But maybe Bryn would like to go."

Trent stiffened. He wasn't ready to spend the hour and a half it would take to go into Jackson Hole and back cooped up in a car with the woman who was tying him in knots. "I'd say she's still tired from her trip. And I can be there and back in no time."

Mac's dark eyes, so much like his son's, held a calculating gleam. "Bryn promised to pick out a new blanket for my bed at the Pendleton store. You know how women are…always shopping for something. I don't want to disappoint her. And you can have dinner before you drive back. Julio and I are going to play poker tonight."

Julio was one of the ranch hands. Trent sighed. He knew when he'd been suckered. But he wasn't going to fight with his dad…not yet.

Moments later, Trent knocked on Bryn's door. It was slightly ajar, and he waited impatiently until she finished her phone conversation.

Bryn ground her teeth when she realized Trent was standing in the doorway. Maybe she should put a cow bell on him so he'd quit sneaking up on her. "What do you want?" The curt question was rude, but she was still stinging from their earlier encounter.

Trent's expression was no happier than hers. His lips twisted. "I'm supposed to take you into town with me to do some errands…a blanket my father mentioned? And he wants me to take you out to dinner."

She cocked her head, reading his discomfort in every taut muscle of his lean body. "And you'd rather wrestle with a rattlesnake…right?"

He shrugged, leaning against the door frame, his face impassive. "I'm here this month to make my father's life easier. And if that means allowing him to boss me around, I'm willing to do so."

"Such a dutiful son," she mocked.

His jaw hardened. "Be out front in twenty minutes."

Bryn fumed as he walked out on her, and she locked her door long enough to change from jeans into nice dress slacks and a spring sweater. She didn't understand Trent at all. But she read his hostility loud and clear. From now on, there would be no kissing, no reliving the past. She was here to right past wrongs, and Trent was no more than a minor inconvenience.

She managed to make herself believe that until she climbed into the passenger seat of a silver, high-end Mercedes and got a whiff of freshly showered male and expensive aftershave. *Oh, Lord.*

Her stomach flipped once…hard…and she clasped her hands in her lap, her feet planted on the floor and her spine plumb-line straight.

The atmosphere in the car was as frigid as a January Wyoming morning. Trent turned the satellite radio to a news station, and they managed to complete the entire journey in total silence.

He let her out in front of the Pendleton store. "I've got some business to attend to. Can you entertain yourself for an hour or so?"

She sketched a salute. "Yes, sir. I'll be right here at six o'clock."

His jaw went even harder than before, and his tires squealed as he pulled away from the curb.

Bryn's brief show of defiance drained away, and her bottom lip trembled. Why couldn't Trent let the past stay in the past? Why couldn't they start over as friends?

She picked out Mac's beautiful Native American–patterned blanket in no time, and visited a few more of the shops down the street, managing to select gifts for her aunt and for Allen. A friendly shopkeeper offered to stow Bryn's bulky packages until Trent returned, so Bryn took the opportunity to stretch her legs.

Back in Minnesota she and Beverly and Allen walked each evening when the weather was nice. The two women enjoyed the exercise, and it was good for Allen to use up some of his energy before bedtime.

Bryn missed her baby. He hated it when she called him that. He was five and would be starting kindergarten in the fall. She wasn't ready. Maybe because it pointed out the fact that he wouldn't always need her. He'd go off to college and meet some scary girl who would take him away for good.

She laughed softy at her own maudlin thoughts. She was twenty-four years old. She was two semesters away from finishing a degree in communications, and as soon as she was able to return home, she would fall back into her familiar, comfortable routine. She had her whole life ahead of her.

So why did she feel despondent?

The answer was simple. She wanted Trent to trust her. To ensure Allen's future, she had no choice but to insist on a paternity test. But everything inside her rebelled at that thought. She didn't want a litigious battle with the Sinclair family.

She wanted Mac, Trent, Gage and Sloan to admit that she was one of them, blood or not. She wanted an apology. She wanted to see more in Trent's face than suspicion and anger.

Her daddy used to say, "Men in prison want out." So what?

She was sitting on a bench, packages tucked beside

her, when Trent returned. Without speaking, he got out, opened the trunk and waited for her to put her shopping spoils inside.

Then he faced her across the roof of the car, his expression stoic. "Where would you like to eat?"

Bryn's temper had a long fuse, but his manner was insulting. She glared at him. "There's a sandwich shop on the corner. We can grab something and eat on the way home...so we don't waste any time."

Her sarcasm hit the mark. He opened his mouth and shut it again, displeasure marking his patrician features. "Fine."

Twenty minutes later, they were on the road. Bryn chewed a turkey sandwich that felt like sand in her mouth. Finally, she gave up and wrapped most of it in the waxed paper and stuffed it in the bag.

Trent had finished his without fanfare and was sipping coffee and staring out the windshield in the dwindling light. Encountering large wildlife on the road was always a hazard, but Trent was a careful driver and Bryn felt perfectly safe with him.

She chewed her lip, wishing she could go back in time and erase every stupid thing she'd ever done. Including the day she invited Trent to take her to the prom. Trent had said no, of course. Bryn had cried her eyes out behind the barn, and Jesse had come along to comfort her.

In retrospect, she suspected Jesse's motive, even from that first moment, had been troublemaking.

When the silence in the car became unbearably oppressive, Bryn put her hand on Trent's sleeve. "I'm really sorry about Jesse. I know you loved him very much." She felt the muscles in his forearm tense, so she took her hand away. Apparently even brief contact with her disgusted him.

Trent drummed his fingers on the steering wheel, his profile bleak. "I still can't believe it. He was such a good kid."

"You weren't around him much in the last several years, though. He changed a lot."

"What do you mean?" The words were sharp.

"Didn't you wonder why he never graduated from college?"

"Dad said he had trouble settling on a major. He was restless and confused. So he switched schools several times. Apparently he decided he wanted to get more involved with the ranch."

Bryn groaned inwardly. It was worse than she thought. Mac clearly must have known about Jesse's problems, but apparently he had done a bang-up job of keeping that information from his other three sons.

Did Bryn have the right to dispel the myths?

She thought of little Allen, and the answer was clear.

"Trent—" she sighed "—Jesse got kicked out of four universities for excessive drinking and drug use. Your father finally made him come home to keep an eye on him."

The car swerved, the brakes screeched and Bryn's seat belt cut into her chest as Trent slammed the car to a halt at the side of the road. He punched on the overhead light and turned to face her. "How dare you try to smear my brother's memory.... You have no right." His dark eyes flashed, and the curve of his sensual lips was tight.

She wouldn't back down, not now. "I'm sorry," she said softly. "I really am. But Mac has done you a disservice. Perhaps you could have helped if you had known."

Trent's laser gaze would have ripped her in half if she hadn't known in her heart she was doing the right thing. Pain etched his face, along with confusion and remorse, and a seldom-seen, heart-wrenching vulnerability—at least not by Bryn.

He ran a hand through his hair. "You're lying again. How would you know anything about Jesse?"

Denial was a normal stage of grief. But Bryn held firm. "I'm not lying," she said calmly. "Jesse called me a couple or three times a year. And every time it was the same. He was either drunk or high. He'd ramble on about how he wanted me to come back to Wyoming."

"If you're telling the truth, it's even worse. He might have wanted to make a family with you and the baby, even if it wasn't his."

"Focus, Trent. He didn't know what he was saying half the time. If anything, he wanted to use me and Allen to win points with Mac…to help cover his ass after whatever new trouble he'd gotten himself into."

"Jesse loved children."

"Jesse offered me money to get an abortion," she said flatly. "He said he had big plans for his life and they didn't include a baby…or me for that matter. That's why I ran into Mac's study that day so upset. I thought Mac would talk some sense into him."

Trent's face was white. He didn't say a word.

"But instead," she said, grimacing at the quiver she heard in her own voice, "Mac put me on a plane to Minnesota."

Please, please, please believe me.

He shrugged. "With your talent for drama, you might have a career on the silver screen."

His flippant words hurt, but they were no more than she expected. He'd been fed a pack of lies, all right. But not by Bryn.

She sighed. "Ask Mac," she begged. "Make him tell you the truth."

Trent shook his head slowly. "My father nearly died. He's grieving over the loss of his son. No way in hell am I going to upset him with your wild accusations."

She slumped back in her seat and turned her head so he wouldn't see her cry. "Well, then—we're at an impasse. Take me home. I want to see how Mac is doing."

She didn't know what she expected from Trent. But he gave her nothing. Nothing at all. His face closed up. He started the engine.

Chapter 3

Trent was appalled by the picture Bryn painted of Jesse. The young brother Trent remembered was fun-loving, maybe a little immature for his age, but not amoral, not unprincipled.

Bryn had unwittingly touched on Trent's own personal guilt. He hadn't been much of a big brother in recent years. Other than Mac's birthday in the fall, and Thanksgiving and Christmas, Trent had seldom made the trip home from Colorado to Wyoming.

His company was wildly successful, and the atmosphere of cutthroat competition was consuming and addictive. He'd made obscene amounts of money in a very short time period, but it was the challenge that kept him going. He thrived on being the best.

But at what cost? Had he missed the signs that Jesse

was struggling? Or had the truth been kept from him deliberately? Gage wouldn't have known. He was usually halfway around the world on any given day. And Sloan was more attuned to the world of numbers and formulas than emotions and personalities. No…Trent should have been the one to see it, and he'd been too damned busy to help.

Of course, there was always the possibility that Bryn was exaggerating…or even inventing the entire scenario. That was the most palatable choice. But though he was far from being willing to trust her, the passionate sincerity in her eyes and in her words would be difficult to fabricate.

When they pulled up in front of the house, Bryn got out and retrieved her packages before he could help her. Her body language wasn't difficult to read. She was angry.

He took her arm before she walked away, registering the slender bones. "I don't want you talking to Mac about Jesse. Not for a while. God knows what you're hoping to get out of this sudden, compassionate visit, but I'll be watching you, so don't do anything to upset Mac or you'll have me to deal with."

She threw him a mocking smile as she walked toward the porch. "I love Mac. And your threats don't scare me. I think your original idea was the best.… I plan to stay out of your way."

Bryn saw little of Trent for three days, which was a good thing. She was still smarting from their most recent confrontation. He showed up in his dad's room several times a day to chat with him, and on those oc-casions, Bryn slipped away to give the men privacy.

Mac was aware of Trent's burdens and complained to Bryn. "Can't you slow him down? The boy works round the clock. If he's not on the ranch, he's holding conference calls with his staff and staying up half the night doing God knows what."

"How am I supposed to stop him? Your sons would do anything for you, Mac, but it must be terribly dif-ficult for a man like Trent to put his life on hold for a month." Trent had built a highly successful company from the ground up, and his drive and intelligence had enabled him to amass his first million before he was twenty-five. Even without the financial largesse he would one day inherit from his father, Trent was a wealthy man.

Mac frowned stubbornly. "He would listen to you, Brynnie."

"I don't think so. You know he doesn't trust me. He's got lawyers flying in by helicopter almost every day with contracts to sign. He's an important, high-profile businessman. He and I might have been close at one time, but I don't even know him anymore." The older boy she remembered—the young man who had seemed like the most wonderful person in the world to her—was long gone. The Trent of today operated in an arena that was sophisticated, intimidating and com-pletely foreign to her.

The change in the man she had once been so close to made her sad.

* * *

Bryn wouldn't have minded the distraction of helping out around the house, but with Mac's revolving staff of cooks and housekeepers, she might as well have been staying in a four-star hotel. Any dirty laundry disappeared as if by magic, and her luxurious bathroom and bedroom were kept spotless.

For someone accustomed to caring for a child, working part-time and keeping up with school, she found herself at loose ends when Mac was resting.

On the third night after the uneasy trip to Jackson Hole, Trent encountered her in the kitchen chatting with the cook.

His expression was brooding. "I thought I might see if Mac is up to having dinner at the table tonight. What do you think?"

She nodded slowly, wishing she didn't feel so awkward around Trent. "It's a great idea. It would do him good to get out of that room for a change." It was really more of a suite than a single room, but even the most luxurious surroundings could seem like a prison.

When the two men reappeared, Mac leaning on his son's arm, Bryn was helping set everything on the table. The menu, by doctor's orders, included as many heart-healthy ingredients as possible, and the aroma was enough to tempt even the most uninspired appetite.

Mac picked at his food to start with, but finally dug in. Bryn watched, pleased, as he cleared his plate.

The conversation was stilted. But Bryn did her best. "So tomorrow's the doctor's appointment, right?"

Mac had his mouth full, so Trent answered. "Yes.

At 11:00 a.m. I'll take Dad. You can stay here and have some time off the clock."

She frowned. He made it sound as if she were the hired help. "But I would be happy to go."

Trent shook his head, his calm demeanor hiding whatever he might be feeling. "No need."

And that was it. The oracle had spoken.

After dinner Mac and Trent played chess on a jade-and-onyx board that Gage had brought back from one of his trips to Asia. Bryn could tell by the quality of the workmanship that the set was expensive. And she wondered wryly what it must be like to never once have to worry about money.

She stood unnoticed in the doorway for several minutes, just watching the interplay between the two men. The Sinclair males had never been the type to wear their hearts on their sleeves, but Bryn knew they loved each other deeply. They were a tightly knit clan.

Unfortunately, she was still outside the circle.

The following morning, Bryn was shooed out of the sickroom so Trent could help his father get dressed and leave. Unbidden, her feet carried her upstairs to Jesse's room. It was as far from Mac's as it was possible to be in the rambling house. On purpose? Perhaps. Jesse would have wanted to avoid his father's watchful eye.

A thin layer of dust coated everything. Mac paid a weekly cleaning service to come in, but they must have been given instructions not to enter this room. Nothing had been touched since the day Jesse died. Even the bed was still unmade.

Though it made her stomach hurt, the first thing she did was to gather a few items that could be used for testing...a comb that held stray hairs, a toothbrush, a razor. She couldn't afford to be squeamish. This was why she had come.

Bryn continued to straighten the mess as her mind whirled with unanswered questions. She had seen the coroner's report. Mac had laid it out in full view on the dresser in his bedroom. She suspected he wanted her to read it for herself so he wouldn't have to say the awful words out loud: *My son was a drug addict.*

What a waste of a young life. She picked up a neon blue iPod, plugged it into the dock, and flipped through the selections. Nostalgia and grief hit hard as she saw one familiar title, "Jessie's Girl." How many times had the two of them played that oldie at full volume, singing along, careening down a Wyoming road?

She had believed it with her whole heart. She had been Jesse's girl, and even though he wasn't Trent, he had made her feel special and wanted. She'd been happy mostly, relieved to know that she would forever be a part of the Sinclair clan.

But it had all been an illusion.

She opened the closet door and reached to put the sports equipment on a top shelf. As she did, she dislodged an old shoe box held together with a rubber band. It fell at her feet. Something about it made a cold chill slither down her spine.

She sat down on the double bed and took off the lid.

She'd been expecting drugs, maybe a gun. Certainly not what she found.

The box held letters, maybe two dozen in all. As she riffled through them, she saw that the earliest ones were dated the year Jesse turned sixteen. The return addresses were all the same...a single line that read *RRIF*. The postmarks were all Cheyenne.

Had no one at the house ever questioned Jesse about them, or were they spaced so far apart that no one took notice? Or had Mac known all along? The three older boys would have been in college when the first ones showed up in the mailbox.

Bryn opened one at random and began reading. Horrified, she went through them all. Her stomach clenched.

What kind of mother would poison the mind of her young son, a boy she had abandoned when he was six years old?

The damage was insidious. A child might have missed the venom behind the words. But what about Jesse? Had he been happy his mother contacted him? Happy enough to not to look beneath the surface? Or as a young adult, had he been able to see the subtext beneath the whining, manipulative words?

Jesse, you were always my favorite.

Jesse, Mac was a tyrant. I was so unhappy. He wouldn't let me take you.

Jesse, I miss you.

Jesse, Trent and Gage and Sloan never loved me the way they should.

Jesse, you have my brains. Brawn isn't everything.

Jesse, you deserve more.

Jesse...Jesse...Jesse...

Bryn couldn't imagine why Mac's wife would have been so cruel. To punish her ex-husband? To bring discord into the family? Why? *She* had left them, not the other way around.

The later letters were the most damning. Etta Sinclair talked about her many boyfriends. She hinted that she'd had affairs while she was married to Mac. And she intimated that Mac might not be Jesse's father.

Bryn's legs went weak, so much so that she might have fallen if she hadn't been sitting down. It wouldn't matter if Trent and Mac ever believed that Jesse was Allen's father. Jesse might not be a Sinclair at all, and if *he* wasn't, then his young son was not, either.

Bryn gathered the letters with shaking hands, tucked them back in the box and went downstairs to her room.

Would there be any point in letting Mac see them? Best to hide them. Until she could decide what to do with them. Surely he had long since become immune to his wife's defection.

The more she thought about the letters, the more confused she became. She had seen pictures of Etta, though they were few and far between. Trent, Gage and Sloan were all carbon copies of their dad—big, strong men with dark coloring.

Jesse was blond and slender, the spitting image of his mother. Was it simply a quirk of DNA, or was there any truth in those letters?

By the time the men returned in the late afternoon, Bryn had almost made herself ill. She excused herself after dinner and hid in her room. After a shower and a long phone call with Aunt Beverly, she curled up in bed and read for hours until she fell into a restless sleep.

Trent's immediate anxieties were eased considerably by the doctor's glowing report on Mac's recovery. The heart attack had been a serious one, but Mac's overall health and fitness had mitigated some of the long-term damage. Mac Sinclair was a tough old bird.

Which emboldened Trent on the way home to press gently for some answers. He kept his voice casual. "Was it really necessary to invite Bryn to come out here? She's bound to cause trouble. You know what she did six years ago. I doubt she's changed."

Mac wrapped his arms across his chest, gazing pensively through the windshield. "I handled things all wrong back then. She deserves a fair hearing. That's why I asked her to come."

Trent was stunned. "But she lied."

Mac shrugged. "Maybe she did, maybe she didn't. But it still does my heart good to see her again."

Trent opened his mouth to protest, but choked back the words with effort. His tough father had never been prone to sentimentality. Trent feared that in this vulnerable state his father might be fooled by a woman who was beautiful, charming and had a not-so-secret agenda.

He spoke carefully. "It would be human nature if Bryn wanted a piece of the pie." Trent's job, like it or not, would be to ferret out the truth and protect his father from doing anything rash.

"Bryn is not a threat," Mac insisted. "She's the same girl she always was."

"That's what worries me. I can't forget what she tried to do to Jesse." Trent, too, felt the pull of Bryn's charisma, acknowledged the presence of nostalgic memories and emotions. But he was not so easily swayed by soft smiles and sweet words. He'd been in business long enough to know that people were not always what they seemed.

"Jesse played a part in what happened six years ago."

"All I'm asking, Dad, is that you don't promise her anything. Bryn might look like a dark-headed angel, but that doesn't mean she isn't out to get what she wants by fair means or foul." Trent would be wise to remember his own advice the next time he had an urge to taste those lush lips.

Mac moved restlessly in his seat, clearly exhausted by the outing. "You're paranoid, boy. Don't be so suspicious."

"I'll try, Dad. For your sake." Trent lived by the adage "Keep your friends close and your enemies closer." Whether or not Bryn was an enemy remained to be seen, but in the meantime, he'd keep an eye on her. She wasn't the only one who could put on an act. He would pretend to be the gracious host, and if she let down her guard, he'd be able to circumvent any mischief she might have in mind.

Tension and stress threatened to turn Bryn into an insomniac. After one particularly restless night, there was a knock at her bedroom door, and she realized with chagrin that the sun was shining brightly through a crack in the draperies.

She cleared her throat. "Come in." She expected the cleaning lady. But it was Trent.

The grimace that crossed his handsome face might almost have been a lopsided half smile. "I owe you a thank-you for coming so quickly when Mac called."

She sat up in bed, covers clutched to her chest, and scraped the hair from her face. Trent was clean shaven and his hair was still damp from his shower. In contrast, Bryn was decidedly rumpled.

He'd brought scrambled eggs and toast. It was all arranged on a tray with coffee, jam and a napkin.

He set it on the dresser and kept his distance.

She tried to clear her sleep-fogged throat. "Thank you."

His brooding gaze studied her. "One of Mac's old college buddies is coming to visit today. I thought you and I should make ourselves scarce. It's a beautiful day. We could take a hike…like we used to."

"A hike?" Her coffee-deprived brain was slow to catch up.

He nodded, still unsmiling. "We got off on the wrong foot this week, Bryn. I appreciate what you're doing for Mac."

"So this is an olive branch?" Her heart leaped in her chest.

He shrugged. "I wouldn't say that. But it bothers him when we're at each other's throats. We can at least put on a good front when we're around him. So maybe we need to clear the air."

The breakfast was delicious, but Bryn chewed and swallowed absently, still pondering Trent's final cryptic statement. He'd left her bedroom abruptly, and he didn't sound like a man who was suddenly convinced she was telling the truth. If anything, he wanted to brush the past under the rug.

She couldn't do that. She had Allen to consider.

She dressed rapidly in light hiking pants and a short-sleeved shirt. She hadn't brought her boots with her on the plane, because they were heavy, so a sturdy pair of sneakers would have to do.

Sunshine must be strong medicine, because she found Mac in good spirits. She smoothed his sheets absently. "Are you sure you'll be okay while we're gone?"

Mac nodded. "I'm fine. No need to hover. You've been in Minnesota a long time. Get out and enjoy the ranch."

Bryn and Trent left shortly thereafter, this time in one of the ranch Jeeps. Trent drove with the quiet confidence that was so characteristic of him.

Bryn wasn't entirely comfortable with his silence. "Where are we going?" she asked.

Trent shifted into low gear as they wound partway up the side of a steep hill. "Falcon Ridge."

There was no inflection in his voice, but Bryn felt a kick of excitement. Falcon Ridge was a family favorite. She and Mac's boys had spent many a happy afternoon there over the years.

Trent parked the Jeep and got out. He attached the quilt like a bedroll at the base of his high-tech pack and stuffed their picnic lunch inside.

"I can carry something," Bryn said.

His motions were quick and methodical. "I've got it."

The trail was only a mile long, but it went up, up, up. Trent led the way, his stride steady, his back straight. Bryn's leg muscles were burning and her lungs gasping for air when they reached the summit.

"Oh, Trent…I'd forgotten how beautiful it is up here."

The valley of Jackson Hole lay before them, breathtaking, magnificent, tucked against the backdrop of the Grand Tetons. A lone eagle soared on thermal currents overhead. Her throat tightened, and she wondered how she had stayed away so long.

"It's my favorite spot on the ranch." For a moment she saw vulnerability in his face and she wondered if he ever regretted moving away.

Trent spread the quilt, and they sat in silence, enjoying the view. Bryn was extremely conscious of him at her side, so close she could feel his body heat. He had leaned back on his elbows, and his flat stomach drew her attention. He was lean and fit and utterly masculine.

She had loved him one way or another for most of her life. When her parents died, it was nineteen-year-old Trent, more than anyone else, who had been able to comfort her. She had cried on his shoulder for hours, and finally, she had believed him when he said the hurt would get better.

If Trent said it, it must be so.

She tried to bridge the gulf between them, wanting some kind of peace. "You taught me to ride a horse… to drive a car. I always wanted you to give me my first kiss. But instead, it was Jesse."

Trent's expression was bleak. "That was a long time ago. Things change."

She pulled her knees to her chest and wrapped her arms around them. She was not the same scared, devastated girl who left the ranch six years ago. She had borne a child, gone back to school, learned to deal with life's disappointments.

But here on this mountaintop, she could feel the pull of emotion. And that was a recipe for disaster.

"What did the doctor say about Mac yesterday?"

Trent sat up, his shoulder momentarily brushing hers. "He was pleased with his physical progress. But he pulled me aside and said he's concerned about Mac's mental condition. There's no real reason Mac needs you or anyone to babysit him anymore. Mac seems to think he's more fragile than he really is. The doc says we need to coax him out of that damned bedroom and get him back to living."

She flipped an adventurous ant from the edge of the quilt. "They say that even for a normal heart-attack patient that can be hard. But on the heels of Jesse's death…" She trailed off. They both knew that Mac hadn't dealt with either the reality *or* the circumstances of Jesse's passing.

Finally, still without looking at her, Trent spoke. "I'm sorry I didn't take you to the prom."

She was surprised that he would bring it up after all this time. "I was a silly girl. You were a grown man. That was bound to end badly."

"Still," he said doggedly, "I could have handled it better."

What could she say to that?

At last he turned toward her. "I was attracted to you, Bryn. And that scared the hell out of me."

"You're just saying that to make me feel better." She couldn't meet his probing gaze. "I was so embarrassed. I wanted to crawl in a hole and die. Literally." Thinking about that long-ago afternoon made her cringe.

He brushed the back of his hand across her cheek. "I'm serious, Bryn. When you started dating Jesse, I hated it."

At last she found the courage to look at him. His eyes were sober, his expression unguarded. His small grin was self-deprecating. "He was my own baby brother, and I wanted to punch him in the face."

Her breath hitched in her throat. "I didn't mean for it to happen that way. I never should have asked you to take me to the prom. But then Jesse found me crying behind the barn and he promised to take me to the dance. He made me feel better."

"Because I had made you feel like nothing."

A jerky nod was all she could manage.

"I've asked myself a million times if things could have turned out differently. If *I'd* taken you to the damn dance instead of Jesse. We might have ended up together."

She rested her forehead on her bent knees. "*I've* questioned a million times why he asked me to be his girlfriend. And in the end, I'm pretty sure it's because he knew I had a crush on *you.* And maybe he thought you had feelings for me. He wanted so badly to be like you and Gage and Sloan. He spent his whole life, I think, trying to measure up. But he was never big enough, tall enough, strong enough. He was always the scrawny baby brother, and he hated it."

"Did he hate *me?*" There was a world of pain in that question.

She reached out blindly and squeezed his hand. "Maybe. At times. But only because he loved you so much."

"Ah, hell, Bryn..." The choked emotion in those three ragged words made her ache for him, but she knew without looking that Trent would be dry-eyed. Stoic. He'd been the eldest, and as such, Mac had trained him in the art of keeping emotion under lock and key.

She turned to face him. "No one's to blame for Jesse's death. No one but Jesse. We make our own road in this world, Trent. He had every blessing, every opportunity."

His jawline could have chiseled stone. "This might have been an isolated event."

"Possibly," she said, trying to keep all judgment out of her voice. "But knowing what I know of Jesse, probably not. He had a dark side, Trent. You never saw it, because you never looked for it. He was your brother and you loved him. I understand that, I do. But Mac protected him and covered for him, and I think that only made things worse."

"You make him seem like a monster."

"Not a monster. But a pathological liar and a user. I know that sounds harsh. But Mac has done you no favors by hiding the trouble. You and Gage and Sloan should have known."

Trent felt the breeze on his hot face. He wanted badly

to believe her, but what she was telling him was tough to swallow. Bryn had a young child to support. And she'd had six years to work on a story that would tug at all their heartstrings and open Mac's checkbook.

If Mac hadn't summoned her, she would have found another way to reinstall herself at the Crooked S. He was sure of that.

Suddenly, he wished his two brothers hadn't left already. Between the three of them they would have been able to determine if Bryn was telling the truth or not.

He let himself look at her, really look at her. A man could lose himself in those eyes. She seemed utterly sincere, but given what he knew, how could he take what she said at face value?

God, he wanted her. And he despised himself for the weakness. She was like a bright, beautiful butterfly, dancing on the wind. But if he reached out and grabbed for what he wanted, would the beauty be smashed into powder in his hand? Would he destroy Bryn? Himself? Mac?

He put his hands on her shoulders and the world stood still. Her eyes were wide. Shallow breaths lifted her chest, drawing his attention to the gentle curve of her breasts.

He laid her back on the quilt…slowly, so slowly. Her gaze never left his. And she didn't protest.

A wave of lust and yearning and exultation swept over him. She was his. She had always been his. Everything in the past was over and done with. There was no Jesse. No death. No suspicion. Only this fragile moment in time.

He shifted over her, resting on his hip and one elbow, leaving a hand free to trace the curve of her cheek, the slender column of her neck, the delicate line of her collarbone.

When his fingers went to the first button on her shirt, she didn't stop him. "Bryn." His voice was a hoarse croak in his own ears.

Finally, she moved. She linked her hands behind his neck and tugged. "Kiss me, Trent."

The invitation was unnecessary. Nothing short of an earthquake could have stopped him. His lips found hers, gentle, seeking. But when she responded, he lost his head.

He plundered the softness of her mouth, thrusting his tongue between her teeth desperately, shaking helplessly when she responded in kind. He was practically on top of her as he yanked her shirt from the waistband of her thin pants.

The skin of her flat belly was soft as silk. His hand moved upward, shoving aside her bra and cupping one bare breast. His head swam. His vision blurred. Her nipple peaked between his fingers, and when he tugged gently, Bryn cried out and arched closer.

Her response went to his head. He was so hard, he ached from head to toe. Ached for her. For Bryn. He hadn't been with a woman in several months…and hadn't really noticed the omission. But now he was on fire, out of control.

As she worked at his belt and found the zipper below, her slight clumsiness tormented him. He groaned aloud when her small fingers closed around his erection and squeezed lightly. *God.* He was in danger of coming in her hand.

What kind of man put sexual hunger ahead of loyalty to his family? What kind of man betrayed the memory of his brother? He panted, counting backward from a hundred, anything to grab a toehold of control. In that brief instant, his ardor chilled and his stomach pitched. Bryn was either a sensual witch or a self-serving liar. And all she had to do was smile at him and he was her slave.

He lurched to his feet, sweating. She stared at him, her cheeks flushed, a dawning misery on her face. With dignity, she straightened her clothes and buttoned her blouse.

She rose with more grace than he had managed and faced him across the rumpled quilt.

He saw the muscles in her throat work as she swallowed. "There's something you're not telling me, Trent. Something important. Something significant. I don't think you're the kind of man to be deliberately cruel. Why start something with me and then back away as if I'm about to infect you? For God's sake, Trent. What is it?"

He told her what he should have said from the beginning. The words felt like stones in his dry mouth. "On the day Mac put you on a plane to Minnesota, Jesse came to me and told me the truth. He said that you had been in his bedroom repeatedly…begging him to have sex with you to make me jealous. But he refused. He told me you probably slept with one of his friends until you were sure you were pregnant, and you planned all along to say it was Jesse's."

Bryn stared at him, frozen, her eyes blank with shock. She wet her lips. "That doesn't even make sense," she whispered.

He gazed at her bleakly. "The damned thing is, Bryn, it worked. I wanted you so much, I was sick with it. And if you had left Jesse alone, you and I might have ended up together. But you made that impossible. And then you tried to make Jesse take responsibility for another guy's kid. You disgust me."

She swayed, and he reached forward instinctively to catch her.

But she backed away, the look in her eyes difficult to see. He felt a lick of regret, a jolt of shame. It was partly his fault. If he had stayed away from her when she arrived in Wyoming, they could have avoided this unpleasant encounter.

She backed up again, her hand over her mouth. Suddenly, his pulse raced. She was too close to the edge of the drop-off.

"Bryn!" He reached for her again, urgently.

He was almost too late. Her foot hit the loose scree at the edge of the steep hillside, her body bowed in a vain attempt to regain her balance, and she cried out as he grabbed for her.

Chapter 4

Trent cursed. In the bare seconds it had taken him to get to her, a dozen horrific scenarios filled his brain. But thank God she hadn't fallen. There would have been little to have stopped a precipitous descent—a small ledge here and there, a few low, scrubby bushes.

He held her tightly as sick relief flooded his chest. "You little fool. You could have killed yourself. What were you thinking?" He held her at arm's length. Her face was white and set. He was rigid, his stomach curling. "Are you okay? Tell me, dammit." The words came out more harshly than he had intended. She flinched, and then her expression went from vulnerable to stoic.

"I'm fine," she said. "No problem. Let me go. Get out of my way."

He ground his teeth. "Don't be stupid. You're standing on loose gravel. I'll help you."

"No." A single word. Two small letters. But the vehemence behind it made him feel like dirt.

Unfortunately, this was not a situation where he was willing to put her pride first. He didn't waste time arguing. He scooped her into his arms and took a deep breath. She went nuts, shrieking and struggling until her flailing knee nearly unmanned him.

"Bryn." His raised voice was the same one he used to put the fear of God into his employees when necessary. "Be still, damn it. Unless you want to kill us both."

She went limp in his arms, and he stepped backward carefully, keenly aware that one misstep on his part might send them hurtling down the mountain. When they were finally on firm, flat ground, he set her gently on her feet.

"C'mon," he said gruffly, grabbing up their belongings and stuffing them in his pack. "We're done here."

Bryn lifted her chin. "I'll find my own way back," she said. And she turned away and started down the mountain while he stood with his mouth open, watching, incredulous, as she did just that.

His temper boiled. He lunged after her, closing the distance in four long strides. He grabbed her arm, trying to keep a lid on his fury and losing the battle. "Don't be an idiot."

When she stopped dead, he had to pull up short to avoid knocking her over. He expected her eyes to be shooting sparks at him, but if she had been angry earlier, that emotion was long gone. Her eyes were dull.

"Are you keeping count of those insults, Mr. Sinclair?" She jerked her elbow from his grasp and kept going.

They walked side by side, traversing the wide trail in silence. He noticed for the first time that she was limping slightly. No doubt the result of a blister from not having the proper footwear for the rough terrain. Stubborn woman. He ground to a halt and stopped her, as well, by the simple action of thrusting his body in front of hers. He put his hands on her shoulders, feeling her fragile bones. "You can't walk back to the house. It's almost five miles. You're not wearing hiking boots."

Her eyes were wet with unshed tears. "I don't care," she cried. "Leave me alone."

"I wish to God I could," he muttered. As they reached the Jeep, he reached in his pocket and extracted his handkerchief. "You've got some dirt on your face. Let's call a truce, Bryn. Please. For twenty minutes. That's how long it will take us to get home."

Bryn knew what it was like to have your heart broken. But the blow-up that happened six years ago paled in comparison to the utter despair now flooding her chest. Jesse's lies had been worse than she thought. He had poisoned his brother's mind so thoroughly, Bryn had no hope of making Trent see the truth.

While he maneuvered the vehicle over the rough trails, she ignored him. They completed the journey back to the house in silence. Without speaking, Trent dropped her by the front door before heading around back to the garage.

Bryn tried to slip inside unnoticed, but Mac caught

her sneaking down the hall past the kitchen. Julio had left, and Mac was fixing himself a cup of coffee.

His bushy eyebrows went up. "What in the hell happened to you, Brynnie? You look like something the cat dragged in."

Hearing the affectionate nickname stung her battered heart. She opened her mouth to explain, but was overtaken by a wave of grief. "Trent thinks I seduced Jesse," she said on a hiccupping half sob. "He'll never forgive me."

And then she broke down. Her body was sore, her feet rubbed raw, her emotions shredded. When Mac enfolded her in his big arms, she put her head on his shoulder and sighed. She hadn't realized until this very moment what a hole there had been in her life without his wise counsel and unconditional love.

He held her in silence for a few minutes, and then they went to his study and sat side by side on the oversize leather sofa.

Mac studied her face. "Talk to me, girl. Are you okay?"

Bryn managed a smile. "I'm fine…really. All I need is a shower and some clean clothes."

Then she bit her lip. "We're going to have to settle some things, Mac. I don't want to be away from Allen much longer. You're recovering on schedule. I know the grief is tough, but physically you're doing well. With lots of rest and healthy food, you'll be back to your old ornery self in no time. But I can't be here with Trent. It's an impossible situation." And with Jesse's parentage now in question her quest to secure Allen's future might be a moot point.

Mac leaned back, his arms folded across his chest. "It's my house," he said gruffly. "I invite whom I please."

She shook her head in desperation. "You don't understand what he thinks of me, Mac."

"He's wrong."

Her heart caught in her chest. Did he really believe her? After all this time? She hardly dared to hope.

Mac's expression was bleak. "I suspected as soon as you left six years ago that I had made a mistake. But bringing you back to marry Jesse would only have made things worse. You deserved far better. And Jesse needed…well, who knows what Jesse needed. So many things…"

"Did you and Jesse ever discuss me?"

He shrugged. "Not directly. But I think he knew I was suspicious of his take on the story."

"But you never put him on the spot and asked outright if he had lied?" That was what hurt so much.

The conversation had tired him. He was gray in the face suddenly and clearly exhausted.

Though it frustrated her, Bryn put her own feelings aside for the moment. She was here to help him, not make his life more upsetting. She took him by the hand. "Never mind," she said softly. "It can wait a few more days. Let's get you into bed for a nap."

He allowed her to lead him back to the bedroom, but he was still agitated. "You can't leave, Brynnie. Swear to me you'll stay."

She tucked him in and smoothed the covers. "We'll have to take it a day at a time, Mac. I can't promise more than that."

After settling Mac for his afternoon rest, Bryn retreated to her room. She had no desire to run into Trent. She was still aching from the knowledge that he believed she had seduced Jesse.

She spent part of the afternoon on the phone with Beverly.

Her aunt picked up on the tone in her voice. "What's wrong?"

"Well, Mac seems to have softened. I think he believes Allen is his grandson, but I haven't had the heart to press the paternity issue yet. Mac's really frail, and Trent is either hostile or suspicious or both."

"You'd think that Trent would want the test to prove that you're lying and let his family off the hook."

"I think he's afraid I'll manipulate Mac's emotions and get him to change the will regardless."

"I didn't get the impression that Mac was so gullible."

"He's not, definitely not. But the heart attack has changed him."

"It will all work out, honey."

"I hope so. But there's more. I found some letters that seem to indicate Jesse might not be Mac's son."

Dinner that evening was painfully uncomfortable. Mac's animated conversation was so out of character that Trent kept shooting him disbelieving glances. Trent never looked at Bryn at all.

Mac cleared his plate and finally dropped the "pleasant host" act. He glared at Trent. "Bryn's talking about going home. And I'm guessing it's your fault."

Trent snorted. "If Bryn wants to go home, she knows where the door is. I'm not stopping her."

Bryn's temper flared. "Charming." Trent Sinclair was a stubborn, arrogant beast.

He lifted an eyebrow and gazed at her coldly. "You can't blame me for wanting to protect my father."

Mac bristled. "I'm not feeble, dammit. Do you really think I'd let myself be manipulated by sentimentality?"

"It's not you I'm worried about." Trent scowled. "It's her."

Bryn felt her cheeks flush, especially because Mac watched the two of them with avid attention. In a flash, she was back on the mountaintop with Trent, his hand warm on her breast, his lips devouring hers. She cleared her throat. "I'm no threat to you or your father, Trent. And if you'd quit being an ass, you'd realize that." Her cutting reply might have been more impressive had her voice been less hoarse.

But remembering what had almost happened earlier that day made her knees weak with longing. The past and the present had melded for one brief, wonderful moment. But it hadn't lasted.

I wanted you so much, I was sick with it. The confession had been ripped from the depths of Trent's soul, and the self-disgust in his voice said more than words what he thought of her.

But fool that she was, despite Trent's obvious antipathy, she wanted him still. It was only sex. That's all. Surely she didn't really crave a relationship with a man who thought so little of her.

She stood up blindly. "Enough me. I have phone calls to make."

Late that evening, Trent sat at the computer in the study, brooding. He could no longer ignore the evidence before him. Jesse had been stealing from the ranch. From Mac.

The knowledge made nausea churn in Trent's belly. Why? Mac would have given Jesse anything he wanted. The old man loved his youngest son dearly. There had been no need to steal.

Cause of death: heroin overdose. The coroner's report wasn't fabricated. Jesse had taken drugs at least once. The little brother Trent remembered would never have done such a thing. But Bryn was right...Trent hadn't been around much in the last few years. Mostly because of a demanding career, but in part because the ranch reminded him too much of Bryn. And the fact that she had slept with his brother, or lied, or both.

He groaned and shut down the computer. If Bryn was telling the truth about Jesse's drug habit, then Trent had not known his brother at all. But if Bryn was lying, why did Jesse die of an overdose? Neither option was at all palatable.

Bryn thought Mac had protected Jesse by covering for him. Would Mac do that? Out of guilt perhaps...because Etta Sinclair had left her young son when Jesse was at such a vulnerable age?

Trent cursed beneath his breath and flung a paper clip across the room, wishing it was something that would shatter into a million pieces. He wanted answers, *needed* them. Was Mac strong enough for a showdown? Trent would never forgive himself if he caused his father to relapse.

He got to his feet and went down the hall, treading quietly. His father's door was open, but the room was dim. Quiet snoring was the only sound. Mac slept like the dead on a good day, and now that he was medicated, he'd probably be out until morning.

Trent retreated carefully, only to find himself staring at Bryn's bedroom door. A light shone from underneath. It wasn't terribly late....

Chapter 5

She was shocked to see him. It was written all over her face.

"I need to talk to you." He shut the door behind him and moved into the room.

Her nightgown lay on the bed but she was still dressed. The lingerie was a silky swathe of cream lace and mauve satin. He swallowed, dragging his gaze away from it and focusing on her face. "I have to leave in the morning."

"So soon?"

"Not for good," he said swiftly. "But I have to fly to Denver for a meeting that I can't handle over the phone. I'll be gone less than twenty-four hours."

Bryn nodded slowly. "I'll keep an eye on Mac. Despite what you think, Trent, I love him."

"Even though he sent you away?"

Her smile was wry. "I'm trying to let go of the past."

He prowled the small space between the door and the bed. "Some of us don't have that luxury."

She stood there staring at him with bare feet and a face washed clean of makeup. Young, vulnerable, sweetly sincere. "You can trust me, Trent. I swear."

His body hardened, and he groaned inwardly. How could he be sure of her when sex got in the way and clouded his judgment?

He shook his head to clear it. But when he looked at her again, she was more appealing to him than she had been mere moments before. His feet took him to her side. Her pull was inescapable.

She stiffened when he wrapped her in his arms. "I'm not playing this game with you, Trent."

The quaver in her voice hurt something deep in his chest. "I can assure you," he said roughly. "This is no game."

He kissed her because it was the only thing he could do. Because if he didn't, something inside him would shrivel and die. Because he was apparently weaker than he thought.

She was everything he had ever wanted and didn't know he needed. Her lips tasted like toothpaste and something else far more exotic. His past and his present woven into one complicated package.

She fit him perfectly, her head tucked against his shoulder, her arms wrapped loosely around his waist. He slid a hand beneath her shirt and stroked the soft skin on her back.

When he tipped up her chin, their eyes met, his searching, hers filled with an emotion he shied away from. He wouldn't let her twist him in knots. This violent attraction was about sex, nothing more.

Slowly, waiting for her to protest, to escape his embrace, he bent his head. Their lips met easily, in perfect sync.

He moved his mouth over hers gently, dragging out the pleasure, making his own heart race with the effort to hold back. What had happened on the mountain only whetted his appetite for more. This had nothing to do with Jesse. This was about scratching an itch. Or at the very least, proving to himself how far she was willing to go. He wanted her.

Clothes drifted away in a sensual ballet. Skin heated. Voices hoarsened with desire. His and hers.

This time Bryn was the one to call a halt. Pale but calm, she slipped from the bed and donned her robe.

"I want you, Trent. But not like this. Not with mistrust between us."

Before he could summon a response, the shrill shriek of the smoke alarm sounded. For one crazed split second, he actually thought about dragging her down on the bed and saying to hell with it.

But the memory of his father jarred him to reality.

He rolled from the bed, groaning and cursing, and shoved his legs into his jeans. "This isn't over," he said.

Bryn knew her blood pressure must be through the roof. To go from desperate arousal to anxiety to fear so quickly made nausea swim in her stomach.

She found Trent and Mac in the kitchen. Trent was swearing a blue streak, and Mac presided over a ruined skillet that contained the charred remains of what must have been eggs.

Trent climbed on a chair to disable the smoke alarm. In the resultant silence, the three adults faced off in an uncomfortable triangle.

Bryn had the misfortune to giggle.

Trent glared and Mac chortled. Soon all three of them were laughing hysterically.

Trent was the first to regain control. "Good God, Dad. What in the hell were you doing? I thought you were sound asleep."

Mac's expression was sheepish. "I was hungry. And nobody will let me eat anything decent. So I was making an omelet…with whole eggs…and butter." He puffed out his chest and tried to face them down with bluster.

"I would have helped you," Bryn said mildly. She took the pan to the sink. "And since when do you know how to cook?"

"Since never. Hence the fire." Trent dropped into a chair.

Mac raked at the tufts of white hair standing in disarray all over his head. "It wasn't actually a fire," Mac muttered, sulking. "I went to the bathroom for just a second, and when I came back…"

"That one's a goner." Bryn gave up and tossed the ruined cookware in the trash bin.

Trent rubbed his forehead, where almost certainly a killer headache was attacking him. He'd not had the best half hour. Bryn felt his pain.

He looked up at both of them. "God knows I don't want to leave you two here alone, but please promise me you'll behave until I get back."

Bryn hugged Mac. "We'll be fine," she said, yawning suddenly. "Let's all get some sleep."

It didn't take a genius to figure out that any sexual overtures on Trent's part would not be repeated…at least not tonight.

There was an awkward moment in the hallway after Mac escaped to his quarters, but Bryn evaded Trent's gaze and slipped into her bedroom with a muttered good-night, closing the door behind her with a sigh of relief. Perhaps it was for the best. She didn't understand Trent's motives. And until she did, self-preservation was the order of the day.

Perhaps understandably, she overslept. She awakened to the sound of a car engine fading into the distance. Already it was clear to her that things were not the same. The house seemed empty with Trent gone. He'd always been a force to reckon with, and the world was oddly flat in his absence.

Instead of moping and trying to analyze the situation, she forced herself to get up and face the day. When Mac appeared in the kitchen, he was chipper and energetic in contrast to her aching head and troubled thoughts.

He ate his egg-white omelet and plain toast without complaint. As Bryn picked at her oatmeal, he cocked his head. "I told Trent this morning to leave you alone so you would stay."

She felt her cheeks heat. Surely…

Mac went on. "I let him know that if he didn't have

anything nice to say to you, he should keep his damn mouth shut."

Her pulse slowed to its normal pace, and she could breathe again. Mac didn't know about last night. How could he?

She twirled her spoon in the bowl. "I can handle Trent. Don't you worry. But we need to talk, Mac."

His bushy eyebrows went up. "Sounds ominous."

"Do you think Jesse's problems had anything to do with his mother's desertion?"

Mac's gaze shifted away from hers. His hands clenched. "Don't know what you mean."

"He was at a vulnerable age when she left. Sometimes kids blame themselves in situations like that."

Mac's complexion reddened alarmingly. "That was a long time ago. Jesse was a wild kid. Can't blame that on a woman who's been gone for almost twenty years."

"But what if she tried to contact him?" Did Mac know about the letters? Was that why he was getting upset?

"Forget his mother," Mac shouted. "I don't want to talk about her...ever."

The change was so dramatic, Bryn was blindsided. One minute Mac was the picture of health. And now...

He shoved back from the table and stood up so rapidly he knocked over his chair.

Bryn reached for him in alarm. "I'm sorry, Mac," she said urgently. "We'll drop it. I never should have said anything."

He backed toward the hallway. "Jesse's gone. Nothing's going to bring him back. End of story."

Mac's knees gave out beneath him. His eyes met hers, imploring, scared.

"Calm down, Mac. Everything's okay. Really." What had she done? But nothing was okay, not by a long shot.

Chapter 6

In that terrifying moment Bryn was desperately grateful that Sinclair wealth meant having access to a helicopter. A 911 call ensured that medical staff at the hospital would be waiting and ready.

Getting in touch with Trent was trickier, and she felt terrible that she was disrupting his important meeting, but she had no choice. She drove herself to the hospital and waited.

Mac was still in emergency when an ashen-faced Trent arrived. "What the hell happened? He was fine earlier. He drank his coffee while I had breakfast, and he was his old self."

Her eyes burned with tears. "I asked about Jesse's mother, and Mac went berserk."

Trent paled. "Dear God. Mac never speaks of her.

Surely you knew that. You lived here for most of your life. Etta's defection wasn't exactly dinner-table conversation. Are you *trying* to kill my father? Dammit, Bryn. What were you thinking?"

The accusation in his eyes was made all the worse by the knowledge that he was right. She should have waited.

"I'm sorry," she said. "But I wanted to get to the truth. This family has too many secrets."

In Trent's gaze, she saw not one whit of the man who had held her so intimately only hours before. He'd come straight from his meeting, and he was wearing an expensive dark suit, perfectly tailored to fit his tall, virile frame. His shoes were Italian leather. The thin gold watch on his wrist could have paid for several semesters of her schooling.

On the ranch, she had allowed herself to think of him as a normal man. But now he wore his wealth and power with a careless confidence that only underscored the gap between them.

She watched as Trent paced the drab waiting room like a caged lion. Her legs wouldn't hold her up. She picked a hard plastic chair in a far corner, sat down and stared blindly at her trembling fingers linked in her lap. Last night she had touched Trent intimately with those same hands. It seemed like a fairy tale now.

The wait was agonizing. What if Mac died? What would happen to all of them? Trent would never forgive her, much less admit that Allen was entitled to part of the estate, if indeed he was. And poor Trent…to lose his brother and father so close together. *Please, God. Let Mac be okay.*

When a young doctor came out, Bryn leaped to her feet, but Trent got there first. She had the impression he might have jerked the poor man to him by the collar if it hadn't been socially unacceptable.

Trent's hands were fisted at his sides instead. "How is he? Was it another heart attack?"

The doctor shook his head. "He's going to be fine. It was an anxiety attack. When his pulse rate skyrocketed, it probably scared him, which merely exacerbated the situation. A frightening cycle, but not life-threatening. Do you know what precipitated this?"

Bryn took a deep breath, trembling uncontrollably. "I asked him a question about his wife. She left the family eighteen years ago. I never dreamed it would still be such a sensitive subject." She stopped, choked up. "Has he suffered any lasting damage?"

The doc shook his head. "No. I want to keep him overnight for observation, but that's merely a precaution. We did a number of tests, and everything looks great. He's a strong old boy, and I predict he'll be around to aggravate you both for a long time. The two of you can go in to visit him now. Room 312."

The doctor excused himself. Trent glared at Bryn. "You stay here. I can't take the chance that seeing you will set him off again."

"But the doctor said—"

"No." He was implacable.

She waited until he took the elevator and then followed him up on the next one. Hovering in the hall, she listened anxiously to hear Mac's voice. Thankfully, he sounded a thousand times better.

Trent's deep, resonant voice was so tender and loving, she almost burst into tears.

"How are you feeling, Dad?"

"Embarrassed." Mac's querulous reply might have made her smile if she hadn't been so fatigued and over-wrought.

Trent spoke again. "I'll stay with you tonight. The doctor says he'll release you in the morning. Apparently you passed all the tests with flying colors. Your ticker's healing beautifully."

"Aren't you going to ask me what caused all this?"

There was a bite in Trent's reply. "No need. I already know."

"Bryn told you?"

"Yes."

"Where is she?"

"I wouldn't let her come in."

"Oh, for God's sake, boy. Don't be a complete ass. This wasn't Bryn's fault."

"It sure as hell was. If that's the kind of loving care she has to offer, we might as well go back to hiring strangers out of the phone book."

"You know the doctor said I don't really need anyone to take care of me anymore."

"So send her home."

Mac snorted. "You'd like that, wouldn't you? You're gonna have to face facts, Trent. I'm ninety-nine percent sure Jesse lied to us."

Trent's voice was icy. "Then we need to get the kid

out here, do a DNA test as soon as possible and find out once and for all."

A nurse, bustling to enter the room, jostled Bryn's shoulder and apologized swiftly. "I apologize, ma'am. I need to go in and take Mr. Sinclair's vitals."

Now Bryn would never know what Mac's reply might have been. The conversation at the bedside turned to medical details.

Bryn slipped away and pulled paper from her purse to jot a note to Trent. She passed it to the nurses' station. "Would you mind to give this to the visitor in 312 as he leaves? Thank you."

Outside, the fresh air was a welcome relief. She was appalled at her own lack of judgment when it came to Mac. Why couldn't she have left things alone?

She checked in to the small hotel around the corner from the hospital. Trent would know where she was. She'd left a note, after all. She wasn't running away.

With no luggage or toothbrush, settling into her standard-issue room was a short process. After a long call home to talk to Beverly and Allen, she eyed the beds. She was running on adrenaline and about five hours of sleep total. Wearing only her blouse and underwear, she climbed into the closest clean, soft bed and was comatose in seconds.

Trent prowled the hallway while an orderly gave Mac a sponge bath. The old man was at full speed already, bossing everyone around, and cranky as hell. But the episode had scared Trent badly.

He owed Bryn an apology. In his fear and upset, he

had been harsher with her than she deserved. She had made a mistake. So what? It might have just as easily been Trent who blundered into a stressful conversation. He and his father butted heads often.

A nurse at the desk handed Trent a folded slip of paper. *I'm at the hotel. Bryn.* The doctor appeared at his side. "I'm going to give your father a light sedative so he'll rest this afternoon. Why don't you go get something to eat and come back around four? We'll call you if anything changes, but he's really doing very well, I promise."

Trent spent a few more minutes chatting with his father, but the medicine in the drip was already doing its job. When Mac's eyes fluttered shut, Trent exited the room and left the hospital.

In a small town like Jackson Hole, the long timers all knew each other. The woman at the hotel desk was a classmate of Trent's. He gave her a tired smile. "Hey, Janine. Bryn checked in a little while ago, right? And she told you Dad's in the hospital?"

"She sure did. Poor thing looked beat. And you don't look so hot yourself."

He shrugged. "We're going to take turns sitting with him. If you'll give me another key to the room so I won't bother Bryn, and a take-out menu from anywhere—I'm not picky—I'll owe you."

He made his way down the hall and around the corner to the room Janine had indicated and swiped the key in the lock. The curtains in the room were closed, and in the dim light, he could see a Bryn-shaped lump in one of the beds. His body tightened. He was determined to have her, even if she had lied. But it would be on his terms. He would be in control. With a low curse for his own conflicted emotions, he kicked off his shoes, collapsed on top of the covers in the opposite bed and closed his eyes.

Bryn awoke to the smell of pepperoni pizza. Her stomach growled.

Her eyes snapped open when Trent's unmistakable voice sounded from close at hand. "The doctor said we could come back at four. I left you a few slices."

She sat up, carefully keeping the sheet at a decorous height, and brushed the hair out of her eyes, deeply regretting the fact that her pants were three feet away on a chair. The covers on the adjacent bed were rumpled, indicating that Trent had napped, as well.

Less than twenty-four hours ago, she had been naked and panting in this man's arms. Now she could scarcely meet his gaze.

She licked her lips, faint with hunger. She had only picked at her breakfast before Mac collapsed. "Close your eyes."

"No."

His answer took her by surprise and she looked at him head-on. Dark smudges under his eyes said he was in no better shape than she was, but he no longer looked furious.

She frowned. "Then hand me my pants."

"No." A faint grin accompanied the negative.

She crossed her arms over her chest, in no mood for a confrontation. "A gentleman would have gotten his own room. You're rich enough to buy the whole hotel. So why are you here?"

He leaned forward, elbows on his knees. "Because this is where you are." He paused and winced. "I have a temper, Bryn. You know that. But what happened with Dad this morning wasn't your fault. You acted swiftly and responsibly. No one could ask for more. I'm sorry I yelled at you."

His unprompted and uncharacteristically humble apology should have made her feel relieved. But she didn't deserve his absolution. "It *was* my fault," she said doggedly. "I never should have mentioned Etta." She had wanted to find out if Mac was aware of the letters. And she was as much in the dark now as before.

"What made you want to talk about our dearly departed mother?"

The macabre humor made her frown. Did anyone really know if Etta was dead or alive? "Well…" She cast about for an explanation that didn't involve the damning letters. She would have to share their contents with Trent, but not yet. "It occurred to me that some of Jesse's troubles could have stemmed from her leaving you all at such young ages. But you and Gage and Sloan turned out okay."

His expression hardened. "We were older. We understood what she had done and why. We didn't weave any fairy tales about her coming back. At least not after the first few days."

"You were *eleven*, Trent. An age when a boy still needs his mother."

He shrugged. "We had Dad. And if Etta cared so

little about her family that she could simply walk out, we didn't need her or want her."

Her heart bled for the stoic little child he had been. He wouldn't even refer to her as *Mother.* "And Jesse?"

"Jesse was different. He was only six. He cried every night for a month. We all took turns sleeping with him so that when he had nightmares, we'd be there to comfort him. He liked Gage the best. Gage would tell him stories about places all over the world…about the adventures the two of them would have one day. Jesse loved it."

"How long was it before he got over her leaving?"

"I don't know that he ever did. But he learned to man up and show he didn't need her to be happy."

But he did. Apparently Jesse had needed Etta a heck of a lot, and when he was a teenager, she wormed her way back into his life and drove him crazy. The thought gave her a shiver. She wanted so badly to unburden herself to Trent, to lean on his strength and counsel.

But with the specter that Jesse might not be a Sinclair, she didn't know what to do. It was naive to expect Trent to believe that Allen was Jesse's son without proof. She had wanted Trent to take her on faith, but *her* feelings were not as important as making sure Allen was taken care of.

Anything could happen to Bryn. And Aunt Beverly wouldn't always be around. Bryn had believed for six years that her son was a Sinclair, heir to a mighty empire that would make his life secure. The truth needed to come out. For all of them.

Once again, she eyed her distant jeans.

Trent stood, arms crossed over his chest, and grinned at her predicament.

"Aren't you being a little ridiculous, Brynnie? I've seen it all."

Her face flamed. "That was different."

"Different, how?"

"We were in the mood."

"I seem to always be in the mood around you."

His self-deprecating smile loosened the knot in her chest. A teasing Trent made her willpower evaporate. "We need to keep track of the time."

"We have all the time in the world."

He glanced at his watch, and her stomach flipped… hard.

He handed her the pizza box. "But never say I seduced you on an empty stomach."

"No seduction," she said primly as she gobbled a slice of pizza with unladylike fervor. "We have to go see Mac."

His eyes were like a watchful hawk. "It's only two-thirty. I can do a lot in an hour and a half."

Every atom of oxygen in the room evaporated as their eyes met. Hunger snapped its bounds and prowled between them. She trembled as each second of the heated moments in her bedroom unfolded in her imagination in Technicolor images complete with scent and sound.

The crust she held fell with a loud thud into the box. Trent took the cardboard container from her numb fingers and tossed it in the trash can. He sat beside her on the bed and twirled a strand of her hair around his finger. "We'll figure this all out, Bryn."

The knowledge that she was lying by omission choked her. "I don't know that we can. Some things can't be fixed."

He kissed her softly, then with more force. "I'll make it all right. You'll see."

She let him hold her, but her heart ached. Trent Sinclair was a man used to winning, to conquering, to molding the world to his specifications. But even the king occasionally had to admit defeat.

He nuzzled her neck. "Don't think so much. Just feel, Bryn. Let it happen."

Their lips met tentatively. Last night everything had seemed new and different. Now she knew the truth. Trent Sinclair was a hard-ass as far as the world was concerned. He kept his feelings under wraps. But beneath that proud, arrogant exterior, he was a man of great passion.

She kissed his chin, his nose, his eyelids. "I feel guilty. We should be at the hospital."

"He's sleeping. The doc said so. Hush and let me love you." He stroked her back as he magically made her reservations disappear.

She heard the four-letter word and managed not to react. It was something men said when they wanted a woman. He didn't mean he loved her. She realized that. She was far too intelligent to delude herself.

Which meant that she had to be smart about this. She wanted Trent. Badly. But now was not the time.

"You nearly convinced me," she said, her heart aching for a multitude of reasons. "But one of us has to be sane. I'll go sit with him. I'm sure you have some business calls you need to make."

Trent pondered what would have happened if they had not been interrupted last night. Today the mood was less mystical, more pragmatic. But she was as much a siren to him as she had been in the quiet intimacy of her bedroom. He reclined on his side, easing her down with him. Beneath her shirt, he traced the lace at the edge of her bra, feeling gooseflesh erupt everywhere his fingers passed.

Bryn studied him, big-eyed, her pupils dilated, her soft breathing ragged. Her chest rose and fell. She lay quiescent, passive. What was she thinking? He liked to believe he was a good judge of women, but Bryn was a conundrum wrapped in a puzzle. Young, but mature beyond her years. Inexperienced, but wildly passionate.

He reached for the tiny plastic hook at the middle that secured the two sides of the bra. As he unfastened it, her breasts fell free, lush, warm, soft as velvet. He pushed up her blouse and buried his face in them, inhaling the scent that was so evocatively Bryn. Her hands played with his hair, sending heat down his spine and making him wish they had all night instead of a snatched hour in an impersonal hotel room.

He would take her…soon. But he would delay his own satisfaction. This particular moment was about establishing control. He stroked her thighs, touched her center still hidden beneath satin and lace. Bryn groaned even at that light caress, her eyes now closed. He rubbed her gently, feeling her heat, the dampness that signaled her readiness for him. He increased the pressure, the tempo. Her hips lifted instinctively.

Slowly, wanting to give her every iota of pleasure, he slipped two fingers beneath the narrow strip of cloth between her legs, and then thrust inside her with a quick motion. Bryn gave a sharp, keening cry and moved against his hand, riding the waves of pleasure that caused her inner muscles to squeeze his fingers.

The eroticism of her release made him sweat. His erection throbbed with a burning ache. But he drew on his iron will and refused to allow himself to be at her mercy. Trent couldn't lie to himself any longer. He was soft when it came to Bryn. And it pissed him off that he didn't really want her to leave. His hunger for her was a weakness. And that vulnerability was trying to persuade him that she was innocent. That she was telling the truth.

Which made him the world's biggest jackass. Powerful men were brought down by scheming women all the time. He hoped like hell she was being honest with him. But if worse came to worst…if she had lied about Jesse…well…Trent's loyalties were clear. Protecting Mac…and protecting Jesse's memory.

But the effort to maintain the upper hand cost him.

He looked down at her broodingly. "You're right. One of us should be at the hospital. And I need to deal with the mess in Denver. I shouldn't have started this right now. I'm sorry."

Her flushed cheeks and tousled hair made her even

more beautiful than usual. He stroked her cheek. "Say something."

Her smile was wry. "What's left to say? I can wait until you trust me...but can *you*?"

Chapter 7

Bryn's heart slugged hard in her chest. She had let herself fall in love with Trent Sinclair.

In the beginning she had fooled herself, thinking that all she wanted was for Trent to forgive her, to believe her and to show her the same gentle camaraderie and friendship they had once shared.

Later, she had told herself it wouldn't be hurting anyone if she dared to enjoy Trent's bed. After all, she'd been living like a nun. She deserved some pleasure.

But now…oh, God…now…

She had done the unforgivable. She had tumbled head over heels, gut-deep in love with a man who was as inaccessible to her as the moon. Trent didn't trust her. Might never trust her. And even if the truth eventually came to light, Bryn had a child. Jesse's son. A boy whose existence might drive a permanent wedge between Bryn and the man she had always loved.

Even if Trent finally accepted her at face value, the situation was hopeless. Even the least intuitive person could see that a happy ending was an oxymoron in this situation.

She turned her head to look at the man who had wreaked such havoc in her life. He was seated on the far side of the opposite bed with his back to her. His voice on the phone was different...sharper, more commanding. She could almost see the employee on the other end of the call scrambling to follow orders.

But Trent was not an ogre. He was disciplined. Fair.

He would hate the description, but he was a beautiful man inside and out. Completely masculine, tough, steady, honorable.

She couldn't fault him, really, for choosing to believe his brother instead of Bryn. Jesse was his flesh and blood. And Trent had spent a lot of years looking after Jesse, making sure he was happy.

Much like Bryn felt about her son. She would do anything for Allen. Including risking Trent's wrath to prove that Allen deserved to be recognized as a Sinclair.

But what she could *not* do was let this thing with Trent go any further. No matter how much she wanted to...no matter how wonderful it was to be in his arms, his life, his bed. Already, her heart was breaking. They had no future...none at all.

She dressed quietly and slipped from the room. Mac was just rousing as Bryn arrived. "You look good," she said. "Let me help you with that dinner tray."

"Hospital food tastes like crap."

Despite his grumbling about the bland food, Mac polished off a piece of baked fish, green beans and carrots. His protest was halfhearted and she knew the collapse had scared him.

Mac sipped tepid iced tea through a straw. "Where's Trent?"

"He was on the phone when I left. He'll be here soon."

"What's going on between you two?"

She winced inwardly, but managed not to react. "Nothing but the usual. He still isn't sure he can trust me."

"The boy's a fool."

"You were on the same page not so long ago," she reminded him gently. "Until Jesse died and you had to face the truth. Give Trent some slack. He's doing his best. Losing Jesse has shaken him. Especially since it came out of the blue."

Guilt washed over Mac's face. He poked at a carrot with his fork. "I didn't want the three boys to know how bad it was. I thought I could whip Jesse into shape, keep a close eye on him. I'm responsible for his death as much as anyone."

Seeing the proud Mac Sinclair with tears streaking down his leatherlike cheeks was almost more than Bryn could bear. She moved the dinner tray and scooted onto the bed beside him, putting her arm around his shoulder. "Don't be a horse's hiney," she said softly. "You were a wonderful father to all four of your boys…and a dear grandfather to me."

"I sent you away." He rested his head against her chest, his eyes closed.

"You did what you thought was right."

"Can you ever forgive me?"

"Of course," she said simply. "Aunt Beverly was so good to me. And Allen adores her. I'm fine, Mac. No harm, no foul."

They sat there in silence, both of them lost in thought.

Finally, Mac gave a wheezing sigh and moved fretfully in the bed. Bryn stood up and smoothed the covers.

He folded his arms across his chest, wrestling with the IV. "Trent thinks we should get a test…as soon as possible. So there won't be any questions. But I don't want to."

The packet of letters in her room mocked her. Would a paternity test destroy her hope of securing her son's future? "Why not, Mac? We all need to know the truth."

"I trust you, Brynnie, my girl."

At that very moment, Trent walked in. If he had heard the end of their conversation, he gave no sign.

"You're looking better, Dad. Nothing like a visit from a beautiful woman to perk up a man."

Mac chuckled, but the bland glance Trent sent Bryn's way made her knees weak. It was hard enough to deal with a suspicious, angry Trent. How on earth was she supposed to find the strength to resist the charming, seductive version? One glance from those dark eyes and she was ready to drag him into the nearest broom closet.

She cleared her throat, forcing herself to look at Trent. "I'm going to stay with Mac tonight. The nurse said they can bring in a cot for me. Why don't you go back to the ranch to check on things and then come back in the morning to pick us up."

"I thought we were both going to stay at the hotel." A frown creased Trent's forehead.

"It was great to have a place to nap, but I'll be fine here. And Mac says he promised several of the men the weekend off. Isn't that right, Mac?"

"Yep. Brynnie will be here if I need anything, and they're predicting storms tonight. I'd feel better if you were at the ranch. Do you mind, son?"

"Sounds like I've been outvoted." Trent's lips quirked. "But sure. If that's what you want, Dad."

Bryn and Trent sat with Mac until almost eight o'clock that evening. Trent brought cafeteria food up for Bryn and him to eat. In some ways, it was almost like old times, the teasing, the laughter. They avoided any and all topics that might be upsetting to Mac.

But finally, it was time for Trent to leave. He touched Bryn's shoulder. "Walk me out to the car."

She did so reluctantly, unwilling to be alone with him but unable to think of a good excuse. They stopped off in the gift shop and Bryn bought a toothbrush and toothpaste. She tucked them in her purse with the sales slip and followed Trent outside. "Call my cell," she said, "and I'll let you know when the doctor says he can be dismissed."

Trent leaned a hip against the car. "Okay. I doubt you'll get any sleep tonight. Are you sure you don't want to keep the hotel room and let us take turns?"

She shook her head. "Mac will feel better about the

ranch this way." A sudden gust of wind sent her hair flying. The skies were darkening as storm clouds built. "You should go," she said. "So you won't have to drive in what's coming."

Trent smoothed her hair behind her ears, both of his hands cupping her cheeks. His gaze was troubled. "I want to believe in you," he muttered.

The husky words went straight to her heart. Was she imagining the caring and tenderness in his voice? She stepped away from him, gathering her courage, though all she wanted to do was rest in his arms. "But you can't," she said, the words barely audible.

He thrust his hands in his pockets. "You expect a lot."

She forced herself to say the words. "I can't be intimate with a man who despises me."

For a split second, he stood, poleaxed, before his face closed up and a mask of arrogance cloaked his inner emotions. "I don't despise you, Brynnie. That's the problem."

She shifted from one foot to the other, wincing as thunder rolled in the distance. "Perhaps in light of Mac's most recent incident, we need to concentrate all our focus on him."

Trent's black scowl sent a shiver down her spine.

She held out a hand. "Let's face it. We have nothing in common, Trent. You're leaving very soon…as soon as Gage gets here. Mac might get the wrong idea if he realizes we've been…"

"Screwing?"

His deliberate crudity hurt. "You were always special to me, Trent. And what we did this afternoon was—"

He grabbed her wrist. "If you say *fun,* so help me, God, I'll shake you, Bryn. But don't worry, sweetheart." A sneer curled his perfect lips. "I get the message. You have a short attention span when it comes to men. Maybe Jesse was right about you after all."

He lowered his mouth to hers, giving her no time to protest. But his lips were gentler than his mood, less combative, coaxing rather than demanding her submission. His tongue invaded her mouth, devastating, as he mimicked the sex act. Her knees went weak. She clung to his arms for support. Even now, with intense emotion radiating from his big frame, she felt no fear, no urge to run.

His hips were melded to hers, leaving no doubt about his state of mind. His erection pressed insistently against her lower abdomen. He was giving her what she craved…perhaps for the last time. And all she wanted to do was meet his raging hunger with her own desperate need for him.

It was over too soon. He shoved her away, his chest heaving. "We're not done with this, Bryn. Not by a long shot."

He got in the car, slammed the door and sped away, leaving her on the sidewalk.

Trent swore violently. How in the hell had she done it to him again?

Was she scared? Or was this part of a Machiavellian plan? Did she think she could turn him into a sex-starved, drooling idiot?

How dare she throw their lovemaking in his face? He'd begun to trust her, to believe in her. And she was deliberately trying to drive him away. He sent the car careening down the road, mile after mile, until reason prevailed and he eased his foot off the accelerator. He'd be no good to anyone dead. Mac was depending on him, and Trent didn't have the luxury of letting his temper reign.

Back at the ranch, he dealt with the various chores on autopilot, his brain racing madly to understand Bryn's behavior. The storm struck with a vengeance, drenching him as he ran from barn to stable to house. When he was finally done for the night, he showered and prowled the halls, wandering from room to room, the electricity in the air keeping him on edge.

He would have bet his entire fortune that Bryn's responses to him had been real…heartfelt. Thinking about last night and this afternoon made him hard as a pike again, and he stood at the large plate-glass window, nude, watching the fury of the storm.

In his memory he saw the smooth perfection of her skin, the way her body responded to his touch. Her warmth. Her scent. His chest hurt, and he rubbed it absently. Jesse stood beside him in the night, a wraith, a painful puzzle.

"Why did you do it, Jesse?" He put his hand on the cold glass. "Why lie about Bryn? Why the stealing? The drugs?"

His only answer was the howl of the wind and the beating of his own heart.

"Hey, boss. Good to have you back."

Trent grinned at the young intern who had the temerity to poke his head into the private office. "Get to work, Chad. Or we'll cut your pay." The cheeky twenty-year-old from the University of Colorado was smart, self-motivated and had fought hard for this unpaid position. He reminded Trent a little of himself at that age.

When the door closed once again, Trent got up from his broad cherry desk and paced the expanse of thick royal-blue carpet. The huge plate-glass window on the opposite wall showcased Denver's downtown skyline, but Trent barely spared it a glance.

After making sure Mac was safely back on his home turf, Trent had come to Denver again to wrap up the business that had been interrupted. He'd half expected the adrenaline of his usual routine to keep his mind off Bryn.

It hadn't worked.

He told himself that he was glad to be back in the office…that the rush of trying to pack two weeks of work into seventy-two hours was exhilarating. And to some extent it was. But for the first time in forever, his personal life took center stage, no matter how hard he tried to pretend otherwise.

His secretary, Carol, was the next to interrupt. "Just wanted to remind you that Mr. Greenfield will be here in twenty minutes. Will you be using the conference room?"

"Yes. And please make sure Ed and Terrence are there."

She nodded and started to leave.

Trent held up a hand to stop her. "Carol…do you think I'm a good judge of character?"

She laughed and then realized he was serious. "I've never seen anyone put anything past you."

"Thanks." He was embarrassed suddenly.

"Is there a problem I can help with?" Her head tilted at a quizzical angle.

"No, not really. Just a situation with a woman."

Her eyebrows went up, and he felt himself go red. "Never mind. Forget I said anything."

The older woman grinned. "One piece of advice, if you don't mind. Don't ever assume you can use business principles in a personal interaction with the female sex. That will blow up every time."

When she closed the door quietly behind her, Trent scrubbed his hands over his face and groaned. He should have a plan before he went home, but he was damned if he could think about anything but getting Bryn in his bed.

He hadn't talked to her once since he left. On purpose. And Mac continued to evade questions about Jesse and the past. Trent felt like everyone was keeping secrets from him, but that was going to end. It was time for a showdown.

When business was tied up and Trent felt comfortable that his staff could handle things for another couple of weeks, he flew home.

It was late when he arrived at the ranch. He'd used a car service from the airport. His first stop was his father's bedroom. Mac was sleeping peacefully.

When Trent stopped at Bryn's door, he called himself all kinds of a fool. Before his knuckles could make contact with the wood, he jerked his hand back. He turned on his heel and headed for the barn, his forehead covered in a cold sweat. If something didn't break soon, he was going to go mad. He saddled one of the powerful stallions and led him outside. Only then did he see the silent figure perched on the corral railing. Had she been there all along?

He led the horse to where she sat. Before he could say anything, she beat him to the punch. Her features were shrouded in shadow. "It's dangerous to ride at night." Her voice was low, musical. He felt it caress him like a physical stroke down his spine.

He shrugged, putting one foot into the stirrup and sliding easily into the saddle. It creaked beneath his weight. "I *feel* dangerous," he said bluntly. "So you'd be smart to stay out of my way."

With him on horseback, they sat eye to eye. Heat shimmered in the air between them, despite the chilly Wyoming night. The emotions that had consumed him…anger…disbelief…disillusionment…all receded, leaving in their wake a sexual hunger so intense he had to grip the reins and clench his teeth to keep from letting her see.

Bryn held out her hand. "Take me with you."

Bryn was done with denying the inevitable. She wanted Trent. She *needed* him. She'd deal with the

fallout later. His big body vibrated with something…
anger…desire. He had every right to be furious with
her. She'd run hot and cold like the worst kind of tease.

Was he still angry? Did she care? She ached with
missing him.

For long, quivering seconds, he didn't move. Then
with a noise that was part exasperation, part muffled
laugh, he edged the animal closer to the rail and extended his arm. "Why not," he muttered, helping her
sling a leg across the horse's back and settle between
his arms.

She felt the warmth of his body against her back
and was excruciatingly aware that his big, hard thighs
bracketed hers. Her bottom pressed intimately to the
area where he was most male. She tried to scoot forward a few inches, but he dragged her back, letting her
feel the imprint of his erection.

Her breath seemed caught in her chest, her lungs
starved for air. All around them, mysterious night
sounds broke the silence, but Bryn could hear little over
the pounding of her own heart in her ears.

Trent held the reins easily, his body one with the
horse. Bryn had ridden since she was four, but she had
no illusions about her horsemanship. Without Trent, she
would never dare attempt a night ride.

They started out slowly, picking their way out of the
yard toward the road. It would be the only safe place
for what Trent had in mind.

He bent his head. She felt his breath, warm and intimate, against her ear. "Forget about everything," he

murmured. "Forget Jesse, my dad, your son. Let's outrun our demons while we can."

She nodded slowly. He was right. They both needed this. In the house, they were always tiptoeing, literally and metaphorically, Mac's welfare foremost in their minds.

Tonight, in the scented darkness, nothing existed but the two of them.

Trent urged the horse to a trot and then a gallop. The powerful animal complied eagerly, his hooves pounding the hard-packed earth, kicking up tiny clouds of dust. The speed should have frightened Bryn, but with Trent's arms around her, she felt invincible.

The horse ran for miles. The air grew colder as the night waned. Bryn's nose and fingers were chilled, but everywhere else she was toasty warm. Her head lolled against Trent's shoulder. She could swear she felt his lips on the side of her neck from time to time.

Finally, the horse tired. They were miles from home when Trent reined the stallion in and lifted Bryn to set her on the ground. Moments later, he joined her.

For a few seconds, she was confused, but then her eyes cut through the darkness. They had stumbled across a cabin far out on the property. The ranch hands used it mostly in the summers, either for work or when they wanted to cut loose and have some fun.

Had this been Trent's destination all along? Or had he come here subconsciously?

She swallowed hard. Trent was right. Danger cloaked them, locked them in a vacuum that allowed nothing in, nothing out. Her heart beat in her throat like a frightened bird's. She wanted him. Even if it led to heartbreak later. Tonight was all that mattered.

A narrow stream, much of the year nonexistent, flowed beside the cabin. Trent tied the animal with access to grass and water, and then turned to face Bryn. He was little more than a phantom in the dark night. Only his white shirt glowed. When he held out his hand, she stepped forward to take it. Their fingers linked... comfortably, naturally.

Once inside, Bryn waited impatiently as Trent lit a kerosene lantern and began building a fire. He squatted in front of the fireplace, his broad shoulders stretching the seams of his starched cotton button-down. His jeans were ancient, but the shirt was one of a dozen just like it. The Trent uniform, as she liked to think of it.

The combination of ragged jeans and pristine dress shirt summed up the mystery that was Trent Sinclair. He could go from polished businessman to rugged rancher in the blink of an eye. And both personas exuded confidence and sexuality.

Bryn felt the first ribbons of warmth from the fire. The room was small. Trent had created a roaring blaze that soon knocked the chill off the unadorned space. Other than the wooden chair where Bryn perched, the only furnishings were the straw tick mattress and the iron bedstead.

Trent opened a metal chest—thankfully mouse-proof—and extracted a couple of old quilts, clean but worn. Bryn's pulse jerked. Trent spread one over the mattress and dropped the second one at the end of the bed.

He stared at her. "You can take off that jacket, Bryn. It's plenty warm in here."

Was there a dare in his voice? She removed the garment slowly, aware that Trent's narrow gaze tracked every movement.

She wore jeans like he did, though hers were newer, and a simple, long-sleeved tee. Because of the jacket, she'd decided to forgo a bra. Trent's hungry expression signaled his approval. Her nipples hardened. He made no pretense of looking away.

He stalked her then, and she hated herself for backing up against the door. She wasn't afraid of Trent Sinclair. But tell that to her ragged breath and trembling limbs.

When they stood toe-to-toe, Trent lifted a hand and touched her chin, just her chin. "Is this want you want? Sex with me?"

A brutally honest question. No euphemisms about *making love*. She inhaled sharply. "Do you believe me about Jesse?"

He stepped back, enough that she could breathe again. "I don't know. Not yet. It's too soon to tell."

Her head dropped. "I see."

He touched the soft fall of her hair. "I'm not sure that you do. He was my brother, Bryn. And I loved him. He died in suspicious circumstances, and I can't wrap my head around that."

"So what are you saying?"

He shrugged. "I don't know what the future will bring. I'm not convinced of your motives or your reasons for being here. But I can put that aside for the moment if you can."

"To have sex."

"Yes. We ache for each other. Don't pretend you don't know it. We've been waiting six years for this. That's a long time to want something. I need you."

I need you. The stark statement was a gift in its own way. The unflappable Trent Sinclair had allowed her a glimpse of his vulnerability. She could throw it in his face…try to hurt him. But any pain she inflicted would ricochet and shred her heart in the process.

She shoved her hands in her pockets, feeling as if she might fly apart. "And afterward?"

A flush of color marked his cheekbones, and his dark eyes glittered with desire. "I don't think once will be enough. I want to take you over and over and over until we're both too weak to stand."

She gasped and covered the sound with a cough. The image painted by his stark words made her tremble with yearning. He wanted her. He needed her. Could she bear it if he turned on her when the deed was done?

"I'm scared."

His wicked grin was a slash of white teeth. "You should be, Bryn. You definitely should be."

Chapter 8

A violent crack of thunder made them both jump. Bryn's shaky laugh held nerves. "At least you're honest."

He sighed raggedly, wanting to make her happy, wanting to reassure her. "Nothing on earth could stop me from taking you in the next five minutes, Bryn," he said. "Unless you change your mind."

His outward calm was hard-won. He wanted to ravage her, rip the clothes from her body, and plunge inside her until the torment in his gut subsided.

"I won't." Her gaze was steady.

Suddenly he was consumed by a wave of tenderness. "Come here," he said, the simple words guttural and low.

She hesitated long enough to terrify him, and then she closed the small gap between them. She lifted her hands to his face, cupping his cheeks, staring into his eyes as if she could delve the secrets of his heart. "I'm here," she whispered. "I'm here."

He lifted her in his arms and carried her to their makeshift bed. He had imagined having sex with Bryn a million times over the years, but in his fantasies, there was always a luxurious bed, scented sheets, quiet music. Reality was a stark contrast, but he couldn't have stopped if he wanted to. His only regret was that Bryn might be disappointed.

He laid her down carefully and stood over her. "If you want to say no, now is the time." If she did, it would cripple him. But he was damned if he'd let her accuse him of forcing her.

She curled on her side, one hand tucked beneath her cheek. "I won't say no. But I'm not sure this is wise."

He groaned, ripping off his clothes and tossing them aside. "It isn't wise. It's insane, Bryn. But to hell with everything else. Surely we deserve this one night."

The bed creaked as he knelt and made short work of undressing her. Her skin was smooth, pure cream. Naked, she looked infinitely smaller and more fragile. Innocent. But she had the curves of a woman, and his hands shook as he touched her reverently.

Her breasts were sensitive, and he spent what seemed like hours kissing them, weighing their plump firmness in his palms, teasing the pert, dark pink nipples with his tongue and teeth. Each gasp and moan fed his hunger.

When he saw her bite her lip, he put the back of his hand to her hot cheek. "Don't be embarrassed. I love watching you respond to my touch. You're beautiful. Even more now than when you were eighteen."

"I have stretch marks." Her eyes shadowed with insecurities.

He stilled, not wanting the intrusion of the past to ruin the present. An unseen little boy came between them for a moment, and Trent's brain shied away from acknowledging the conflict that lingered just offstage.

With a shaky hand, he swallowed hard, forcing himself to trace one faint silvery line at her hip. "No mother should ever apologize for that. You are young and lovely and sexy as hell."

He wasn't sure if what he saw in her eyes was gratitude or doubt. "No regrets," he said huskily. "Tonight's all about pleasure."

The pupils in her eyes were dilated, her breathing rapid. "Then I want to touch you," she said. She pushed at his shoulders. "Lie on your back."

Bryn hadn't seen a naked man in six years…and in truth, Jesse had been more a boy than a man. So, the reality of Trent's tough, toned body was enough to make a woman swoon. His skin was a light golden-tan all over except for a paler strip at his hips.

She paused a moment to wonder jealously if he vacationed in the tropics at some wildly expensive private island with a string of girlfriends, but she doggedly pushed the thought away. He was here with *her* now.

He tucked his hands behind his head, leaving her free to explore at will. His chest was firm and lightly sculpted with muscle. A smattering of silky, dark hair emphasized his upper chest, slid between his rib cage, and arrowed all the way down to his… She gulped, feeling gauche and in way over her head. Trent was an experienced man with sophisticated tastes.

What did she know about pleasing him?

Hesitantly, she placed her hands on his shoulders. His skin was hot and smooth. His chest rose and fell once… sharply. He closed his eyes. She leaned over him awkwardly, kissing his eyelids, his nose, his full, sensual lips. She didn't linger at his mouth. Too much danger of him taking over and derailing her mission.

Even his ears fascinated her. She traced them with a fingertip and repeated the motion with her tongue. She was shocked when her simple caress made him groan and shake.

His sharp jawline bore the evidence of late-day stubble. She liked the rough texture, because it made him seem more human, less polished. With his eyes closed, he appeared docile, but she was not stupid. Trent Sinclair was powerful in every way. For him to allow her such intimate access was a concession that was only temporary.

She moved her splayed fingers lightly down his chest, pausing to rub her thumbs over his small, brown nipples. He flinched, but didn't open his eyes. His jaw could have been chiseled stone.

Her palms burned from the heat he radiated. She reached his hip bones and lost her courage.

Trent moaned and, still with his eyes closed, took one hand from behind his head and grasped her wrist. Gently, but inexorably, he placed her fingers on his erection. He was long and thick and fully aroused. She gripped his hard flesh and felt a rush of excitement fill the pit of her stomach.

Carefully, she stroked him. His flesh tightened and flexed in her grasp. He was hot as fire, hard as velvet-covered steel, and so amazingly alive. Without weighing the consequences, she bent her head and tasted him. His hips came off the bed, and he gasped.

His eyelids flew open. He looked at her with an expression that sent heat pulsating wildly between her thighs. He managed a tight smile. "That feels good, Bryn. So damned good."

The guttural words bolstered her confidence. She had no experience to guide her, but she wanted to know everything about Trent Sinclair. What made him smile, what made him shiver, what made him shudder in passion.

She loved the intimacy of the act, the feeling of power, the exultation of being able to please him despite her naïveté. But he stopped her too soon, his expression rueful. "Not all the way. Not this time. I want to be inside you when I come."

Her face went scarlet. She could feel it. And for a moment, she panicked. Trent was a male in his prime, a dominant animal, a man set on a course with only one possible outcome. What was she doing? What was she thinking? Could she seriously spend one night in Trent Sinclair's arms and not pay the consequences?

His smile was more a grimace as he lifted her on top of him. "My turn. And this way I can see all of you."

The position made her feel horribly vulnerable. He

had not joined their bodies. His erection brushed the folds of her damp sex and made her quiver helplessly.

He studied her body intently, his gaze drifting from her face to her breasts to the place where their bodies were so close to consummation. IIis hands gripped her hips. "You're beautiful, Bryn. But back then you were so young.…"

His voice trailed off, his expression troubled.

She was the one to take *his* hand this time. She placed it on her breast. "Nothing matters outside this room, remember? We're taking this night for us. Don't think about the past or the future. Touch me. I've never wanted anything more."

Her impassioned speech broke the spell that held him still. He toyed with her breasts, plucked at her taut nipples, tugged them until she cried out. His eyes flashed, and he came to life suddenly, dragging her down to crush her breasts against his chest as he kissed her wildly.

He thrust his tongue between her teeth, taking what he wanted. She tasted the wine he had drunk earlier in the evening, felt the urgency of his hunger as he explored the recesses of her mouth.

Her head swam dizzily. The acrid smoke from the lantern and from the fire mingled with the scent of aroused male. She smelled his familiar aftershave and the tang of his soap.

For a split second, as he put her beneath him, fear pierced her muddled senses. She should tell him…

"I want you, Bryn." His voice cracked as he nibbled her earlobe. "I can't wait." He reached blindly for his pants on the floor, found his wallet, and extracted three condom packets, still linked.

Her stomach clenched. "Are you always so prepared?" she asked petulantly.

"No. Actually, I'm not." His eyes locked on hers with determination. "But I've been carrying these around since the first day you arrived…for insurance. I knew how I felt about you. I've always known. And I wasn't going to let bad planning on my part put you at risk. Do you believe me?"

His eyes were warm. She saw the essence of the man he was in their depths. "Yes," she whispered. "I believe you."

She flinched involuntarily as he parted her thighs and she felt the tip of his erection enter her.

"Relax, sweetheart. I won't hurt you," he said gruffly. He stilled and kissed her eyelids.

But he did. It was inevitable. When he pushed forward, filling her steadily, he met resistance, tightness.

A half-dozen years of celibacy made her body unused to penetration. She gasped once, and then clenched her teeth. It was getting better already. The painful fullness was morphing into a stinging sensation that might be pleasure.

He reared back in shock, but didn't disengage their bodies. "Brynnie?" His incredulous gaze bore a hint of panic.

She squeezed her eyes shut, wanting to concentrate on the incredible sensation of having him fill her completely. "It's okay," she panted. "Really. I can handle it."

But something changed. He continued to take her

in deep, long thrusts, but he was so gentle, so protective, that her eyes stung with tears. He wouldn't say the words anytime soon, perhaps never, but his body was making love to hers.

His hips pressed her to the mattress, but he kept his considerable weight on his arms, looming over her in the flickering light. Sweat sheened his chest. He was breathing like a marathon runner, his eyes glazed with hunger. She whimpered as he ground his pelvis into hers, putting maximum pressure on the tiny bundle of nerves that controlled her release.

She wrapped her legs around his waist, needing to be closer still. This was what she wanted, what she had dreamed of for years. And the reality far surpassed her limited imagination. She hovered on the edge of climax.

She wouldn't have objected if he had maintained the incredible sequence of penetration and release all night. It was that good. But his body got the best of him. She felt his sudden tension, heard his muffled shout, and then groaned with him as he took his release in a rapid-fire series of thrusts that toppled her over the edge, as well, into a starburst of sensation that seemed to last forever. Trent Sinclair was well worth the wait.

Trent felt remarkably similar to the time he'd been half trampled by one of his father's prize bulls. He could barely catch his breath and his heartbeat wouldn't slow down, no matter how much he tried to relax.

In contrast, Bryn slept in his arms like a limp, weary, dark-haired temptress. He brushed a strand of hair from her cheek and sighed. He was in big trouble, because now that he'd had her, there was no way in hell he'd be able to let her walk away. She was his. That much he knew with a visceral, inescapable certainty.

He looked down at their bodies. The way she clung to him was natural. Right. His arm tightened around her waist, and he wondered how long a gentleman would let her sleep before instigating round two.

He wasn't a completely terrible son. His cell phone was in his jeans pocket, so if Mac woke and needed anything, Trent was accessible. But the truth was, Trent and Bryn had the whole night to themselves, and some invisible, pivotal moment had occurred…though he wasn't quite sure what it all meant.

Bryn was almost a virgin…if there was such a thing. Her body hadn't accepted his willingly. She'd been fully aroused, no doubt about that. But he'd had a difficult time penetrating her incredibly tight passage.

Which must mean she had gone without sex for a very long time. And that picture sure as hell didn't jive with Jesse's description of Bryn as a seducer and a promiscuous teen.

He tucked the quilt around her bare shoulder, lingering to smooth the faded fabric against her warm body. He was in deep now. He'd made such a big deal of trusting his brother because of blood ties, but more and more it was becoming apparent that Jesse was not what he seemed.

Jesse had stolen from the ranch, from Mac. And the money had been used to buy drugs…at least once. Though Trent fought the sickening knowledge with everything in his heart, it only made sense to admit that

Jesse had funded a secret addiction via his access to the ranch accounts.

Jesse had described Bryn as a manipulative, sexually active girl. But the woman to whom Trent had just made love was innocent and inexperienced, her body barely able to accept his at first. So in all likelihood, Jesse had lied about that, as well.

For the first time, Trent allowed himself to think about Bryn's little boy. Somewhere in Minnesota there was a kid who might be a Sinclair. If Bryn was telling the truth, then Mac and Trent had treated Bryn abysmally. But what motive would Jesse have had for lying about his relationship with Bryn? Surely Jesse knew that Mac would have welcomed Bryn as a permanent member of the family.

Perhaps for Jesse the answer was painfully simple. Perhaps Jesse hadn't wanted the responsibility of a wife and child. Trent would never know for sure.

Too many questions. Too few answers.

He eased carefully from the bed and stoked the fire. It was 3:00 a.m. Soon he and Bryn would have to go back to the house. And then what would happen? Nothing was resolved. Was Trent going to confront his sick father with the evidence of Jesse's perfidy? Or should he clean up the mess and say nothing?

The trouble was, the Sinclairs had too many secrets already. Secrets that had caused pain and heartache. And Trent was no closer than ever to knowing how to sort it all out.

He slid back into bed, chilled, and groaned his appreciation when Bryn's soft, warm body pressed up against his. Unfortunately for her, his cold skin wasn't nearly as welcoming.

She stirred and sat up. "Trent?"

His heart stopped. The firelight danced across her face, her shoulders, her full breasts...painting an impossibly lovely Madonna. Her dark hair fell in soft waves, framing her face. She was like a vision, a fantasy...

But when he touched her, his heart beat again. She was real. She was here. And he would take what he could, give what he could...as long as the night survived.

He was on his back looking up at her. All it took was a smile to make him hard. Her eyes were shadowed with exhaustion, her tousled hair a testament to their earlier lovemaking.

"I'm glad you came with me tonight." He couldn't resist stroking her leg.

"Me, too. I missed you while you were gone." She pulled her knees to her chest and laid her head on them, regarding him sleepily.

Despite the awkwardness of the question, he took a deep breath and made himself ask it anyway. "Why was it so difficult for you to..."

"Have sex with you?"

He grimaced. "Yeah."

"Why do you think?"

She was asking for something from him. But he felt as if he was traversing a minefield. "I don't think you've been with a man in a very long time. Is that right?"

Her lashes fell, and he could no longer judge her expression.

"I've had sex in my life a total of five times…all with Jesse. I had already decided to break it off when I found out I was pregnant." She sighed. "Since then… well, *you* try being an unwed mother, a full-time student and a grateful niece. Boyfriends were way down on my radar."

A sharp pain in his chest made it hard to breathe. She had been through a hell of a lot, and the responsibility for all of it lay firmly at his family's door. They had all let her down. Mac. Jesse. Trent.

He couldn't bear to think of it anymore. Not right now. Not with the epitome of every one of his fantasies just a hand's width away.

"Come here, Bryn. It will be better this time, I swear."

A smile flitted across her expressive face, but she allowed him to pull her beneath the covers. "It wasn't all that bad before," she teased gently.

She insisted on being the one to put on the condom. Her clumsiness was both amusing and arousing. He moved half on top of her, shuddering at the sense of homecoming. "I can do better."

He put his hand on her thigh, between her legs. She was wet already and warm, so warm. Being with Bryn was like basking in front of a fire on a rainy winter's night. She chased away the cold. And she filled him up in places he never knew were empty. Why was he so afraid to take her at face value? What more proof did he need?

She wasn't content to be passive. As he caressed her, she set about to drive him over the edge. She was a fast learner, and she was uncannily attuned to his body's responses. Her small, soft hands touched him everywhere. He burned. He ached. He struggled to breathe.

He heard her laugh once, and a shiver snaked its way down his spine. It was the sound of a woman discovering her power. And his weakness.

In the distance, the sound of rain drummed steadily on the tin roof. The seclusion lent a surreal note to the night's events. A wild, windswept ride, a deserted, ramshackle cabin. A man and a woman discovering each other's intimate secrets.

If he hadn't known better, he might have thought it was all a dream. He leaned on his elbow, winnowing his fingers through her hair. His body insisted he seal the deal, but he was desperate to make the night stretch beyond its limits. He brushed a thumb across each of her eyelids, replacing urgency with tenderness. Passion slowed to a quiet burn.

"I wish we could go back and change the past," he muttered.

Her expression, even in the firelight, was bleak. "I have a child, Trent. I wouldn't change that if I could. Whether or not you can come to terms with Allen's existence will decide how all of this plays out. I won't hide my son and I won't apologize for him."

He was struck by her quiet confidence. She might be a novice in bed, but she was a mature woman with undeniable strength...an appealing mixture of vulnerability and determination.

Already her taste was like a drug he couldn't resist. He slid an arm beneath her neck, pulled her to him and kissed her. He shoved aside all the questions, the problems, the uncertainties. One thing he knew for sure. Bryn Matthews was his. He'd worry later about the details.

Tonight was not the time.

Their tongues mated lazily. He was on his side with Bryn tucked to his chest. In this position, he could play with her breasts at will, could caress the inward slope of her waist, the seductive curve of her hip. One of her legs slid between his, and his heart punched in his rib cage.

The hunger blindsided him, not blunted at all by earlier release. "Bryn," he said hoarsely, "let me take you."

She spread her legs immediately. A rush of primordial exultation burned in his chest. He lost the ability to speak. Softer emotions were incinerated by his drive to find oblivion in her embrace.

He tried to remember her lack of experience, wanted to be careful with her, but his control had reached the breaking point. He thrust hard and deep, drawing groaning gasps from both of them. Her tight passage accepted him more easily this time, but still he saw her wince.

"I'm sorry." His voice was raw, his arms quivering as he tried to still the unstoppable pendulum.

She lifted her hips, driving him a half inch deeper. "Don't stop." She whispered it, pleading, demanding. "I want it all."

He snapped then, driving into her again and again, feeling the squeeze of her inner muscles as she climaxed, and still he couldn't stop. Over and over, blind, lost to reason or will.

The end, when it came, was terrifying in its power.

He'd built a life on control...on dominance. But in those last cataclysmic seconds, his body shuddered and quaked in a release that was like razor blades of sensation flooding his body as he emptied himself into hers. It went on forever. He lost who he was. He forgot where he was.

All he could see through a haze of exhaustion was Bryn.

Bryn was everything.

Chapter 9

They made it back to the ranch before daybreak, but only barely. The storm had passed on, leaving only faint flashes of light in the distance. Bryn was boneless with exhaustion. Were it not for Trent's strong arms surrounding her, she might have fallen from the horse.

The return was no mad gallop. The horse was tired, as well, and they made the trip at a slow amble. Bryn wanted to cry with the knowledge that their stolen moment in time was over. Tomorrow, in the harsh light of day, all the problems would still exist. Mac's illness. Jesse's tragedy. Allen's paternity. The letters.

Just before they reached the barn, Bryn turned and buried her lips at Trent's throat. She felt his heart beating in time with hers. Awkwardly, she curled one arm around his waist, wanting to hold on, craving one last moment of believing that he cared about her.

Perhaps some of his hostility had been erased for good. But she was under no illusions. Trent hadn't said he believed her. Not yet.

He helped her down from the horse and held her close for several seconds before he bent his head and kissed her.

His voice was hoarse with fatigue. "Go get some sleep. I'll see you later this morning."

She knew he had to tend to the animal, but she felt rebuffed even so. Was that how it was going to be? Trent being his usual aloof, self-contained self, Bryn desperate for any scrap of affection he might offer. The picture that painted made her wince. She'd spent six years proving to herself that she was a strong woman who could put her life back in order. She couldn't let her feelings for Trent make her lose sight of the fact that she was first and foremost Allen's mother.

She had come here to secure her son's future. And to care for Mac. What happened tonight changed nothing.

Trent recognized the watershed moment in his life. As much as it hurt, he had to admit that Jesse was not what he seemed. Trent's baby brother had lied to, stolen from and hurt the one woman who had always been dear to the Sinclair family. The woman who above all deserved their support and protection. But Jesse wasn't the only villain. By their cruel actions, Trent and Mac were partly to blame.

Mac had begun the process of reconciliation. It was up to Trent to carry it through.

He decided on the front porch as neutral ground. When Mac headed off for his usual post-lunch nap, Trent lingered for a heart-to-heart with Bryn. She seemed oblivious to the gravity of the moment, and followed him outside without question.

Trent took her wrist. "Sit down for a minute. I want to talk to you."

She sank into a chair, her expression cautious.

"I realize that you were telling the truth all along about Jesse. Your son is Jesse's boy."

Her smile was watery. "Yes. Thank you for believing me."

He shrugged. "I still think we need to do some testing. For legal reasons. But Mac seems reluctant. Do you have any idea why?"

She shook her head. "I really don't know. He's admitted that he believes me, too. But I get the feeling there's something he's not telling me."

Trent took a deep breath. "Is there anything *you're* not telling me?"

Her unmistakable hesitation sent an arrow of astonishment to his gut followed by a painful shaft of disappointment. He knew her well enough to see the little flash of guilt…the way her gaze shifted from his. *Well, hell.*

The sense of betrayal he felt was crushing. He could persuade himself to believe her response was nothing important, but even his increasing desire for her couldn't make him ignore her telling reaction.

He clenched his jaw. "Bryn?"

She was pale, and her eyes implored him to understand. "There *is* something we need to talk about…but not in Mac's hearing."

"Well, that's convenient. When were you going to tell me this big secret?" Acid churned in his stomach.

She bit her lip. "It's not that simple. People can be hurt."

"People?"

"You. Mac. Your brothers."

His blood pressure spiked. His hands fisted. "Tell me. Now."

She held her ground, though she was trembling all over. "I will. I swear. But now is not the time."

"Dammit, Bryn." He slammed a fist on the unforgiving wood of the railing.

"Your family destroyed my world," she cried. "And I've managed to forgive you all. But I won't let you boss me around. Your money has spoiled you, Trent Sinclair. It's turned you into an arrogant jerk. You think you can make everything and everyone dance to your tune. But you can't. Not me, anyway."

When she stood up, he took her arm, halting her progress. "Tell me."

She nodded slowly. "I will. Soon."

They maintained an unspoken truce throughout the afternoon and during the evening meal. Trent's frequent absences from the house made things a lot easier, though he did show up at the dinner table on time and carried his end of the conversation.

Bryn avoided looking at him, her attention fixed on Mac. But she was hyperaware of Trent sitting only a few feet away. He was rumpled and weary, his jeans stained, his white dress shirt no longer crisp. But in a room of tuxedo-clad men, he would still command attention.

He was an alpha male, and he had the confidence of twenty men. She wondered bleakly what it must be like to always be so self-assured. She'd second-guessed herself a hundred times as a new mom, and even now, she often worried at night, when sleep came slowly, if she could give Allen everything he needed.

Not so much *things*. Between her and Aunt Beverly, they had a nice life of modest means. But sooner or later, Allen would need a father figure to guide him. Someone to toss a football with, to go on Scout outings, to learn what it meant to be a real man.

Mac might fill that role in part, if he were willing. But he was getting older, and his heart attack pointed out the reality that he would not always be around. Bryn couldn't bear to think of the Crooked S without him.

It was a relief when the two men left her to her own devices and headed off to the study. Bryn decided to make her evening phone call a little earlier than usual. She missed Allen fiercely, and she wanted to listen to his high-pitched voice telling her all the silly inconsequential things that made his day special.

In her bedroom, she shut the door, not wanting to be overheard. Her throat was tight, and if she got emotional talking to her son, she didn't need any witnesses.

Before she could dial the number, her phone rang,

and the caller ID was Beverly's. Bryn smiled to herself. *Great minds think alike....*

"Hey, there," she said, her heart lifting. "What's up?"

Beverly's voice was solemn. "Don't freak out, my love. Little Allen is in the hospital."

Bryn's legs collapsed beneath her. She sat down hard on the bed. "What happened?"

"He's going to be okay. It was a severe asthma attack. I had to call an ambulance. He's stabilized, but he's crying for you."

Bryn had never felt so helpless. She swallowed hard. "Can you put him on the phone?"

"Of course."

There was a small silence, and then her son's weak, pitiful voice said, "Hi, Mommy."

"Hello, my sweet boy. I'm so sorry you're sick. Is the hospital taking good care of you?"

"I got ice cream for supper."

She closed her eyes. "That's nice."

"I miss you, Mommy."

The knife in her heart twisted. It was hard to speak. "I'm going to get on a plane, and I'll try to be there when you wake up. I promise."

"Okay." He sounded drowsy now.

Beverly came back on the line. "Don't panic, Bryn. He's perfectly fine. They'll probably release him in the morning. But I do think he needs you."

"I'll be there as soon as humanly possible."

Trent seated his father in the leather desk chair and pulled up a stool beside him. He put a hand on Mac's, feeling the slight tremor of his dad's fingers. Trent had gone back and forth about what to do, but the doctor had reassured him this morning that Mac was more than strong enough to face the truth about Jesse.

Trent pulled up the file he had saved on the computer and sighed deeply. "Dad, I don't know how to tell you this without just blurting it out. I've been working on the books every day during the last two weeks. I've combed through the accounts repeatedly. And I keep coming up with the same answer. Jesse was stealing from the ranch. From you."

Mac's expression didn't change. He turned his palm upward and squeezed Trent's hand. "I know, son. I know."

Trent gaped. "You knew?"

Mac took his hand away and leaned back in the chair, his gaze pensive. "I wanted him here so I could keep an eye on him. Offering him the so-called job of keeping the books straight was supposed to give him direction. But I track every column of those ledgers. I saw the first instance where he shifted funds—I knew what was happening from the beginning."

"And you couldn't confront him?"

"I was scared. He'd developed a terrible temper, exacerbated by the drugs, I'm sure. He was trapped in a downward spiral, but I couldn't seem to find a way to stop it. I was a helpless old fool."

"Why didn't you ask Gage and Sloan and me for help?"

Mac rubbed his eyes. "I didn't want you to think badly of him. You were his big brothers. He idolized all three of you. And I knew how much you loved him in return. If he had managed to get clean, he would have been so embarrassed that you knew, so I kept his secret."

"But Bryn knew."

Mac winced. "Apparently so. I didn't know it at the time, but Jesse often called her when he went on one of his binges."

"She told me. And I called her a liar."

"Aw, hell, son. We didn't deserve that little girl. She hit the first crisis of her adult life, and we kicked her out."

Trent didn't protest being included in the *we*. He could have stood up for Bryn six years ago, but he hadn't. His jealousy and pride had blinded him to the truth of Jesse's poisonous lies.

"We really need to get a test done right away." Trent stood at the window staring into the dark night. "I think we both know that Bryn was telling the truth all along, but I want everything to be on the up-and-up."

"We'll tell her we believe her…that we're sorry we ever fell for Jesse's innocent act. And we'll redo my will to include the boy. But I think doing a test would be insulting to Bryn."

"She will probably welcome the idea."

Mac shrugged. "We'll see…"

"You'll want the boy to spend some time here."

"Of course. Maybe Bryn can stay over while Gage is here, bring the kid out, and she and Gage and I can show him the ropes."

A sour feeling settled in Trent's stomach. He didn't

want his brother bonding with Bryn's little boy…or worse yet, Bryn.

Suddenly, the door to the hall flew open, and Bryn stood framed in the archway. Her dark eyes burned in a face that was ghostly pale. "I have to go." Her chest rose and fell with her rapid breathing. In one hand were the keys to her rental car, in the other, her purse.

Trent was at her side in one stride, gripping her shoulders. "What is it? Are you hurt?" He ran his hands down her arms, searching for clues to her near hysteria.

She put her head on his shoulder, her voice a pained whisper. "Allen's in the hospital. He's had a terrible asthma attack. He's asking for me. And I'm not there."

It was a mother's worst fear. Trent felt her anguish as if it were his own. His eyes met Mac's over Bryn's bent head, both men thinking the same thing. How many nights had they kept vigils at a young Jesse's bedside when he had struggled so pitifully to breathe?

Trent held her close, stroking her hair. "Don't panic. I'll take you. We'll use the next thirty minutes to pack and check plane schedules, and we'll be out of here."

Mac held up his hand. "Wait a minute. Let me order the jet, Bryn. You call the doctor and see if the boy's stable enough to fly. We'll bring Allen and your aunt out here and I'll hire the best private nurse money can buy to accompany them. It will give the kid something to be excited about and you'll enjoy showing him the ranch."

"I can't ask you to do that. It's too expensive." Bryn's face was tearstained.

"I'm an old coot." He lumbered to his feet and laid a hand on her shoulder. "What am I going to do with all that money, anyway? Let me do this, Bryn. It won't make up for the past, but it would make me feel better. It's late now…they probably have him sleeping. In the morning your aunt can tell him he's going on an exciting journey."

"Would he be comfortable on the plane?" Bryn looked at Trent, her expression troubled, vulnerable.

"It's damned luxurious." Trent chuckled. "He can play video games if he feels like it. There's a bed where he can lie down. He'll be pampered, I promise."

She nodded slowly. "I'll have to call the doctor right away."

"Use my BlackBerry. You don't mind us listening in, do you?"

She frowned. "Of course not."

Trent carried on a conversation with Mac while Bryn was on the phone. "We can give the aunt and the nurse and the boy the suite of rooms at the end of the hall. They'll be close to Bryn, and she can keep an eye on her little one."

Mac gave him a narrow-eyed, knowing gaze. "Staking out your territory, are you?"

Trent didn't rise to the bait. "It's healthy for children to have their own rooms. Even I know that."

"Well, I'll tell you this, boy. If you have designs on Bryn, you'll have to move fast." Mac snorted. "She won't be here much longer."

Bryn finished her call. The doctor had given the go-ahead, so Mac got on the phone in turn and started barking orders. Trent did his part, as well, and soon all the pieces were in place. By 8:00 a.m. the plane would be staffed with a nurse and every medical convenience necessary to make sure Bryn's young son would receive top-notch care.

Trent went in search of Bryn. He found her huddled in a quilt on the front porch swing. The night air was crisp and the stars numbered in the millions. He sat down beside her and pulled her against his chest. "He'll be okay, Bryn. Try not to worry."

She shrugged. "It's what mothers do."

"Did you ever think about getting an abortion?"

She didn't answer for a long time, and he wondered if he had offended her. "I'm sorry. That was very personal."

She tucked the quilt more tightly around her neck. "No, it's okay. Honestly, I don't remember ever thinking of that as an option. I'd wanted for so long to be a real Sinclair. You five were the only family I knew. I had a hazy memory of meeting Aunt Beverly, but the ranch and you and Mac and your brothers were my real family, at least in my heart. So when I realized I was pregnant, my first emotion was joy."

"But that didn't last long, thanks to us."

"I knew Jesse and I were young, but we were in a better position than most kids our age. Finances wouldn't be an issue, and we had all of you to support us."

"So you intended to keep the baby all along."

"Yes. I assumed Jesse would be happy. But that was naive. He wanted to be with me because he thought *you* wanted me. A baby made everything too real. So he lied."

"And we believed him."

"Yes."

"What did your aunt do?"

"She was wonderful from the beginning. No questions, only her unconditional love and support. Which was amazing, because I was almost a stranger to her. She did want to sue Jesse for child support, but I convinced her not to."

"Was she financially comfortable?"

She put her head on his shoulder, her body limp. "No, not really. But I held out this faint hope that one day I'd be able to reconcile with all of you, and I was afraid if we sued for child support, you'd hate me."

"Ah, Bryn." He held her close, feeling sick to his stomach as he realized anew how badly the Sinclair clan had played their part in this scenario. She had believed herself to be one of them, and they had tossed her out on the proverbial street.

Bryn yawned hugely as he stroked her hair. He nuzzled her cheek. "You need some rest, Bryn. It's been a tumultuous forty-eight hours."

She yawned again. "I know."

The memory of all that had transpired between them hovered in the sudden awkward silence.

Bryn stumbled to her feet, nearly tripping on the quilt. He scooped her up in his arms, bedding and all.

"Trent…" she protested halfheartedly.

"Let me pamper you," he muttered, holding her close. "Relax. I've got you."

He carried her all the way to her bedroom and laid her gently on the bed. She was already in her nightgown, and her hair was clean and damp from her shower.

He smoothed her cheek with the back of his hand. "I want to stay with you tonight."

The only light in the room was a dim lamp on the bedside table. But he could see her expression clearly. "Trent, I don't think I can—"

He bent to kiss her. "I'm not talking about sex. Give me some credit. I only want to hold you, I swear."

She nodded. For a moment, shy pleasure replaced the worry in her eyes. She scooted over on the mattress, making room for him. He shed everything but his knit boxers and climbed in beside her. It would be hell not to make love to her, but she needed him tonight, and he was going to be here for her. He had a lot to atone for, and maybe this would be a start.

She nestled in his arms as if they had been lovers for years. The pain in his chest returned, and he rested his chin on her head, inhaling her scent and keenly aware of her soft body and silky skin. He cared for her. Bone deep. It had begun as an invisible tie between them as she grew up. And when she reached womanhood, he'd known deep in his psyche that he wanted her.

But he hadn't been smart enough to understand that some opportunities weren't always available. His ambition and drive to succeed had taken precedence. As an arrogant young buck out to conquer the world, frequent sex had been available and plentiful. Perhaps in the back of his mind he'd assumed Bryn would always be waiting.

It would never have occurred to him to try to win her from Jesse. He loved his little brother too much. But he'd been well acquainted with Jesse's attention span, and he knew, even then, that one day in the near future Bryn would be free. Jesse didn't have it in him to settle down with one girl.

But nothing had turned out like it should.

Bryn cared for him now, he knew that. Otherwise she never would have let him make love to her. But a mother's love and loyalty were fierce commodities, and she would stand by her son first and foremost.

Whether Trent had a shot at convincing her he would welcome Jesse's son was by no means a sure thing. And honestly, he had qualms about being a dad. His own father had lived by the "make 'em tough" model, but Trent doubted that was what Bryn wanted for her son.

And what if Trent had children of his own? Would he be able to love Jesse's son in the same way? He and his family had hurt Bryn in the past. It would be inexcusable to compound that mistake.

Bryn moved restlessly, turning in his arms to find his lips. She moved her mouth over his drowsily, murmuring her approval when he slid his tongue between her lips and deepened the kiss.

His shaft hardened, but the lust he felt was overlaid with a patina of contentment, seemingly an odd match-up, but true nevertheless.

He wanted her, but the need to protect her was stronger.

As she lay on her side, her breast nestled in his palm. He felt its weight and ached to undress her and caress her everywhere. She had become as necessary to him as breathing, and for once in his life, he didn't have a course mapped out. He didn't know if determination was going to be enough. No business model existed to tell him what a woman was thinking. No amount of money could buy her trust.

And there was still a secret between them...something she was hiding.

She fell asleep, her breathing slowing to a gentle rhythm. He reached for the lamp and plunged the room into darkness.

It was hours before he slept.

Chapter 10

Bryn woke with a dull headache and a sensation that something was wrong. Then it all came flooding back. Her aunt's phone call. Her son's illness.

She scrambled out of bed and dressed haphazardly, pulling her hair into a messy knot on top of her head. It was almost nine. For God's sake, why had Trent let her sleep so long?

She made her way to the kitchen, dialing her cell phone as she walked. Mac was there, drinking coffee, looking old and tired. Corralling Jesse would have been his main focus for many years, a drain on his time and energy. With Jesse gone, and once the grief dulled, surely Mac would regain his customary vigor.

She clicked her phone shut and paced. "Beverly's

not answering her phone. What if something has happened?"

Mac reached for her hand as she passed his chair for the third time. "Relax, Brynnie. The plane is in the air. They'll be landing in a little under two hours. And all reports are good."

Bryn couldn't sit still. She went to the sink and stared blindly out the window. Allen was on the way…and Beverly. Now if only Gage and Sloan were here, she would have everyone she loved under one roof.

When she had herself under control, she sat at the table. The cook set a scrambled egg and some toast in front of her. Bryn was too excited to eat, but she forced herself to get it down. Mac passed her a section of the morning paper. One of the ranch hands' jobs was to make a run into town early every weekday to pick up the three papers Mac devoured without fail. It was an expensive habit given the gas consumption, but Mac refused to read newspapers online, though he was fairly computer savvy.

Bryn was too jittery to concentrate on the printed words for long. "When should we leave?"

Mac grinned. "Trent's going to bring the car around in thirty minutes or so. Think you can be ready?"

She punched him on the arm. "Very funny."

The trip to the airport lasted forever. Trent drove, of course, and he and Mac sat in the front seat talking ranch business. Trent had kissed her briefly when he appeared, but there hadn't been time for anything more personal or intimate. Bryn sat in the rear, her legs tucked beneath her, and leaned her head against the window, watching the world go by.

She loved Wyoming. And as much as she missed her son and her aunt, she wouldn't have traded this time for anything. Being home—and it *was* home—had healed the dark places inside her. She didn't know what the future would bring, especially because of the unrevealed letters, but it was enough to be here for the moment and to know that Mac and Trent no longer mistrusted her.

There had been no overt apologies, no verbal acknowledgment that Jesse had lied repeatedly, but she sensed in Trent and Mac a softening, a willingness to listen.

Soon, maybe tonight or tomorrow, she would pull Trent aside and show him the letters, even if it meant finding out that Allen wasn't a Sinclair. Trent, as Mac's eldest son, would have to make the decision about whether or not to let Mac see what his ex-wife had written to Jesse. And after that, who knew what would happen.

They pulled in to the parking lot of the small Jackson Hole airport and parked. Mac stayed in the car, but Trent and Bryn got out and leaned on the hood, hands over their eyes as they watched for landing aircraft. Prop planes were common. Occasionally a larger, commercial airliner.

But it was the sleek, small jet with the blue-and-green stripe and the Sinclair logo that caught Trent's attention. "That's it," he said. He tapped on the window. "C'mon, Dad."

Bryn walked on shaky legs, Trent and Mac at her

side. This was more than just a normal visit. A new Sinclair was about to step foot onto the land of his heritage. And if he wasn't a Sinclair by blood, he was still Jesse's son.

She waited impatiently in the small concourse. Another jet had landed moments before, and Bryn had to clench her fists and bide her time as the stream of tourists meandered inside from the tarmac.

At last Bryn saw the familiar outline of Aunt Beverly's gray head, with its short, tight curls. Her heart leaped in her chest. An unfamiliar woman in a white uniform walked at Beverly's side, but it was the third member of the entourage who spotted Bryn first and shouted at the top of his lungs.

Allen broke free of Beverly's hold and, despite her admonitions to go slowly, raced forward. "Mommy, Mommy!" His face was aglow.

She ran to meet him, scooping him up in a tight hug as she went to her knees. "Hello, my little sweetheart. I've missed you so much." He smelled of sweat and peanut butter and little boy.

He suffered through a moment of Bryn scattering kisses on his freckled cheeks, but then pulled away impatiently, already asserting his manly independence even in the middle of a reunion. His skin was pale. Dark smudges beneath his eyes emphasized his pallor, but he had certainly recovered his high spirits.

"Who are they, Mommy?" He tugged her to her feet and looked past her with curiosity.

Tears clogged her throat and she had to try twice to speak. "That's Trent and his father, Mr. Sinclair."

She lowered her voice to a whisper. "Remember how I taught you to shake hands."

Allen grinned at the two strange males, his head cocked slightly to one side as he held out his tiny palm. "Very nice to meetcha."

Trent stood silent, unmoving, his features carved in stone.

Mac rubbed a hand across his face. "Oh, my God." He took Allen's outstretched hand and pumped it. "Welcome to Wyoming, son."

Chapter 11

After that, chaos reigned. They all made their way outside. Aunt Beverly and Allen were installed in the backseat with Bryn. Trent hadn't missed a trick. The booster seat he had purchased for Allen was exactly the correct size and model.

The nurse rode behind in a rental car with a hired driver. All the bags went with her, as well.

By the time the caravan got back to the ranch, Bryn was frazzled. Allen was hyperexcited, Aunt Beverly was exhausted and Trent had yet to say more than a couple of terse words to anybody.

Mac was the one to show the new arrivals to their quarters and to help Bryn get everyone settled in. She was pleased that Allen's room was so close to hers. Even with two other caregivers watching out for him—one highly trained—she liked knowing that her son was where she could check on him during the night.

Lunch was quick and simple, sandwiches and fruit. Allen begged to explore the ranch, but the three women who controlled his fate insisted on a nap.

Mac took pity on the boy. He smiled down at him, his eyes misty. "How about I tell you a couple of stories about your—" He stopped short, sending Bryn a visual SOS. His face creased in distress.

She ruffled her son's blond hair, automatically trying to smooth the eternal cowlick. "Mac raised four sons on this ranch, Allen. Trent was one of them. I'll bet Mac can tell you lots of great stories about the trouble they got into."

That seemed to convince Allen, and the old man and the young boy wandered down the hall to Allen's new bedroom.

Which left Bryn and Aunt Beverly alone in the kitchen. Trent had disappeared, and the nurse was taking a much-deserved hour for herself.

Beverly hugged Bryn for the dozenth time. "I missed you, honey. The house was empty without you."

"I missed you, too. Did Allen really do okay...until he got sick?"

"He was a sweetheart." Beverly eased into a chair at the table. "I'm stiff from the plane ride, even if it was the equivalent of being treated like a queen. Good grief, Bryn. These folks have some serious money. They should have been helping you all these years."

Bryn bent her head. "It was complicated." Aunt Beverly knew most of the story, though she had no clue that

Bryn had harbored a crush on Trent. She sat down beside her aunt. "Mac hasn't said so, but I can tell from his face that he thinks Allen is Jesse's son. He practically melted, just like a doting granddad should."

Beverly extended her feet, clad in sensible walking shoes, and stretched. "How long will we be staying?"

Panic welled in Bryn's chest. Mac was back in fighting form. Once Allen had a chance to immerse himself in ranch life and the nurse declared him fully recovered, there would no longer be any reason for Bryn and her son to stay.

Which meant Bryn had to confront Trent with the letters. Soon.

And that was problematic, because Trent had reverted to the coolly reserved, impossible-to-read man she had first encountered in Mac's sickroom when she arrived. She no longer detected hostility from him, but his utter lack of emotion was even worse.

He either refused to believe the evidence of his own eyes, or he had no interest in getting to know his nephew.

When Allen woke from a long nap, he was grumpy, but a juice box and a cookie soothed him. The nurse checked him over, and soon, Mac and Bryn were on horseback, with Allen—wearing a mask as a precaution—riding in front of his grandfather. They covered a lot of ground, and Mac's transformation was miraculous. No longer an invalid, he was suddenly hale and hearty again, his skin a healthy color and his eyes sparkling with enthusiasm.

At one point when Allen was occupied playing with

puppies on the front porch, Mac took Bryn's arm. "We need to talk this evening."

Bryn nodded solemnly, a lump in her throat. "Okay. After I get Allen settled for the night, I'll come find you."

"Trent will need to be there, also."

She nodded again, but couldn't think of a thing to say. Trent's feelings on the subject of Jesse's son were an unknown quantity.

Allen tired quickly. They whisked him back to the house and Beverly occupied him with a simple board game while Bryn talked to the nurse. The prognosis was promising. They would have to be vigilant about inhalers and the like, but there was a very good chance Allen would outgrow the worst of his asthma.

After dinner Allen was allowed to watch one of his favorite Disney DVDs, and then it was bedtime.

When Bryn entered Mac's office a short while later, he was already there. And so was Trent. Mac greeted her with a smile. Trent barely noticed that she'd entered the room. He sat in front of the computer, his forehead creased in concentration as he studied the screen.

For a moment she flashed back to that dreadful day six years ago. But she was not here to plead her own case on this occasion. She was an advocate for her son. Bryn wanted nothing for herself from the Sinclairs unless it was freely given. Not money, not love, not anything.

Mac motioned for her to sit in the big, comfy armchair. It was a man's chair, and it dwarfed her, but she complied. Still, Trent remained apart from the conversation. Mac reached in a drawer and pulled out a five-by-seven silver frame.

He handed it to Bryn. She stared at it, but it took a few moments for understanding to click. The birthday cake in the picture was decorated with five candles. And the gap-toothed birthday boy with the wide grin and the cowlick was Jesse.

He could have been Allen's twin. Her throat tightened. "I don't know what to say."

Mac's eyes glazed with wetness, but he coughed and tried to cover his emotion. "I think you know how sorry we are for what happened six years ago, but Trent and I want to make a formal apology and ask you to forgive us. Isn't that right, Trent?"

Finally, Trent revolved and faced her, his expression unreadable. "Yes, of course."

Bryn squirmed in the chair, bringing her knees up beside her in an effort to get comfortable. For years she had thought an apology was what she wanted, but now that the time had arrived, she realized that it changed nothing. "I appreciate the thought," she said slowly. "But I understand why you did what you did, especially Trent. Jesse was the light of this family…the heart and soul. You all poured your love into him, and it would never have occurred to you that he was capable of such bare-faced lies."

Mac scowled. "Trent can be absolved on that account, but even back then I realized that Jesse's sweetness and compliance was an act. I was trying to protect him and you, too, Bryn. But I handled it badly. If I had encouraged you to stay and had challenged Jesse to own up to the truth, I'm convinced that things would have gotten very ugly, very fast."

"So you sent me to Beverly."

"Your mother spoke highly of her older sister, and after you ran out of the study that day, I contacted Beverly to explain the situation. We both agreed that you needed to be with a woman during your pregnancy." He came over to the chair and laid a hand on her shoulder. "But it wasn't that I didn't love you, darlin'. I never stopped loving you."

Bryn reached up to stroke his hand. "Thank you, Mac. And I'm sorry I was such a brat and sent all your presents back."

He grinned. "They're in a closet in my bedroom. You're welcome to them."

Her eyebrows went up. "Ooh…an early Christmas. I might have to take you up on that."

Mac sobered. "Allen is your son, and any decisions about his future are up to you. But I want you to know that I already have my lawyers preparing the paperwork to make him a legitimate heir to my estate."

Bryn looked at Trent, begging him without words to say something, anything.

He was stoic, watchful.

Her stomach churned with tension. What did Trent's silence mean? Was he angry? Would he challenge the will?

She straightened. "I assume you'll want to do DNA testing to establish the relationship between Jesse and Allen."

Mac snorted. "Allen's a mirror image of Jesse at that age. Any fool can see it. I don't think we need a test."

At long last, Trent spoke up. "It might be important to the boy one day to have the proof positive. So no one can ever doubt him."

Bryn's heart sank. Trent still wasn't sure she was telling the truth. "Does this mean you don't believe me, Trent?" She had to know.

Impatience darkened his features. "Of course I believe you, Bryn. Even before I saw the boy I believed you. But I deal in legalities, and it never hurts to dot the *i's* and cross the *t's*."

She nibbled her lower lip, not at all certain what was going on inside his head. It seemed as though he couldn't even bring himself to say Allen's name. Was he angry that Bryn had borne Jesse's child?

Mac raked a hand through his thick silver hair. "Today was a big day, and I'm almost as wiped out as the kid. I'll say good night. See you both in the morning."

His departure left an awkward silence in the room. Bryn had hoped to approach Trent in a better mood when she revealed the letters, but the time had run out. No wills could be notarized, nor big declarations made, until the truth about the letters from Etta came to light.

She took a deep breath. "Trent, there's something I need to show you. Something important."

He lifted an eyebrow. "What is it?"

"It will be easier if I show you. It will only take me a minute. Please wait here."

His gaze followed her out of the room, and she went rapidly to extract the shoe box from its hiding place.

When she returned, Trent hadn't moved. His eyes narrowed suspiciously. "What is that?"

She held the box to her chest. "Not long after I arrived—the day you took your dad to the doctor and I was here alone—I realized that Jesse's room had not been cleaned since his death. I did some laundry… straightened up the mess. And in the process, I found a box of letters written to him by Etta. As far as I can tell, they started arriving about the time he turned sixteen."

Trent's eyes blazed with emotion, and he took the box from her hands with a jerk. "Let me see that."

She hated showing them to him, knowing it would cause him pain. "They're bad, Trent…wicked in cases… and cruel. Perhaps Jesse's self-destructive behavior was being fueled by something none of us knew anything about."

Trent reclaimed his original seat at the desk and opened the box. He riffled through the contents for maybe ten seconds before selecting an envelope and extracting the enclosed piece of notepaper. As he read it, his scowl blackened.

She could only imagine what he was thinking. She, herself, had been shocked and dismayed the first time she had read the letters. How much worse would it be for Trent, knowing that his own mother had been so intentionally mean-spirited?

No, it was actually worse than that. A child was supposed to be able to know that his parents loved him unconditionally. Jesse would have been better off thinking that his mother had left for parts unknown and was never coming back. Desertion was a terrible blow to a vulnerable boy. But in writing the series of notes designed to manipulate Jesse's fragile emotions, Etta had moved from abandonment to deliberate harm.

Trent read every word of every letter. Bryn sat in silence as the clock ticked away the minutes. The house was quiet. Everyone else had gone to bed. Trent's face was terrible to see. His shoulders slumped, his skin grayed, his lips tightened.

When he finished the last one and turned to face her, his eyes were damp. She had expected him to be angry…and perhaps that would come…later. But at this precise moment, he was in so much pain, he was unable to hide it, even from her.

He swallowed hard. "Why? Why would she do such a thing?"

Bryn clasped her hands in her lap, searching in vain for the right words to ease the torment etched on his face. "I don't know, Trent. Maybe she thought that if she could worm her way back into Jesse's life, Mac would let her come home."

He dropped his head in his hands, elbows on his thighs. "Jesse must have been so confused, so torn. He adored Dad, but she insinuated—"

Trent had seen it, too. Bryn squeezed the arms of the chair. "Etta made it sound as if Mac wasn't Jesse's father." The words scraped her throat raw. "And if that is true, then Allen is not a Sinclair. Not at all."

Trent was so still, he worried her. She went to him and put her arms around his neck from behind. "I'm so sorry," she whispered, putting her cheek to his. "She was your mother. I know this hurts."

He shrugged out of her embrace and got up to pace, his hands shoved in his pockets. She took the seat he had vacated and wrapped her arms around her waist, trying not to let him see how upset she was. Trent had enough to deal with at the moment without comforting her.

Intense emotion blasted the air in unseen waves. He ranged around the small space like an animal trapped in a cage. He paused finally and leaned against the wall, fatigue in every line of his posture. "Why didn't you show them to me when you first found them?" he asked dully.

"I was afraid. Afraid of hurting Mac...hurting you."

"Afraid of losing your quarter of the Sinclair fortune?"

Her actions hadn't been blameless. She shouldn't have been surprised by the question. But Trent's question sliced through her composure and left her bleeding.

"Fair enough. I understand why it might look that way. But I was always going to show you these eventually. I had to. You deserved that from me. Because sometimes the only way to help with grief is to find answers."

"Did you think about destroying the letters?"

"No," she said bluntly. "I would have had to live with guilt for the rest of my life. I *want* Allen to be a Sinclair, but only if it's true. If Jesse was not Mac's son, we'll deal with it somehow."

"You didn't show these to Mac." It was a statement, not a question.

"No. He's been so frail. I did wonder if maybe he knew about them already. They weren't exactly hidden. The box fell off the top shelf in the closet when I was putting things away."

"But Mac wouldn't have snooped in Jesse's room."

"No, I guess not."

They both fell silent.

When Trent didn't say anything more, apparently lost in thought, she pressed him. "Do you think we should show them to him now? He's like a new man since Allen came."

Trent frowned. "True. But if he *didn't* know about them, then the contents might give him another heart attack. And I don't know if I can risk that."

"We can't let him change the will if he's not Allen's grandfather. It would be wrong...unethical..."

"But if bringing Allen into the family makes Mac happy, who are we to stand in the way?"

It was her turn to frown, her stomach knotted. "You made it clear six years ago that being a Sinclair is a bond all of you shared, and I didn't. My growing up here meant nothing. So what would make you soften that stance now?"

Trent's expression was inscrutable, his mouth a grim line. "Six years ago I hadn't lost my baby brother to a drug addiction. Six years ago I hadn't watched my father nearly die of a heart attack. Six years ago, I was a self-centered jackass."

His unaccustomed humility made her uneasy. She counted on Trent to be a rock. She didn't need his self-abnegation. Not now. Not with so much riding on the outcome of the next several days.

She glanced at her watch. The hours had flown. It was midnight—the witching hour. That dark moment when everything bad in life was magnified into a crushing burden. No longer able to sit still, she stood up and went to the window, her back to Trent.

Her breath fogged up the chilled glass. "So what do we do?" She wanted him to come to her, take her in his arms and tell her everything would be all right.

But as always, Trent was not a man to be easily understood or bent to a woman's will. She sensed him watching her, but he remained where he was. "I have to think," he said gruffly. "Too much is at stake to make any snap decisions. Will the boy take a nap tomorrow?"

The boy. Trent still couldn't say her son's name. "Yes." She drew a heart in the condensation on the windowpane.

"Then let's you and I take a ride in the afternoon. We'll go to the far side of the meadow…where the creek cuts through the aspen. No one will interrupt us. We'll talk and decide what to do."

Trent was speaking matter-of-factly. Nothing in his tone or demeanor suggested a hint of passion. But unbidden, her mind jumped to memories of the night they'd shared in the cabin, and she felt her face heat. It might as well have been happening again at this very instant, so vivid was the recollection of each perfect minute.

Her moans and cries. His hoarse shouts. The rustle

of the straw beneath the quilt. The snap and pop of the fire. The comforting drone of rain on the metal roof.

His touch lingered on her skin. She breathed in his crisp masculine scent. His hard body moved over her and in her. Soft sighs, ragged murmurs...pleasure so deep and swift-running she drowned in it.

She was glad they weren't facing each other. Her face would have given her away. She stiffened her spine, drawing on every ounce of self-possession she could muster. She turned to look at him and almost flinched at the intensity of his gaze.

For one blazing instant she saw raw, naked hunger beyond comprehension in his narrow gaze. A predatory declaration of intent. But he blinked, and it was gone.

Had she imagined it? Did he still desire her, or had her actions in concealing the letters destroyed the fragile bond between them?

She bit her lower lip, unsure how to proceed.

Trent's posture had relaxed somewhat. He leaned against the wall, looking tired and discouraged. Seeing him so vulnerable hurt her somewhere deep in her chest. He had taken on so much responsibility in the last few weeks. And her revelation about the letters, necessary though it was, had only added to the load he carried.

She toyed with the cord that controlled the wide-slatted wooden blinds, unable suddenly to meet his gaze. "I'll be glad to go with you tomorrow," she said quietly. "To talk things through. But in the end, it has to be your decision, Trent. Mac is your father. You know what's best for him and your family. I think he could help us get to the bottom of Etta's correspondence and what it means. But if you think he can't handle it, we'll destroy them and no one will be the wiser."

He ran a hand through his rumpled hair. "This is a hell of a mess. I need to call Gage and Sloan."

"Can they come back so soon?"

"Gage is due here in a week anyway, because we all agreed to give the old man a month of our time to help get things at the ranch back up and running. And Sloan, well, I'm pretty sure he'd come back under the circumstances. They deserve to know the truth about Jesse's problems, but I don't know if we can wait to talk to Dad about the letters."

It hit her suddenly that Trent was planning to leave... and soon. His month was up. He'd be going back to Denver. Without her. She'd known it was going to happen... eventually. But she had deliberately closed her mind to the thought of it. It hurt too much.

She went to him and laid her head on his chest, circling her arms around his waist. "I'm so sorry, Trent."

His hand came up to stroke her hair. Beneath her cheek she felt his heart thundering like a freight train. "Go to bed," he said softly. "Get some rest. I'll see you in the morning."

Chapter 12

Trent saddled his horse and headed out, following the route he and Bryn had taken to the cabin. But tonight Trent pushed his mount, skirting the edge of recklessness, trying to outrun the barrage of thoughts whirling in his brain. Every word of the damn letters was emblazoned in his memory. And it hurt. After all these years, his mother's betrayal hurt.

And then there was Bryn. What was he going to do about Bryn? From the moment he'd set eyes on Allen, he'd been consumed by guilt. The kid was Jesse's son, no question. Yet, six years ago they had thrown Bryn out in the street. Like she was some sort of sinner. And all along, Jesse had stood by and let it happen.

Dammit. What an unholy mess.

Trent couldn't lie to himself any longer. He was head

over heels in love with Bryn. And it wasn't something that was going to magically go away. Hell, he'd been half in love with her for years. She was his heart, the very essence of who he was. And whatever it took, he couldn't lose her.

He'd been an ass about Allen. He didn't know much about children, and the fact that the boy was Jesse's son hit Trent hard. He was only the uncle, but the bare truth was, he wanted to be the boy's father. And if Jesse wasn't Mac's son… Good God.

And still he rode on, paying penance, seeking answers, looking for absolution.

Bryn barely slept. Every time she rolled over to look at the illuminated dial of the clock, only an hour had passed…sometimes less. Her whole life hung in the balance. For years she had assumed that her son would one day take his place as a Sinclair. And she had believed that such a moment would cement the fact, once and for all, that the ranch would always be her home, no matter where she actually chose to live.

Deep in her soul she recognized a connection to the land here. Perhaps it was unwarranted. Her parents had been no more than hired help on the Sinclair ranch. But that reality couldn't change the way she felt.

And Trent…dear, complicated Trent. She loved him beyond reason. Loved him enough to know that no other man would ever measure up. She didn't want to spend her life alone, but it would take a long, long time to forget the imprint Trent had made on her soul.

Jesse might have been the one who took her virginity, but Trent had showed her what it meant to be a woman.

An early morning walk calmed some of her agitation and made it possible for Bryn to greet her son and aunt across the breakfast table with some degree of equanimity. Beverly and the nurse carried on a lively conversation. Mac's mood was jovial, and no one remarked on Trent's absence. An empty cereal bowl and coffee cup were evidence that he'd been up early.

Allen finished off his pancakes and turned, bright-eyed, toward his mom. "What are we going to do today?"

Bryn had thought about letting him explore the attic—she'd loved doing that as a child—but she worried that the dust might aggravate his asthma. He wasn't going to be content with puzzles and board games now that he was feeling better. Inspiration hit her. "Come with me," she said. "I have a surprise for you."

With Allen bouncing along beside her, she went to the large family room and opened the cabinet that stored all the leather-bound picture albums. Gage, Mac's second son, had developed a passion for photography early in life, and Mac had indulged him with fancy and expensive cameras, lenses and developing equipment. Mac could never have imagined in those early days how Gage's love of photography, combined with a strong wanderlust, would take him to far-flung places across the globe.

Bryn opened one of the early albums and spread it in Allen's lap. Her throat tightened as she recognized a long-forgotten photo. It was one of the rare instances where Gage was actually "in" the picture, and Mac had been the photographer. Five children, four boys and a girl, sat on the top corral rail, their legs dangling. The three older brothers bore a striking resemblance, though Trent, probably twelve or thirteen, stood out as the eldest.

Bryn and Jesse sat side by side with the bigger kids, their arms around each other's shoulders. Bryn's hair was in pigtails...Jesse's blond head gleamed in the morning sun. All five children looked healthy, happy and carefree.

When Allen wasn't looking, Bryn took the photo and slipped it in her pocket. Soon, very soon, she'd tell him about his father. And she wouldn't lie, if possible. There were plenty of good memories to share.

She flipped the pages...showing Allen a montage of county rodeos, family Christmases, impromptu picnics on the ranch...all chaperoned by a much younger Mac. Allen drank it all in with avid interest.

The final album was smaller than the rest. Inside the front cover was a faded Post-it note in Mac's handwriting that read *For Bryn.* Every photo inside was of her parents, sometimes together, sometimes smiling alone for the camera, many times holding their little girl.

She touched one picture she barely remembered. "That's my mom and dad," she said softly. "I wish you could have known them. But they died a long time before you were born."

A frown creased Allen's small forehead. "Did my daddy die, too? Is that why he doesn't live with us?"

The question came out of the blue and took her breath

away. Allen had never once asked about his father. Bryn had been prepared for some time now to launch into an explanation when Allen seemed old enough to understand, but until today, he'd never questioned their nontraditional family.

She had lain many nights, sleepless, wondering how to explain to a small child that his father didn't want him. Now she didn't have to.

She swallowed the lump in her throat, desperately wanting to point to a photo of Jesse and say, "That was your dad." But she couldn't. Not yet. Not until things were settled.

"Yes," she said simply. "Your father died. But he loved you very much." Perhaps God would forgive her for the lie. A son needed to know that his father thought the world of him. Even if it wasn't true.

In the way of five-year-olds, Allen suddenly lost interest in the past. "Can we go see the puppies now?" he asked, wheedling in every syllable of his childish plea.

"You bet." She laughed. "I'll get Julio to bring them up from the barn."

Lunch was a scattered affair. Bryn and Allen took sandwiches out into the sunshine to eat, spreading a quilt on the ground and enjoying their alfresco meal. It had been a long, hard winter in Minnesota, and the spring warmth was too appealing to resist. But by one o'clock, Allen was flagging. Bryn turned him over to Beverly and the nurse.

When she left her son's bedroom, Trent appeared

suddenly in the hallway, his expression somber. "Are you ready?"

She nodded, her stomach flip-flopping with nerves. "Yes."

One of the ranch hands insisted on helping Bryn saddle her horse, though she could have done it on her own. Trent mounted a beautiful stallion and waited for her to put a foot in the stirrup and leap astride the gentle mare assigned to her. She was self-conscious about Trent watching her, but she managed not to embarrass herself.

They rode side by side in silence, crossing a meadow bursting with flowers and sporting new green in every shade. Trent had rolled up Bryn and Allen's luncheon quilt and tied it to the back of his saddle. He'd also brought along a couple of canteens of fresh water.

When they reached the creek, Trent helped her dismount and tied both animals to trees so the horses could eat and drink as needed. He spread the faded blanket and dropped the canteens to anchor the fabric against the capricious breeze.

Nearby, the crystal-clear, frigid water burbled gently over smooth stones that were as old as the mountains themselves. Trent faced her, his expression unreadable.

The breeze tossed her hair in her face. She took a rubber band from her pocket and bound the flyaway mess at the base of her neck. "Where do we start?" she asked. The calm in her voice was a complete fabrication. Her knees were the consistency of jelly, and her heart fluttered in her chest.

Trent took one step in her direction. "With this," he

said gruffly. He took her in his arms, and instantly her fear and anxiety melted away to be replaced by heat and certainty. It was a homecoming, a benediction, a warm, wicked claiming.

Did he know? Did he have any idea that she was his in every way that mattered? She met the urgency of his kiss eagerly. The hunger that consumed both will and reason no longer frightened her.

She would have followed him into hell for the chance to have him again, to know the searing touch of his hands on her damp flesh.

He was inside her jeans, his big hands cupping her bottom, drawing her tight against the hard, pulsing ridge of his erection.

"Trent. Oh, Trent." She wanted to say more, needed to say more. But it was all she could do to remain standing.

They ripped at clothing, hers and his, unashamed to be naked beneath the gentle afternoon sun. Bits of shade dappled their bare skin.

She barely noticed when he drew her to the soft caress of the quilt. He went down on his back, taking any discomfort from the rocky ground and making it his, while she sat cradled astride his hard thighs.

His thick, eager erection was impossible to miss. It lifted boldly between them, filled with life and purpose.

The gleam in his eyes made her blush. "Stop that," she hissed, unable to hold his gaze. She looked around, knowing they were alone, but feeling bashful nevertheless.

He gently traced the curve of one breast, lingering to coax the nipple to hardness. "Stop what?"

The innocence in his question might have been more convincing if he hadn't simultaneously brushed his finger in the wetness between her legs. Where his touch trespassed, her body went lax and soft, ready to take him. Eager for more.

She cleared her throat. "I thought we were going to talk," she said. It seemed as though one of them should make an effort to be sensible, but it was difficult for a woman to be taken seriously when she was sprawled in erotic abandon beneath a cloudless sky.

A shadow darkened his face for scant seconds, but he shook it off, his hands clenching her hips hard enough to bruise.

"Later," he groaned, rolling on a condom and lifting her to align their bodies. "Watch us," he muttered. "Don't close your eyes."

He entered her inch by inch, and though she squirmed and shivered, her gaze never wavered from the spot where his hard flesh penetrated her. The act was as elemental as the cry of the hawk overhead, as life-affirming as the advent of new life in the wild.

He filled her completely, his mighty arms straining as he lifted her repeatedly. Her knees burned, her thighs ached. The intentionally lazy tempo drove her mad with longing. She bore down on him, squeezing, pressing his shaft so he would go faster.

But Trent Sinclair had an iron will, and his control was frustrating for a woman whose patience unraveled with every upward thrust of his hips. She was so close to the moment of release, she held her breath.

Acting on instinct, she lightly touched his copper-colored nipples, circling them and making Trent flinch and groan hoarsely. Within her, he grew. Harder. Longer. More insistent.

She was stretched. Impaled. Held captive to the madness that drove them both to the brink of insanity. And it *was* insane. There was no future for them. No hope for a positive conclusion.

All they had was the present.

She put her hands on his shoulders. He reached behind her, and with a brutal twist of his fingers, snapped the band that held her ponytail. The long silky strands tumbled over her breasts and onto his chest. He stroked her hair with wonder and reverence in his gaze.

Then his hands fisted in the silken fall and he dragged her down so his mouth could ravage hers. Teeth and tongues and clashing breath. His sweat-slicked chest heaved, her thigh muscles quivered. He tortured them both, making them wait, drawing out the anticipation of the end until she wanted to scream at him and scratch his bronzed muscles with her fingernails, anything to hasten the promised pleasure that shimmered just out of reach.

He seized her face in his hands, his fingers sliding into the damp hair at her nape. His rapier gaze locked on hers. "You should have been mine, Bryn. He didn't deserve you. You should have been mine." Something in the rough, aching words made her heart hurt. But then he kissed her again, and the joy returned.

They were helpless, lost in the windswept eroticism of the moment. He laughed at her, laughed at them both. Nothing could have torn them apart. She lay on his chest, exhausted. The new angle sent tingling sensations from her core throughout her body.

His strength and stamina amazed her. He grunted and thrust more wildly. She was limp in his embrace, desperately aroused, but unable to summon the energy to sit up again.

"Tell me you want me, Bryn. I need to hear you say it." He rolled them suddenly, coming on top of her, but bearing most of his weight on his forearms.

She licked her lips, her throat parched. "I want you."

"Tell me you need me."

"I need you."

"I wish I had been your first."

Her slight hesitation sent lightning flashing in his dark gaze, dangerous, potent.

"I was immature," she said softly. "I think I used him to make you jealous. And I am so sorry for that. But I was never *in love* with Jesse."

She waited for him to say he loved her. Prayed with incoherent desperation that he would say the words that would change her life forever. The simple phrase that would make all her dreams come true.

But no such words were forthcoming.

Trent's face was unreadable. He was a man in the throes of passion…nothing in his features to express anything other than a dominant drive toward completion.

And finally, when she was boneless in his embrace,

he rode her hard and took his own release with a ragged shout that echoed across the plain.

Trent pulled the edge of the quilt around the sleeping woman in his arms and checked his watch. The minutes ran away from him like rivulets of water on a rain-soaked windowpane. He wanted to preserve this slice of time, keep it pristine in his memory. But the moment of reckoning was fast approaching and it might be very ugly indeed. No matter how much he wanted to protect Bryn and her son from pain, his efforts might be futile.

He closed his eyes, feeling the sun burn into the skin of his eyelids and face.

He stroked her hair, abashed to realize that he was no longer jealous of his dead brother. Jesse had held Bryn like this…had made love to her. The knowledge was painful. But he loved his brother. Would always love him. And Jesse's premature death was a tragedy that would forever mark their family.

He was hard again. It seemed to be a perpetual, inescapable condition in her presence. He shifted her gently onto her side so they were face-to-face. Carefully, he lifted her leg across his hip. Breathing hard, he probed gently at her swollen entrance.

Bryn murmured, and the ghost of a smile teased her lips as her eyelids fluttered and opened. He pushed until he was seated fully in her still-slick passage. He moved slowly, savoring the way her body grasped his shaft. She felt small and fragile in his embrace, but she was strong in ways he could never match. She'd made a home for her son as a single mother.

Beverly had been a source of strength…true. But Bryn was a good mother, a woman of backbone and grit, much like the pioneer females who helped settle the wild and dangerous West.

She kissed him and murmured soft words of pleasure. He gritted his teeth as his climax bore down on him. He'd taken her like a crazy man less than a half hour before, and already he was at the edge again.

He slowed his strokes, relishing the position that enabled him to kiss her as he moved in and out with deliberate thrusts. Dark smudges beneath her eyes tugged at his heartstrings. Sleepless nights. Endless worry. But her smile was pure sunshine.

When he thought of the way he and Mac had thrown her out six years ago—a naive, pregnant eighteen-year-old—he was sickened. He'd never be able to make that up to her, but God knows, he could try.

He shuddered as his brain ceded control to his baser instincts. Tremors shook him. The base of his spine tightened.

"Bryn…" He spoke her name urgently, needing to see her forgiveness, wanting absolution.

She caught her breath. "Trent…ohh…"

Their position was intimate, sensual. He put his hand on the soft curve of her bottom and pulled her in to his downstroke. Her back arched. Her eyes closed. She was so beautiful, he was blinded. He told himself it was the sun.

But it was her. It was Bryn. Until she came back to the ranch, he'd had no clue his life was an empty shell.

But she had shown him the truth. And all she'd had to do was be herself…pure, generous, charming.

He'd been lost from the first moment, though he'd fought hard to believe she was a liar and a cheat. It was much easier that way.

He brushed a kiss across each of her cheeks, her nose, her eyelids. The urgent need for climax had retreated to a muted simmer. His primary emotion at the moment was quiet contentment. And for a man unused to examining something as hazy and insubstantial as feelings, it was a significant shock to realize that the woman in his arms was as necessary to him as breathing.

The knowledge was exhilarating and scary as hell.

He pushed her over onto her back and urged her legs around his waist. Her skin was soft and luminous in the unforgiving light of day. What would it have been like to be her pioneer husband, bound inside a tiny log cabin for weeks at a time as blizzards howled?

Isolation. Nothing to diffuse the interaction between male and female. Nothing to run interference when one of them was in a bad mood. Nowhere to escape when tempers flared.

He'd have taken her night after night, wrapped in a world of only two. And it would have been as close to heaven as a man like him was liable to get. He'd said Jesse didn't deserve her, but the truth was, neither did he.

She smiled at him, a secretive curve of soft pink lips that made him shake. Her gaze was slumberous. The look of a woman who had been well loved. Any man in his right mind would move heaven and earth to make her his. He'd grown up believing that everyone and everything had a price. But not Bryn. She had never asked for a single thing.

And he wanted to give her the world.

He moved in her, wanting to imprint his touch on her heart so that she could never forget him.

She dug her heels into his lower back. "Whatever happens, Trent, I'll always remember this." Her gaze was solemn, melancholy.

He nuzzled her neck. "I'll work it out. Trust me."

A slight frown appeared between her perfectly arched brows. "Work what out?"

He withdrew almost completely and chuckled when she said an unladylike word. He dropped his head forward, resting his brow against hers. "Mac. Jesse. Allen. The letters. You'll see."

She tightened her legs around his waist with surprising strength. "Less talk. More action."

He tried to laugh, but it came out as a groan. He let it snap...the cord he'd bound so tightly around his need, his control. Again and again, he entered her, holding back until he heard her sharp cry and felt her body spasm around his rigid flesh. And then he buried his face in her neck and leaped into the unknown, feeling only the soft pillow of her breasts and knowing that there was nowhere else he wanted to be.

Sweat dried on their skin. The sun moved lower, brushing the mountains with gold and lavender.

He came so close to blurting out his love for her. But the habits of a lifetime were deeply ingrained. Never operate from a position of weakness. Make a plan. He'd get everything worked out in his head, and then he'd tell her. When the time was right.

Bryn was so silent and still beneath him, he felt panic tighten his throat.

He sat up and gathered her in his arms, warming her skin with his hands. The words rushed from his mouth, shocking the hell out of him. "Marry me, Bryn. Make Allen my son."

Chapter 13

Over the years Bryn had entertained dozens of fantasies in which Trent declared his everlasting love for her, went down on one knee to offer her a ridiculously extravagant ring and begged her to marry him. None of those scripts bore any resemblance to what had just happened.

She stood up awkwardly, painfully aware of her nudity, and scrambled to pick up her clothes and put them on. In one quick glance she saw that Trent was frowning. No less magnificent and commanding in the buff than he was fully clothed, he stood with his hands on his hips.

When she was ready, she folded her arms across her waist and made herself look at him. She managed to swallow against a tight throat. "Thank you for asking," she said quietly, "but no." He hadn't technically asked her at all. It had been more autocratic than that. An order. The mighty Trent Sinclair telling a minion what to do.

She hated that she was suspicious of his motives, but her instinct for self-preservation had kicked into high gear. She couldn't be one of his *acquisitions*. Her heart couldn't bear it.

Trent's scowl was black enough to make a grown man cower, but Bryn held her ground. His jaw was clenched so hard, the words bit out in sharp staccatos. "Why the hell not?"

The naive Bryn grieved for the ashes of fairy-tale romance. But practical Bryn had more to consider than hurt feelings. "If Allen is a Sinclair, then of course I want him to get to know his grandfather and you and Gage and Sloan and the ranch. But if it turns out that he's *not,* I'll take him back to Minnesota with me and we'll make a good life there with Beverly."

His eyes narrowed. "You said that whether or not to show Mac the letters was my decision. I say we destroy the damn things and move on…as a family."

The temptation to give in was overwhelming. She would be Trent's wife. Allen would be his son. There might be other children.

She bit her lip and shook her head. "I was wrong. I've had all night to think about it. Secrets are never the best course of action. Mac needs to know the truth. And afterward…"

He shoved his legs in his pants and buttoned his shirt.

"And afterward, your son will either be very rich, or just another illegitimate kid being raised by a single parent."

She flinched. His deliberate cruelty shocked her. Was this his response to not getting his own way? "It's about more than the money," she whispered, her throat raw from the effort not to cry. "You know that."

He faced her, barefooted. Most people would appear vulnerable in that condition. Not Trent. "The world revolves around money, Bryn. And if you don't realize that, you're more of an innocent than I thought."

She was chilled to the bone though the day was warm. "Why are you being so hateful?" What had happened to tender, caring Trent? Had the gentler, kinder man been no more than a ruse to get her into bed?

He shrugged, the smile on his face mocking. "If I'm not in the best of moods, Brynnie, you'll have to take the blame for that. It's not every day I get a marriage proposal tossed back in my face. Forgive me if I'm not so cavalier about it as to go on with life as normal."

For the briefest flash of a second, she thought she saw hurt flicker in his cold gaze, but then it was gone. She couldn't hurt Trent. He was impervious, thick-skinned. That was the only way to make it to the top.

She bit her lip. "Why did you ask me to marry you?"

He propped his foot on a stone and bent to put on the left boot, then the right.... Was he hiding his expression deliberately? His voice was muffled. "We owe you. Maybe not Gage and Sloan, but certainly Jesse and Mac and I. You suffered at our hands, and that can't be erased. Sinclairs always repay their debts."

Disappointment and grief tangled in her stomach,

destroying any last hope that Trent felt something for her beyond simple lust. "I absolve you," she said dully. "There's plenty of blame to go around. I kept Allen away from you all for five years. So let's call it even."

She picked up the quilt and rolled it with jerky motions. "I need to get back to the house."

The hours until Bryn and Trent could meet with Mac in private passed like molasses on a cold day. Allen's high spirits frayed Bryn's nerves, yet finally, by nine o'clock, Allen was sound asleep. Bryn didn't waste any time. She retrieved the box of letters and made her way to Mac's study.

The two men were already there.

Her heart thumping, she entered hesitantly, searching out Trent with her gaze to see if his face gave any indication of what was to come. What had he said to Mac? Anything? She sat down and waited.

Trent ran a hand over the back of his neck, looking uncustomarily frazzled. "How are you feeling, Dad?"

Mac frowned. "I'm great. What's all this about?"

At Trent's almost imperceptible nod, Bryn smiled wanly. "We have some things to tell you, but we don't want you to get upset."

Mac snorted and rolled his eyes. "I may have a contrary ticker, but I'm not some damned pansy who's going to wilt over a little bad news. For God's sake, spit it out. You're making me nervous. You and Trent look like you've swallowed bad fish. Tell me what it is. Now."

Bryn gripped the box in her lap. When she looked at Trent, he was no help at all. He simply shrugged.

She stood up and moved to where Mac sat in the leather chair that was his version of a throne. "I found these," she said. "When I was cleaning Jesse's room. They're letters. From Etta. Did you know Jesse's mother had been writing to him?"

"God, no." Mac paled.

Bryn winced. "I was afraid of that. They're bad, Mac. She tried to poison his mind. And her deliberate mischief-making may have contributed to the drugs. Jesse would have been confused. And hurt."

"Let me see." He tried to take the box, but she held on to it for a moment more.

"That's not all." She was surprised she was able to speak. Her throat spasmed painfully. "Jesse may not be your son."

Mac's big hands trembled. He jerked the box away from her. "Damn it, girl, quit coddling me."

The room was silent when Mac tossed the last letter in the box and replaced the lid. He set the innocent-looking cardboard container on the desk and laid his head against the back of his chair. His eyes were closed. Bryn was not in the mood to indulge him.

She got to her feet and paced. "Talk to us, Mac. Please."

He scrubbed his hands over his face and turned his head in her direction. His entire body had deflated. He looked like an old man.

Trent exhaled an audible breath. "Dad. Come clean with us. What's going on?"

Mac sighed. "I didn't know about the letters, but I've known where Etta was every day since she left."

Trent looked thunderstruck.

Bryn managed to speak. "I don't understand. I thought she ran away. Left her kids. Left you."

Mac nodded. "She did that for sure. And I checked her into a mental facility, because she had a complete, devastating breakdown. She split with reality. Etta has been a patient at the Raven's Rest Inpatient Facility in Cheyenne for almost two decades."

Trent gaped. "For God's sake, Dad. Why did you never tell us? Why did you let us think she ran away?"

"She did run away. At first. But when I found her, she was cowering in a bus station like a wounded wild animal." Mac's voice broke, and Bryn saw that even after all the years that had passed, he still loved her.

He continued, his voice thick. "I took her to the hospital. And she was never able to come back home. She was a danger to herself and others. There were a few good days here and there, but for the most part, she lives in an alternate world. I'm honestly shocked that she was able to remember Jesse well enough to be able to write to him."

"You think Jesse inherited some of her mental instability, don't you?" Trent's face had paled, as well.

Mac nodded slowly. "I wanted him to see someone… to get help…medication. Anything that he needed. But he never gave me an inch. Denial was his friend."

Bryn leaned forward. "So the other men she talks about in the letters? Did they exist?"

Mac's silence dragged on for tense moments. He was suddenly the epitome of an elderly man. "Yes." His tone was flat. "She never leaves the facility now. But before…when she was still living on the ranch…there were a couple of episodes. Jesse is probably not my biological son. I'd been gone for a few weeks to a cattle show. The timing…well…let's just say the odds are against it. But it doesn't matter anymore. Jesse is dead."

He got to his feet, almost stumbling, and leaned a hand on the back of the chair. "You were right to show me the letters. I'm sorry I didn't tell you the truth about your mother, Trent. But when you were all boys, I didn't want you to know. And by the time you were old enough to understand, I'd kept the secret so long, I couldn't bring myself to expose the truth."

He hugged his son, and Bryn was relieved to see that Trent gave as good as he got. She had feared he'd be furious. But whatever his emotions, he kept them in check for now.

Mac hugged Bryn, as well. "I love you, Brynnie, my girl. And you've always been family to me, with or without Jesse."

She kissed his cheek. "Sleep well, Mac. I'll check on you before I go to bed."

When it was just the two of them, Bryn studied Trent's face. He wasn't doing well. She could see it in his eyes, though he stood as proud as ever, his spine straight and his broad shoulders squared off against the world. She took his hand. "Come to the kitchen with me. I'll fix you something to drink. And I'll bet Beverly tucked away some of those sugar cookies."

He cocked his head, pulling his hand out of her grasp and stepping backward behind an invisible fence. "You don't have to pamper me. I'm not dying. But I guess you were smart to say no to my proposal. Who knows what crazy genes are rattling around inside me? I don't know which is worse—a mother who will abandon her children on a whim, or a raving maniac."

His sarcasm made her flinch. "Don't do that, Trent," she said urgently. "Give yourself time to process this. You've had a shock." She turned to Mac's desk. He'd been known to keep a flask for emergencies. "I'll pour you some whiskey. You deserve it after the day you've had."

Trent's laugh held little amusement as he took the tiny shot and tossed it back. He wiped his mouth with the back of his hand, his eyes bleak. "There's not enough whiskey in the world to fix this."

"It will be okay," she said, trying to believe it.

It was as if he never heard her. "I'm going to have to be the one to call Gage and Sloan. I can't make Mac do it. He could barely tell me. Damn it to hell." Trent hurled the small glass against the wall and smiled with grim satisfaction when it shattered into a dozen pieces.

"You don't have to do anything tonight," she insisted. "It can wait until morning. When you've calmed down."

"I'm perfectly calm," he said, his tone blistering. "Go to bed, Bryn. This doesn't concern you."

"*You* concern me," she said. He was trying to hurt her…and he succeeded. But her own concerns had to be pushed aside temporarily for his sake. He needed to let go, let the anguish out, and hang on to someone else for a few minutes. But such perceived weakness wasn't in his repertoire. He was a Sinclair male. That particular animal was trained not to show weakness. Not to anyone.

She knelt to clean up the mess, and Trent barked at her.

"I said…go to bed." His eyes blazed in a white face.

She finished her task and dropped the pieces into the trash can. "I don't want to leave you right now. You need me."

He went still, and in that split second, she knew she had made a mistake. His lip curled. Any tenderness she'd ever imagined in his steely gaze had been obliterated by fury and suffering that was painful to witness.

"I don't *need* anyone, Brynnie. So leave me the hell alone."

Bryn gave herself and her son one last, precious twenty-four-hour period to enjoy the ranch. Their return flights, along with Beverly's and the nurse's, were booked for the following day.

She did her best to make her mind a blank. All that mattered now was ensuring that Allen and Mac spent time together and that Allen had one last opportunity to explore the ranch. She was the one making a decision to leave this time, but the end result was the same. She had to say goodbye to the two men she loved. And to the home where she had grown up with so many happy memories.

Allen ran circles around her when she lagged behind on their walk. Her sleepless night was catching up with her. She held up a hand. "Mommy needs to rest a minute." They were climbing a slight rise, and the two or three hours of sleep she'd had during the long, bleak night weren't enough to give her any energy at all.

She spied a boulder up ahead near the trail, one of many left behind when the glaciers retreated, and made a beeline for it. They were in sight of the house. Their trek had taken them in a big circle.

They sat down and Allen put his head in her lap, a move that said louder than words that he wasn't entirely back to normal. She stroked his hair. "I have something to tell you, sweetheart."

He yawned and swiped at his nose with a dirty hand. "Okay."

She hadn't expected it to be quite so hard. "You know how I told you I lived here when I was growing up?"

He nodded.

"Well, Mac had a son, Jesse, who was my age. I fell in love with him and that's how you were born."

"But my daddy died."

"Yes."

"Why didn't we live with him?"

This was the tricky part. Allen sat up and looked at her with big curious eyes. She bit her lip. "Ah, well… your dad was very sick and he couldn't help take care of a little boy."

Allen cocked his head. "Like strep throat?"

"No. Something that never got better. But you were very lucky because you had me and your aunt Beverly."

"Why didn't my dad ever invite me to come here?" Allen was sharp.

"He didn't want you to see him feeling bad. And he didn't tell Mac and Trent that you were his little boy.

But now that they know, Mac wants you to visit as often as we can."

"Can we live here?"

Bryn groaned inwardly. "We already have a place to live…you know? And Aunt Beverly would miss us if we were gone."

Allen grinned. "Yeah. I guess." Then as usual, his focus shifted. "Can we go back to the house now? I'm hungry."

She ruffled his hair. "You're always hungry."

They took off at a trot, and Allen pretended to race her, giggling when she panted and bent to put her hands on her knees. She took a deep breath and made one last sprint.

Two steps later, she cried out in shock when she stepped in a hole and her body kept going. There was a sickening crack, dreadful pain shot up her leg and she catapulted forward to meet the ground with a thud.

The first thing she remembered was her son's little hand patting her cheek. When she opened her eyes, she realized he was crying. "I'm okay," she said automatically.

He wasn't stupid. Fear painted his face. "Mommy, your phone's not in your pocket."

Oh, God. "I left it at the house." Throbbing pain made it difficult to enunciate.

"I'll go get help," he said, looking sober and not at all childlike.

"No. You'll get lost." She blurted it out, terrified at the possibility of letting her baby boy wander alone.

Allen took her face between his hands, his expression earnest. "Mommy, I can see the house. It's over there."

He was right. The roof was visible through the trees. Her brain spun. What choice did she have? If she passed out and it was a good possibility given the way she felt—she'd be leaving Allen unattended anyway. Was there any difference in the two scenarios? The pain made nausea rise in her throat as sweat beaded her forehead.

Desperately, she gazed at her small, brave son. "You must stay on the trail. And if you get confused, stop and come back. Be careful. Promise me."

He stood up. "I'll bring Trent, Mommy. He'll know what to do."

Trent was in the corral, examining the left rear shoe on his stallion, when a small figure out of the corner of his eye caught his attention. It was little Allen. Alone. Trent ran to meet him, his heart in his throat. "What happened? Where's your mother?" He dropped down on his knees, so the two of them were at eye level. Allen was wheezing a little bit, but his color was good. He was scared and trying hard not to show it.

He laid his head on Trent's shoulder in an innocent gesture of trust. "She stepped in a hole. Her ankle might be broken. I can show you where she is. It's not far."

Trent's brain buzzed. He scooped the little boy into his arms and tucked him up on the horse. "Hold on to the saddle horn. We're going to ride fast." Allen's eyes were huge, but he nodded. Trent put a foot in the stirrup and vaulted up behind him. "Let's go. I'm counting on you to show me the way...."

One arm wrapped around Allen's waist, Trent rode hell for leather. Thinking about Bryn, hurt and alone, made him crazy, so he did his best to concentrate on getting to her as quickly as he could.

Thankfully, the kid was right. It was less than a quarter of a mile. But when they reached Bryn, she was unconscious. Trent felt his world wobble and blur. She had to be okay. She had to be okay. She had to.

He jumped down and set the boy on his feet. While Allen hovered anxiously, Trent took a handkerchief from his pocket and wet it with water from the canteen on the ground beside Bryn. He wiped her face gently. "Wake up, Bryn. I'm here. Wake up, sweetheart."

It was a full minute before Bryn responded. She was ghostly white, and her lips were pale. "You came."

The words were so low he had to bend his head to hear them. He reached out his hand for Allen, pulling him close. "Your son is a hero," he said softly. "I'd never have known where you were without him."

She tried to wet her lips. "I've hardly seen you speak to him. I thought you were angry because he was Jesse's son," she whispered, her voice almost inaudible.

He lifted the canteen to her lips and made her drink. "Angry?" Had she hit her head after all? She wasn't making sense.

"Because he's not yours and mine."

It was his turn to frown. "Don't be ridiculous. I love Allen. He's my flesh and blood. I'll always love him."

It was a nightmare ride that took far longer than it

should. The sun dropped lower in the sky as they made their halting way back toward the house.

When they finally reached the edge of the corral, Trent barked out orders, and ranch hands came running. Beverly took charge of Allen, and the nurse was at Trent's side as he carried Bryn into the house. He put her in his bedroom. It was larger and more comfortable than hers, with a massive king-size bed. Bryn moaned as he laid her carefully on the embroidered, navy silk duvet.

There was really no choice what to do. The ankle was clearly broken. The nurse confirmed Trent's amateur diagnosis. Mac summoned a helicopter and Trent and the nurse boarded with Bryn for the brief trip to Jackson Hole.

Chapter 14

"How is she, son?" Mac, Beverly and Allen had lingered at the ranch for a couple of hours, not wanting Allen to get restless at the hospital during what could be a lengthy surgery.

"She should be coming out of recovery any minute now." Trent was hollow inside, feeling the aftermath of adrenaline. The sterile waiting room had been a cage he'd prowled for several hours. "Why don't you go on in so she can see Allen first thing. It's room 317. I'm going to grab some coffee and a sandwich."

He didn't linger at the snack machine. It was almost nine and he knew Mac and Beverly wouldn't want to keep Allen out too late.

When he approached the room a quarter hour later, he could hear Allen's excited chatter and Bryn's softer voice. He drew in a sharp breath, swamped with a wave of relief to hear concrete proof that she was okay.

He hovered in the hall, wanting to give the others plenty of time to reassure themselves that Bryn had come through the surgery with no ill effects. Finally, the door opened, and Bryn's visitors exited. The nurse would ride back to the ranch with them.

Mac squeezed his shoulder. "Take care of our girl."

Now Bryn was alone. Trent took a deep breath, knocked briefly on the partially open door and stepped into the room.

Bryn shifted in the bed and winced. Even with really wonderful drugs, her ankle throbbed mercilessly.

When Trent appeared in the doorway, her heart jumped. She hoped he couldn't tell on the monitor. She was in pain. It had been a terrible, stressful day. And she felt in no condition to hold her own with him.

He looked like hell. "You should have gone home with the others," she said quietly. "You're exhausted."

He pulled up a chair beside her bed. "I'm not leaving you." His angular face was creased with fatigue, his eyes shadowed. She wanted to smooth a hand over his hair, but she felt the invisible wall between them.

"There's no need for you to stay. I'm fine...really." She touched the neck of her hospital gown and sighed inwardly. Her hair was a mess. She would kill for a shower. And Trent had to see her like this. It wasn't fair. She always seemed to be at a disadvantage when it came to their interactions.

He took her hand in his, examining the shallow cuts and scrapes that covered the palm. She had tried to catch herself when she fell. It was a wonder she hadn't broken an arm. He ran his thumb gently over the worst of the wounds. "I lost ten years off my life today."

He looked at her, for once his dark gaze completely unguarded, and her breath caught in her chest. Was she imagining the agonized concern she saw there?

She curled her fingers around his palm. "I'm so sorry. I should have had my phone with me."

He shrugged. "Reception is sometimes spotty once you get away from the house. It might not have been any help. Your son, on the other hand, is one hell of a smart kid."

She might have taken offense at the "your son" reference, if not for the fact that Trent's face beamed with pride.

No mother could resist praise for her offspring. "He *is* pretty amazing," she said smugly. The she sobered. "I was terrified to let him go off on his own, but what choice did we have?"

"He took me right to you. He was a trouper."

The room fell silent. She was tremblingly aware of the fact that Trent stroked the back of her hand, almost absentmindedly.

He stood and reached forward to tuck a strand of hair behind her ear…then kissed her cheek. "Why did you turn down my marriage proposal, Bryn?" He propped one arm on the bed rail and stared at her intently.

She plucked at her IV nervously, unable to meet his eyes. "I'm able to provide for my son."

"That's not what I asked."

She slanted him a sideways gaze. "I didn't want to be an obligation to you...a wrong you have to right."

He frowned. "That doesn't even make sense. I offered to make you my wife."

"Like a business merger." She heard the petulance in her own voice and winced inwardly.

A smile began to draw up the corners of Trent's sensual mouth. "I may be good at a lot of things," he muttered, "but that was my first proposal. It possibly lacked finesse."

She pouted. "It lacked *something.*"

He grinned fully now, picking up her hand and kissing each scrape. "Would it have helped if I told you I adore you...that I've loved you since you were a little girl in ragged shorts and scabbed-up knees. That what I felt for you changed over the years into something far deeper. But that I was too much of a self-centered, ego-driven jerk to recognize what I had before I lost it. That I need you so much it hurts, and I didn't even know there was anything missing in my life until you showed up in Wyoming."

Bryn lay, openmouthed, and thought her heart might break. For Trent, the self-contained, tightly controlled man that he was, to humble himself in such a way was a gift she had never expected. She was speechless.

His smile was wry. "Is that a second *no?*"

She gulped. "No. I mean yes. Oh, Trent, I don't know what to say." She sniffed, blinking rapidly.

He shook his head and wiped her cheeks tenderly with the edge of the sheet. "You're killing me, little one. Any kind of answer would be appreciated. A man can only stand so much suspense."

She grabbed his hand in hers and squeezed. "Are you sure?" She couldn't bear it if he was confusing affection with love.

He kissed her again. Harder this time. With echoes of the passion they had shared. "Do I strike you as indecisive, Brynnie? *Yes*—I love you. And I promise you I'm not going to change my mind in five minutes or fifty years. So you might as well get used to it."

She tugged him closer. "Sit on the bed."

He lowered the bed rail and complied, but he pretended to look toward the hall with apprehension. "I'm scared of that nurse. Please don't get me in trouble."

She wanted to laugh, but her chest was a huge bubble of happiness that made it hard to breathe.

He put an arm around her shoulders and settled her against his chest, her cheek over his beating heart. She decided there and then that a broken ankle was a small price to pay.

"Yes," she said with a soft sigh.

He kissed her temple. "Yes to what?"

"To everything. To laughter. To forever. I love you, Trent."

He stretched his long legs out on the mattress, one ankle propped over the other. "Are you sure?"

He was mocking her, but she was too happy to care. "I'm sure," she said, grinning uncontrollably. "So kiss your calm, ordered life goodbye."

He nuzzled the top of her head and sighed from deep in his chest. "I can't wait, Brynnie. I can't wait."

* * * * *

We hope you enjoyed reading

MIXED MESSAGES

by #1 *New York Times* bestselling author

LINDA LAEL MILLER

and **THE SECRET CHILD AND
THE COWBOY CEO**

by *USA TODAY* bestselling author

JANICE MAYNARD

Both were originally
Harlequin Desire stories!

Harlequin Desire stories feature sexy, romantic heroes
who have it all: wealth, status, incredible good looks…
everything but the right woman. Add some secrets,
maybe a scandal, and start turning pages!

HARLEQUIN®

Desire

Powerful heroes…scandalous secrets…burning desires.

Look for six *new* romances every month
from **Harlequin Desire**!

Available wherever books are sold.

SPECIAL EXCERPT FROM

HARLEQUIN®

Desire

Here's a sneak peek of
CHRISTMAS IN THE BILLIONAIRE'S BED
by USA TODAY *bestselling author*
Janice Maynard

His mother had won the war without firing a single shot. The last thing Aidan wanted to do was visit Silver Glen, North Carolina, during the holidays, but Maeve knew he wouldn't miss his own brother's wedding.

It wasn't that he didn't love Silver Glen. He did. But going home for Christmas brought back too many ugly memories. So he chose to visit his large, close-knit family at other times of the year: Easter, Mother's Day, the fourth of July.

But December? No.

He stood and stretched, tossing the offending invitation on his desk. The view from his office window stretched from the Statue of Liberty to the George Washington Bridge. Aidan loved New York City. The constant pulse of life. The anonymity. No one here cared about his past. The emotional breathing room had become as essential to him as food or water.

But knowing his mother, she had planned a series of social events to fill the days leading up to the wedding and Christmas, which meant two weeks at home. Might as well be a lifetime.

For a moment, he flashed back to the past. Two young women. Both beautiful. Both charming. Both full of life and fun. And he had lost each of them.

HDEXP1114-2

The familiar burning in his gut was more than guilt and regret. It was a longing for what he would never have. Absolution. A woman and a family to call his own.

The memories lived with him everywhere. The painful part of going home was having other people *share* the memories. His family's empathy would be his downfall.

He didn't want their love to heal him. He didn't deserve that.

Aidan Kavanagh was a charming shell of a man, interested only in closing a deal or cashing a check. Ask anyone. The persona was one he had crafted carefully to keep people away. After loving and losing twice in his life, he was through with emotion…with caring.

In Silver Glen at the holidays, he would have to open himself up to the warmth of celebrations that would make him terribly vulnerable. Loving his family was a given. But beyond that, he had nothing to offer.

Loving and losing meant vicious, unrelenting pain. Only a fool would walk that path again.

Find out how Aidan feels when his ex turns up as a
guest at his brother's wedding in
CHRISTMAS IN THE BILLIONAIRE'S BED
by USA TODAY bestselling author
Janice Maynard.

Available December 2014,
wherever Harlequin® Desire
books and ebooks are sold!

HARLEQUIN®

Desire

Powerful heroes…scandalous secrets…burning desires.

Save $1.00 on the purchase of

CHRISTMAS IN THE BILLIONAIRE'S BED

by Janice Maynard,

available December 2, 2014,
or on any other Harlequin® Desire book.

Available wherever books are sold, including most bookstores,
supermarkets, drugstores and discount stores.

Save $1.00

on the purchase of
CHRISTMAS IN THE BILLIONAIRE'S BED
by Janice Maynard
available December 2, 2014,
or on any other Harlequin® Desire book.

Coupon valid until February 4, 2015. Redeemable at participating retail outlets
in the U.S. and Canada only. Limit one coupon per customer.

52612057

Canadian Retailers: Harlequin Enterprises Limited will pay the face value of this coupon plus 10.25¢ if submitted by customer for this product only. Any other use constitutes fraud. Coupon is nonassignable. Void if taxed, prohibited or restricted by law. Consumer must pay any government taxes. Void if copied. Millennium1 Promotional Services ("M1P") customers submit coupons and proof of sales to Harlequin Enterprises Limited, P.O. Box 3000, Saint John, NB E2L 4L3, Canada. Non-M1P retailer—for reimbursement submit coupons and proof of sales directly to Harlequin Enterprises Limited, Retail Marketing Department, 225 Duncan Mill Rd., Don Mills, Ontario M3B 3K9, Canada.

U.S. Retailers: Harlequin Enterprises Limited will pay the face value of this coupon plus 8¢ if submitted by customer for this product only. Any other use constitutes fraud. Coupon is nonassignable. Void if taxed, prohibited or restricted by law. Consumer must pay any government taxes. Void if copied. For reimbursement submit coupons and proof of sales directly to Harlequin Enterprises Limited, P.O. Box 880478, El Paso, TX 88588-0478, U.S.A. Cash value 1/100 cents.

5 65373 00076 2 (8100)0 11991

® and TM are trademarks owned and used by the trademark owner and/or its licensee.
© 2014 Harlequin Enterprises Limited

NYTCOUP1114